A
Garland Series

VICTORIAN FICTION

NOVELS OF FAITH AND DOUBT

A collection of 121 novels
in 92 volumes, selected by
Professor Robert Lee Wolff,
Harvard University,
with a separate introductory volume
written by him
especially for this series.

JOHN BULL AND THE PAPISTS

A. H. Edgar

Garland Publishing, Inc., New York & London

1976

Bibliographical note:

this facsimile has been made from a copy in the
Library of Congress
(PZ3.E22J)

Library of Congress Cataloging in Publication Data

Edgar, A H
John Bull and the papists.

(Victorian fiction : Novels of faith and doubt ; 3)
Reprint of the 1846 ed. published by T. Richardson, London.
I. Title. II. Series.
PZ3.E22Jo10 [PR4639.E298] 823'.7 75-447
ISBN 0-8240-1527-4

Printed in the United States of America

JOHN BULL AND THE PAPISTS.

JOHN BULL AND THE PAPISTS;

OR,

PASSAGES IN THE LIFE OF

AN ANGLICAN RECTOR.

BY A. H. EDGAR.

"England of Saints! the peace will dawn,—but not without the fight:
So come the contest when it may,—and God defend the right."

NEALE'S *Hierologus.*

LONDON:
THOMAS RICHARDSON AND SON,
172, FLEET STREET; 16, DAWSON STREET, DUBLIN;
AND DERBY.
1846.

TO

THE RIGHT REVEREND DR. MURDOCH,

BISHOP OF CASTABALA,

AND COADJUTOR VICAR APOSTOLIC IN THE WESTERN DISTRICT OF SCOTLAND,

THE KINDEST OF FRIENDS, THE WISEST OF DIRECTORS,

AND THE FIRMEST SUPPORT IN AFFLICTION;

THIS TALE

IS HUMBLY DEDICATED BY ONE WHO OWES HIM MORE THAN CAN EVER BE REPAID.

PREFACE.

Some friends, to whom the manuscript of this work has been read, have imagined that it was intended to portray individual characters, particularly among the Puseyite party. The writer disclaims all intention of the kind; having only attempted to sketch a class, and in no one instance an individual. With regard to the Methodists, any one who is in the habit of reading their biographies and magazines will see that their peculiarities have not been exaggerated.

JOHN BULL AND THE PAPISTS.

CHAPTER I.

> "These are the church-physicians; they are paid
> With noble fees for their advice and aid,
> Yet know they not the inward pulse to feel,
> To ease the auguish, or the wound to heal." CRABBE.

"How the rector did expose himself last sabbath forenoon!" exclaimed Mrs. Benson, a leading character among the Methodists of Eaglesham, to her sister Dame Blount, a farmer's wife, who patronized the church by law established.

"He hesitated, stammered, turned red and pale time about," she continued, "and made every body think he was going to take a fit—at least so they told me. At last he shut the book and said he was ill; but it was all because he did not choose to read the communion service! I am up to him! He has a bad conscience! His heart has never been made right with God! He has never been born again! His dry bones have never been made to live! Even Balaam's ass would have cut a better figure in the pulpit; for certainly that admirable beast once spoke to the purpose, and that is more than the rector ever did!"

"You speak of what is above your compos mentis, Sister Benson," replied the dame, a dumpy little woman with a pug nose and great dignity of manner.

2

"Dissenters, and all such low creepers, are unfit to judge of the sublime affairs of church and state. A bishop is altogether above their comprehensitiveness, and a rector is a Chinese puzzle to them! No wonder that Parson Feversham's conduct is strange in their eyes—has he not the whole weight of the English church entablature upon him?—Is he not girt round about with the thirty-nine articles?—Do not pistols, gospels, and rubrics prey upon his mind, not to speak of his cares for the surplices, widows and orphans of the parish? It would be a bad sign of our rector, and of the church and state by law established—of which I am proud to say I am a pillaster—if his conduct was lowered to the comprehensitiveness of sectaries. No, no! he walks in a mysterious way, does his reverence the rector."

"Your head is turned about church and state," replied Mrs. Benson. "Every man that is a clergyman by law established, of course, is faultless! But wait a bit till the rector is found out! Can he pray extempore? Has the sword of the Spirit divided his marrow? Did he ever cry Abba Father? Is he a converted, regenerated, sanctified, born-again, out-and-outer? Answer me that, if you please! And tell me if he is anything better than a mere marrying and christening machine? A fruitless, leafless, withered branch, no more to be compared to that budding rod of Aaron under whose ministry I sit, the Reverend Mr. Longab, I mean, than you are to the widow of Tekoah, or Solomon in his glory!"

"Well, well," cried the dame, "go on as you like! I can always make acts of magnanimousness towards poor misguided sectaries! They know no better, poor things! If they had the benefit, like me, of collects in abundance every Sunday, or if they had the blessed rubric to console them, not to speak of the service for ordaining priests and deacons, and that beautiful epigram on the Gunpowder Treason, which is the best bit in the prayer-book, I might expect better things from them. But as it is, they have no aristocratical advantages; nothing to raise them above the common herd—I'll not say herd of what—but I am thinking on the Prodigal Son's flock just now! However, let that pass! If they cannot comprehend and admire the mysterious, supernatural, and hysterical connection between church and state, they are more to be pitied than blamed! Yes! I that am a church and state going woman, spits from an eminence on the likes of dissenters!"

"Come, come, let us have no more wrangling," exclaimed the husband of the dame, a sensible good-natured farmer, who now entered the apartment. "Would it not be far better never to talk on religion, when we all know you cannot agree about it?"

"I don't agree with you there, farmer," replied Mrs. Benson. "It is against my conscience to hide my light under a bushel! I feel called upon to raise up my testimony against Parson Feversham! That care-worn face of his conceals something not good! It may be only a bilious conscience, for many a one swallows the Thirty-nine Articles, that has little stomach for them; but I fear it is worse! The devil is doubtless busy with him, laying nets and mouse-traps for your precious souls, and baiting the snare with the cheese of legality and good works! However, as he is a friend of yours, farmer, I'll say no more, but open the subject which led my steps hitherward.—So Jacob is come! Jacob Hogg, I mean!"

"Well," replied the farmer, gruffly, "what is that to me?"

"Only that he is your son-in-law by the wife's side," replied Mrs. Benson, "married to your wife's first husband's daughter, my niece Sarah! A consanguinous relative if ever there was! It is a shame in you, farmer, to take no notice of him. You know the text, 'Let brotherly love continue.' I have called to-day for no other reason than to make an Esau of you, and get you to kiss Jacob. We all know what a sinner Jacob has been, but that is nothing to the purpose. He is converted now, and thoroughly evangelized. The new birth took place about three weeks ago in the meeting-house at Overbury, with a strong and bitter cry of 'What shall I do to be saved?' Since that time he has been singing, praying, and praising continually; so that, during the still watches of the night, his neighbours in the cottages adjacent are awakened by shouts of 'Hallelujah!' And last Sunday, while Mr. Longab was preaching, there were few in the congregation that could hear what he said, so powerful was Jacob's accompaniment of 'Glory! glory! glory!' The Lord's ways are wonderful in plucking such a brand from the burning. And now I feel marvellously stirred up and impelled to improve the occasion for all our spiritual profit, and for this end have contrived a banquet of tea, coffee, and cakes, for the nourishment both of soul and body. Mr. Longab and Jacob will expound the Scriptures, and hold spiritual converse, to be concluded with extemporaneous prayer, which doubtless Jacob, being but a new hand, will compose before coming. I myself will improve the occasion by making spiritual remarks on the creature comforts, as Mr. Interpreter did when Christian visited his house. What say you, farmer Blount, will you and my sister, and that little scapegrace, your son Neddy, spend the evening with me and my friends on Wednesday?"

The farmer laughed and consented; while his wife tossed her head, and said that if she came at all she would bring the common prayer-book with her, and amuse herself with the thirty-nine articles while the praying went on. Mrs. Benson now took leave; and the farmer, putting on his hat, strode towards the fields. He had scarcely gone many steps when he met the rector of the parish, Mr. Feversham, of whom his sister-in-law had expressed such a bad opinion.

Before detailing their conversation we shall describe the footing on which they stood with regard to each other; and for this purpose must relate some of their early history. The rector was a younger son of a very ancient Catholic family in a distant part of England. His parents died before he was grown up, so that he and his brother were left to the management of guardians, one of whom was an indifferent Catholic, the other a Protestant. The family chaplain, Father Lefevre, who had watched over their early years, was obliged to return to France; so that the good seed he had sown in their bosoms was, in one of them at least, speedily choked with tares. The elder brother, on coming of age, took possession of the family estate; and a commission in a fashionable cavalry regiment was purchased for the younger brother, Edward. Farmer Blount was about the same age as the young officer, and was the son of a respectable yeoman, who farmed a portion of old Mr. Feversham's estate. His relations were Protestants, and as such he had been brought up till the age of fourteen. One day, when the young gentlemen were bathing in a river not far from the hall, the younger was seized with cramp, and would have been drowned, had it not been for the timely assistance of John Blount, who was fortunately passing at the time. This occurred about a year before the death of old Mr. Feversham, who was so grateful for the good service rendered to his son, that he determined henceforward to befriend the lad; and, of course, the first step was to give him a good education. During the succeeding year he was permitted to join the boys in their studies under Father Lefevre, and was instructed in the Catholic religion. John was a fine, frank, good-natured fellow, but too thoughtless to think seriously about anything. When the young gentlemen were sent to school after their father's death, and when old Father Lefevre, with whom he had been a great favourite, had gone back to France, John still called himself a Catholic, but speedily forgot all he had been taught, and scrupled not to attend a Protestant church with his parents.

When Edward Feversham entered the army, Blount took it into his head that he would like to be a dragoon also; and much against his father's will, set off to join his young master, who took him immediately for his private servant. Young Feversham speedily found that his religion was much against his interest; for some years past he had only been a nominal Catholic—nothing was easier now than to change. He mentioned his intention to Blount, who said that of course his honour should know best, and that he would change also in compliment to his master. It was done. They soon afterwards went abroad, and saw a great deal of actual service. Mr. Feversham distinguished himself by his bravery, and his reckless gaiety rendered him a general favourite. When he returned to England, after a number of years, it was as colonel of his regiment. He soon afterwards sold out, and married Lady Harriet Malvern, the daughter of the Earl of Hillsdale, a frivolous woman of fashion, with a considerable fortune. They lived in great style for a few years, during which Lady Harriet gave birth to a daughter, the only child she ever had. Her habits were far too expensive for the income which her own and the colonel's fortune afforded them. They became involved in debt. The old earl was by this time dead; but Lady Harriet's brother, a good-natured man, who would have assisted them had he not likewise been embarrassed, proposed a very simple expedient. He had a valuable living in his gift; this should be the colonel's, if he would drop his military title, and take holy orders. Edward Feversham agreed, and for the last twelve years he had been rector of Eaglesham. By a strange coincidence, John Blount had also settled in that parish. He had left the army and become a farmer, having married a widow with a little property of her own. She had one daughter by her first husband, who by his will had left Sarah two hundred pounds. Farmer Blount in all respects treated his step-daughter as though she had been his own child, but never succeeded in gaining her confidence or affection; she was an unamiable and peevish girl, whom it was impossible to please. When grown up, she formed an intimacy with a journeyman tailor, Jacob Hogg by name, a man of very indifferent character, and total disregard for truth. Her step-father did all in his power to break off the connexion; but when the thankless young woman began to hint that he opposed her marriage, because it was inconvenient to pay her dowry, the farmer instantly gave in, and allowed the match to proceed. On the marriage-day, in the presence of two respectable witnesses, he paid down the money, and received the acknowledgment for it in writing. Some very disgraceful circumstances relating to Mr. Hogg coming to light within a few months after his marriage, he prudently withdrew to a neighbouring town, where, with his wife's money, he succeeded in entering into partnership with a London haberdasher, lately come from the metropolis, who distinguished himself by selling flashy goods at extremely low prices. They failed, but cleared a good deal of money; and Jacob, with his share of the profits, was now about to open a shop in the large village of Eaglesham, where most of the inhabitants were methodists. It was, indeed, a lucky coincidence that Jacob's conversion should have taken place immediately before his arrival, as a great deal of patronage was thereby secured to his new shop.

But to return to Mr. Feversham. For some years after entering on his ministerial duties, the greater portion of his time was taken up in field sports, and in visiting and receiving visitors, for Lady Harriet and he kept open house. About three years before the commencement of our story, he fell from his horse and received an internal injury, which shattered his health, and from which he never wholly recovered. Soon afterwards, he and his family went abroad, in order to economize. They had but lately returned; and every one remarked with surprise the change which had taken place in the rector's appearance; he looked twenty years older, and was evidently a sufferer both in mind and body. His gaiety had entirely fled; he avoided society, and when obliged to enter it, his manner was abstracted and moody. On one occasion only, during the last three months had he read the church service, and then he was obliged to do so by the unexpected absence of his curate. It chanced to be a communion Sunday, and Mr. Feversham, who had appeared ill and agitated during the whole service, gave way entirely as he was about to dispense the sacrament, and was assisted out of the church nearly fainting.

"Well, John," said the rector, as the farmer advanced, hat in hand, to greet him, "how well and hearty you are looking! Who ever could believe that you were the same age as myself! The world goes on smoothly with you I see, or your smiling and ruddy cheeks belie you."

The farmer laughed as he replied, "I ought to be happy, Sir, for I have plenty to eat and drink, I sleep soundly, and have no care; my dame, though a little queer in her ways sometimes, is no bad wife on the whole; and my heart is bound up in my little son—so altogether I have much to be thankful for. You see, Sir, I enjoy my blessings, because I am no scholar, and never was given to thinking, which, to my mind, makes a man plaguy unhappy. I hope your reverence will excuse me—but it came into my head last Sunday, when you were looking so ill, that if you had been an ignoramus like me, you would, may be, have been as hearty."

"The thing is possible," replied the rector with a sigh. "Still, it is very dangerous to live in indifference, and never think at all; for then the subject of most vital importance, our eternal salvation, is neglected. If you are happy because you never trouble your head about religion, your happiness is but very hollow, and will not last; and when on your death-bed, you will regret having neglected so utterly the concerns of your soul."

"What would your Reverence wish me to do?" asked the farmer, who by no means liked the subject. "I am sure I go to church once a week, besides listening to the dame on the Sunday evenings when she teaches Neddy the Catechism. Whenever a collection is made, I give a penny; and I regularly treat the farm servants to a goose at Michaelmas, not to speak of a merrymaking and lots of mince pies at Christmas."

"That is all very well," said the rector, "but I should like you to understand what you are about. Do you know what your church teaches? Can you tell me what you believe?"

"Well, now, really your Reverence is mighty hard upon me this morning," replied Blount. "Nobody ever asked me before what I believed. I can't say as how that I know it, unless it be in the Lord's prayer and the catechism."

"But what made you change your religion, Blount, when you and I were young?" continued the rector; "why did you leave the Catholic church to enter the Protestant one, if you know so very little about the latter?"

"Faith, Sir," replied the farmer, "it's a simple story to explain. I had a wonderful respect for Papistry, because the family at the hall were Papists. Then I loved good old Father Lefevre, so it was no wonder that you all got round a lad of fourteen, as I was then, and made a Roman of me. But a year's schooling is not enough to make a good Christian; so, of course, when the family was scattered, and the priest away, I forgot all I had learned. Then I heard from my friends that the Papists were idolaters, and their religion a mummery; so that opened my eyes a little. And afterwards, when I joined your regiment, and you spoke seriously to me and told me your own intention of changing, in compliment to you I could do no less than follow your example; and I have never had anything but satisfaction in the Church of England ever since. It seems to be the motto with her to 'let well alone,' for not a soul belonging to her has troubled me about religion from that day to this, except, indeed, my wife. And as for you, Sir, have you not had cause to bless the day when you turned Protestant? If I remember right, Providence rewarded you very quickly, for you got your promotion a month after; even I myself had better luck after I changed."

The rector winced under the unconscious sarcasm, and paused a moment ere he replied, "Supposing now that you were to make the discovery that the Church of England was wrong, and that some other church was right—do you think you would leave her?"

"What a strange question!" exclaimed Blount. "Well, I would not countenance deceit under any form; though I can't say exactly what I would do till I am tried. May be I would give up church going altogether. But how can the Church of England be wrong when so many of the first gentlemen in England—witness your Reverence's own self—are her ministers, and have a fine income for looking after her? No, no! I see plain that your Reverence is humbugging me."

"No, John, indeed I am not," replied Mr. Feversham; "I ask you a simple question, because I am curious to hear your answer. If you were to discover that the Church of England was not God's own true church, and if you were morally certain that another one was, would you hesitate to embrace that one?"

The farmer considered a few minutes—such a startling question had never been put to him before; but he had an honest mind, and he grappled seriously with the difficulty. The colour left his face, and then he became redder than before, as he exclaimed, "Why then, dang it, rector! I would not hesitate!"

CHAPTER II.

> "Louder and louder grew his awful tones,
> Sobbing and sighs were heard, and rueful groans;
> Soft women fainted." CRABBE.

ON the next day, Wednesday, Farmer Blount and his wife set off at four o'clock to the house of Mrs. Benson. The dame was as fine as red ribbons and a gay silk gown, much too tight, could make her; and in her hand she carried her best prayer-book, wrapped up in a pocket handkerchief. Mrs. Benson, who received them at the door, was in every respect a contrast to her sister; she was a tall angular woman, with marked features, a Roman nose, and piercing eyes; her fluency of speech was wonderful, and she prided herself on her talents. Jacob and his wife had already arrived. The former was a sleek, comfortable looking man, with a brilliant complexion and sleepy black eyes; a honeyed smile played unceasingly about his thick lips, and he gave a sanctimonious shake of the head whenever he talked of his own spiritual experiences. The Reverend Mr. Longab was a dark man, with bushy eyebrows and a thundering expression of countenance and eyes, which darted forth lightnings from the pulpit when he spoke on his favourite topic, hell-fire. In all respects he was a contrast to the oily-tongued Jacob, who was particularly anxious at this moment to curry favour with him; and for this purpose frequently during the evening propounded spiritual riddles, which Mr. Longab dexterously solved. The following may be taken as specimens. "What is the taste of the bitterness of sin?"—"Is there marrying and giving in marriage among the devils?"—"Is it better to commit every species of actual wickedness, and all the time have the heart right with God, or to practice good works and be unregenerated?"—"Whether is the guilt of the present Pope of Rome, or of Herod that murdered the innocents greatest?" There were many others equally interesting and edifying.

One young woman whose parents were gospel christians, but who herself had not been born again, ventured after the evening meal was despatched, to propose that the table should be drawn aside, and that the young people, of whom several were present, should dance. Jacob Hogg, who was not as yet thoroughly initiated into the ways of a sanctified character, seconded the proposal, on the pious grounds that both Miriam and David danced. But Mr. Longab sternly rebuked him, enunciating in his most thundering voice, that the holy people of old leaped to the sound of sackbuts and psalteries, and not to the squeaking of profane fiddles; besides the ancient worthies were careful always to dance by themselves, there being no Scripture mention of their partners.

Several of the leading methodists now gave their experiences, and accused themselves of being hell-deserving sinners. They alluded to their faults in general terms, while they specified their virtues and the graces they had received from God with the most edifying minuteness. Mrs. Benson, according to her promise, made very original spiritual remarks on corporeal blessings; and the entertainment of the evening concluded with Mr. Longab, Jacob, and several others praying by turns, while their listeners groaned, wept, and ejaculated, "Glory!" and "Hallelujah!" at the proper intervals. The dame, who was very indignant at any one daring to pray in other than the words of the prayer-book, quietly put on her spectacles, and during the most vehement supplications thundered forth by Mr. Longab, very coolly read aloud the thirty-nine articles for the benefit of all who chose to listen. No one paid the least attention to her however — not even Neddy, who, planting himself on his knees behind the minister with hands outstretched, mimicked every motion and every groan; and at each pause, like a good boy who had all his life reverenced the establishment, ejaculated Amen as well as the clerk in the parish church could have done. His father, who did not like anything, however ridiculous, connected with religion to be mocked, punished him afterwards by sending him supperless to bed. At last the young woman previously mentioned, giving a loud shriek, fell to the ground in a fit. Mr. Longab hastened to raise her up, and the pious methodists around her exclaimed in triumphant accents, "The new birth! the new birth! This is the Lord's doing, and it is marvellous in our eyes!" Meanwhile the honest farmer, exceedingly disgusted, made a sign to his wife to follow, and taking Neddy by the hand, slipped away during the confusion which ensued.

The next day, as the farmer was leaving his work to go home to dinner, he again met the rector, who walked up the lane with him. After the customary salutations, Mr. Feversham enquired if the curate, Mr. Hounslow, had been in time the previous evening to baptize the sick child of a young couple who lived within five minutes' walk of Blount's farm. The latter replied in the affirmative, adding, that the infant had died within an hour after the clergyman's departure.

"Thank God it was baptized," exclaimed the rector, "the parents have much reason to be grateful."

"Well, now, your Reverence, I don't see that at all," replied the farmer. "A little squalling thing! It would have saved a deal of pain and grief to the mother had it died sooner. Considering that she was to lose it at any rate, she could not have been much up or down, because it lived to be baptized. However, baptism is a fine old custom, and I am far from thinking little of it."

"It is not as a custom merely that you should regard it," said the rector; "Christ positively commanded it, and we learn from scripture that unless we are baptized, we cannot enter heaven."

"You don't surely mean to say, Sir, that if that little soul had never been baptized, it would have been kept out of heaven! Where do you get scripture for that?"

"In the third chapter of St. John's gospel, Jesus says, 'Verily, verily, I say unto thee, except a man be born of water and of the Spirit, he cannot enter into the kingdom of God.'"

"Are you sure, Sir," asked the farmer, "that this being born of water means baptism?"

"What else can it mean?" rejoined the rector; "no other explanation presents itself; besides, the primitive church so interpreted it."

"And where does Christ command it, your Reverence?" continued the farmer.

"In the twenty-eighth chapter, and nineteenth verse of St. Matthew's gospel," replied Mr. Feversham, "when He said to His apostles, 'Go ye therefore and teach all nations, baptizing them in the name of the Father, and of the Son, and of the Holy Ghost.'"

"These texts are very plain too," replied Blount, "now that your Reverence points them out; but I don't see the exact use of baptism; what good does it do?"

"It communicates grace to our souls," said the rector; "the apostle Paul terming it in his epistle to Titus, 'the washing of regeneration, and renewing of the Holy Ghost.' It remits and washes away our sins, as St. Peter testified when he said, 'Repent and be baptized every one of you in the name of Jesus Christ for the remission of sins.' (Acts ii. 38.) Ananias commanded St. Paul, 'Arise and be baptized, and wash away thy sins, calling on the name of the

Lord.' (Acts xxii. 16.) The latter tells us in his epistle to the Ephesians, that 'Christ also loved the church and gave himself for it, that he might sanctify and cleanse it with the washing of water by the word.' And in Hebrews (x. 22,) he says, 'Let us draw near with a true heart, in full assurance of faith, having our hearts sprinkled from an evil conscience, and our bodies washed with pure water.' Ezechiel also prophesied in his 36th chapter and 25th verse, 'Then will I sprinkle clean water upon you and ye shall be clean.' Thus you see from these texts, that baptism cleanses from sin and washes it away."

"Why don't they baptize oftener if it does that?" rejoined the farmer; "I've committed a plaguy sight of sins since the day I was baptized, and would give anything to have them washed away, if it could be done. Though it is not the custom, could I not be baptized over again?"

"Baptism," replied the rector, "can only be administered once, as it imprints a spiritual mark on the soul which can never be effaced. God has in His mercy, however, provided another remedy for sin, by which sinners may be cleansed and get quit of the load of their guilt."

"Yes, Christ's blood washes away sin; I know that," said the farmer.

"You are right," continued the rector, "but Christ has instituted a certain method of applying that blood to our souls, and washing away our sins in virtue of His divine pardon."

"I do not understand your Reverence," said the farmer. "Since baptism washes away sin, I think that the Baptists, who put off their baptism till they are grown up, show more sense than we do—for indeed I cannot believe that you will find in scripture any other institution so convenient; however, Sir, I'd be glad to hear it if there is."

"What did our Saviour mean," answered the rector, "by saying to his apostles, 'Whosesoever sins ye remit, they are remitted unto them; and whosesoever sins ye retain they are retained,' (St. John xx. 23,) and again, 'Whatsoever ye shall bind on earth shall be bound in heaven; and whatsoever ye shall loose on earth shall be loosed in heaven.' (St. Matthew xviii. 18.) Was that not giving them power to pardon sins?"

"To be sure it was, Sir," said the farmer, "but what the better are we? the apostles are all dead, and who is to give us pardon now?"

"Their successors," answered the rector, "with whom the same power continues."

"If your Reverence could prove from scripture that the power continues, it would be a fine thing for us; but I suppose that is hardly possible," said Blount.

"If our Saviour," replied Mr. Feversham, "had not intended that this power should belong to the successors of the apostles as well as to themselves, what could He have meant by saying, 'Lo I am with you alway even unto the end of the world?'" (Matt. xxviii. 20.)

"So that is what is meant by the minister giving absolution in the prayer-book," replied the farmer. "That beats every thing! I never thought of it before! But it seems odd to forgive sins in a lump, without knowing what they are."

"You are right there, John," said the rector, "sinners, before receiving absolution, ought to confess to the priest appointed by God. Confession is plainly commanded in scripture by the apostle St. James."

"Oh, Sir," interrupted the farmer, "I know what you mean, but he only says, that we should confess 'one to another.'"

"Would you not prefer going to the priest who had power to give absolution?" continued the rector. "If you only confessed your sins to your neighbour, I fear you would not get much satisfaction."

"That is true, Sir," replied the farmer thoughtfully, "but is not that contrary to the church of England?

Surely it is safer to stick by the prayer-book, and not take new fangled expositions of scripture."

By this time they had reached the farmer's door, and the rector offered to go in and point out an applicable passage in the prayer-book. He was accordingly ushered into the best parlour, and the book being got, he turned over some pages and read as follows from the visitation of the sick, 'Here shall the sick person be moved to make a special confession of his sins, if he feel his conscience troubled with any weighty matter. After which confession, the priest shall absolve him, &c.' "You see now," continued the rector, "that the prayer-book authorizes this practice."

"So it does," said the farmer, scratching his head and looking very doubtful, "but it seems to me that we should have heard more about confession in the scriptures, had God meant it to be done."

"There are a great many passages in the Bible relative to confession," replied Mr. Feversham. "For example, the precept of God himself in the fifth chapter of Numbers; 'When a man or woman shall commit any sin that men commit, to do a trespass against the Lord, and that person be guilty, then they shall confess their sin which they have done,' &c. We find such to have been the practice of the first Christians likewise. After the preaching of John the Baptist, the people 'were baptized of him in Jordan, confessing their sins.' (Matt. iii. 6.) And during the preaching of Paul at Ephesus, 'many that believed came and confessed and showed their deeds.'" (Acts xix. 18.)

"Well, we have good example for confession any way," said the farmer, "and it stands to reason, that if the ministers of the church of England have a right to give absolution, in virtue of Christ's words 'whosesoever sins ye remit, they are remitted,' sinners ought certainly to tell them their sins first."

"Clearly so," replied the rector. "Now you see,

John, how it is not necessary to be baptized a second time for the remission of sin, because Jesus Christ has provided another means of cleansing our souls when we sin after baptism."

"Why do not all the ministers of the church of England hear confessions, Sir, since that is the case?" demanded the farmer.

"It has been occasionally done in the church of England," replied the rector, looking rather odd.

"I never before heard, your Reverence, of any but Catholic priests hearing confessions," responded the farmer. "Father Lefevre took great pains, I remember, to prepare me for confession. Surely it is a remnant of popery."

"There are many 'remnants of popery' as you term them," continued the rector, "both perfectly scriptural, and clearly authorized by the English church. However, I see I am keeping you from your dinner, so good morning to you." And so saying Mr. Feversham departed.

"Whew!" exclaimed the farmer, giving a long whistle, "his honour has never forgotten what Father Lefevre taught! But if these things are found in scripture that is everything."

CHAPTER III.

"Some feelings are to mortals given,
With less of earth in them than heaven;
And if there be a human tear,
From passion's dross refined and clear—
A tear so limpid and so meek,
It would not stain an angel's cheek,
'Tis that which pious fathers shed,
Upon a duteous daughter's head." SIR WALTER SCOTT.

THE rector's only daughter Mary, was an amiable girl and highly accomplished. Pretty and agreeable, her father doated upon her. She was engaged to marry Mr. Harvey, a young clergyman, who at present had an Oxford fellowship, but who shortly expected a living. Before the commencement of her engagement, which had now lasted a long time, she had been very gay and lively, but latterly she had been much changed. The suspense and anxiety inseparable from her position, and a certain estrangement which seemed latterly to have arisen, apparently without cause, between her and her father, preyed upon her mind, and she was not happy. She had no one to speak to, no one at home with whom to open her heart, for her mother was the wreck of a frivolous woman of fashion, vain as in her youth, and concentrated in self; while her father, during the last few months, evidently avoided being alone with her, and never talked confidentially, as they had been accustomed to do before. Poor Mary was bewildered, while a dull and heavy misgiving of some approaching evil weighed down her spirits.

One morning she and her father were breakfasting alone together, for lady Harriet, who was very nervous, and had a thousand imaginary ailments, seldom came down stairs till after mid-day, and frequently kept her room for a week together.

"Papa," said Mary, "I have just been thinking how long it is since I received communion from you! It seems so odd! To be sure, when we were abroad it was not so strange; but since we have come home, something always happens to prevent you performing the service."

The rector looked hard at his daughter, while a shade passed over his face.

"Indeed, dear papa," she continued, following up the attack, "something must be the matter with you, you are so changed. Why don't you read the service occasionally as you used to do? People are beginning to make remarks about it. And then you are so dull and grave, you never walk with me and talk the way you did formerly. And as your bad health has made you give up field sports, you make that an excuse for not seeing your old friends. Do, dear papa, tell me what is wrong with you; I am sure I would sympathize with you, and perhaps could do you good."

The rector pressed his daughter to his bosom, but he could not speak; at last he controlled his agitation.

"Not now, Mary, not now!" he exclaimed; "the time is not ripe; you will hear all too soon, when you and your mother are beggars!"

Mary, dreadfully shocked, implored her father to explain himself, but in vain; he tried to laugh and turn away the subject, as though his previous words had escaped him unawares, for he had said more than he intended. Mary, however, still persisted, and at last the rector, trying to smile, replied, "The truth is, my love, we have all been too extravagant, and as it is just possible that my failing health, joined to other causes, may induce me to give up my living, I fear the change of circumstances may prove painful to you and Lady Harriet."

"And is that all?" said Mary, with the air of one

much relieved. "We can manage very well to live on Mamma's fortune; we shall send away half the servants, and still have as many as we require. I will be housekeeper myself, and we shall be as comfortable as possible: I am so glad it is nothing worse."

The rector sighed as he kissed his daughter. The tears were in his eyes, but he had not the courage to tell her the painful truth that her mother's fortune had been spent long ago—and that his living was all the family had at present to depend upon. Luckily for him, further explanations were avoided by the entrance of a servant who came to summon Mary to Lady Harriet.

"What has become of the box I expected, Mary?" were her mother's first words. "You ought to have written again to Madame La Fleur about it. But you have no consideration for your mother's feelings! None in the world!—I might as well be dead as here for anything you care! How can I make calls till the bonnets come from London! However, you regard your mother's appearance as little as you do her health! A mere dowdy yourself, you think of no other body!"

Mary was inclined to laugh as she good-naturedly replied, "Indeed, Mamma, I am almost sure the box will arrive to-day; however, I can write if you like, and enquire what is detaining it."

"If it is not too much trouble," replied Lady Harriet, with mock humility. "Don't think to deceive me," she continued, "it is all of a piece; you and Mr. Feversham are in a conspiracy together to rob me of my happiness! I can see through you both—the very soup I ate this morning might have opened my eyes, had they been blinded before! There is no attention paid to my comfort! And then that unfortunate dog," she added, pointing to an apoplectic little spaniel, lying at her feet, "yesterday when he was washed, you did not see him properly dried, and the consequence is, he has a wretched cold to-day! Love me, love my dog! A mere straw will tell how the wind blows! As the poor dumb animal is neglected, so is his mistress! And the bonnets are in keeping with the rest. Mr. Feversham hates to see me looking well, and grudges even the money to pay poor Madame La Fleur's little account for the last six months!"

"It was a hundred and fifty pounds, Mamma," said Mary, deprecatingly, "not including what is coming in the box to-day!"

"So you are turning against me, too!" exclaimed Lady Harriet. I am a poor neglected ill-used being! No one to feel for me, or sympathize with me! No kindred soul! No heart to beat in unison with my own! No second self to whom I can outpour my sorrows! I am a miserable, over-sensitive, and misunderstood woman! But it has always been so— I might have anticipated what would happen, when I married a man with more obtuse feelings than my own! The dog, the soup, the bonnets! Woe is me!"

And here Lady Harriet consoled herself by taking a good fit of weeping, which lasted for ten minutes, when luckily the missing box arrived, and the excitement of unpacking it made her forget her sorrows.

While Mary was talking with her mother, Mr. Feversham strolled down towards Blount's farm, and soon met the honest man himself.

"I have been thinking a great deal of all your Reverence has been telling me," said the farmer, "and the new light I have got about baptism and confession seems very satisfactory. But there is a question that has come into my head more than once since, and puzzled me. If that little squalling soul we were talking of, had not been baptized, you don't mean to say that it would have gone to hell-fire, do you, Sir?"

"Certainly not," replied the rector. "God is too merciful to punish a being that has never committed actual sin, even though not having been 'born again of water,' it could not enter the kingdom of God. A third place is mentioned in Scripture, neither heaven nor hell, and there we may suppose are the souls of unbaptized infants—a place of rest and probably of happiness, where the souls of the saints were detained before the coming of our Saviour."

"And where may that be mentioned in Scripture?" asked the farmer.

"St. Peter tells us that Christ 'went and preached unto the spirits in prison; which some time were disobedient, when once the long-suffering of God waited in the days of Noe,' &c." (1 Peter iii. 19, 20.)

"Is that what the Romans call purgatory?" asked the farmer.

"The middle state," answered the rector, "of which purgatory is a part, is called Limbo."

"But you never can find purgatory in the Bible, Sir!" exclaimed the farmer. "That is where the Roman Catholics are purified by fire!"

"It is in the Bible, nevertheless," said the rector; "for St. Paul informs us in 1 Cor. iii. 13, 14, 15, that 'every man's work shall be manifest' by a fiery trial; and that they who have built upon the foundation, which is Christ, wood, hay, and stubble, (that is, whose works have been very imperfect and defective, though not to the degree of losing Christ) 'shall suffer loss: but he himself shall be saved, yet so as by fire.'"

"That is a very striking text, indeed, Sir," said the farmer.

"Then, again, our Lord says, in Matt. xii. 32, 'And whosoever speaketh a word against the Son of man, it shall be forgiven him: but whosoever speaketh against the Holy Ghost, it shall not be forgiven him, neither in this world, neither in the world to come.' Now our Lord, who never said anything without a purpose, would not have mentioned forgiveness in the world to come, if some sins, not forgiven in this world, could not be forgiven in a future state; and there must be a third place where this takes place, because no sin can enter heaven to be forgiven there, and in hell there is no forgiveness."

At these words the farmer appeared very much struck; he did not reply for a few minutes; his naturally rosy face flushed still more—he began to speak, and then stopped short; at last, he articulated, "Your Reverence is making game of me. I can assure your honour that I'm a good Protestant now; but although I have forgotten nearly all the papistry I learned, there is something in this that puts me in mind of Father Lefevre."

The farmer paused, and looking up at the rector as he said this, was surprised to see him turn away his head, for the tears were in his eyes.

"God help me! Is your Reverence ill?" he exclaimed. "Was I wrong to speak of Father Lefevre?"

"No, John," replied Mr. Feversham, repressing his agitation, "you were right—quite right. You have a claim upon my candour, for I was the unfortunate instrument of misleading you in the thoughtless days of your youth. I have thought deeply during the last two years, while absent abroad; I have studied both sides of the great question with care and deliberation; and the result of my investigation is, that I now firmly believe the Church of Rome to be the One Holy Catholic and Apostolic Church, and the Church of England to be a false one."

"For God's sake think of your family!" exclaimed the farmer, horror-struck.

"I have thought of my family too long," said the rector, with a sigh. "And God knows whether I do not think too much of them still; for, though I certainly shall give up my living ultimately, yet I do not consider the present to be the fitting time to send my wife and daughter penniless into the world. However, let me not speak of this at present. I have long felt that it was a duty I owed to you, to make you acquainted with my change of sentiments, knowing that I could depend upon your secresy. You are now responsible for yourself; it is for you to judge what you ought to do."

"Very well," said the farmer, a good deal affected. "I followed your Reverence when I was young very faithfully, because I loved and respected you; but I was thoughtless then, and would have followed you for evil as well as for good, not to say that your honour ever led me into evil. Now-a-days, Sir, I am old, but my heart beats as warmly for your Reverence as it did then. So, if you can prove to me that the Catholic Church is true, I'll join her, and never heed the taunts and jeers of the neighbours, who would rather see me a Turk than a Roman. However, if I do what pleases God, they'll laugh on the wrong side of their heads at the day of judgment. Bnt, Sir, it is only fair to tell you that I'm grown very obstinate since I have been married to my dame, and it won't be so easy now to make me change opinions as it was long ago."

CHAPTER IV.

"Canst thou not minister to a mind diseas'd;
Pluck from the memory a rooted sorrow;
Raze out the written troubles of the brain;
And with some sweet oblivious antidote,
Cleanse the stuff'd bosom of that perilous stuff,
Which weighs upon the heart!
Doctor. Therein the patient
Must minister to himself." SHAKSPEARE.

"WHAT is the meaning of this, Sister Blount?" inquired Mrs. Benson, as she came in to chat half an hour with the dame. "They say the rector is very ill; and it is only last Tuesday that I watched him from my window, turning down your lane, going to see your good man, and have another mystification with him, I'll warrant you. They say he was not ten minutes home after that, till he took to his bed. There's Satan's work going on, Mrs. Blount, you may see that written on the rector's face; there is no peace of mind there: and if you don't keep a sharp look-out on John Blount, the rector will make him as bad as himself. I've been watching him since Tuesday last; and instead of singing and whistling in his ordinary ungodly fashion coming up the lane, he has been looking as grave and solemn as the late Ezekiel Benson's bass-fiddle case—which, now that we are speaking of it, I have regretted ever since my good man's death, that I did not use for a coffin for him, seeing he was but small, and with the knees doubled up a bit, it would have fitted him to a hair."

"It is a thing I'll not allow, sister Benson, replied the dame, "that any of my family have the imperance to compare my husband to any man's fiddle-case, or far less to his coffin lid. To my mind, it be no disimprovement to John Blount, that he should look more grave and seductive after speaking to his honour the rector. They have not put the honour on me yet to take me into their intrigues or private talks; and though I would not take it well that my husband carried on this privateering with any other individual, yet with a minister by law established, I take it as a compliment to be kept out of the affair. We are not like sectaries, Sister Benson, that lets their women speak in churches; no, no, we keeps women in their proper place, thanks to the rubric and the homilies! And you need not think to make me jealous about my husband's face sobering, as long as Mr. Feversham consults him in affairs of church and state, and the authorising of bishops, and archiprelagy, for I am content and proud to see him like a Corinthian pillaster, supporting his Reverence, and spitting from an eminence on the likes of dissenters."

"If your husband is such a useful man as you say," rejoined Mrs. Benson, whose face had become very red, "why does he not keep up Mr. Feversham's spirits? And how does it happen that the longer they take counsel together, the worse gets the minister by law established? He has only preached once since he came from abroad; and then, I hear, it was a papistical sermon. When he was to dispense the Supper of the Lord, he took ill and left the church; and now he leaves your house on the Tuesday, and takes to his bed. Far better for a converted, regenerated, and sanctified woman, with a saving knowledge of the Scriptures, and a tongue piercing the ears like the flourish of the last trumpet—far better, I say, for a chosen vessel like *that* to fill the ministry, than for a dead dog, pottage without salt, or mattress without stuffing, like your famous rector."

"Thanks to the divine abundance," replied the dame, "our glorious church by law established is in no danger of falling into scandalous overtures of that kind. Though womankind was exalted in Eve, yet she is not the stuff to make bishops and curates of; and though I cannot go so far as to propound that women should hearken to their husbands at home, as I never do to John Blount, except he fly in a passion, yet on no account would I sanctify by countenancing them, your female preachers."

"And why not?" rejoined Mrs. Benson, drawing her thin spare form up to its height. "Has Miriam sung, and Deborah led the Israelites in vain? Did Sarah take her own way with Abraham, and did Jael knock the right nail on the head, for nothing? No, no; while the Apostle Paul lived, I grant you he was strict, and having so much to say himself, had no time to listen to women, and therefore forbade them to speak in churches; but now-a-days it is a different thing, and I opine that the Holy Spirit knows best, so that if He move a woman to lift up her testimony in the meeting-house, lo! who shall gainsay her?"

"I would," replied the dame. "Spirit, or no spirit, I'd be the first to leave the place if she did."

"You forget, Mrs. Blount, who is the head of your own beautiful establishment," continued her sister. "The queen may very well act as minister any day she likes. I hold she has got what you call holy orders already. She is above priests, deacons, bishops, and archbishops; she is the tip-top head of the episcopacy, and if that does not prove that she is a beneficed clergyman in holy orders, and therefore fit to administer the sacraments, take church fees for baptism and matrimony, collect tithes, hold a glebe, and preach on Sundays, my name is not Deborah!"

"I'll have no privy treason spoken in my house, Sister Deborah; so, unless you change the subject, I'll trouble you to walk. Goodness gracious! just to think that our blessed queen in her robes of state should ever be humbled so far as to set up as a preacher! No, no, Sister Benson, I am royal to my queen, and there must be no conspiratures spoken here."

"Well, and how you do flare up," said her opponent, "when I only mentioned the queen's privileges. Bless me! you may be sure the queen of Sheba, who was at least as fine a woman as our Queen Victoria, mounted the pulpit in the temple, and gave a sermon, taking for her text Solomon's wisdom—at least, I don't think that if she were worth her ears, as she had doubtless a fine discourse, that she would miss that opportunity of making herself heard. It's more than I'd have done any way! However, as you are in bad humour, Sister Blount, I'll say good-bye, praying the Lord to open your eyes, which you keep so obstinately closed, with His own sharp scissors; and that the Spirit may pound you with His pestle in His own mortar, until you come humbly seeking admission into our fold, a veritable crushed lump, and a bruised methodist."

Shortly after Mrs. Benson's departure, the farmer entered, and was greatly vexed and surprised to hear from his wife of the rector's illness. He did not altogether believe it, as he sometimes suspected his good sister-in-law of amplifying news; but, in any case, he felt he could not be at rest until he had walked to the rectory, and satisfied himself. On his enquiry for Mr. Feversham, the man who opened the door informed him that he was unwell, and had given orders that no one should be admitted. The farmer turned away disappointed, when the library bell rang violently, and the rector's voice was heard directing that Blount, whom he had seen coming up the avenue, should be shown up stairs.

Mr. Feversham was in his dressing-gown, and looked exceedingly ill. His brow was even more deeply furrowed than heretofore, his eyes were blood-shot, and his cheeks were pale and haggard. He rose at the farmer's entrance, and shaking his hand warmly, led him to a seat. "I left you abruptly the other day, my good friend," he said, "for I could stand the interview no longer. Harassed with care as I am, to add to my other misfortunes, my health is giving way; when, alas! to steer myself out of my present difficulties, and weather the storm about to burst over my head, I would require to have nerves of iron. However, God's will be done.........Were you surprised, Blount, at the disclosure I made so unexpectedly?"

"Yes, your Reverence," replied the farmer; "I was surprised, and I may say shocked a good deal too. However, the more I consider it, the less strange I think it; though, to be sure, it took me all of a heap at first. Your Reverence had been preparing me too, for a while before, if I had but had the sense to see it. Is your Reverence better now, if I may make bold to ask?"

"Yes, John," said the rector, "I am somewhat better; but I never can be well until this is off my mind. I have a number of things to arrange, before I can declare openly to the world my change of opinion, and till then I can neither expect health nor mental peace. Above all, I am uneasy about my daughter. Poor girl! she is engaged to marry a very worthy man. If that marriage were only concluded, and proper settlements made upon her, my mind would be more at ease. However, we'll see what can be done when the bishop comes home; that will be some time yet."

"And is your Reverence quite decided, then," inquired the farmer, "to turn Papist, and give up your living?"

"I am, John," replied the rector, "God bestowing upon me grace and strength."

"May God grant you His best blessing, and strengthen you to do it!" ejaculated the farmer. "Whether you be right or wrong, He only knows, and a poor man like me cannot judge; but this I know, that God must be pleased with truth of purpose, and will surely reward a sacrifice made for Him. I could almost cry myself; so, if you please, your Reverence, don't be angry with me for telling my mind."

During these words, the rector had risen, and was pacing up and down the room, as men are wont to do when they are uneasy. When at last he sat down, the farmer continued, "If I am not detaining you too long, Sir, I have a great curiosity to ask you a question. How does it happen, your Reverence, that, instead of opening your mind to one of your own family, or to some of your grand friends, or the learned men of your acquaintance, you have so far condescended as to speak frankly and openly to me, that can be of almost no use to you, although I was ever so willing."

"I have not spoken to my family, John," replied the rector, "because I wish to spare them needless pain, until the decisive moment for acting comes. Neither have I mentioned the matter to the learned men of my acquaintance, because they would ply me with arguments; whereas I need none, being no longer in doubt. Nothing they could say would shake me; I have been studying the subject, and reading the best authors for and against Catholicity, during nearly three years. The consequence has been that I have only ended where I began, with the conviction oppressing me, that I left the true church of Christ and entered a false one from mercenary motives; and that, however I might lull my conscience to sleep for a time with folly and vanity, I never could think seriously for a moment without confessing to myself that I was a hypocrite. The reason I spoke to you is very obvious; because the guilt of having persuaded you to take a false step is on my conscience, and I wish to set you once more on the right path. Besides, John, I must confess that it is a great relief to me to give vent to my pent-up feelings, and though my efforts in making the disclosure to you on Tuesday gave my health a shock, yet, on the whole, my mind is more at rest since I spoke."

"So your Reverence would like to make a Catholic of me again, because you believe it to be the true religion," rejoined Blount. "I am ready and willing to be convinced, if so be it is a religion that agrees with the Bible, and I look to your Reverence to show me that. The neighbours will say I am an old fool should I turn Papist; however, right is right any day, and what need I care if I prove to be no fool at the day of judgment?"

"I am delighted to find you in such dispositions, Blount," said the rector. "If you are sincerely anxious to know the truth, and will be deterred by no fear of consequences from embracing it when you discover it, I think it will not be a difficult task to show you that the Catholic is the only true religion. One of the most important points on which Catholics differ from Protestants, is on the subject of the holy communion, so, if you please, we shall discuss that first."

Yes," said Blount, "I should like it of all things, for I can't say that I have very clear ideas about the Lord's Supper. I have mixed with a good many sectarians in my time, and though they all hold by the Bible, there are hardly two of them agree about it; some say there is nothing particular in the bread and wine, and that it is merely for a commemoration like, of the last supper. When I was a dragoon, I remember our regiment was ordered to Scotland; your honour had got leave of absence at the time. Well, there was a parish a few miles from the town where we were, and I happened to hear that the sacrament was to be given the next Sunday. These presbyterians, your Reverence, don't give the sacrament more than once or twice a year, but people come from all the neighbouring parishes to see it done. It is just like a fair, all but the dancing and the buying and selling—as many fine clothes, as much merry-making and drinking at the public-houses! Well, it so happened, Sir, that after the people had got the sacrament, or rather the bread and wine, for I have my suspicions that little was done in the way of consecrating it, there was a good deal of the bread left that the minister had been distributing, so I asked a young woman near me, who chanced to be the minister's own servant, what they would do with it. 'Oh!' says she, 'it is gathered up and brought to the manse, where Missis and I generally makes a pudding of it.'* Well, Sir, that struck me all of a heap! It gave me a mighty shock! And says I to myself, 'That's no sacrament!' I was mightily pleased, your Reverence, though, the other Sunday, when your curate gave us a sermon on the Spiritual Presence of Jesus Christ in the Sacrament; for that showed me that it was not common bread and wine which is received. I always thought so myself, and for that reason I never took the sacrament but once, in the English church, for I felt I was not worthy of it."

"Well, John," said the rector, "we shall not discuss any farther the different opinions with regard to the Eucharist, but go at once to the Bible, and see what is said there. You are willing, of course, to abide by that, and to correct any vague or erroneous opinion which you have previously held, if you find it disagree with Holy Writ."

"Certainly, your Reverence," said Blount.

"Well," continued the rector, "the institution of the Lord's Supper is mentioned four different times in the New Testament in the most explicit terms, and unless we perversely choose to misunderstand it, there is no fear of our going wrong, if we only take the literal meaning. In the twenty-sixth chapter of St. Matthew, at the twenty-sixth verse, we find the following, 'And as they were eating, Jesus took

* This actually happened some years ago, at a manse in Perthshire.

bread and blessed it, and brake it, and gave it to the disciples, and said, 'Take, eat; this is my body.' Do you believe what Christ says, John? He does not say this signifies my body, but he says, 'This *is* my body.' In the twenty-eighth verse again we have, 'For this *is* my blood of the New Testament, which is shed for many for the remission of sins.' Observe, Christ does not say here, this signifies my blood, but, 'this *is* my blood.'"

"But it is very hard to believe, Sir," replied the farmer, "that what we see is bread and wine, should be in reality Christ's body and blood!"

"I grant you it is, John," rejoined the rector, "very difficult to believe, and beyond our comprehension; but it appears to me that you must either believe it, or make out Christ to have said what was false."

"Is it the Protestant Bible, Sir, or the Catholic, that you are reading, for that may make a great difference?"

"It is the Protestant one, John, which I now use, as it will, of course, be more satisfactory to you to get proofs from it."

"Well, your Reverence, I confess that I am posed here—but you see I am an unlearned man, and no hand at explaining the Bible; yet it strikes me that Protestant ministers say that Christ spoke figuratively! How is your Reverence sure that he did not?"

"Because Christ could have no object in speaking figuratively at the time; He was alone with His most confidential friends, the twelve apostles, and though He was accustomed to speak in parables to the people, He was always in the habit of explaining what He meant to *them*. To prove this, on one occasion He said to them, 'Unto you it is given to know the mystery of the kingdom of God; but unto them that are without, all these things are done in parables.' Mark, 4th chapter, 11th verse. And in the 34th verse, alluding to the people in general, it is said,

'But without a parable spake he not unto them; and when they were alone he expounded all things to his disciples.' Had Christ been speaking to the multitude when he said, 'This is my body,' and 'This is my blood,' I allow these might very possibly have been figurative expressions; but He would have been acting in an extraordinary and unusual manner had He spoken ambiguously to His apostles. You must remember also, Blount, that these apostles were the chief individuals chosen by Jesus Christ to preach His gospel; if He did not mean them to understand Him literally, what possible motive could He have had for using an expression likely to put wrong not only them, but afterwards so many millions of christians who take the words in their literal sense? I will go farther even," continued the rector, "and say that if Christ did not mean literally the words, 'This is my body,' and 'This is my blood,' it would have been deceiving the apostles; because He had previously given them reason to suppose that whatever He might do to others, He made known to them everything without reserve. See His words in the 15th chapter, 15th verse of St. John, 'Henceforth I call you not servants; for the servant knoweth not what his lord doeth; but I have called you friends; for *all things* that I have heard of my Father, I have made known unto you.' Observe, John, Christ says, '*all things;*' you see there no keeping back, no reservation, and no hint of enveloping the truth in mysterious language."

"I see that, Sir," said Blount; "but your Reverence said that the institution of the Lord's Supper is mentioned four times in the New Testament; will you have the goodness to read the passages, for I should like to know if our Lord's body and blood are as clearly mentioned in the other places. If they are not, it would make a difference."

"Well," said the rector, "let us see. We have already quoted St. Matthew, we shall now look what

St. Mark says on the subject, in the 14th chapter and 22nd verse of his gospel: 'And as they did eat, Jesus took bread and blessed and brake it, and gave to them and said, Take eat, *this is my* body.' Not, this signifies my body, but 'this *is*.' In the 23rd and 24th verses we find, 'And he took the cup, and when he had given thanks he gave it to them, and they all drank of it. And he said unto them, this *is my blood* of the New Testament which is shed for many.'

"Now we shall take St. Luke's testimony, 22nd chapter, 19th and 20th verses. 'And he took bread and gave thanks, and brake it, and gave it unto them, saying, This *is* my body which is given for you, this do in remembrance of me. Likewise also the cup after supper, saying, This cup *is* the New Testament in my blood which is shed for you.' In case the record of the Evangelists is not sufficient, we shall quote also from St. Paul's description of the Last Supper, in the 11th chapter of his first epistle to the Corinthians. He likewise mentions our Saviour having said, 'This *is* my body which is broken for you,' and 'This cup *is* the New Testament in my blood;' while, to make assurance doubly sure, he adds, in the 24th verse, 'For he that eateth and drinketh unworthily, eateth and drinketh damnation to himself, not discerning the Lord's body.'"

"These are strange texts of scripture," said the farmer, "enough to make me tremble; they are hard to believe, and yet if I am not to believe them, it would almost shake my confidence in Christ altogether, for I think He would have been wilfully deceiving us, thus saying over and over again by the mouths of the Evangelists what is false. I cannot believe your doctrine, for it goes against my senses that what I see is bread and wine, should be the body and blood of Christ: but I am loth to disbelieve it too; for it strikes me that if I deny it, it would be making Christ Himself a liar. Is there no way, your Reverence, of getting out of the scrape?"

"There is no way, John, for an honest and simple mind that acknowledges Christ to be the Son of God, but to believe implicitly what Christ has said."

"It is a hard thing, your Reverence," replied Blount; "you bring me forward good proofs, such as would satisfy me were I on a jury about matters of law and business—and yet, hang it, I can't believe it. You see, Sir, those notions were so laughed out of me when I was a young man, and they were made to appear to me so ridiculous, that though you were to give me all the Bible authority in the world for it, and though I would wish to believe what is plainly stated there, yet I can't."

"I suppose, John, that you don't like to believe what you cannot comprehend, or what you think goes against common sense?"

"Just so, Sir; I think God gave us sense to guide us, and that we are bound to use it, and to reject what goes against it. For example, Sir, though I am not just perfectly sure, yet I would find little difficulty in believing that God has enjoined us to confess our sins, and that the successors of the apostles have authority to remit them; because not only there are texts in the Bible for it, but it does not go against reason. The other thing, however, is different; though your Reverence has given me much stronger Bible proof for the bread and wine becoming the body and blood of Christ, yet somehow it goes against me to doubt my eyes, and my taste, and my common sense."

"And yet, John, you are inconsistent, for there are some things which you believe at present, quite as incomprehensible and as opposed to common sense, as the doctrine of the real presence of Christ in the Blessed Sacrament."

"For example, your Reverence, if you please."

"You believe," said the rector, "that there is but one God, that in this God there are three persons, that they are *entirely distinct*, and yet the three are but one God. How can three distinct persons be one? You cannot comprehend it, but because God has taught it you must believe it, although common sense will not assist you there. If you refuse to do so because you cannot understand it, then you are no Christian. So I would advise you, John, to take care not to say that you will not believe what you do not comprehend, or you will get yourself into a scrape."

"Well, well, your Reverence, perhaps I went too far in saying so. I have not the same difficulty in believing the doctrine of the Trinity as that about the Sacrament. Though the Trinity is above my comprehension, yet I can believe it if God has taught it; for it is a thing altogether apart from every day common sense, and to my mind common sense has no business to judge of it, for it is God's affair, and He is not to be judged by man's reasoning; but my objection to your doctrine of the Sacrament is, that it goes against nature to believe a thing different from what you see it."

"Is not God everywhere?" inquired the rector; "are we not told that such is His immensity, that heaven and earth cannot contain Him? and yet this infinite being came down from heaven and took the form of a little infant. The Almighty was concealed under the appearance of a poor and helpless child. Take example, then, by the shepherds and by the wise men of the east, who did not hesitate to believe a thing contrary to the evidence of their reason and of their senses, and who came and adored the God of the universe under the form of a weakly and tender infant."

"That *was* faith," said Blount, "I allow, and I don't see that it should be much harder for me to believe in the body and blood of Christ, than for them to worship God in the shape of an infant. But you see, Sir, some people are differently constituted from others; you have given me authority for it in scripture, far clearer authority than for baptism and confession, and yet these doctrines are not difficult for me to believe, but this one is. Perhaps when I get more accustomed to it, Sir, I shall feel differently; it is strange to me just at first, and yet when I was a boy I believed it firmly."

"You believe in the Bible, Blount, and you allow that I have given good scripture proofs for this, so that in one way at least your understanding is satisfied. All the proofs in the world would do you no more good, unless God gave you the grace of faith. Pray earnestly then, my dear Blount, that He would open your eyes and make you see clearly what is truth. He never refuses to hear those who ask Him. Beseech Him then, with the greatest confidence, to assist you, and to show you who are right, whether those who believe the words of Jesus Christ, 'This is my body,' and 'this is my blood,' or those who 'eat and drink damnation to themselves, not discerning the Lord's body.' I must send you away now, Blount, for I have not time to continue the conversation, but I hope you will come to see me very soon again, particularly if it be not in my power to go to you."

CHAPTER V.

"The Jews therefore strove among themselves, saying, How can this man give us his flesh to eat?......From that time many of his disciples went back, and walked no more with him.—*St. John's Gospel*, vi. 52, 66, *Protestant version.*

THE next day the farmer, having more leisure than usual, saddled a powerful grey horse which he kept partly for riding, partly for the lighter work of the farm, and proceeded to Overbury, where he went straight to the house of a Mr. Sharples, a clergyman of the established church, who had lately been appointed there, and who had already made some noise by his preaching. This gentleman was of evangelical principles, and was thought particularly calculated to make friends among dissenters, whose acquaintance and society he very much courted. He had lately commenced preaching against popery, being incited to do so by the great increase of Catholicism in Overbury, and by the opening there of a new Catholic chapel, chiefly for the Irish workmen, which drew crowds every Sunday from the novelty of the worship. We shall not describe the conversation which took place between the honest farmer and Mr. Sharples, it being sufficient to mention the fact of his making that gentleman's acquaintance, to account for the numerous objections to Catholicity, which without this assistance would not have entered his own head, but with which he henceforward answered Mr. Feversham.

"Will your Reverence be angry with me," said the farmer next time they met, "if I make some objection to one of the proofs you gave me from the Bible about Christ's body and blood?"

"Certainly not," replied the rector; "on the contrary I shall be glad to have the opportunity of answering them, and I am pleased to find that you have studied the subject sufficiently to discover objections; far better that, than to subside into indifference."

Blount's face became red as he replied, "Why, your Reverence, I must tell you the truth; the objections I have found would never have come into my head, had they not been put there by a cleverer man than I am—Mr. Sharples, of St. Luke's church in Overbury."

"You don't mean to say," exclaimed the rector starting, "that you told him the subject of our present conversations; to say the least, John, it was very indiscreet, and I consider it breaking bargain with me; of course, I should be the first person to make known my own change of sentiments to the world."

"Not so fast, your Reverence, not so fast," replied honest John. "I never mentioned your name at all to him, Sir. I merely told him that in my youth I had been a Catholic myself, and that now some misgivings were coming across me that my old religion might be right, and that as I heard he was the great man against Papists, I came to him for advice. He did not even know my name, Sir, for I go but seldom to Overbury, and when he asked it, I mumbled something about my name being of no consequence, and in that way put him off. No, no, your honour! I am not such a fool as to tell tales, particularly after you placed confidence in me. Mr. Sharples began a long tirade about popery, and told me a number of things that I knew myself were not true; but I cut him short by saying, that if he had no objection we would just take the thing bit by bit, and if he would answer me the Catholic arguments for transubstantiation, that was all that I wanted at present. I had some difficulty in bringing him to the point, for he had so much to say on every thing; but at last I managed to get from him two or three objections which I have ready for you. If I mistake not, Sir, you quoted 1 Cor. xi. 23, 24, 25, to prove that the bread and wine become the body and blood of Christ; I think I am right, Sir, for I took down all the texts with a pencil, just as you gave them. Well, your Reverence, when Mr. Sharples and I turned up the place, he pointed out to me how Paul three times over in the verses following calls it *bread;* saying, 'For as often as ye shall eat this bread,' and again, 'Wherefore, whosoever shall eat this bread and drink this cup of the Lord unworthily,' &c. &c. Now if our Saviour really meant 'this is my body,' why does Paul call it bread immediately after?"

"This certainly is an objection which I think never would have struck you, John, had you been unassisted, for I consider it mere quibbling. Nothing is more common than to call a thing by the name of that out of which it was made or changed. For example, it was said to Adam in Genesis, 'Dust thou art;' because, though a living man, he was made of dust. In Exodus, speaking of the magicians, it says, 'They cast down every man his rod, and they became serpents; but Aaron's rod swallowed up their rods.' It was no longer a rod but a serpent when it did so, and yet it is called a rod. I could give many other examples of the same kind were it necessary. However, if you are still in doubt, let St. Paul explain himself. After he has, as you say, three times called by the name of bread the Sacrament which he describes our Lord to have consecrated, he goes on as follows: 'For he that eateth and drinketh unworthily, eateth and drinketh damnation to himself, not discerning the *Lord's body.*' In making such objections, John, are *you* not refusing also to discern the Lord's body?"

Blount did not reply, so the rector continued, "Lest we should mistake him, St. Paul has already expressed himself clearly on the point in the previous chapter, the 10th of 1st Cor. 16th verse. 'The cup of blessing which we bless, is it not the communion of the blood of Christ? The bread which we break, is it not the communion of the body of Christ?' And to crown all, our blessed Saviour says, in St. John 6th and 51st, 'The bread that I will give is my flesh,' &c."

"Well, your Reverence," said Blount, "there was another objection that Mr. Sharples made. I am sure it is a wonder that I remember it, but he took so much pains, your honour can't think, to knock it into my head, that I might be sure not to forget it; for I told him, Sir, I was in the way of meeting with a Catholic now and then. I hope I did right, Sir?"

"A Catholic in heart at least, John, who will soon

declare himself openly I hope," replied the rector, smiling; "but what is this new objection?"

"Why, Mr. Sharples said, that in Luke our Saviour calls the Sacrament the fruit of the vine; which was as much as to say, that whatever it might mean figuratively, it was not really his blood."

"Though our Saviour called it so, it would mean no more than the expression of St. Paul which I have already explained. But Jesus Christ did not call the holy Sacrament the fruit of the vine; for he spoke of what was in the cup before it was consecrated, and before it became his blood, as you will see in reading the passage beginning at the 14th verse of the 22nd chapter of St. Luke. 'And when the hour was come, he sat down, and the twelve apostles with him. And he said unto them, With desire I have desired to eat this passover with you before I suffer. For I say unto you, I will not any more eat thereof, until it be fulfilled in the kingdom of God. And he took the cup and gave thanks, and said, Take this and divide it among yourselves: for I say unto you, I will not drink of the fruit of the vine, until the kingdom of God shall come.' This is the passage to which you refer, Blount, and you see there is as yet no mention of the consecration of the sacrament, though there is in the 19th and 20th verses which immediately follow. To mark the difference I shall quote them likewise. 'And he took bread and gave thanks and brake it, and gave unto them saying, This is my body which is given for you: this do in remembrance of me. Likewise also the cup after supper, saying, This cup is the New Testament in my blood which is shed for you.' Thus you see that it was not the sacramental cup, but that which was drank at the passover, which our Saviour called the fruit of the vine."

"You have the best of it, rector, by far," replied Blount. "To say the truth, though I have given you Mr. Sharples' objections with great pain and difficulty to myself, for it took me two hours and a half to get them by heart, so as decently to put them before your Reverence; yet I did not think much of them myself, for I thought they were too much in the style of quips and quibbles for my taste, and that your Reverence argued in a more solid manner. It is a strange thing, Sir, that though I cannot answer your arguments, and though Mr. Sharples does not do it satisfactorily either, to my way of thinking, yet I cannot believe altogether in the real body and blood of Jesus Christ being in the sacrament. There is a somewhat against it to my judgment, though I cannot just lay hold of it, to argue with your Reverence."

"God has not yet given you the grace of faith, John," replied the rector. "Your head is in the process of being convinced, but your heart is not touched. Pray, I beseech you, to God, to lead you aright, and all will go well. If you pray earnestly, God will hear you for the sake of our Blessed Redeemer, and there will be no fear of your either remaining in error or falling into it."

"I shall do so, your Reverence," said the farmer, rising to depart, "but I sometimes fear that God will not listen to the prayers of an old sinner like me, that have neglected Him so long."

"Never fear John," replied the rector, "no one in a contrite spirit ever applied to God in vain. Our Saviour forgave the dying thief; He raised Mary Magdalen by His grace from the lowest degradation, and He says Himself that He came not to call the just but sinners to repentance."

The farmer now left the rectory, and on his way home pondered deeply on all he had heard. He could not deny that there was a great deal in the proofs brought forward by Mr. Feversham in support of the doctrine of the real presence of Christ in the sacrament; but he felt as though he could more easily disbelieve the Bible altogether than adopt an opinion which so daringly outraged all common sense. "I am loth to believe," said he to himself, "that the Bible is untrue; but why then does it prove such an extraordinary doctrine? . . . Father Lefevre believed it though, and he made me believe it once, when I was under him! True, I was a boy at that time, and easily swallowed every thing I was told; but I was better then than I have ever been since, and I would believe in transubstantiation again most willingly if I could, were I only sure of becoming as good a Christian as in Father Lefevre's time! But then, if I can't, I can't; the rector makes it out that the Bible goes so awfully against common sense! After all I must take another trip to Overbury and see Mr. Sharples, though he again goes too far the other way!"

"Mr. Jacob Hogg was here asking for you while you were out," cried little Neddy, running to meet his father. "He told mother that he was getting a beautiful new shop full of pretty things, and he says that if you will let me go and see him and Sarah, that he will give me a drum and a fife! Won't it be nice, father? If you'll go and see him you will get a drum too! He gave me a gingerbread lady and a horse to-day! I likes Jacob, father, for he is good now, though he once pinched me long ago when you wasn't by, and made me cry."

"What nonsense is that you are talking, Neddy?" cried Dame Blount, as her husband and son entered. "You missed a wonderful sight of things, farmer, with gadding about to-day. Jacob, or I should better say Mr. Hogg, for he's turning the genteel man now, is setting up the most splendiferous shop that has been seen yet in the village. It will take the shine out of Overbury, if not out of Lunnun itself. Silks and satins, and damasked prints, thread, needles, tapes, cotton velvets, red maroon hangers, tapestry, carpets, tea, sugar, wine, and spirits, French plums, carraways, ball dresses, and candles—in short, as Jacob says, he is going to sell all that the imagination of man, which is evil from his youth, can conceive. He brought me patterns and exemplars of some of the most beautifullest gowns I ever saw. You must encourage his trade, John, by giving me a gown at Christmas."

"And what was his business with me?" enquired Blount. "None of the things you mention are in my line, so I should think I was not much missed."

"He is getting everything for you too," said the dame, "coats, great coats, shirts, all ready-made; whips, walking sticks, gaiters, &c.; he has promised to buy my butter and my cheese, and give me articles of virtue in exchange."

"Articles of what?" asked the farmer.

"Articles of virtue—some of the fine new-fashioned things they make at Brummagem, I guess," said the dame.

"Are you sure they are not the thirty-nine articles mentioned in the big prayer-book?" rejoined the farmer, laughing.

"None of your imperance now, Blount," replied his wife. "It would be good for your soul if you practised the thirty-nine articles only half as well as your missis does. But I have no time to stand here mangling and wrangling when I have got a message to tell. Jacob Hogg bid me say that he will thank you to call up at the new shop any time, and see the goods and other combustibles. He has somewhat to tell you about a profitable vesture of money, that he thinks will be a great benefice to the family."

"If Jacob Hogg likes, he can come down himself again to speak about it," said the farmer; "but as for me, I shall not stir a step. I have no opinion of his investments; and the less any of us have to do with him the better, I think."

"He was speaking of a school, too, for Neddy," said the dame. "It seems he is agent for a virtuous and respectuous man, Mr. Longab's cousin, who brings up little boys by the fear of the rod in the love of God, and teaches them Latin and strict morals for twelve pounds a year — food, washing, the use of the globules, and a university education included: nothing extraneous but two pair of sheets and a couple of towels. I asked Jacob if his friend was illicit, or connected with church and state, for it struck me that we could not do better than invest Neddy there; but as he said he was a 'pendant congregationalist, I tossed my head and told him freely that I would have nothing to do with dissent."

"No, no, Neddy," said the farmer, taking his curly-headed darling on his knee; "when we send thee to school, it must be to a good one—thy mother was right this time."

CHAPTER VI.

"Blessed are they that have not seen and yet have believed."

St. John's Gospel, xx. 29.

It was some days ere the farmer had time to go to the rectory again, as he was engaged with business about the farm; and he had determined also not to call on Mr. Feversham until he had seen Mr. Sharples, and learned a few more objections. Had the rector spoken to him of almost any other doctrine than the real presence of Jesus Christ in the sacrament, he would have been open to conviction, always supposing that reasonable proofs had been brought forward; and he would never have taken the trouble to go to any other clergyman to propound his doubts. The present case, however, was very different; he was hemmed in by arguments which he could not answer. They appeared to him to involve an absurdity; and yet his honest mind could not deny them without denying the Bible altogether. He was glad to attribute his present difficulties to his own ignorance and want of knowledge; and fondly hoped that Mr. Sharples, who had already so much distinguished himself in controversy, could remove his difficulties. And yet no vulgar prejudices against Catholicity reigned in his mind; he considered Catholics to be at least as good as their fellow Christians, though his judgment refused to yield its assent to transubstantiation, the key-stone of their faith.

It was about ten days after the conversation last described, that farmer Blount again called upon the rector, who, although his health was improved, had not gone to see him, thinking it better to leave his good sense to revolve what had been said, than to urge any more arguments. In the great question between Protestants and Catholics, argument is useless after a certain point; for, though the judgment of the former is often led captive by the reasoning of the latter, God does not give them sufficient grace to believe Catholicity with that firmness and ardour which is necessary to enable them to *dare* to change their religion. A conversion is the work of God, and not of man; human reasoning is powerless without His grace softening our hard hearts, and enabling us to become in docility and humility, like those little children of whom are the kingdom of heaven. Let us pray earnestly, then, for the conversion of those who differ from us; it is neither human learning nor skill in argument which will convert our antagonists, though these are powerful adjuncts, but it is prayer which must be our great weapon in the conflict. Perhaps, if our honest friend Blount had prayed more at this time, he would not have been in such perplexity.

"I have brought your Reverence another objection from Mr. Sharples," said he to Mr. Feversham, the next time they met. "Though I'll not deny that it looks rather flimsy, yet, maybe there is something in it; so if you, Sir, will please to answer it, I'll be obliged."

"What is it, John?" enquired the rector.

"Why you see, Sir, Mr. Sharples repeated again that our Saviour often spoke figuratively. So I replied that he did so to the Jews, but not to his particular friends, the apostles and disciples; and then Mr. Sharples said that he could prove that Christ did speak in figures to them also. So I said, 'Prove it, Sir, if you please.' And with that he turned up the 15th chapter of John's Gospel, and sure enough our Saviour compares Himself there to a vine, and them to the branches; and what is more, if I mistake not, He is speaking *only* to the Apostles, for it was at the last supper."

"You are quite right, John," replied the rector, "in saying that our Saviour compared Himself to a vine after the last supper in the presence of his Apostles only. But there is all the difference between that and when He said, 'This is my body,' and 'This is my blood.' After comparing Himself to the vine, He explains the metaphor in the 5th and 6th verses: 'I am the vine, ye are the branches: he that abideth in me, and I in him, the same bringeth forth much fruit, for without me ye can do nothing. If a man abide not in me, he is cast forth as a branch, and is withered,' &c., &c. Here is a complete explanation of the ambiguous term. Now, after the institution of the sacrament, our Saviour in no way explains His extraordinary language, 'This is my body,' and 'This is my blood.' You have nothing for it but to believe Him implicitly, for He gives no clue to the solution of the mystery. Another reason you may give Mr. Sharples against what he urges in this: when our Saviour says, 'I am the true vine,' He is merely delivering a sermon to His Apostles, when a metaphor, particularly as He explains it afterwards, is surely allowable; but when Christ says, 'This is my body,' and 'This is my blood,' the moment is one of the most tremendous importance to the whole human race—our Saviour is enacting a law which is to be observed for ever in the church, He is instituting a sacrament to be always frequented by the faithful, and He is making His last will and testament by leaving us a pledge of His love. Away, then, with such utter nonsense as to say that, because our Saviour once spoke metaphorically to His Apostles, He would do it when the happiness and salvation of the whole human race were at stake, and when He must have foreknown that, if He did not mean His words literally, He would deceive, with scarcely an exception, the whole body of Christians throughout the world who lived before the Reformation. I consider such arguments as the present the most paltry trash; and so do you too, Blount, in your heart of hearts, I am convinced."

"Yes," replied the farmer, "I must say I agree with you, for your Reverence speaks with force; but, supposing that we give up this, for I allow that the argument about the vine is a mere quibble, what the better am I, if I cannot for my life be convinced that what I see to be bread and wine is really the body and blood of our Lord?"

"Continue to pray to God earnestly, John," said the rector, "and I hope that, in a short time, you will not have the same difficulty. Are you aware that in our Saviour's days there were people who, like you and the other Protestants, refused to believe that Christ would really give His body and blood?"

"No Sir," replied Blount, "but I should like to hear about it, in case it would give me some encouragement."

"Well then, John, in the 6th chapter of St. John's gospel, beginning at the 51st verse, you will find that our Saviour says, in speaking to the multitude, 'I am the living bread which came down from heaven, if any man eat of this bread he shall live for ever; and *the bread that I will give is my flesh*, which I will give for the life of the world.' Here, you see, is another proof of the doctrine of transubstantiation;

now hear what the first Protestants replied. 'The Jews therefore strove among themselves, saying, How can this man give us his flesh to eat?' Is not this the very question which the Protestants have been asking ever since the reformation? Our Saviour replies, 'Verily, verily, I say unto you, except ye eat the flesh of the Son of man and drink his blood, ye have no life in you. Whoso eateth my flesh and drinketh my blood hath eternal life, and I will raise him up at the last day. For my flesh is meat indeed, and my blood is drink indeed. He that eateth my flesh and drinketh my blood, dwelleth in me and I in him. As the living Father hath sent me, and I live by the Father, so he that eateth me even he shall live by me. This is that bread which came down from heaven; not as your fathers did eat manna and are dead. He that eateth of this bread shall live for ever.' Now, John, can anything be plainer than that the Blessed Sacrament is the fulfilment of the words of our Saviour, 'Except ye eat the flesh of the Son of man and drink his blood, ye have no life in you?'"

"Well, Sir," said Blount, with an awkward smile on his lips, "did the Protestants as you are pleased to call them, say and do no more about it? Were they convinced by what our Saviour said?"

"No, John, they were not; like those who in the present day have separated themselves from the Catholic church, because they will not discern the body of our Lord in the Eucharist; so in like manner did these first Protestants withdraw from our Lord's communion, as you will see in the 66th verse: 'From that time many of his disciples went back and walked no more with him.'"

"Well, Sir," said the farmer, scratching his head, as he always did when at a loss what to say, "you argue almost as well as you fought at Talavera; there is no standing against you, no more than the Frenchmen did. But if I may make bold, I have got what the Colonel used to call 'a *corpse* of reserve.' Mr.

Sharples said to me, 'Sir,' says he, 'if your Catholic friend proves to you that he is right and that you are wrong, which is very likely, seeing you are both an ignorant man and more than half inclined to popery already, in that case tell him, that though Jesus Christ be really present in the sacrament, which I (Mr. Sharples) deny, yet even then, that is no reason for leaving the English church, because many Episcopalians hold nearly the same thing.' 'Well, Sir,' says I, 'how is that?' So he said that Luther and his followers who founded the church of England, maintained the real presence of the body and blood of Christ in the bread and wine. Or, in short, your Reverence, that the body and blood, and the bread and wine are together. This would make it easier for me to believe, so what does your Reverence say to that?"

"I say," replied the rector, "that it is not the meaning of the plain words of scripture. Christ does not say 'along with the bread is my body,' or 'together with the wine is my blood;' but He says, 'This *is* my body,' and 'this *is* my blood.' Why should not we believe Him? Again, He does not say, 'In the bread that I will give is my flesh,' but He says, 'The bread that I will give *is* my flesh.' The whole Catholic church before Luther's time believed in the literal meaning of our Saviour's words, and what authority had Luther, may I ask, to give a far-fetched meaning of his own?"

"Well, Sir," said the farmer, "I was wrong in mentioning about Luther, because Mr. Sharples told me that I was only to speak of him in case I had given all his other objections and been worsted in every one them. But you see, Sir, I have got one or two of Mr. Sharples' objections yet, which have only just come to my mind, so if your Reverence please, I'll just tell what they are. If you would turn up, Sir, Luke 22nd chapter and 19th verse—I have got it down on paper, your Reverence."

"Well," said the rector after reading it, "this is one of the proofs I mentioned already, where our Saviour, at the institution of the sacrament, says, 'This is my body which is given for you.'"

"Will your Reverence read on, if you please," replied Blount.

"'This do in remembrance of me;'—well, John, what about it?"

"Mr. Sharples said that this ought to clear up all difficulties, since it shows that the sacrament was no more than a remembrance."

"It is a remembrance of our Lord, undoubtedly," replied the rector; "but though it does in the most forcible manner remind us of Him, does that fact in the slightest degree contradict His other words, 'This is my body,' and 'This is my blood,' or His promise, 'The bread that I will give is my flesh?' Excuse me, John, for saying it; but I think some of Mr. Sharples's arguments utter nonsense—I wonder that you remember them."

"Oh! for that matter," said Blount, "he gave me them all on paper last time I saw him; but the mischief is, I have taken them out of my pocket in the wrong order."

"Well, Blount," continued Mr. Feversham, what next?"

"Why, I think your Reverence will say that my next argument is a better one," said Blount, perusing his paper. "Mr. Sharples says it is absurd to suppose that the real body and blood of Christ can be at the same time in heaven, where He ascended, and in all the churches throughout the world, where the sacrament is kept."

"If we believe, John," answered the rector, "that God is almighty, of course we must allow that this is quite possible to Him."

"But, Sir, Mr. Sharples says, that one body cannot be in two places at once."

"Why should it be impossible to God, Blount?

Is there any more difficulty in believing it than that one God is in three persons—or that one person should have two natures? Were not two bodies in the same place at once, when Christ's impassable body after the resurrection, penetrated to where the Apostles were sitting, the doors being shut? Or is it more extraordinary, than the fact that after our bodies shall have crumbled to dust, and perhaps been scattered by the four winds of heaven, they shall rise again immortal at the last day?"

"I cannot say that it is," replied Blount.

"And now," continued the rector, "I shall give you, in my turn, a question to ask Mr. Sharples—How can a minister of the Church of England deny the real presence of Jesus Christ in the sacrament, when the Church to which he belongs confesses in her catechism, 'The body and blood of Christ are *verily* and *indeed* taken and received by the faithful in the Lord's Supper?' And if you think you can remember it, you may also ask Mr. Sharples, how it happens that Protestants are scarcely so well off as the Jews were? For, during the first part of the history of the world, the servants of God had striking images and memorials of the promised Messiah, of which they could participate, and which benefited their souls; such as the tree of life in the garden of Eden, the sacrifices of the patriarchs and afterwards of the Jews, the manna which fell from heaven, and above all others, the Paschal Lamb. These were signs and promises that God would bestow upon His people the thing signified by them. While our Saviour lived on earth, I grant that the world received the fulness of the promise; but in what are the Protestants more privileged now-a-days, than were those who only enjoyed these types and figures? If they receive bread and wine merely as a commemoration of Jesus Christ, in what are they better off than the Jews, who ate the Paschal Lamb? And yet the reality ought to be better than the symbol; and the new law ought to afford greater advantages than the old. Ask him also what Protestants have to compensate them for the want of the Holy of Holies in the Jewish temple, where it is believed God was more immediately present? And tell him that it is only Catholics who can possibly lay claim to the possession of privileges greater than the Jews. Instead of eating the Paschal Lamb and the manna in the wilderness, they receive the real body and blood of our crucified Lord—and instead of the mysterious Holy of Holies, into which only the high priest was allowed once a year to enter, they have the perpetual presence of their Redeemer among them in the Blessed Sacrament on their altars, to which not only the priests have access, but also the poor and the lowly, the sick and the sorrowing. No matter how wretched, no matter how guilty, they may have recourse to Him at all seasons and in all circumstances, sure of finding in His real presence, support and consolation, and of being able personally to make known to Him their wants and their miseries."

"And does all this come," asked the farmer, "from believing that the bread and wine is changed in the sacrament into the body and blood of Christ?"

"Yes," said the rector, "for we believe that where the body and blood of Christ are, there also must be His soul and divinity; and considering this, it is no wonder I attribute such glorious privileges to the possession of the Blessed Sacrament."

"Then," said the farmer, could I once believe in the real presence of Jesus Christ in your sacrament, I would willingly become a Catholic, even though I could not agree with the rest of your doctrines; for it must be a great thing to have Christ always among you!......It seems to me strange, your Reverence, to think that I once had the happiness of believing this! May God, in his mercy, grant that if it be indeed true, I may receive the grace of faith! I dare say your Reverence thinks me another Thomas, because it is so hard to make me believe."

"I am not at all dissatisfied, John, to find you dispute the point with me so sturdily. I believe you have an honest mind, so that I don't think you will willingly cleave to falsehood; and if you pray earnestly, there is no fear but God will lead you to the truth. By all means hear what Mr. Sharples has to say, it is as well you should know both sides of the question. I must warn you, however, that recognising the real presence of Jesus Christ in the sacrament, supposing even that God give you grace to do so, will not make you a Catholic; there are many other things which you must believe before a Catholic priest would admit you to his communion."

CHAPTER VII.

"I have of late ....lost all my mirth, forgone all custom of exercises."—HAMLET.

"I WISH, dear Papa," said Mary, one morning, "that you would sometimes take a walk with me to visit the sick poor of the parish."

"My dear child," said the rector, "may the same God who inspires you with this pious desire, bless and reward you for it! But I cannot, my dear child; no, I cannot accompany you in these visits of charity, however much I might desire it! Perhaps, by-and-bye, a month or two hence, it may be in my power to do so; that is, if you still wish it; but at present, my love, you see yourself that the state of my health prevents it, not to speak of other reasons."

"But, dearest papa," said Mary fondly, "it is chiefly on account of your health that I propose it; it would do you so much good to walk with me in the forenoons the way we used to do long ago. And, then, how pleasant it would be, at the end of our ramble, to rest in some cottage where the people were sick, or poor, or even only ignorant, and do them good by talking to them and assisting them. And, dear papa, will you not be angry if I say something that is on my mind? I wish to show people how truly good you are, and not to let them continue to think that you take no interest in their salvation. Dearest papa, you will not be angry with me, surely, for saying so."

"No, my own child, I will not," replied the agitated rector. "Speak to me always as frankly and as honestly as you do now. Poor Mary! You have been much tried lately, and you will be more so. Give me rest, Mary—give me peace and quietude a little longer, and all will be well by and bye. Do not urge me, Mary, to take an active part at present; I must keep myself quiet, calm, and collected, for I have a great deal before me. Pray for me, my sweet child, that I may do my duty, for I am in trying circumstances."

The rector paused for a moment, and then continued, "You must feel very lonely, now that your mother is so constantly in her room, and that you have no longer your old father to study, walk, or ride with you. I would be your companion if I could, but my spirits are not equal to it at present; besides, I have a great deal to occupy me at this moment. I have been thinking, however, Mary, that it would do you a great deal of good, and give you an interesting occupation, if you had courage to put the plan you mentioned in execution by yourself—always in the hope that by and bye I might be able to join you. A servant should at all times accompany you, so there would be neither danger nor impropriety in going alone, and you might ride or walk all over the parish, relieve the old and the sickly, and by your good deeds make amends for what seems the remissness, but which is in reality the misfortune of your father. Of course, you would be supplied liberally from this house with everything you might wish to give away. Rely upon it, my child, that you may thus do a good work in the sight of God, which He will not allow to pass unrewarded, since Jesus has promised so much to those who even give away a cup of cold water in His name. The very angels, too, will rejoice in heaven to see you performing a filial duty, and by your piety and charity making up for the omissions of your parent."

"Dear, dear papa, I shall be delighted, but you must first speak to mamma on the subject, for she thinks it unladylike to go rambling about the country, even with a servant behind me; and she would like it still less, if she thought I was going to play the Lady Bountiful."

"Do not be afraid, Mary, I shall arrange all that with your mother," said the rector, smiling.

"And I shall be more happy than I have been for a long time," continued Mary, "for I was much in want of a pleasant occupation; besides, dear papa, I confess that sometimes I used to feel low and dull, thinking I was of no use in the world. You had ceased to make me your friend; mamma prefers a good novel to my society at any time; with the exception of Harvey, who seemed to derive pleasure from my letters, I was neither of comfort nor use to any human being. But now, dearest papa, instead of avoiding me as you so long did, you have taken me again into your friendship, and what is more, you are procuring for me an occupation and a means of doing good."

While saying so, poor Mary's eyes, that had so long been heavy and sad, beamed with joy as she looked up in her father's face.

"Poor child!" said the rector, gazing tenderly upon her, "what a sin it is to neglect you when you are so easily made happy!"

We shall now follow Mr. Feversham into his study

and take the liberty of looking over his shoulder as he reads a letter. It was dated Rome, and signed by Monsignore Geroni. For the benefit of our readers, we shall translate it from the Italian.

"My dear Friend,

"It was with the most unfeigned pleasure I received the intelligence, that at last you are resolved to enter boldly that Holy Catholic and Apostolic Church, which you so thoughtlessly abandoned in the giddy days of youth. But why, my friend, do you speak of 'necessary delay?' You say that your scruples are now set at rest, that your mind is made up, that you have no longer any doubt as to the propriety of the step you are about to take. Is it not dangerous, then, is it not trifling with God's grace, to defer giving up your living and announcing to the world the change in your sentiments? As I do not know your motives, I have no right to judge; but, Oh! my friend, excuse an old man for giving you advice. If a sick person were about to undergo a painful operation, how much would their annoyance and suffering be increased by putting off from day to day having it done! Imagination conjures up a thousand terrors and a thousand pains, perhaps far worse than the reality, and instead of one day of suffering, the poor timid one has a hundred! Just so is it with you, my friend. How often, during the last three years, by your own confession, have you been on the eve of acknowledging Catholicity, and how often by procrastination and want of moral courage to make use of the day of grace, has the light of faith been withdrawn from you, and your mind obscured once more by doubts and fears, while the gnawing of your conscience prevented you enjoying a single happy hour! I allow that at present things look more promising, and that you never before appeared so determined to take the decisive step; but why pause even for an instant? You know, from sad experience, your own weakness and vacillation. Arise, then, and act while there is yet time! The night cometh when no man can work. God will not be trifled with! He stands at present like a merciful Father extending His arms to embrace and receive His penitent child! Fly to Him, then my dear friend, and by a public recantation of your errors, nobly and generously make amends for the scandal caused by the great false step of your youth! There is more joy in heaven over one sinner that repenteth, than over ninety and nine just men that need no repentance. That God may strengthen and assist you to *dare all* for Him, is the constant prayer of your faithful friend, ALFONSO GERONI."

It was with uneasy and dissatisfied feelings, that Mr. Feversham perused this letter. "Geroni does me injustice!" he ejaculated. "And yet, after all, why should I say so? Does not my present conduct seem to give reason for his anxiety? His letter is nearly a month old, and am I one step farther on, towards declaring myself Catholic, than I was when I wrote the epistle which he now answers?"

We shall now leave the rector for a little, and return to Farmer Blount, who on this day, soon after breakfast, saddled his horse and set out for Overbury. On his way through the village he was observed by Mr. Jacob Hogg, who was standing at the door of his new shop, and who insisted that the farmer should dismount and come in to see it. Blount refused at first on the plea of want of time; but Hogg was so urgent, that without giving great offence it was impossible not to yield, and accordingly the farmer entered in very bad humour.

"I have a brilliant assortment of gentlemen's garments, under and upper, Farmer Blount," said Jacob, "and I shall be happy at all times to accommodate you on the lowest terms; I consider it a matter of honesty, Farmer, to sell my goods at the minimum price, trusting to the number of the customers who will patronise the shop to reimburse me. Here are gentlemen's neck-handkerchiefs of the most brilliant colours, absolutely thrown away! Stockings of the finest and most durable material, warranted to last an indefinite period! Trowsers, garters, and other unmentionables, really given for nothing, and vieing with the things done in the tailoring department for the children of Israel in the desert, which we are told never wore out! Here are watches that go more correct than the dial! Wash-hand basins warranted not to crack! Tea and sugar at extraordinarily low prices! Gowns for the ladies! Razor-strops for the men! Warren's blacking and all sorts of confectionary!"

"You seem a universal dealer, Jacob," said the farmer, "if you had been living in old Noah's times, you might have taken out a contract for supplying the ark!"

"And a very profitable spec it would have been," said Jacob, rubbing his hands.

"Are you sure you could have resisted the temptation of palming off sour hay and musty oats on old father Noah, for his cattle?" asked the farmer, laughing. "And would you not have watered the treacle, sanded the sugar, and mixed the tea with hedge-leaves for the ladies of the family?"

Jacob Hogg's face turned red, but he tried to assume a smile as he replied, "You are at your old tricks again, father-in-law! Always for a joke and never shewing signs of becoming a converted character!"

"These cups and saucers there, what's the price of them?" asked the farmer, as though he had not heard him.

Mr. Hogg named a sum considerably higher than their apparent worth. The farmer laughed. "You have charged a few additional shillings, I suppose," said he, "in consideration of so many of them being chipped at the edges as if a dog had bitten them! And what may be the price of the walking sticks in the corner?" Mr. Hogg named a trifle, and the farmer took one; but happening to lean upon it for a moment, it snapped in two, to the great confusion of the proprietor of the shop.

"Let us see your gloves," said Blount.

A package was opened accordingly, but the farmer could find none to satisfy him, for they were all more or less soiled, and had evidently been damaged when they were purchased.

"I do not think much of your articles, Mr. Hogg," said Blount, "they make a very fine show from the street, but when you look near, few will bear inspection."

"I have good things for those who will pay me good prices," said Mr. Hogg, drawing himself up, "but of course there are inferior articles for skinflints, who will not give a just value."

"Well, well, Mr. Hogg, no offence," said the farmer. "Your articles are just rather flimsy for my taste, though I allow they have a great show; so wishing you all the success you deserve, I'll say good bye, for I am going to Overbury, and have not too much time."

Mr. Hogg bit his lips at hearing the very ambiguous good wishes of Blount, but instead of returning his salutation and bidding him adieu, he took his arm and led him into the back shop.

"I have a matter of business, father-in-law, about which I wish to consult you, as I know you are a safe man in these matters. We are anxious to find an honest well-doing person, who will consent to enter into partnership with us. We don't want an active partner but a sleeping one; an individual with five or six hundred pounds or so, for which he would get from us twenty per cent. merely for letting it lie in our hands. No risk and no trouble in the matter—his money keeping warm and comfortable here, in the shape of silks, satins, velvets, and what nots, and a hundred pounds dropping into his pocket every year for the use of it. My partner and I should like, if possible, to secure a God-fearing man, one who would not glory save in the cross of Jesus Christ, to enter into this intimate union and connection with us. However, if we cannot hit upon one born of the Spirit with five hundred pounds chinking in his pocket, then a plain decent man, strictly honest, and of excellent character, even though not yet regenerated and sanctified, will serve our turn. In that case, however, we would require a little more of the filthy lucre of this world; say eight hundred pounds, and our business is done."

"So by your account, a converted man with five hundred pounds, or a reprobate with eight hundred, will equally serve your purpose," said the farmer.

"Not equally well," replied Mr. Hogg; "of course my partner and myself would much prefer five hundred pounds from the purse of one of God's elect, to eight hundred from an ordinary sinner. But you see, father-in-law, those persons here in whom God's image is plainly to be discerned, I mean born-again out-and-outers, though many of them are comfortable warm men, yet they don't just happen to have the money ready to lift. Now, to speak plain, I know that you have. You could not do a more profitable thing than advance the money; I would supply you with groceries for a mere nominal price. You would have twenty per cent. coming in yearly, and the Lord would bless all your undertakings, even to your going out at the front door and coming in at the back, in consideration of your being connected with His chosen people."

"Is it five hundred or eight hundred you want?" asked the farmer drily.

"Why, as you are a friend," said Hogg, "we would admit you into the firm with only the five hundred, though it is against our rule. Or if you choose to be in no partnership at all, and would merely lend the money at fifteen per cent. why, I leave it to your own good sense to see that it would be more advantageous to lend a large sum at that exhorbitant interest, than merely to invest a small one."

"And a pretty profit you will need to make on your flashy goods, Jacob, before you can afford to pay such an interest. However, I suspect that is not your tack at all. Some ten months hence we shall see your shop shut up, and Mr. Jacob Hogg travelling on the continent playing the fine gentleman, or perhaps in America with my five or eight hundred in his pocket. No, no, Mr. Hogg, much obliged to you for your favours, but would rather not accept of them just at present. Good day to you, Sir." And so saying the farmer put on his hat and left the shop, leaving Mr. Hogg in what is called a white rage; for the blood had left his face, he bit his lips till they nearly bled, and forgetting his late conversion, he cursed the farmer from the bottom of his heart, and muttered threats of revenge.

When Blount arrived at Overbury, he left his horse at a small inn, and walked straight to the house of Mr. Sharples. He was shown into a back drawing-room, and as the folding doors which separated it from the front were ajar, he had ample opportunity for seeing and hearing all that passed there. Three ladies, one old and two young, had come to call on Mrs. Sharples, and in the absence of their hostess, were discussing the sermon of the previous Sunday.

"Well, it is wonderful," said one of them, "that the Papists can be so blinded to the enormity of their system. How clearly Mr. Sharples exposes it! Did you ever hear anything more thrillingly appalling, than the secrets of the confessional, such as he disclosed them. What a masterpiece of subtlety it must be, by which the Catholic priests allure souls to perdition!"

"Oh! it was beautifully handled by dear Mr.

Sharples," rejoined the other young lady, who appeared to be the friend of the first speaker, "but to my mind I preferred our good pastor's eloquence in showing up the sublime horrors of the Spanish Inquisition. It surpassed the most frightful ghost story, or narrative of robbers, in its power over the imagination. I declare to you, I could not sleep at night afterwards, from a horrid vision of the grand Inquisitor impaling me on a bodkin."

"It shook my nerves too, I confess," said the elder lady, "and put me all in a tremble. Just to think that miscreants like these should have perpetrated their misdeeds in a Christian country; and that others of the same, (Catholic priests I mean,) should be in this very town of Overbury! It is well for us they are so few in number, for I have little doubt that if the Catholics once more got the ascendancy, we should all wake some morning murdered in our beds. Arabella, my love," she continued, addressing the young lady who had first spoken, "what was it you so acutely observed had been omitted by Mr. Sharples, in his account of the Spanish inquisition? Something that you said might have been introduced with a sublime and tragic effect."

"The bull-fights, I believe it was, Mamma," replied the young lady. "You know, Miss Jervase," she continued, turning to her friend, "these bull-fights were an engine of fearful power in the hands of the inquisitors. After the poor sufferers had been stretched on the rack for several days at a time, they were brought into the arena, and there tossed by bulls for the amusement of the Spanish ladies. Polycarp was one of these martyrs you may remember, if you have read church history. It was only after they were so disfigured that their friends could not recognize them, that they were mercifully delivered to the stake, to find in fire a release from their torments."

"How very dreadful!" replied Miss Jervase, "and how thankful we ought to be for our own religious freedom, and that we are born in a country where every one interprets the Bible as he has a mind."

"Yes, and there is another thing for which to be thankful," said the old lady; "that the Bible is not kept from us, as it is from the poor benighted Papists."

"Well, at any rate *that* is not true," thought the farmer, "for here am I getting Bible proofs from the rector for everything."

At this moment Mr. Sharples entered the room where Blount was sitting, and first closing the folding doors, advanced and greeted him very cordially.

"Your name is Blount, I believe," were his first words as he seated himself.

"Yes, Sir, I'll not deny it," replied the farmer rather taken by surprise; "but may I make bold to ask, Sir, how did you come to know it?"

"It was easily found out, my good man," said the clergyman smiling, "one of my servants saw it written in large characters in the inside of your hat, which was left in the lobby the other day. But what made you wish to conceal it, I should like to know? you have *as yet* done nothing to be ashamed of."

"No Sir, I hope not," replied the farmer, colouring and drawing himself up. "But you see, Sir, to be honest with you, I did not wish to mention the name of the Catholic I had been speaking to. And I thought, Sir, that if you heard my name, you might perhaps make inquiries of some one that knows me, and maybe find out the other."

"No honest man ought to be afraid to avow his sentiments," said Mr. Sharples, "and it by no means leads me to think highly of your Catholic friend, that while he poisons your mind with insidious sophistry, he recommends you to conceal his name."

"I did not say that he did," replied the farmer, and I don't come here, Sir, to have my friends abused. If you, as a minister of God, are kind enough to throw a little light on my perplexities, I am deeply obliged to you; but, Sir—and I hope you won't take offence at it—I beg you will spare my friends."

"Well, well, Mr. Blount, I should be sorry to give you offence; for, though I regard you as a pig-headed and illiterate man, I respect your honesty. So, if you please, we will change the subject. What sort of rector have you at your parish? And why did you not think of consulting him or his curate in your difficulties?"

"Why, Sir," replied Blount, "I—I really don't know. It was a ticklish subject, Sir. People in one's own neighbourhood might take offence, you know, Sir. I got more satisfaction, in short, coming to you, Sir, about the matter."

"Do you know a Mr. Longab from the same neighbourhood?" enquired Mr. Sharples. "A most worthy and pious individual of the methodist persuasion. A very powerful speaker, I hear, in his own way. He is local preacher, if I mistake not."

"Yes, Sir, I know him slightly," replied Blount.

"He was telling me something of your rector," continued Mr. Sharples. "He says he is a gloomy and reserved man, one who pays little attention to his flock, scarcely ever mounts the pulpit, and, even though he did, would not preach the gospel. Does that agree with your opinion?"

"I think, Sir, it is a great want of charity to judge our neighbours harshly. And what I would not do to people of my own standing, I would still less do to Parson Feversham, both because he is a clergyman, and is in a station above me."

"I myself," said Mr. Sharples, "have not the pleasure of Mr. Feversham's acquaintance, having only come here lately, and we have besides missed each other when we called; but I cannot help thinking it a blessed thing that you did not go to him for advice, since Mr. Longab informs me that it is more than half suspected that he has a leaning to popery—that masterpiece of the devil's invention."

CHAPTER VIII.

"Submit thyself to God, and humble thy sense to faith, and the light of knowledge shall be given thee as far as shall be profitable and necessary for thee." THOMAS à KEMPIS.

"WELL, your Reverence," said the farmer, the next time he saw Mr. Feversham, "I asked Mr. Sharples your question, what he makes of the Church of England Catechism declaring that the body and blood of Christ are verily and indeed taken and received in the Lord's Supper."

"And what did he say, John?" asked the rector.

"Why, Sir, he coughed, and blew his nose, and cleared his throat, and took a pinch of snuff. I thought he was not going to answer it at all; when, at last, he said that these words bore a spiritual meaning, and we were all bound to understand them figuratively. 'So,' says I, 'Sir, why does it affirm that the body and blood of Christ are *verily and indeed* taken, if it does not mean it?' So upon that he said that the founders of the English Church, though very good men, were much more papistical than they ought to have been; and that the church has gradually purified herself since their time from Romish errors. He allowed that the words of the catechism were a little too strong, but that, when properly explained, they could do no harm."

"And do you not see from this, John, the inconsistency of the members of the English Church, and how they disagree with each other? Those who compiled the catechism could not be right if Mr. Sharples is right; and, on the other hand, Mr. Sharples cannot be right if they were so. What confidence can you have in a church whose teachers are at variance among themselves?"

"The more is the pity, your Reverence," replied Blount; "but what can poor folks like us do? There is no finding two living clergymen that hold the same opinion; and, of course, we can't tell which is right and which is wrong. Considering all things, I was not in the least surprised that Mr. Sharples differed from the manufacturers of the catechism—great divines though he called them."

"And how did he reply, John, to the other query I put: what is to compensate Protestants for the loss of the advantages the Jews enjoyed under the old law, such as the holy of holies, &c?"

"Oh, your Reverence, you may as well not ask," replied Blount. "He gave me a long answer, but I could neither make head nor tail of it; and to tell you the truth, my head was running upon something else, though, at the same time, I don't think he could answer your Reverence. I heard a precious deal of nonsense going on, Sir, in the front parlour before Mr. Sharples came to speak to me at all. There were some ladies calling, Sir, and they were talking about Spain, and the cruelties practised there by the Catholics. Some other day I must ask your Reverence about it; but I heard one big lie any way, so that made me doubt the rest."

"As you please, John," said the rector; "but, at present, we had better resume the same subject we were discussing last day—I mean the blessed Eucharist. Did Mr. Sharples urge no more objections?"

"Indeed he did, Sir," replied the farmer. "I told him, your Reverence, about the first Protestants mentioned in St. John's Gospel; and he was very ill pleased, indeed, that such a venerable name as Protestant should be applied to unbelieving Jews. However he bid me take notice of the 63rd verse, where Jesus, after asking those who murmured at it, 'Does this offend you?' says, 'It is the Spirit that quickeneth:

the flesh profiteth nothing. The words that I speak unto you, they are spirit and they are life.' Well, he said, your Reverence, that this entirely explained away what Christ had said before about giving His flesh to eat."

"It appears to me, John," said the rector, "as indeed I think I formerly mentioned, that we should explain one passage of Scripture by another. The institution of the blessed sacrament, where Christ says 'This is my body,' and 'This is my blood,' leaves us no longer in doubt as to what He meant by the promise that He would give His flesh to eat. As to the text you quote, I cannot do better than read you the words St. Augustine has written in treating of this very passage. 'What means *the flesh profiteth nothing?* It profits nothing as they understood it, for they understood flesh as it is torn to pieces in a dead body, or sold in the shambles, and not as it is animated by the Spirit. Wherefore it is said, the flesh profits nothing, in the same manner as it is said, *knowledge puffeth up*. Must we then fly from knowledge? God forbid: what then means knowledge puffeth up? That is, if it be alone without charity; therefore the Apostle added, *but charity edifieth*. Join therefore charity to knowledge, and knowledge will be profitable, not by itself, but through charity: so here also the *flesh profiteth nothing;* viz. the flesh alone. Let the Spirit be joined with the flesh, as charity is to be joined with knowledge, and then it profits much. For if the flesh profited nothing, the Word would not have been made flesh, that he might dwell in us.' (St. Augustin. Tract 27 in Joan.) You see, John, our Lord only adds the words you quoted to correct the misconception of the Jews, who thought he meant dead flesh, separated from the soul and divinity."

"Mr. Sharples said too, Sir," rejoined the farmer, "that Christ being alive at the time He instituted the sacrament, plainly proved that it could not have been His real body which He gave to His Apostles."

"It seems humanly speaking impossible, I allow, John, and to us it is altogether incomprehensible. Still, that is no reason against it, because with God all things are possible; and even Protestants are content to believe on God's authority what seems equally incomprehensible—such as the Trinity, our Saviour being born of a virgin, &c. &c. Mr. Sharples's argument is either null, or would go against these doctrines also. Let us now see if it be a credible person who asserts it. *It is our Lord Himself;* who, taking the bread in His hands, says, 'This is my body.' Are we to disbelieve His plain words, and make Him out a liar? If Christ did not give His real body, but only a bit of bread to His Apostles, why did He call this morsel of bread His body? What inducement could He have had for doing so? An ordinary honest man would have been ashamed on so serious an occasion to use a deceitful mode of speaking, and to call bread by a name it never had before, so as to lead into error millions and millions of human beings. You know yourself, John, this could never have been the case; then why refuse any longer simply and candidly to throw yourself at the feet of your Saviour, and say, 'Lord, I believe; help thou mine unbelief:' for with thee all things are possible?"

"I wish I could, Sir; I wish I could!" said the farmer, with much feeling. "Mr. Sharples, Sir, is always harping over and over again about the folly of distrusting the evidences of our senses in the matter. He says, 'You see with your own eyes that it is not the body and blood of Christ, so what would you have more?' Now, Sir, when he says that again, what am I to answer him?"

"Tell him," said the rector, "that there are many examples in Scripture where they who trusted to the evidence of their senses were misled. The Jews, seeing only a common man, could not recognise the

Son of God. 'Is not this the carpenter's son?' they exclaimed; 'Is not his mother called Mary?' (Matt. xiii. 55.) In like manner Joshua thought that he saw a man (Joshua v. 13); Abraham that he eat with three men (Gen. xviii.); and Jacob that he wrestled with one (Gen. xxxii. 24); when, in each instance, they were no real men that were present, but disembodied spirits, the senses of the patriarchs misleading them. Again, we find that the eyes of the disciples going to Emmaus were holden, so that they did not know Jesus. (Luke xxiv. 16.) The same thing happened to Mary Magdalen and the Apostles. (John xx.) But I need not multiply examples. In common life do we not also find that the senses are but erring guides after all? A stick seen in the water, appears crooked, though in reality straight; and who, trusting to his senses merely, would believe that the sun and the fixed stars are all larger than the earth? These cases are perhaps not exactly to the point, as we are treating of a thing wholly supernatural. But, at all events, you may mention them to Mr. Sharples as overthrowing his assertion that the evidence of our senses is always to be believed."

"Well," said the farmer, "to own the truth to you, rector, I am sick and tired of all this quibbling. The Bible texts you bring forward to prove the body and blood of Christ in the sacrament, seem to me entirely convincing. Mr. Sharples' objections are to my mind, pitiful; twirling and twisting the words into meanings never intended. Your explanations are those of an honest, down-right man, anxious to take the plain meaning out of plain texts. And if the Catholic church explains always in that style, I hold her to be an upright church, and I wonder that she has not smashed with the weight of her truth, all the other churches that set up to put new fashioned pettifogging interpretations on what is as plain as a pikestaff. And so I tell you honestly, rector, that I will ask Mr. Sharples for no more objections to Transubstantiation, for his objections are too fine, feathery, and spider-web-like for an honest man like me, to be much up or down of them."

"Then, John," said Mr. Feversham, "am I to understand that you believe in the Catholic doctrine of the real presence of Jesus Christ in the Blessed Sacrament?"

"I believe that the Bible proves it clearly, Sir;" replied Blount, "but I don't feel that conviction of it in myself, that I should like to have, though I hope it may come. I must do as you say, Sir, throw myself humbly on God's mercy, and say, 'Lord, I believe, help thou mine unbelief!'"

"And God will undoubtedly hear your prayer, my honest friend; for he never rejects the humble and earnest supplicant. Have you any other questions, John, that you would like to ask me before we separate?"

"Well, your Reverence, if you will have patience with me, I will just mention another thing Mr. Sharples said; that the body and blood of Christ in the sacrament, is comparatively a new invention, and that in the first ages it never was heard of. He, could not exactly fix when the notion first started, but he said it was believed by a good many, to have arisen in the eighth century. Now, Sir, even though the Bible proves it, I should think that the first christians would not have refused to believe it unless they had some good reason for it."

"You will be surprised, John, to hear that I flatly deny this assertion of Mr. Sharples," replied the rector. "Fortunately for us, the works of the first fathers and doctors of the church are still in existence, and are open to the researches of both Catholic and Protestant. Were I to collect from their writings every testimony they give in favour of the real presence of our Saviour, it would fill a large folio volume. I fear my quoting from them will not make you much the wiser, as you probably never heard their names before; yet I shall mention a few, as it may be satisfactory. St. Ignatius, who was bishop of Antioch, and lived in the first century, having been the disciple of St. John the Evangelist, says, in describing some heretics of his time: 'They do not admit of Eucharists and oblations, because they do not believe the Eucharist to be the flesh of our Saviour Jesus Christ, who suffered for our sins.' In the second and third centuries, St. Justin Martyr,* St. Irenæus,† Tertullian,‡ St. Cyprian,§ and Origen, have all borne the same testimony. I shall quote the words of the latter, as I happen to have them near me. 'Manna was formerly given as a figure; but now the flesh and blood of the Son of God, is specifically given and is real food.'‖ In the fourth century we find similar examples in the works of St. Hilary,¶ St. Basil,** St. Ambrose of Milan, &c., &c. I shall quote from a treatise of the latter, explaining christian doctrine to his young neophytes. 'Perhaps you will say, Why do you tell me that I receive the body of Christ when I see quite another thing?

"'We have this point, therefore, to prove.—How many examples do we produce to show you that this is not what nature made it, but what the benediction has consecrated it: and that the benediction is of greater force than nature, because by the benediction nature itself is changed! Moses cast his rod on the ground and it became a serpent's tail, and it recovered the nature of a rod, &c.

"'Thou hast read of the creation of the world: if Christ, by his word, was able to make something out of nothing, shall he not be thought able to change one thing into another?'†† I may also mention the

* Apolog. to Emp. Antonin.
† S. Irenæus, l. 4. c. 3, 4.
‡ L de cor anilitis, c. 3.
§ Ep. 54. ad Cornel.
‖ Hom. 7. in Levit.
¶ Eighth book of the Trinity.
** Moral Rules, Reg. 1. c. f.
†† St. Ambrose of Milan, de his qui Myst. Init. c. 9.

testimony of St. Cyril of Jerusalem, on a similar occasion to that of St. Ambrose. 'Since Christ himself affirms thus of the bread, *This is my body*, who is so daring as to doubt it? And since he affirms, *This is my blood*, who will deny that it is blood? At Cana of Galilee, he by an act of will, turned water into wine, which resembles blood; and is he not then to be credited when he changes wine into blood? Therefore, full of certainty, let us receive the *body and blood of Christ;* for under the form of bread is given to thee his body, and under the form of wine his blood.'* In the fifth century, St. Jerome, St. Augustine, St. Gregory of Nyssa,† St. Chrysostome, all bear witness to the same truth."

"Oh! stop, stop, your Reverence, if you please! that is enough to quote from men I never heard of before, though I dare say they were great divines in their time! But I think you mentioned St. Chrysostom; I have heard of him—does not he write the prayer of St. Chrysostom in the prayer-book? I should like to hear what he says about it, if your Reverence please."

"Most willingly, John; St. Chrysostom writes as follows: 'Let us always believe God, and not contradict him, though that which he says seems to contradict both our thoughts and our senses. For His word cannot deceive us, but our *senses* may easily be deceived. He never errs, but we are often mistaken. Since, therefore, he says, *This is my body*, let us be fully persuaded of it.' "‡

* St. Cyril of Jerusalem, Catech. Mystagog, 4.

† St. Gregory of Nyssa writes thus, "I do therefore now rightly believe, that the bread sanctified by the word of God, *is changed* into the body of God the Word." And again soon after, "Here likewise the bread, (as the apostle says,) is sanctified by the word of God and prayer. Not so that by being eaten it becomes the *body* of the *Word*, but because it is suddenly *changed* into his *body* by this word. *This is my body*. And this is effected by the virtue of benediction, by which the nature of those things which appear are *transelemented* into it." In Orat. Catech. c. 37. t. 3. Edit. Par.

‡ S. Chrysostome, Hom. 83. in Matth.

"Thank your Reverence for your trouble," answered the farmer. "But I think we have had enough of quotations now, Sir, if I may make bold to say so. Nevertheless, I am highly pleased, for I think these authorities ought to be very satisfying to learned men, seeing that even to my capacity they speak to the purpose. I suppose, Sir, you could go on till to-morrow-come-never quoting from them, if you liked."

"Certainly, John, it would be a most voluminous subject," said the rector; "for the later we come down, the writings of the ancient fathers which have been preserved increase, and we have consequently a greater body of testimony; much having been lost in the first ages. In short, the christians of every nation in the world, Greeks, Latins, Africans and Europeans, all except Protestants and a few Vaudois peasants, have believed in the real presence of Christ in the Sacrament, and in Transubstantiation.* Even some of the chief Reformers held the doctrine of the real presence. Luther himself, confesses how anxious he was to deny it, although he could not; 'Because,' he says, 'I clearly saw how much I should thereby injure Popery: but I found myself caught without any

* Witness the synods held against Berengarius, the decrees of the general councils of Lateran, Constance and Trent. See also the general consent of the Greeks and all the Oriental Christians demonstrated by Mons. Arnaud and the Abbé Renaudot, in their books bearing title "La Perpetuité de la Foi," in which we have the testimony of the Greek patriarchs, bishops, and abbots, &c; also the orthodox confession of the oriental church, and to crown all, the testimony of the Armenians, Muscovites, Jacobites or Surians, Cophts, Maronites and Nestorians, touching the real presence and transubstantiation. In the same book is quoted the testimony of the Greek fathers of the first six centuries, and the proofs of the same doctrine in the oriental liturgies. We find even protestant writers acknowledging this universal concurrence of testimony; see "Sir Edwin Sandy's relation of the Religions of the West," p. 238. "Dr. Potter's answer to Charity Mistaken," p. 225. "Bishop Forbes de Euch." l. l. c. 3. p. 412. Dr. Philip Nicolai, a protestant, in his first book of the kingdom of Christ, p. 22, writes as follows, "Let my Christian readers be assured, that not only the churches of the Greeks, but also the Russians, and the Georgians, and the Armenians, and the Indians, and the Ethiopians, as many of them as believe in Christ, hold the true and real presence of the body and blood of the Lord," &c.

way of escaping, for the text of the gospel was too plain for this purpose.' In another of his writings also, speaking of the Zuinglians, who explain the words of the institution in a figurative way, he says, 'The devil seems to have mocked those to whom he has suggested a heresy so ridiculous and contrary to scripture as that of the Zuinglians.' In short, the first English Reformers very generally held the tenet of the real presence of our Saviour in the sacrament;* though it must be confessed they differed from Catholics as to the mode, instead of taking our Saviour's words literally 'this is my body,' explaining them in this manner 'along with the substance of the bread is my body.'† Archbishop Bramhall among the rest, makes a curious admission, saying, 'We find no debates or disputes concerning the presence of Christ's body in the sacrament, and much less concerning the manner of his presence, for the first eight hundred years!'"

"And is it not a strange thing then, your Reverence," said the farmer, "that so many ministers now-a-days of the Church of England, should explain away entirely the real presence?"

"Some do and some do not;" replied the rector, "however there is one thing certain, that as truth is but one, that church must be in a bad state which nourishes so many contrary opinions in her bosom. You will be surprised when I tell you, John, that even the Liturgy, I mean the Book of Common Prayer, has been changed several times with regard to this very subject. At first, when Cranmer, Ridley, &c., drew it up in 1548, the communion service expressed the real presence in the words, 'the whole

* See the works of bishops Andrews, Bilson, Morton, Land, Montague, Sheldon, Gunning, Forbes, Cosin, and Hooker.

† It is curious enough that Calvin, Zuinglius, Beza, and the defenders of the figurative sense, in short, all but the Protestants, have confessed that if the real presence be admitted at all, the Catholic doctrine is more conformable to scripture than the Lutheran.

body of Christ is received under each particle of the sacrament.'* When the Calvinistic party prevailed, the 29th of the 42 Articles drawn up by the same prelates in 1552, expressly denied the real presence. Ten years afterwards, Queen Elizabeth, patronising the Catholic doctrine on this point, desired this declaration against it to be left out of the prayer-book.† The Liturgy remained thus a hundred years. And in the time of Charles the Second, the old rubric against the real presence and the adoration of the Blessed Sacrament was restored as it is at present."

"Well, your Reverence, is it not a pitiful sight," said the farmer, "to see an old and venerable church, as I have been accustomed for so long to consider the Church of England, changing her belief so often in a thing of such importance? I think if people knew it, they would have less respect for her! She must have been far wrong some time or another!"

* See Burnet, p. ii. b. 1. † See Heylin, p. 124.

CHAPTER IX.

> "When poverty, with mien of shame,
> The sense of pity seeks to touch,
> Or bolder, makes the simple claim,
> That I have nothing, you have much.—
> Believe not either man or book,
> That bids you close the opening hand,
> And with reproving speech and look,
> Your first and free intent withstand."
>
> R. MONCKTON MILNES.

MEANWHILE Mary commenced her visits of charity, and her affectionate heart found it in some respects exceedingly delightful to alleviate the sufferings of the distressed, the aged, and the poor. Nevertheless, it must be confessed that they were generally by no means so grateful as she had expected. Where she gave much, they almost invariably asked for more; and where she gave little, they were dissatisfied at being worse off than their neighbours. She found it very difficult to convey spiritual instruction: for the more grossly ignorant they were, the less they cared for acquiring information; and the sick poor generally preferred discoursing on their ailments to hearing from her about the mercy of God, or the sufferings of Jesus Christ. There were many minds so brutish, that it was nearly impossible to make them in the least degree understand spiritual things, as they were unable to realize any idea but what appealed to the evidence of their senses. Notwithstanding England's boasts, there are few countries in the world where the peasantry are more lamentably ignorant of the common truths of religion, believed alike by Catholic and Protestant: such as the doctrine of the atonement of Jesus Christ, the blessed Trinity, &c., &c. Not unfrequently people might be seen living in open vice, who yet did not seem to know they were doing wrong. In many instances, the field so long neglected by the clergy of the church of England, had been taken possession of by the methodists and other dissenters; more devotion was certainly observable among them than among those of the establishment, but at the same time an immense increase of spiritual pride. How often did they not say, "God, I thank thee that I am not as other men are, extortioners, unjust, adulterers, or even as this publican!" And yet how often did not God hurl the proud from their seat, by allowing them to fall into sins which gave open scandal, but which their dissenting brethren did all in their power to hush up and conceal. Of course, Mary at first saw but little of this, as her observations were necessarily, from her age, sex, and inexperience, rather superficial. Still, she gradually beheld enough to discover that there was a great want somewhere. She felt convinced that it was not the intention of God that the poor should be so generally vicious and ignorant; and she could not help thinking that, were proper means taken, the evil might be greatly remedied. The question then arose, what means? But this, which has puzzled many wiser heads than hers, she knew not how to answer. She sometimes ventured to hint at her new ideas to her father, and in reply she often got from him what seemed to her very curious pieces of information.

"Papa," said she to him one day on her return from an excursion, "the more I see of the labouring classes in this part of the country, the more I am astonished at their excessive ignorance, and the grossness of their ideas. Very few pay attention to religion at all; and even from those who think they know something about it, I receive the most extraordinary answers. For instance, when I ask how many Gods there are, I am very frequently told *three*—

Father, Son, and Holy Ghost. And seldom do I find any one able to inform me which of the three persons of the Godhead died for us. Ten to one they reply, 'God the Father,' or 'God the Holy Spirit.' I wonder what England must have been during the middle ages before the invention of printing; the people could scarcely have been more ignorant than at present."

"In Catholic times," replied her father, "'Merrie England,' as she was then called, supported a vast number of chapels, churches, convents, monasteries, hospitals, and other religious foundations, for the purposes of charity, and for the education of the people. Philips, in his Memoirs of Cardinal Pole, informs us that* 'The abbeys in England were public schools for education, each of them having one or more persons set apart to instruct the youth of the neighbourhood, without any expense to the parents.'"

"Then the people," replied Mary, "could scarcely have been more ignorant than they are now, if so much so. The question is, whether all these pains did them any good, when they could be taught nothing but popery. There is another thing, papa, which I constantly hear about, and which seems a great evil. When I have spoken to any of the farmers' wives, or indeed to the farmers themselves, I hear nothing but grumbling about the poor rates. At first I thought that they had no right to find fault, for, of course, they ought to assist in supporting the poor. But it turns out that stout, able-bodied men think it no disgrace to be upon the parish-books, and receive weekly assistance; that young men even marry for the sake of getting a greater allowance in consideration of wife and children, than they could receive while single. The farmers, seeing this imposition, give less wages than they ought, and insist that the parish should

* Philips' life of Cardinal Pole, part I. p. 220.

make out the difference. In short, everybody complains, and no one is satisfied; none complain louder than those who are received into the workhouse, because, among other grievances, the husband is separated from the wife, and the parents from the children. It seems extraordinary that so much expense should do so little good, in the way of making people happy and comfortable. How were things managed in old times? Were the poor laws always in existence?"

"No, Mary, they were not," replied Mr. Feversham. "In Catholic times there was no need of poor laws, in consequence of the splendid endowments left by private individuals for the purposes of charity, and the princely munificence of the monks and other religious, who were in the habit of supporting as well as instructing the neighbouring poor. Some other day I will read you an account of the habits and occupations of the monks of the olden time, which, I think, will highly interest you."

"Do, dear papa," said Mary; "nothing excites my curiosity more than such topics. But it seems very strange that blinded Papists should have excelled us so much in charity, the first of virtues. And were there really no poor laws needed?"

"No, my child, they were not; and what is more, the poor were infinitely better off than they are at present. In speaking of Catholic times, however, I must not forget to mention what was done by the parish clergy; and for this purpose shall read you the orders contained in a canon issued by a Bishop of York:.

"'Let the priests receive the tithes of the people, and keep a written account of all that have paid them; and divide them in the presence of such as fear God, according to canonical authority. Let them set apart the first share for the repairs and ornaments of the church; let them distribute the second to the poor and the stranger, with their own hands in mercy and humility; and reserve the third part for themselves.' At different times, and under different bishops, regulations somewhat different were adopted, but there were always *two-fourths* at the least of the annual produce of the benefice to be given to the necessitous, and to be employed in repairing or ornamenting a church."*

"How extraordinary, papa, that such admirable regulations should have existed amongst men whom we blame so much! Who would put in practice such precepts now-a-days!"

"The thing would be altogether impossible," replied Mr. Feversham, "among married clergy, who have their families to support, as we have. Of course it was a comparatively small sacrifice for a priest to give up two-thirds of his income, when he was both unencumbered by family ties and when, from the more simple habits of the better classes, there were fewer ways of spending money on personal gratifications."

Mary looked very grave; and her mother sending for her, she soon left the room.

"Really, Mary," said Lady Harriet, "the way you neglect me now is intolerable. It is not that I miss your company at all in the forenoon when I have a good novel to read. But, then, one likes to know you are in the house, in case anything goes wrong. It is most unlady-like, the quantity of exercise that you are taking now. Coming in from your rides smirking, and looking so provokingly happy! Your cheeks like a milk-maid, and your forehead marked with a red stripe by your hat. I wonder you can disfigure yourself so. And then going into those dirty cottages! There is no saying what you may bring home from them. Don't sit near me; I feel quite uncomfortable. Remember, Mary, I strictly forbid you to go to see sick people. I am quite in the horrors!

* Letter 2nd, Cobbet's Protestant Reformation.

You will have your mother dying of small-pox or typhus fever some of these days. And, ungrateful creature, it will be all your doing!"

"Indeed, mamma," replied Mary meekly, "I am very particular about whom I go to see; and I think I should be wrong did I visit such sick as you describe. Papa particularly cautioned me not to enter any house where there was an infectious disorder, for fear of bringing it home to the family."

"Well, I am glad he has so much good feeling," replied Lady Harriet; "but I wish he would put a stop to your excursions altogether. You are getting so stout, and instead of being pale and interesting, you are absolutely becoming rosy! It is a great trial for a poor weak invalid like me, to have a person in rude health bustling about them. I suppose you have become so virtuous lately, it would be a terrrible hardship for you to give up your pious excursion to-morrow forenoon, in order to do a commission for your mother."

"On the contrary, mamma, I shall be most happy to put off my ride, in order to do anything you like," replied Mary.

"Well, I am glad to see that you have some filial duty left. I want Delphine to make an alteration in my green velvet dress; and you must take the carriage, and go to Overbury to try if possible to get it matched; or if not, to get some of the shopkeepers to send to London for it."

Mary was very glad thus to oblige her mother, as she was anxious to show that her new occupations in no way interfered with her former duties. She was likewise pleased to have an excuse for visiting Overbury, as she wished to see an intimate friend, a Mrs. Egremond, who lived there. This lady was a widow, old enough to be Mary's mother. At the age of three-and-twenty she had made a love-match, with the full concurrence of her friends and relations. Her husband, who like herself, belonged to the established church, was a sensible, kind-hearted, and religious man. Though well-informed, he was not a deep thinker; tolerably satisfied with the church in which he had been brought up, it had never entered into his head to examine the tenets of another, in hopes of finding a nearer approach to truth. It was his opinion that, as all the different sects of Protestantism belonged to the fold of Christ, it was not even necessary to believe precisely what the particular church held, to which one outwardly conformed; it being sufficient to be faithful to the private teaching of the Spirit in one's own soul. He was an affectionate husband and kind master, charitable to the poor, and obliging to his friends; so, at his death, he was universally regretted. Though still a young woman at the period of her husband's decease, Mrs. Egremond received a shock from which she never wholly recovered, and which tinged the entire course of her future life. Years elapsed before she could even mention his name without painful agitation. Before this event took place, being of a very happy, gay disposition, she had enjoyed the world much; her loss, however, thoroughly sobered her; she henceforward found her great consolation in religion, though gradually she was again able to take pleasure in the society of her friends, and in the pursuit of her various accomplishments. She appeared to least advantage when she talked of religion, because her ideas were somewhat confused on that subject. This proceeded, in great measure, from having adopted her late husband's notions, and having mingled with them a number of set phrases picked up from her evangelical friends, which, though they may express much to the enlightened, yet to ordinary listeners convey no definite ideas. It is nearly impossible to argue with a person who speaks this language; because his words convey no precise and obvious meaning to lay hold of and combat. For instance, when he speaks of 'the truth as it is in Jesus,' if you interpret this differently from what he does, you are at cross purposes in argument.

To this lady Mary went, after transacting her other business in Overbury. Mrs. Egremond was delighted to see her, and kissed her most affectionately.

"How was Mr. Harvey when you heard from him last?" she enquired. "I hope you have brought me some of his letters to read, as you promised; you know how much I am interested in all that concerns your happiness."

"Indeed, dear Mrs. Egremond," replied Mary, "I am ashamed to say I have not done so. I knew that I should have very little time, and I hoped to persuade you to accompany me in a little excursion which I was proposing to make, before I should order the carriage to take me home."

"Certainly, my love, I shall be happy to go with you. But where?"

Mary then described in a few words the nature of the new occupation which had afforded her so much interest, and added that, being inexperienced, she feared that she often missed opportunities of giving instruction, or doing good, where her aid was most wanted.

"But how can I assist you in this, my dear?" asked Mrs. Egremond, smiling.

"You can very much," replied Mary; "for I am sure you are in the habit of visiting the poor yourself, and I wish you to take me along with you, and show me how you do."

Mrs. Egremond looked puzzled as she replied, "The truth is, Mary, there are no poor families whom I visit at present. I do certainly lay aside a certain portion of my income yearly for the purposes of charity; but I generally prefer assisting those individuals, who from birth and education are entitled to move in good society, but who have not sufficient fortune of their own to maintain a respectable appearance. When I give to the poor, I always employ either a clergyman or an experienced person, for I find myself very apt to be deceived."

"And must I then give up my plan?" asked Mary, "to which I have been looking forward with so much pleasure."

"Not so, my love," replied her friend. "Though I am a very bad guide, yet I am most willing to indulge your curiosity. So, if you like, we will walk to a very poor quarter of the town, where an old servant of my father's lives, whom I found a year ago in great distress, but whom I have enabled to set up for herself in a small grocery business. I have no doubt she will be able to give us information about her poor neighbours, and then you can see if there are any among them whom you would like to visit."

"Thank you, dear Mrs. Egremond; you are truly obliging," exclaimed Mary.

During their walk to the grocer's shop, Mrs. Egremond took occasion to say, that she thought it was perhaps a dangerous occupation which Mary had chosen for herself, as it must have a tendency to make her set a value upon works; whereas works are nothing but filthy rags, and by faith alone we are saved. Mary replied, that she thought works were useless, except through Jesus Christ; but that through Him God would reward us on account of them. Mrs. Egremond was horrified at this doctrine, and quoted several passages from St. Paul to prove that by faith alone we are saved. Mary repeated the promise of Jesus Christ, that a cup of cold water given in His name should not be without its reward. Her friend did not know very well how to answer, except by quoting St. Paul again, who certainly spoke very strongly in her favour. Mary tried to prove from St. James that works are enjoined; but, to her surprise, Mrs. Egremont urged that many eminent Christians, Luther among the rest, had doubted the authenticity of this epistle.

"What would I give," exclaimed Mary, "to have

any means of knowing for certain what I ought to believe on this, as well as on many other questions, and how to reconcile what appears almost contradictory in Bible texts! Did it never strike you, Mrs. Egremond, what a great deal of doubt, uneasiness, and sorrow it would have saved in the world, had God given a peculiar grace to any set of clergy, so that by His Spirit they should never go wrong in explaining Scripture?"

"What an absurd notion, my dear child!" said Mrs. Egremond, laughing, "the thing is impossible!"

"I don't know that," replied Mary. "It has often struck me that it must have been the case under the Jewish dispensation; and it seems nearly certain that the Jews had an infallible guide to explain the law in the persons of the priests and doctors."

"What an extraordinary and unfounded notion!" exclaimed Mrs. Egremond. "Have you forgotten the extreme corruption of the lives of the Jewish priests and rulers in our Saviour's times, and that they had made the law of God of no effect through their traditions?"

"Very true," replied Mary; "but I cannot help thinking that on all important matters God preserved their faith true, whatever their actions may have been; otherwise Christ would not have said, 'The scribes and Pharisees sit in Moses' seat: all therefore whatsoever they bid you observe, that observe and do; but do not ye after their works, for they say and do not.' Now, I think from this, that the Jews could not go wrong so long as they obeyed those who sat in Moses' seat; and I wish with all my heart that we had Moses' seat still, or something in place of it."

"You are a strange girl, Mary, and I cannot argue with you, not having studied these subjects," said Mrs. Egremond; "but I think, even supposing the Jews had this infallible guide, we are still better off than they, because we have the teaching of the Spirit

—the Spirit witnessing to our Spirit that we are the sons of God."

"But," said Mary, "I never could be sure that it was the right Spirit that witnessed in me. Satan might deceive me."

Mrs. Egremond would have replied, but at this moment they reached the petty grocer's shop, where they were to make enquiries. After talking a few minutes to the woman behind the counter, and purchasing a trifle, Mrs. Egremond asked her about her poor neighbours. She mentioned in reply the names of several, who were in great distress, and offered to send a little boy to guide the ladies to their habitations. They immediately accepted her offer, and set out. After going half-way up a filthy back lane, they mounted a long and dilapidated stair-case, with several doors opening off every landing-place. When nearly out of breath they reached the top, the boy pointed to a crazy door full of chinks, through which loud and sharp sounds of altercation, in the shrill tone of women's voices could be heard. The moment they knocked all noise ceased, and a dead silence ensued; they knocked again, but not a breath, not a movement could be distinguished. Had it not been for the previous sounds, they would have turned away in the belief that there was no one in the house.

"Come, come, Judy Roberts, none of your tricks! Moll Fitzsimmons, open the door, I tell you!" cried the boy who accompanied them, at the pitch of his voice. "A pretty like thing to be quarrelling there, when the quality are standing waiting at the door, and can't get in."

"Blessings on us! the quality did you say?" cried a harsh cracked voice. "It's many a long day since the quality crossed this door. But sure I am glad to see them now; may be they'll bring good luck!"

The door was speedily unbarred, and the ladies entered. But what a scene of squalor and desolation met their eyes! The roof was so dilapidated, that the clouds could be discerned, coursing through the heavens; and the floor in many parts was so rotten, that there was some risk of falling through into the room below. The only furniture consisted of an apology for a table, two old boxes, and one three-legged stool. Bed there was none. In the corner of the apartment best sheltered from the weather, lay a heap of shavings, for straw would have been too great a luxury. On this was stretched a miserable object that looked scarcely human, with her head wrapped in a handkerchief, the original colour of which could not be discovered. As the ladies advanced, she drew more closely round her an old and very small piece of carpet—her only covering.

"Good heavens! this is dreadful!" ejaculated Mrs. Egremond.

The other occupant of the room was a woman about fifty, swarthy in her complexion, with black eyes and marked features. Her appearance denoted the shrew, but this was counterbalanced by a look of sense and honesty; her clothing was decent, though exceedingly scanty. On inquiry they found that the bed-ridden sufferer, Judy Roberts, had entirely lost the use of her limbs, and was dependent on the kindness of her cousin, Molly Fitzsimmons, for support.

"Can she not get into the poor-house?" asked Mary.

"To the poor-honse!" cried the voice from among the shavings. "Do you think I would go to the poor-house—where they tell me they sleep three in a bed, where they give diseased meat to the poor to eat, and where the doctors run off with the body to their butcher chopping houses, within an hour after you are dead? No, no, I'll not go to the poor-house! I know *she* wants me to go—Molly, I mean. She wants to be quit of me! I am up to her! She grudges the trouble and the expense of maintaining me. But I tell her and *you* too, ladies, that I'll die lying in the corner of the street sooner than go to the poor-house. I know her tricks, ladies. She gave me bad butter to my breakfast this morning; my stomach turned at it!"

"Why do you give the poor woman such disgusting food?" asked Mrs. Egremond.

"Sorra better could I, Ma'am!" replied Molly Fitzsimmons. "I spent my last halfpenny in getting butter for her at all, Ma'am, to tempt her appetite—let alone bad butter."

"And what had you for your own breakfast?" asked Mary.

"Just nothing, Ma'am," replied Molly. "I am used to want; and I would not let the poor cratur on the shavings there, go without her butter if I could help it, for she has a delicate appetite, Ma'am, that requires to be tempted."

"And pretty-like tempation you give me! a piece of rancid butter, smelling like whale oil, and no bigger than a penny piece!" exclaimed the voice from the corner.

"Have you had anything at all to eat to-day?" asked Mary, turning to Molly. "You have at least dined, I suppose, though you did not breakfast?"

"'Deed, Ma'am, sorra a bit of me has tasted meat this day; but I was just thinking, Ma'am, to go out to borrow a penn'orth of bread when your ladyship came in."

"Cruel wretch that she is!" cried the voice from the corner. "She was going out to leave me all alone in the cold; and when I asked her to warm a brick to put to my cold feet that are perishing with the shivers, she told me to wait till she came in."

"Now, now, Judy, just be aisy!" cried Molly. "Have not I warmed the brick five times for you this blessed day already? and yet I think you would cry to the day of judgment for a hot brick."

"Oh, Ma'am, Ma'am," cried Judy, addressing Mrs. Egremond, "just come here till I complain of her. She put a scalding hot brick to my poor senseless feet this very morning; and the skin peeled off my toes as it would do off potatoes."

"And just you, Ma'am, hear me," cried Molly. "She's the ungrateful woman. Do I not toil for her, and slave for her, and starve myself for her, and all to keep her out of the poor-house because she does not like to go?"

The ladies made a few enquiries, and found that the two women were second cousins. They had been great friends in their youth; and on Judy becoming bed-ridden, Molly had received her into her house, and supported her. Latterly she had required so much attendance, that Molly had been obliged to give up her humble trade, that of apple-woman, in order to be constantly beside her.

"How then do you support yourselves?" asked Mrs. Egremond.

"I have a shilling a week from the parish," said Molly; "and we can't expect more, when Judy won't go to the workhouse."

"Hear the unfeeling monster!" cried Judy.

"The clergyman has twice visited us," continued Molly; "and his honour always left a shilling The neighbours give us a trifle now and then, and hitherto I pawned the clothes and the furniture; but there is little left now."

"Think of her!" said Judy; she bought me two sour apples yesterday, but I would not look at them."

"And indeed, your ladyship," continued Molly, "my second last penny went for those very apples."

"Have you no relations that could assist you?" asked Mrs. Egremond.

"Judy has none," replied Molly; "but I have a son well to do in the world. He is mate of a vessel, and has a house in Liverpool."

"Can he not assist you?" enquired Mary.

"Yes, Ma'am," replied the poor woman; "he is

a good son, and willing to assist me. But in his last letter, when he sent me something, he told me to get quit of Judy there, and come to live with him in comfort."

"Hear that! hear that!" cried the voice from the shavings. "She wants to get quit of me; but I tell her that only main force shall take me to the workhouse, where they lie three in a bed."

"You would be much more comfortable there than you are here," said Mrs. Egremond, turning towards her. "You would have a mattress to lie upon, and blankets to cover you, which you have not at present."

"And do you think I would go to the workhouse, Madam," replied Judy, "to have my body chopped into small pieces by the doctors after I am dead: for I have no relations to claim me, but Molly there, and she would be off to Liverpool to her son."

"Have you written to your son again, Molly, since your present distress?" enquired Mary.

"No, Ma'am," she replied. "You see I could not find in my heart to do as he asked, and send away Judy. Besides, he has a wife; and the pride, Ma'am, the pride keeps me from telling him the real truth about our poverty, for *she* would see it—his wife, I mean."

"She does not do a hand's turn for herself," cried Judy. "She might go about and beg for us, or at least take her basket and sell apples if she liked. So, I say Molly is not to be pitied, though I am."

Molly upon this pulled down her stocking, and showed her leg to the surprised visitors, who perceived a long, open wound, about a finger in length, where diseased matter seemed to be gathering.

"Judy would not let me leave her, Ma'am, though I could, for she is always wanting some little thing. Even though I were to try to go I am not able, for I am lamed entirely, with this wound which I got from the hot brick falling on it."

Mrs. Egremond relieved the poor women; and gave Molly orders to proceed immediately to a dispensary to get her wound dressed. She also promised to send them bread and butcher-meat as soon as she got home. The women both appeared grateful, particularly Molly.

"How old are you?" said Mary to the latter.

"Just fifty, Ma'am; and Judy there is sixty, but she looks the youngest, though she is bed-ridden; for you see, Ma'am, she was always of a gay and cheerful disposition, while I was melancholy and took on care."

"You ought to keep the poor creature cleaner, Molly," said Mrs. Egremond.

"Indeed I would if I could," replied she, "but it is not so easy, Ma'am, when she has not a rag to change."

"Her hair is far too long," said Mary; "in her state of filth it would be better to cut it short."

"Sorra would I, Ma'am," said Molly. "Though she is past sixty now, there is not a grey hair in her head. That hair, Ma'am, reminds me of the ould ancient days, when we was both young. She was very pretty then, and well to do in the world; her father was a decent innkeeper, though she is lying now, like a beast in a dirty cage. Her hair was very fair, Ma'am, and greatly admired. They used to call her then Silver Judy."

"Get the brick warmed for my feet directly, Molly," cried Judy, "and don't stand gossipping there."

"Indeed, Judy," exclaimed Mrs. Egremond, advancing towards the heap of shavings in which the poor object lay half buried, "you are far from doing your duty with regard to your cousin; she supports you from charity, so why do you assume that tone of command and insolence when you address her? Indeed, Judy, you do very wrong."

"Speak to *her*, Ma'am, speak to *her*, Ma'am!"

answered Judy. "She vexes me, and contradicts me from morning till night, and never gives me a soft answer."

"And who could," retorted Molly, "when you are always aggravating me?"

"You are both in the wrong," said Mary, now addressing them. "Do you not know that you ought to imitate Jesus Christ, our Divine Master, who was gentle, long-suffering, and patient, and bore with the faults of His friends. Judy, it is evident from your state that you cannot live very long, and when you come to die, you will regret that you have not practised patience and gentleness a little more."

"Whew!" cried Judy, giving a long whistle, and peering at Mary through the shavings. "Just what I expected when you came in, ladies. Not a soul, even among the neighbours, comes to see us, but what is all for legality and good works—bothering and tormenting an old bed-ridden woman like me, to practise patience, long-suffering, and other fal-de-rals! I tell you, Ma'am, by faith alone we shall stand or fall. And does not St. Paul say in Romans: 'A man is justified by faith without the deeds of the law.' So you see, ladies, there is no need of preaching to me. I hold by faith, and leave the filthy rags of good works to Molly there, who is but a poor hand at practising them when all is done."

"As good as yourself any day!" exclaimed Molly.

"Hear her, hear her!" cried Judy; "that is the way she always aggravates me, with her evil tongue and her bad butter!"

"And you aggravate her quite as much, Judy," said Mrs. Egremond, when it is far less your part to do it, since she from kindness chooses to support you. You quoted St. Paul just now about faith: listen, then, while I quote him in my turn on a subject most applicable to you. In his Epistle to the Ephesians he says: 'Let all bitterness, and wrath, and anger, and clamour, and evil speaking be put away from you with all malice. And be ye kind to one another, tender-hearted, forgiving one another, even as God for Christ's sake hath forgiven you.' "

"Well, Ma'am," replied Judy in her shrill voice, "I allow that is a beautiful text that your ladyship has quoted. But you know, Ma'am, that there is no manner of doubt that the Bible is different in different places; so just do you take your favourite texts, and let me take mine: we will both be right in the end, since we stick to Scripture. Does not St. Paul say in Galatians, 'The just shall live by faith.' Now I sticks to faith, and casts works to the dogs!"

At this speech Mary, who had great difficulty in keeping from laughing, gave a look to Mrs. Egremond, as though to remind her of their previous conversation, and whispered, "Who shall decide when doctors disagree? Oh, for a sure and certain guide!"

Meanhile Molly, clasping her hands, exclaimed, "Did you ever hear anything better spoken? Judy is the boy after all! She was always a fine discoursed woman, ever since I knew her. She has read a power of books, and got the larning."

The ladies now hurried away, promising to return another day; for Mary just then discovered that it was already the hour at which her carriage had been ordered.

CHAPTER X.

"Dear bairns, gie ower askin me the reason for this, an' the reason for that; folk that maun hae reasons for everything, aye turn infidels, or what's waur, Papists." *My old Nurse.*

"HAS your Reverence time to talk a bit with me to-day?" asked Farmer Blount, as he entered Mr. Feversham's study, after an interval of more than a week. "I was in Overbury yesterday, selling potatoes; and Mr. Sharples met me in the market-place, and insisted on me going to his house with him. He began asking how I was coming on with my Catholic friend, and then gave me a good deal of information about which I should like to talk with you."

"On what subject, John?" inquired the rector.

"On several, Sir," replied Blount; "but chiefly on the infallibility of the pope. He said, your Reverence, that Catholics hold that the pope can do no wrong, which assertion bears a lie on the face of it, since some of the popes have been the worst of men."

"I am surprised, John, to find that Mr. Sharples is so ill informed on this subject. The infallibility to which the Catholic Church lays claim, merely regards matters of faith, and has nothing whatever to do with the conduct of any of the popes. Some of them, but very few in proportion to the whole number, were indeed most scandalous sinners; and yet, strange to say, the Church was as infallible during their lives as at any other period, because she still continued to teach what Christ had taught, without change or variation."

"You are a candid man, Mr. Feversham," replied

Blount, "therefore you allow the bad lives of some of the popes; but do you think the Catholic clergy in general would be honest enough to confess it?"

"Certainly they would," replied the rector. "It is a well-known fact, which no one would try to deny. At the same time, Protestants have no more reason to adduce it as an argument against Catholicity, than the Jews would have had to question the authority of the Apostles because a Judas had been among them."

"Then it is not true," rejoined Blount, "that Catholics hold that the Church can do no wrong. I wish, Sir, that you would particularly explain what they do mean by infallibility."

"Simply," replied the rector, "that the Church cannot go wrong in deciding what we are to believe."

"That is a bold claim, your Reverence, but assertion is not proof; even though it is the Catholic Church that speaks. I would think now that it is impossible to give any sort of reasonable grounds for maintaining such a ridiculous thing, and still less to find Scripture warrant for it."

"We shall see," replied the rector. "In Matthew, 16th chap. 18th verse, Christ says, speaking of the Church, 'The gates of hell shall not prevail against it.' The gates mean the powers of hell; and do you think Christ would be keeping His promise if the Church taught what was false? Would that not be the most signal triumph of the powers of darkness?"

"Yes," answered Blount; "if the Catholic Church is the true one, then Christ would be breaking His promise, were He to permit her to teach error. But there's the rub: I never allowed that the Catholic is the true Church, for Protestants have quite as good a right to claim that title, and say that the promise about the gates of hell, applies to them."

"It would be very well, Blount, to argue in this way, if Protestantism had always been in existence;

but, unfortunately, it is little more than three hundred years old. Who, then, reaped the benefit of the promise during the previous fifteen hundred years, if not the Catholic Church? And if the Catholic Church had it so long, on what grounds can you assert that the promise was transferred?"

"Faith, I don't know," said the farmer; "your Reverence is far too 'cute for me, but I'll go to Mr. Sharples to-morrow, and get to the bottom of this."

"At any rate, Blount, before you go, you may as well hear a few more passages of Scripture which apply to this subject; it may save you two walks to Mr. Sharples."

"As your Reverence pleases," replied Blount; "though I think that 'The gates of hell shall not prevail against it,' is a sentence enough to pose Mr. Sharples, or any other man, without being pressed hard with more texts."

"When our Saviour," continued the rector, "consoled His disciples with the promise of the Comforter, He goes on to say, in John xvi. 13, 'Howbeit, when He, the Spirit of truth, is come, he will guide you into all truth.'"

"But," replied Blount, "it was to the disciples Christ was speaking, as your Reverence observed, and not to the Catholic Church."

"If it had only been to the disciples that the promise was addressed, Blount, how did it happen that our Saviour prayed the Father, that this Spirit of truth might abide with them for ever, as you will find in John xiv. 16, 17? Did the disciples live for ever? If, on the contrary, they died like common men, how was the promise kept, unless by the Spirit of truth remaining for ever with their successors throughout all ages?"

"There is some reason to say that, rector, if every text of Scripture is to be taken literally; however, I don't just think it necessary to follow up words so uncommon close. At that rate there would be new lights found continually in the Bible; and many a thing spoken in a general sort of way by Jesus Christ, if taken to the letter, would upset our old notions altogether."

"And yet some time ago, Blount, you expressed your satisfaction at finding that the Catholic Church interpreted Scripture so literally."

"Why, I did so, certainly, I confess," replied Blount; "and I do think still that we ought to take Scripture literally, wherever it treats of important matters—such as the real body and blood of Christ being in the sacrament—because then it would not be according to God's mercy to speak ambiguously, and let us be deceived. But it is a very different thing to take Scripture literally on the smallest things; and there would be no end to the confusion if we once began."

"Do you not therefore see, John, the great necessity for having an authority to which we can refer whenever we are puzzled with Scripture?"

"Why, as to that, Sir," said Blount, "I should always take the opinion of great doctors and learned men."

"I quite agree with you in thinking it the best thing you could do," answered the Rector, smiling "And now I am sorry that a particular engagement at this hour, calls me away, so that I must bid you good-bye—which, perhaps, is just as well, for you can go to the learned doctor in Overbury meanwhile, and get him to explain Scripture for you."

"No, no," cried Blount, "your Reverence is making game of me. I don't count Mr. Sharples alone, much authority; I only wish to get at the truth, and I hope your Reverence is not angry with me for making a sturdy defence of my old opinions."

Blount now departed, and the following day went to see Mr. Sharples; but as his conversation with that gentleman can be best gathered by his next interview with the rector, we shall at once pass over the intermediate circumstances, and return to Mr. Feversham's study, after the lapse of a few days.

"I have been talking again to Mr. Sharples, Sir," commenced Blount as soon as he entered. "I was telling him that your Reverence said, Protestantism began little more than three hundred years ago. To my mind, Sir, he gave a very pretty answer. He said, Sir, that though Protestantism was not visible until Luther tore the veil off it like, yet it always existed in the hearts of true believers; and that those Protestant believers were the true Church that has been ever since the Apostles lived, and that the gates of hell never prevailed against them."

"So Protestantism was not the visible church till Luther's time. Is not that what you mean?" said Mr. Feversham.

"Yes, Sir," replied Blount; "but a thing can be strong and active before it is visible, like the fire in my new hay last season."

"Very true, John," replied the rector. "And from time to time there has arisen heresy in the Church, which, like the fire in the hay, smouldered in secret for a little while, till it was discovered, and means taken to extirpate it. If God had chosen that the true Church should be an invisible one, of course He could have made it so. But He did not choose such to be the case; for I have proof in Scripture that the true Church must be visible. Isaiah in his second chapter, speaking of the Church, says that it shall 'be established in the top of the mountains, and exalted above the hills, all nations flowing to it.' Can this be an invisible Church? Micah says the same thing in his fourth chapter. Isaiah likewise describes the Church in the 62nd chapter as a city whose watchmen 'shall never hold their peace day or night.' But indeed our Lord Himself is explicit enough on this subject, when He desires us, in Matthew xviii. 17, '*to tell the church.*' And I may therefore well ask you if the Church were at any time invisible, how you would be able to find her out, so as to obey Christ's command, and tell her anything?"

"Oh, your Reverence, do stop, and have pity on me; you know very well I am not up to these fine reasonings. However, Mr. Sharples said that I ought not to mind though you proved me wrong, seeing I am no hand at argument; but that, whenever I was posed, I was to transfix you with a smasher."

"What do you mean, John?" asked the rector, laughing.

"I mean, Sir, that facts are worth twenty argument. And Mr. Sharples told me to give you an instance of the invisible Church in the Old Testament. The Church, your Reverence, had so far disappeared in Elijah's time, that even that holy man was convinced that he himself was the only one left, until God told him that there were seven thousand in Israel who had not bowed unto Baal, (1 Kings xix. 18.) Now, was not that a first-rate invisible Church?"

"Yours is not a good argument, John," replied the rector, "because, at the very time you mention, the Church was visible and most flourishing in its proper seat—the neighbouring kingdom of Judah—under the good king Jehosaphat."

"Well, that is most uncommon provoking, Mr. Feversham," said Blount; "for I had considered it a special good bouncing argument."

"But surely, Blount, if you are only anxious to know which is the true religion, you need not care whether I overturn your reasoning or not. Do you not agree with me in thinking that the great point is to find truth in the end?"

"Certainly," replied the farmer; "but I am a foolish man too, your Reverence, and sometimes for the minute lose sight of the main thing. But if you please, Sir, tell me some more of your reasons for believing that the true Church must be visible."

"I have already given you a few," said the rector; "and I can only add that the injunctions to hear and obey the Church, and to follow our spiritual guides, are far too numerous and explicit in the New Testament to allow us to suppose that it could, by any chance, be invisible, and hence difficult to find."

"Well, it is very hard, Sir, to be told to obey the Church, and yet not know which Church is meant. Though it is just my case! But, if you please, would your Reverence be good enough to quote Scripture for it."

"Willingly," replied the rector. "Our Saviour alludes to a visible Church, whose voice can be heard when He says, (Matt. xviii. 17.) 'And if he shall neglect to hear them, tell it unto the Church; but if he neglect to hear the Church, let him be unto thee as an heathen man and a publican.' Again, in Luke x. 16, when He sends out the Apostles He says, 'He that heareth you heareth me; and he that despiseth you despiseth me, &c.'"

"Yes, yes, Sir," interrupted Blount, "but that applies only to the apostles."

"Not so," replied the rector; "their successors have the same powers, commission, and authority; because, as I told you before, Christ promised to remain with them till the end of the world, and that the Spirit of truth should be with them for ever. St. Paul also gives his testimony, calling the Church the 'pillar and ground of the truth.' (1 Tim. iii. 15.) Likewise, in Hebrews xiii. 17, he says, 'Obey them that have the rule over you, and submit yourselves.'"

"Then I should submit myself to the pastors of the Church of England, because I am a member of it," said the farmer, smartly.

"Certainly, if it be the true Church," said the rector. "We shall come to that question by and by, however. Meanwhile, I am only quoting these texts to show how we are enjoined to submit to the Church, and obey her, which would be an unreasonable command, had she been for any time invisible. Now, to go on: St. Paul, writing to the Ephesians, tells them that God has not only placed in the Church apostles, prophets, and evangelists, but also pastors and teachers—for what end? 'For the perfecting of the saints, for the work of the ministry, for the edifying of the body of Christ.' Till when? 'Till we all come in the unity of the faith,' &c., &c. Why? 'That we henceforth be no more children, tossed to and fro and carried about by every wind of doctrine.' You will find all this, and more which I have no time to quote, in Ephesians, 4th chapter, beginning at the 11th verse. From this Scripture we gather that God has appointed pastors to guide us to unity, in order that we may not be tossed about with conflicting opinions. Surely, I need say no more to prove that the Church is visible."

"Well, I will be candid," said Blount, "and own that your Reverence has pretty well convinced me that the Church is visible, and must always have been so; otherwise Christ would not have been so unjust as to pronounce sentence against those who will not hear her. But it seems to me, Sir, that God is not so narrow-minded and prejudiced as we poor mortals are. So is it not possible that he embraces all the different denominations of Christians in the one true Church, seeing they all trust in Christ, which, to my notion, is the great thing?"

"You have frequently been in a court of justice, John," replied Mr. Feversham, "and have often heard witnesses swear contradictory statements. How many of these statements can be true?"

"Of course, Sir, said Blount, "truth is but one; we all know that. There can't be more than one story right; but, indeed, where all the witnesses contradict each other, I should be greatly tempted to think them a set of blackguards, and believe none of them."

"And yet, Blount, in a much more important matter, you are willing to believe that some hundred different bodies of Christians, contradicting each other, are all in the right!"

"Not exactly," said Blount; "I don't mean they are perfectly in the right in little things, but in important matters they are perhaps right, and thus form the one true Church."

"And do you really think that Christ's Church, if composed of such contradictory elements, has any right to be called the pillar and ground of truth? Or, in such a case, is she so strong that the gates of hell should never prevail against her?"

"Well, your Reverence," replied Blount, "I will just frankly and honestly tell you the whole truth. If I judged solely by the Bible, without having any private experience or knowledge of my own, I would say that there is but one true Church—that that Church is visible—and that we are not only strictly commanded to hear and obey her, but to get instruction from her pastors whenever we are in doubt or difficulty as to what we should believe. I think, too, that Christ has promised pretty plainly that she should not teach error, because the Spirit of truth is always to remain with her—which, if I mistake not, is what you call infallibility. This is what I should gather from the Bible alone. But bless your soul, Sir, these things are enough to drive an honest man mad. I am becoming more and more of an infidel every day. I tell you frankly, Mr. Feversham, that though I allow all you have asserted to be proved in the Bible, yet I am inclined not to believe one word of it."

"What do you mean, John?" asked Mr. Feversham. "Do you deny the authority of the Bible?"

"I hope not just yet," replied poor Blount, very gravely and sadly; "but I don't know what I may do by and by. I will confess to you honestly, Sir, what makes me have doubts. If there is but one true and visible Church which has always existed, even a child might see very clearly that it will be an easy thing for you to prove that it can be no other than the Catholic Church. Now, if I know from good authority that the Catholic Church is guilty of many corrupt practices—such as idolatry, superstition, refusing half the communion to the people, and using a language which cannot be understood, in order to hide her secrets from them; besides a great variety of other things which Mr. Sharples told me—hearing this, is it not enough to drive me distracted to think that a Church which sanctions such a lot of abuses has the best side of the argument, and can quote Scripture to prove that she is the pillar and ground of truth? Supposing even that she cannot prove herself to be the true Church, what the better am I? It is enough to make me lose respect for the Bible, if there is so much in it that is all fudge and mere words."

"Well, John," replied the rector, "I respect your honesty, and I hope by and by to get you out of your difficulties. You must state all these accusations against the Catholic Church in detail. I shall try to answer and satisfy you; and if in the end there be no one of her practices and doctrines which seems opposed to the Bible, or of which you disapprove, will you then refuse to acknowledge that she is the church mentioned in Scripture as the pillar and ground of truth, against which the gates of hell shall never prevail, and with which the Spirit of truth shall remain until the end of the world?"

"Right glad shall I be, rector, to acknowledge her the pillar and ground of truth, if you will do your part completely, and satisfy me as to the falsity of what I have heard. And there's my hand on it, rector; it is a bargain."

CHAPTER XI.

"And is there care in heaven, and is there love
In heavenly spirits, to these creatures base,
That may compassion to their evils move?
There is; or else more wretched were the case,
Of men than beasts. But, oh! the exceeding grace
Of highest God! that loves his creatures so,
And all his works with mercy doth embrace,
That blessed angels he sends to and fro,
To serve to wicked men—to serve his foe."
SPENSER.

"THERE is a thing, your Reverence, which I don't at all like," said Farmer Blount; "and that is the custom Catholics have of worshipping the saints. We are forbidden very distinctly in the Bible to commit idolatry; and after that, it is past my comprehension to understand how you can, with any face, persist in it."

"Catholics do not commit idolatry, and do not worship the saints, Blount. We merely beg them to pray to God for us, knowing that they have no power to help us, independently of God's will and pleasure."

"But, rector, I beg your pardon; Mr. Sharples showed me prayers to the saints, in which there were petitions for mercy and defence."

"Very likely," replied Mr. Feversham. "We ask the saints to show mercy to us by praying for us; and we think they can defend us from the powers of darkness and from other dangers, because we know that God has given his angels charge over us. In the same way, were we travelling through a country infested with wild beasts, or what is worse, with robbers and plunderers, and if the king of the country had given us a guard of soldiers to defend us, it would only be natural, whenever we approached a particularly dangerous place, to ask the soldiers to take especial care, and defend us valiantly."

"Well, I have heard, Sir, that the angels do take care of us. We have Scripture for that; but it is the worship of the saints I am speaking of."

"As to that, John, what applies to the angels applies to the saints; for we are told by St. Matthew that we shall be as the angels."

"And indeed, rector, it comes much to the same thing; for, if it is right in the one case, it is right in the other; but, somehow, I should always like to go straight to God Himself through Jesus Christ whenever I wanted anything. The roundabout way of going to the saints first, is not to my taste."

"You disapprove then, perhaps," continued the rector, "of the custom in the Church of England of recommending sick people to the prayers of the congregation?"

The farmer stared with surprise at the question, and replied, "Not a whit—not a whit, your Reverence. On the contrary, I think it very proper; but what has it to do with what I was saying?"

"A great deal," said Mr. Feversham. "Because if you think it beneficial to recommend those in distress to the prayers of a mixed congregation, how much more advantageous must it be to obtain for them the prayers of the glorified saints in heaven!"

"Certainly, if you can," replied the farmer; "but how in the universe are you sure of making them hear? There is no speaking-trumpet to reach their length, I'll bet."

"We believe," replied the rector, "that they both hear and know what passes on earth; for, in Luke (15th chap.) it is said, 'Joy shall be in heaven over one sinner that repenteth,' &c. And again, a few verses further on, we find that when a sinner repents, 'there is joy in the presence of the angels of God.' The glorified spirits cannot rejoice over a circumstance of which they know nothing; they must hence be aware of these conversions, and probably know not only what happens outwardly, but even what passes in the heart, since the conversion of a sinner often takes place in an entirely interior manner, when God speaks to the soul through the voice of conscience."

"It's all very well talking this way, your Reverence; but still it goes against me to believe that the saints know so much—it is like making them into Gods."

"And for my part, John, I think you have far too low an idea of what the spirits of the blessed become. Are we not told in 1 John iii. 2, 'that when He (God) shall appear, we shall be like him; for we shall see him as he is?' Now they who see God face to face, by contemplating Him who knows all things, will surely not be unaware of what passes here below; for as the Psalmist says, 'In thy light shall we see light.' You may learn also from St. Paul not to judge of the capabilities of the saints by our own limited faculties, since he says in 1 Cor. xiii. 12, 'For now we see through a glass darkly; but then face to face: now I know in part, but then shall I know even as also I am known.'"

"Your Reverence is too much for me with your Scripture," replied the farmer. "I must give up the point, and confess that it is most likely the saints know all about us. Still, I should like to hear what Bible reasons you have, for thinking that they take such a great interest in us, as to make it worth our while bothering them with asking them to pray for us."

"We find in the Bible," answered the rector with much good humour, "that they offer our prayers to

God—which, by the way, is another argument in proof that they hear them. In Rev. v. 8, it is said that they fall down before the Lamb, 'having every one of them harps and golden vials full of odours, which are the prayers of the saints.' I shall also read you Rev. viii. 3, 4.—'And another angel came and stood at the altar, having a golden censer; and there was given unto him much incense, that he should offer it with the prayers of all saints upon the golden altar which was before the throne. And the smoke of the incense, which came with the prayers of the saints, ascended up before God out of the angel's hand.'"

"These are very applicable texts, Sir," answered the farmer. "But I would just like to hear them in the Protestant Bible."

"It is the Protestant Bible which I always quote," answered the rector. "Of course it must be more satisfactory to you than the Douai edition, of which, I assure you, in my conversations with you I have not once made use, nor do I intend to do so."

"Thank you, Mr. Feversham; I am then perfectly satisfied. But have you any other instance in Scripture of the angels or saints praying for us?"

"Yes, Blount. I shall read you Zechariah i. 12: 'Then the angel of the Lord answered and said: O Lord of hosts, how long wilt thou not have mercy on Jerusalem, and on the cities of Judah, against which thou hast had indignation these three-score and ten years?'"

"It is a different thing, however, your Reverence, simply to ask a saint or angel to pray for you, from begging them in an idolatrous fashion, as Mr. Sharples showed me in a Catholic prayer-book, for their blessing."

"Mr. Sharples need not have gone so far," replied the rector, laughing; "he might have found an instance nearer home. What say you to one of the patriarchs giving the example? On Jacob's death-bed, as you will see in Gen. xlviii. 15, 16, he blessed Joseph and said, 'God, before whom my fathers Abraham and Isaac did walk—the God which fed me all my life long unto this day, the angel which redeemed me from all evil, bless the lads.' St. John also conveys a blessing of the same kind to the seven churches: (Rev. i. 4.) 'Grace be unto you and peace from Him which is, and which was, and which is to come, and from the seven Spirits which are before His throne.'"

"These are certainly not bad examples, your Reverence," said Blount. "But without going into particulars, will you not agree with me in a general sort of way, that it is best always to have recourse to Christ at once, and that having other mediators is like taking from His office?"

"By all means, John, fly to Christ at once as you say: but that does not hinder you asking the saints to pray to Him along with you. There can be no more harm in doing so, than in St. Paul constantly asking the prayers of the faithful, as you may see at the end of his Epistles. By getting as many as possible to pray for us, God has more honour and we more profit; at the same time neither the saints nor ourselves obtain anything, except through Jesus Christ. God must be pleased with it, since He so often spared the Israelites at the intercession of Moses, and since He expressly commanded the friends of Job to get that holy man to pray for them." (Job xlii. 8, 9.)

"How does your Reverence make all that agree with what St. Paul says in 1 Timothy ii. 5: 'There is one God, and one mediator between God and man, the man Christ Jesus."

"The words that follow explain it," said the rector: "'Who gave himself a ransom for all.' There is, therefore, only one mediator who ransomed us—that is, Jesus Christ; and as I have already quoted St. Paul's example for asking the prayers, or (if you like to call it so) the mediatorship of others, I think I need say no more."

"Well," said Blount, "we shall now, if you please, rector, let the question rest, as to its being lawful to ask the prayers of saints; for I think you have proved it pretty clearly. And I also agree with you in thinking there is no reason why they should not hear us, since it appears they know when a sinner repents. Now you see, Sir, I am honest; I so far give in as to say I have no objection to all that; but you Catholics go an immense deal further—popping down on your knees whenever you address them. Is not that giving them divine worship?"

"No more, Blount, than a child gives to its parents in kneeling down to get their blessing."

"I got two texts from Mr. Sharples which I have not yet mentioned to you, Sir," continued the farmer. "In Rev. xix. 10, it is said that John fell at the feet of the angel to worship, who immediately forbade him; and in Colossians ii. 18, Paul cautions against the worship of angels."

"The angel," replied the rector, "did not forbid John to ask his prayers, but to give him idolatrous worship, which the Apostle, probably mistaking what he was, seemed about to do. In like manner, St. Paul forbids giving angels the adoration due to God."

"Thank you, Sir, I am pretty nearly satisfied now," said the farmer; "but before I say good day to your Reverence, I wish you would give me any other texts of Scripture which you remember referring to saints and angels. It would, may be, add a clencher to all you have been saying."

"Most willingly," replied Mr. Feversham. "St. Paul says (1 Cor. xiii. 8.) that charity never faileth," though the gifts of tongues, of prophesy, and of knowledge shall cease or vanish away. Now, if the saints have prayed for their brethren on earth, as their charity will never fail, they must continue to do so in heaven. Christians, even in this world, have a communion with them; for St. Paul says, addressing the Hebrews: (xii. 22, 23, 24.) 'But ye are come unto Mount Sion, and unto the city of the living God, the heavenly Jerusalem, and to an innumerable company of angels. To the general assembly and church of the first-born, which are written in heaven, and to God the judge of all, and to the spirits of just men made perfect, and to Jesus the mediator of the new covenant,' &c., &c. This fellowship, which Christians have with the glorified spirits in heaven, is mentioned in the Apostles' creed, when we say that we believe in 'the communion of saints.' And how close does the Catholic religion draw this communion! We not only speak to them, but receive obligations from them! As to the communion of saints, in the Protestant acceptation of the term, it is but an empty name."*

"It is curious enough, your Reverence, that I never thought about the meaning of 'the communion of saints' before. But tell me, if you please, Sir, is it perfectly certain that the apostles composed the creed?"

"The Catholic Church has always believed so," replied the rector, "and the English Church like-

* So numerous are the passages in the writings of the ancient fathers in favour of the invocation of saints, that the labour of transcribing them would be endless. We shall therefore content ourselves with the testimony of Protestant authors. Dr. Fulk, in his Rejoinder to Bristow, p. 5, says, "I confess that Ambrose, Austin, and Jerome, held it to be lawful."

Chemnitius, a Lutheran and a man of learning, maintains that the invocation of saints was brought into public assemblies about the year 370, by St. Basil, St. Gregory Nyssen, and St. Gregory Nazianzen, in Exam. Conv. Trid. part 3rd. p. 200.

Mr. Thorndike, not to speak of many others who bear a similar testimony, writes thus: "It is confessed that the lights, both of the Greek and Latin church, St. Basil, St. Gregory Nazianzen, St. Gregory Nyssen, St. Ambrose, St. Jerome, St. Austin, St. Chrysostom, St. Cyril of Jerusalem, St. Cyril of Alexandria, Theodoret, St. Fulgentius, St. Gregory the Great, St. Leo, and more, rather all, after that time have spoken to the saints and desired their assistance." In Epil. part 3, p. 358.

wise, since she calls it in her prayer-book the 'Apostles' creed.'

"Well now," said Blount, "I call that fact very convincing. The Apostles, if they had meant nothing particular by the 'communion of saints,' would never have stuck it into their creed. I'll mention it to Mr. Sharples. But if you please, Sir, will you go on now with the texts, for my time is short, and Dame Blount will be grumbling if I keep her pot boiling too long. I can stay a quarter of an hour yet," he continued, pulling out his watch, "if your worship ben't tired."

"I am not tired, John, at all, and shall be happy to go on as long as you have time to stay. We find, in Revelations ii. 26, that the saints are powerful, since it is said, 'And he that overcometh, and keepeth my works unto the end, to him will I give power over the nations.' And in the 9th chapter, 10th verse, St. John hears the glorified Spirits singing, 'And hast made us unto our God kings and priests; and we shall reign on the earth.'"

"These are texts that come home to one, Sir," interrupted the farmer. "There is Scripture too for the angels taking charge of us, if I remember right; and if we are to become like unto the angels when we get to heaven, why then it is applicable to the saints also; is it not, Sir?"

"Certainly, John; and I shall now repeat the passage to which you refer. Christ, speaking of the children that were brought to Him to bless, says: (Mat. xviii. 10.) 'In heaven their angels do always behold the face of my Father which is in heaven.' From this we see that angels were appointed to take care of them. St. Paul writes: (Heb. i. 14.) 'Are they not all ministering spirits, sent forth to minister for them who shall be heirs of salvation?' A good deal more could be quoted to the same effect; but on this point I see you are satisfied. I shall now show you in what veneration angels were held by the servants of God. When Joshua was before Jericho, an angel, calling himself captain of the Lord's host, appeared to him. In the 14th verse of the 5th chapter, we find that Joshua fell on his face to the earth, and did worship. Of course by this is not meant divine honours—merely a religious respect; though you must allow that the expression is pretty strong. In the Old Testament we likewise find the angels invoked, as when Jacob blessed the sons of Joseph, which I mentioned before; and Hosea, (xii. 4.) speaking of the same patriarch, writes: 'Yea, he had power over the angel, and prevailed; he wept and made supplication unto him; he found him in Bethel, and there he spake with him.'"

"Well, Sir, I think you need quote no more," said Blount; "I must own that you have good reasons on your side. While your Reverence was speaking, a droll idea came into my head that I would just like to mention. There's a set of foolish people, Sir, that believe there are certain spells or forms of words for calling up the devil. Now, Sir, if Satan can hear them while at that wickedness, I don't see how the angels and saints should not hear us, particularly when the Apostles themselves give us a hint to make friends with them when they speak of the communion of the saints."

"I agree with you so far, John," replied the rector, "that those who believe the devil can be summoned by certain formula, have no right to say that the saints and angels are unable to hear us."

"Well, good-day, Sir, and many thanks for the instruction. Blessings on us, it is late! and my dame's temper will be none the better for wanting her dinner so long."

"Is dinner ready, dame?" asked the farmer on reaching home.

"That it is I trow," replied Mrs. Blount, "and a pretty time you have kept it waiting. I've finished mine long ago; for it was better to eat, than to get my corruption set up against you for making me, as sister Benson would say, 'like the young lions that lack and suffer hunger.' Here, man, there's your bacon and beans. I've been taking some spiritual consolation in my lonesomeness, while you were out."

"Aye, what was that?" asked the farmer.

"I've been reading the thirty-nine articles," replied the dame with dignity. "There's a fund of the useful and ornamental in them things. Says I to myself when I heard your knock, there is nothing wanting in these small articles to make them equal to the book of Job in tragic effect, except the mention of that highly sublimated beast the behemoth, not to speak of the wild cony."

"What is my dame raving at?" exclaimed the farmer, raising his knife and fork in astonishment.

"Aye to be sure, I forgot," said the dame; "one must suit their discursiveness to the low capacity of their auditory listeners. I was a pitch above thee, farmer. Now I'll lay a bet, notwithstanding all your argumentations with his Reverence the rector, your better half has got a few dictionar words more than you, and a picturesquer flight of elocutionary power."

"Plague take the woman!" muttered the farmer. "I say, my dame," continued he aloud, "once for all I beg you to keep your balderdash for sister Benson and folks like her, but speak plain English to a decent man like me."

"Easier said than done, Mr. Farmer Blount," replied the lady. "Pegasus' wings be not so easy clipped as those of a laying hen. Thou shouldst rather feel proud and Luciferish, farmer, at having a wife that can feel the beauties of the thirty-nine articles and other literary compendiums."

CHAPTER XII.

"So mighty art thou, lady, and so great,
That he who grace desireth, and comes not
To thee for aidance, fain would have desire,
Fly without wings; nor only him who asks
Thy bounty, succours, but doth freely oft,
Fore-run the asking; whatsoe'r may be,
Of excellence in creatures—pity mild,
Relenting mercy, large munificence—
Are all combined in thee." DANTE.

"Hear us, sweet Mother! thou hast known
Our earthly hopes and fears,
The bitterness of mortal toil,
The tenderness of tears." CALABRIAN SHEPHERDS' HYMN.

"I HOPE I don't trouble your Reverence coming so soon again," said Farmer Blount, entering Mr. Feversham's study; "but I have just been at Overbury, holding argumentations with my friend there. In some things I have had the best of it, where I quoted your Reverence's instructions; and in other things Mr. Sharples has fairly set me dumb, leaving me not a leg to stand on; but I'll tell you, Sir, all about it, if you please, beginning at the beginning."

"Do so, John; I shall be happy to listen," replied the rector; "and instead of being wearied by your coming so often, it gives me the greatest pleasure to see you take an interest in the subject."

"Well, Sir, Mr. Sharples said that we never can be sure of those to whom we pray being real saints; and for aught we know they may not be in heaven at all. So, says I to him, Catholics only pray to those who have led very holy and good lives on earth, and as a good tree is known by its fruits, it is likely they are but seldom wrong."

"An excellent answer, John," replied the rector. "For it is only those who have practised heroic virtues, and led lives of extraordinary, nay, preternatural sanctity, to whom the Holy See sanctions our supplications. Before this permission is granted, numerous witnesses of unblemished veracity must be called upon for their testimony. So particular is the enquiry on this subject, that frequently a body of evidence, sufficient to establish a point of law in any ordinary court of justice, is rejected as inadequate."

"What does your Reverence mean by preternatural sanctity, and what sort of witness proves that?"

"I shall defer explaining this till another day," said the rector, "for I think it a pity not to finish, in the first place, the subject we are discussing at present."

"As your Reverence pleases," said the farmer. "So, as I was saying, Sir, the next thing Mr. Sharples attacked was the idolatry of the custom altogether. Says I to him, 'Sir, the church of England is more idolatrous in asking the prayers of sinful congregations, as you yourself often give out to be done on Sundays, than the Church of Rome is, in asking the prayers of those in heaven.' Upon that, he went on to say that at any rate we had no warrant in Scripture for it. So I settled that point by showing him your Scripture texts. And then says I to him, 'Sir, since you go by Scripture so mightily, what warrant have you in the Bible for calling one day St. Michael's day, and another St. Matthias's, besides many more, as I see in the prayer-book? And why did you read morning prayers on All Saints' day, as I heard tell from one of your congregation? Had you Scripture for honouring the saints on these days, when you disapprove of it on others?'"

"Excellent!" exclaimed the rector. "I scarcely gave you credit for this. And what did he reply?"

"Why, Sir, he made no hand of an answer; but he changed the subject directly, and said, 'At any rate I'll give you a text to prove that the saints know nothing about us. What say you to this? "Doubtless thou art our Father, though Abraham be ignorant of us, and Israel acknowledge us not,"' &c., &c. (Isaiah lxiii. 16.) I could not answer him, your Reverence, for I did think it a strange thing that Abraham should be ignorant of the children of Israel."

"St. Jerom* explains this for us," replied the rector, "telling us that Abraham will not own wicked Israelites to be his children. In the same sense our Saviour will say to the reprobate at the last day, 'Verily, I say unto you, I know you not,' (Matthew, xxv. 12.)

"Thank your Reverence, I understand it now," replied Blount. "Well, the next thing he said was that there is but one mediator between God and man, Christ Jesus. I don't know if I answered him right, Sir, for I said that Catholics also hold that there is but one mediator who ransomed us, and that the very saints in heaven use the mediation of Christ in offering our prayers to God."

"You did perfectly well, John," said Mr. Feversham.

"And now, Sir," continued the farmer, "I'll tell you a subject where I was completely posed, and where I think Mr. Sharples had really the best of it; and that is the extravagant honour that you pay to the Virgin. I would have no objection to honour her as much as you do the other saints; but there is a medium in all things, and I think Catholics go too far."

"But do you not agree with me in believing," said

* Jer. in C. 63. Isa.

the rector, "that God honoured the Virgin Mary infinitely more than any other of His creatures, by choosing her to be the mother of His divine Son—the mother of God?"

"Ah, Sir, that is just it!" said the farmer. "It sounds strange to my ears your calling a mere woman the mother of God."

"It may sound strange or not," replied the rector, "but there is not a Protestant among you that can deny that she was so."

"Yes, Sir," rejoined Blount; "but it is just these very sort of expressions that startle one. However, as I must allow the fact of her being mother of God, we shall let that pass."

"Well," continued the rector, "since you admit that God thus honoured her infinitely more than any other creature, why should not we, in like manner, honour her more than the rest of the saints?"

"Your Reverence reasons well, but yet I don't feel quite satisfied, for I am on strange ground. However, I should like to go into particulars, and ask you the meaning of some of the prayers to her, which Mr. Sharples was criticising. To begin at the beginning, I may as well enquire why addresses to her and the other saints are called prayers at all? Surely, you ought to pray to none but God."

"As far as I can understand," replied the rector, "a prayer and a humble request are much the same. How often do we see in petitions, this expression, 'the deponent humbly prayeth?' Do we not also in common conversation speak of a son praying his father to forgive him, or of a beggar praying for relief?"

"All very true, your Reverence, so we won't quarrel on that point. Still, I should like to hear the exact footing on which Catholics place the Virgin."

"Catholics," replied the rector, "condemn those who refuse to honour her as mother of God, as well as those who would pay her divine worship. No honour which can be given to a mere creature is too great for her; and whatever reverence and devotion we feel towards her, redounds to the glory of her divine Son. By the way, I forgot to mention that we have Scripture precedent for calling her the mother of God, since St. Elizabeth, in St. Luke's gospel, styles her 'the mother of my Lord.'"

"All you have said, Sir, is very good," rejoined Blount; "but, if I mistake not, Catholics go farther even than you have mentioned. In a prayer that Mr. Sharples read to me, called 'The Litany of Loretto,' she is called 'mother of divine grace.'"

"Certainly, John, because she is the mother of the fountain of grace, and has the greatest interest with her Son to obtain it for us."

"But she is also called 'queen of all saints,' and in another prayer that I have seen, they style her 'queen of heaven.'

"Well," replied the rector, "as she is the greatest of all the saints, she may properly be styled their queen; and she has, besides, a further claim to the title, as being the mother of the King of heaven."

"But I should like to see Scripture warrant for paying her so much honour," interrupted Blount.

"You shall have it, John; and for this purpose I need only quote from a very common Catholic prayer called the 'Ave Maria,' 'Hail, full of grace,' (or as your Protestant version has it, 'Thou that art highly favoured') 'the Lord is with thee; blessed art thou among women.' These are the words of the angel Gabriel to Mary, when he announced the birth of our Saviour; (Luke i. 28.) and surely, Blount, you cannot say that Catholics do wrong in repeating such expressions in their prayers."

"I suppose not, Sir," said Blount, scratching his head.

"The cousin of the blessed Virgin, St. Elizabeth, uses the same words in addressing her: 'Blessed art thou among women.' She also adds the next part of the Ave Maria, 'and blessed is the fruit of thy womb.' (Luke i. 42.) Now, as neither the angel nor St. Elizabeth were idolaters, I don't think Catholics can be so while they follow their example."

"Nor I, your Reverence, if they go no farther," replied the farmer.

"The blessed Virgin herself," continued the rector, "inspired by the Holy Ghost, said in answer to St. Elizabeth, 'From henceforth all generations shall call me blessed.' (Luke i. 48.) The great bulk of Christians, since the days of our Saviour, have fulfilled this prophecy. It is now only the Protestants who refuse to comply with it."

"Why, you are right there, answered the farmer; "for I scarcely ever heard a Protestant mention her name, except to find fault with honour being paid her. Some, Sir, will not even allow that she remained always a virgin. Mr. Sharples was just saying that, after the birth of Christ, she had other children to St. Joseph."

"This is a heresy, condemned by the Church more than fourteen hundred years since. At that time it was contrary to the general voice of tradition. The Apostles' creed, besides, styles her Virgin; and I leave it to you to decide whether Mr. Sharples or the Apostles should know best."

"Your Reverence is bantering me; for you know well that I'll stick to the Apostles. But if you please, Sir, explain how, in Mark, 6th chapter, Jesus is called the brother of James, Joses, Juda, and Simon."

"Any one, Blount, knowing something of Jewish manners and customs, could inform you that it was the habit among them, to call those near of kin brothers and sisters. Those you mention were the sons of Mary, the wife of Cleophas, who is called in Scripture the sister—at any rate, the near relation—of the blessed Virgin."

"But how do you know that, Sir, may I ask?" enquired Blount.

"Because Matthew (xxvii. 56.) mentions Mary, the mother of James and Joses, as one of those beholding the crucifixion; Mark relates the same thing; and St. John (xix. 25.) informs us that she was the sister of the blessed Virgin, and the wife of Cleophas."

"Thank your Reverence, I understand the thing now about James and Joses. But Mr. Sharples pointed out to me also, how Christ is often called her first-born son, which certainly looks as if others had followed."

"This is a Hebrew expression," answered the rector, "not signifying that any were born after, but rather that none were born before him."

"Well, I am much obliged to your Reverence for explaining all this to me," said Blount. "I am getting rather more clear on the subject now, I think. In the first place I see that, as there is no harm in asking you to pray for me, so there must be still less in asking the glorified saints, whom God delights in honouring, to do me the same good turn. They must have a deal of power too, since God has promised to make them kings over the nations. When I am at it, at any rate, I think I may as well speak to the angels likewise, for God has given them charge over us. And, though last not least, I'll try my hand in asking Mary, the mother of Jesus, to pray for me; as the more I consider, the more it seems to me that she could do a great deal, if once I could move her to begin praying for me. I should think now, Mr. Feversham, that as our Saviour must have been a very dutiful son to His mother on earth, and would do any thing she asked Him then, so it is likely He will do as much for her now in heaven."

"Yes, John; and in the conclusions you have drawn, you have very tolerably expressed Catholic belief. I am glad that you find it so easy to overcome your prejudices against addressing the blessed Virgin and the saints. It is generally the last point on which a Protestant gives way. In order to be admitted into the Catholic church, it is sufficient to recognize its lawfulness, it being optional to do it or not; but I have frequently heard it remarked, that there never was a devout Catholic who did not practise it; the very fact of employing the intercession of the blessed Virgin and of the other saints procuring a great increase of grace, and the true spirit of piety and devotion."

"I am thinking," continued Blount, "that if such be the case, I should beg the mother of Christ to ask her Son to help me to believe the Bible."

"Explain yourself, Blount, I don't quite understand you," said Mr. Feversham.

"I mean," replied the farmer, "that I think it clearly laid down in Scripture, that the sacrament is the actual body and blood of Christ, and that, unless we eat His flesh and drink His blood, we shall not have eternal life. (John vi.) Now, as I have a difficulty in believing it, though in a sort of way I am convinced that it is true, I think I shall try my hand at speaking to the saints by going to the greatest first, and begging Mary to ask Jesus to make me believe firmly what I ought to do on the subject."

The honest farmer now departed, and left Mr. Feversham alone to revolve the preceding conversation.

"My God!" he exclaimed, after considering a few minutes, "would that I had courage to imitate this man's simplicity! O Mary, mother! I have never recurred to you as I ought. Procure me now, by your powerful intercession with your dear Son, boldness to do what is right; and despising the world, to sacrifice all for God!"

Poor Mr. Feversham was agitated; but, alas! a few minutes afterwards he added, "Not yet—not yet! O my God, I am not yet ready! But, when the suitable time comes, give me strength to act."

The suitable time never arrives to the man who,

convinced in his heart of the truth of the holy Catholic religion, delays taking a decisive step until circumstances become favourable for declaring himself. Difficulties always increase; the meshes of the net with which the devil impedes his motion grow thicker and more complicated; day by day it becomes more impossible to burst through them. The opposition of friends and relations goes on steadily increasing, the longer they have time to contemplate and dread the threatened step; nay, what is worst of all, God, displeased at his cowardice, gradually withdraws from him the light of faith. He loses that certainty of being right, which would have carried him triumphantly through his difficulties in the first instance; he begins to be assailed by doubts and fears; and though convinced by his reason that the arguments of the Catholic church are good, he has no longer that divine faith, the gift of God, which would enable him to embrace Catholicity with his whole heart. Terrible, most terrible are the mental tortures of the coward on the brink of Catholicity! He has but two choices: forward to the rock of ages, to the one holy Catholic and Apostolic church, where alone his weary heart and his restless mind can find peace and joy; or to remain behind, not still, but gradually receding—for so a righteous God has decreed—sure to meet the punishment of the dastard—eternal death in the next world, and misery in this! In vain will he try to drown care in society, amusement, or dissipation! He cannot fly from himself; the worm that dieth not, a conscience ill at ease, is gnawing unceasingly at his heart; and weary of life, he dares not seek repose in the grave!

As the farmer approached his own door, little Neddy ran to meet him. "Papa," he cried, "I would like to be a parson, or mayhap a bishop! And to preach to grand ladies and gentlemen in fine clothes, and to ride in a coach and six!"

"Would you not like to preach to the poor, Ned;

and let those that could not afford to pay, hear for nothing?" asked his father.

"I could not keep my coach and six then, father," said Neddy; "no money, no corn for the horses. Besides, mother says that if I was a bishop, I could make all my uncles and aunts vicars and curates. Would not that be a grand thing? And then to see me with a little black apron before me, like the bishop that was here last summer, getting as plump as you'd like to see, and doing nothing, just like any other gentleman. I'll make a man of you, father, if you'll let me be a bishop!"

"We'll see, we'll see," replied Blount laughing. "But you would make a bad parson, Neddy, after all, if you won't preach to the poor. Don't you know that Jesus Christ preached chiefly to the poor; and that almost all those that followed Him were poor people?"

"Well then, father," said Neddy, putting his little hands into his breeches pockets, "I guess there were no pews let for money, in the church where Christ preached, or the poor would not have got in. He had free seats, I'll warrant you."

"He did not preach in a church at all," answered his father; "but he sought out the poor wherever He could find them."

"Still I could not do that," said Neddy, thoughtfully, "for my coach and six would need a deal of corn for the horses, and the poor folks would not pay. No, I don't think much of the poor, father."

"My dear child," said his father solemnly, "I am sorry to hear you speak this way, for the poor in this world will be great in the kingdom of heaven. Jesus Christ was poor Himself, and loved the poor with His whole heart. You must try also to love the poor, because if you love the poor for Christ's sake, He will reward you in heaven."

Neddy looked very doubtful, for his imagination had been quite captivated with the idea of being a bishop, and preaching to lords and ladies; so his father continued:

"You love Jesus Christ—do you not, my boy?"

"Yes," replied Neddy, looking somewhat like to cry.

"Then you shall do something to please Him," said his father. "Put on your cap, and get a quart of new milk from your mother, and run with it to the poor widow at the corner of the lane, and give it to her for Christ's sake, and He will reward you in heaven, for He has promised it."

"Yes, Papa," shouted Neddy, and ran off with great alacrity.

CHAPTER XIII.

"Paul did us an ill turn when he hinder'd women that hae sic a gift o' the gab, frae waggin' their pows in a pu'pit." *My old Nurse.*

THE farmer no sooner entered than he heard the sound of loud voices proceeding from the inner room, and became aware of the presence of Mrs. Benson.

"So, as I was saying," were the first words which he distinguished, "Jacob Hogg heard him with his own ears repeat that they had seven sacraments."

"Who?" asked the farmer, entering the room; "who said so?"

"Who?" repeated Mrs. Benson in a tone of derision; "who else could it be but the Babylonish priest at Overbury? Jacob went to hear him t'other day—on a week-day I mean, when they had a festivity of some kind in their chapel; not on the Sabbath you may be sure, for Jacob knows better nor to commit no sort of abomination on the Lord's day. Well, there were several present performing in beautiful robes of scarlet, purple, and fine linen—one that took the lead like, and the rest boys. Oh, it is an awful sin to introduce the young idea, that should be learning how to shoot, thus early into the mysteries of iniquity! At last the head priest mounts the pulpit, and maintains—yes, gravely maintains—that there are seven sacraments! Blessings on us! the smallest child in our connexion, that knows what is what at all, could have told him that there are but two."

"And to think of the imperance of the individual," said Mrs. Blount, "to maintain that he had seven, when church and state from economic motives keep but two! I'd have no objection to the English church entablature having seven sacraments for dignity's sake; but as for the dissenters and other varmint, I'd confine *them* to two."

Mrs. Benson, with a piercing glance, looked as though she could have annihilated her misguided sister, and was preparing to launch forth a torrent of her usual eloquence, when the farmer interposing, reprimanded his wife for her indiscreet language, and begged the offended lady to go on with what the Catholic priest had said.

"*Priest* do you call him!" said she, "though I did let that name slip myself, yet I allow no man to be a priest who does not offer sacrifice. We are done with priests now-a-days since Caiaphas' time; and thank goodness! any man or woman, illuminated by the Holy Spirit, can mount the boards and exhort, expound, or entreat, in season and out of season."

"Out of season, indeed, like oysters in July!" muttered Dame Blount.

"Well, but tell me," continued the farmer, "what did the clergyman say about seven sacraments? what are their names?"

"That is what I can't tell you exactly. I heard of

two new ones at least—matrimony was one, and extreme unguent was another."

"Extreme unction, you mean," said the farmer.

"Yes, that was it," replied Mrs. Benson. "Though it is of little consequence how it is called, for my mind is all in a state of absorption from a new idea that fills it, to the rooting out of all things sublunary and temporal. And that is, that the seven sacraments are the seven hills upon which the Babylonish woman sits, corresponding to the seven days of the week, the seven deadly sins, and the seven golden candlesticks. Don't say a word about it, brother Blount, nor you, sister. It is of great importance that it should be kept the profoundest secret; for," she added, drawing herself up, and shaking her head mysteriously, "the wise providence of God is about to call me to a new state of life."

"Is the woman mad?" exclaimed both the farmer and his wife at once. "You are not going to marry again—think of your children."

"I am not going to marry again," said Dame Benson solemnly. "No, I am a pitch above that. Nor yet will I mind my children; for though 'the young lions do lack and suffer hunger,' yet the children will doubtless be cared for, since God finds worms and slugs for the young ravens who cry. No, I am going to give up the world; and, like another Debora, or a giant flushed with wine, girding my loins, and with a staff in my hand, I will embrace the ministry in the methodist connexion. This day, by a wonderful providence, Mr. Longab has been called to his native county to bury his father; so that next Sunday, God willing, and by the aid of pectoral lozenges, my throat being free of cold, the vacant pulpit shall be mounted by me; and then, sinners, reprobates, lambs in sheeps' clothing, and other delinquents, shall hear thunder! The idolatrous church of Rome shall be the first object of my attack, because people like better to hear the faults of others than their own; for you see, my good brother and sister, one must, in some things, adopt the wisdom of the serpent in order to get on. Once I shall have reformed the Catholics—particularly by pointing out the seven deadly sins under the veil of the seven sacraments, and the rank idolatry of bell-ringing, and other abuses—I shall go nearer home, and take a fling at the establishment. No offence meant, sister Blount. If God mercifully give me breath to finish my speech, I shall conclude with a eulogistic elegy on the methodist connexion, and the bright, shining, and burning lights which have therein been produced."

"Brands for the burning, I suppose," ejaculated Dame Blount, anxious to give a hit at her offending sister.

The farmer had some difficulty in pacifying the ladies. Several minutes elapsed before this could be effected; and in the end, Mrs. Benson took her leave, by no means altogether satisfied at the cold reception with which the announcement of her new ministerial dignity had met.

The next day the farmer hastened to the rectory, and after the ordinary salutations thus addressed Mr. Feversham: "Will your Reverence have the kindness to explain to me why the Catholic church has seven sacraments?"

"I shall do so with pleasure," replied the rector; "but, in the first place, it would be well to understand clearly the meaning of the term sacrament. Can you explain it?"

"An outward and visible sign of an inward and spiritual grace, as the English catechism has it," replied the farmer.

"Not a bad definition," said the rector, "for a sacrament is an outward sign or action instituted by Christ to give grace."

"Since we are enquiring into the meaning of words, your Reverence, would you be pleased to explain exactly what is grace?"

"Grace," replied Mr. Feversham, "is that divine assistance communicated by the Holy Spirit, without which it is impossible to please God, and which the sacraments are the most powerful means of obtaining."

"Well, now I understand what I am about," said the farmer; "grace means the divine assistance. I have often heard, Sir, that prayer was the way to get grace; is prayer a sacrament, Sir?"

"No, John, it is not; though undoubtedly a great means of grace, particularly to those who frequent the sacraments, or who, if unable, at least desire to do so. To constitute a sacrament, there must be three conditions: firstly, an outward or visible action or sign; secondly, this must have the power of conveying grace to the soul; and, thirdly, the whole must be in virtue of the ordinance of Jesus Christ."

"What are the names of the seven sacraments, Sir?"

"Baptism, confirmation, eucharist, penance, extreme unction, holy orders, and matrimony. We shall now return again to the subject of baptism, which I once discussed with you, and see if the three conditions are fulfilled in it. The washing by water with the form of words prescribed by Christ, is the outward sign; the inward grace is 'the washing of regeneration, and renewing of the Holy Ghost;' (Titus iii. 5.) and the whole is the ordinance of Christ. (Matt. xxviii. 19.) 'Go ye, therefore, and teach all nations, baptizing them in the name of the Father, and of the Son, and of the Holy Ghost.'"

"Supposing the words were changed, your Reverence, as I hear tell they do in some places, saying, 'In the name of the Father, through the Son, and by the Holy Ghost,' would it make any difference?"

"A very great difference, John; because it cannot be reckoned a sacrament at all, unless we keep exactly to the ordinance of Jesus Christ."

"There is another question I should like to ask,"

continued the farmer. "How much water is necessary? John the Baptist baptized in the Jordan; now, must we be dipped in a river?"

"Not necessarily, John," replied the rector, laughing. "Baptism can be administered either by dipping the individual into water, pouring it on him, or sprinkling him with it. It is enough that the action of washing be expressed by there being enough of water applied, to flow."

"I suppose," said the farmer, "your Reverence holds that only Catholic priests can give good baptism."

"You are mistaken there, John," replied the Rector, "for even heretics can give baptism, if they comply with the conditions I have mentioned, and have the intention of doing as the church does."

"But, Sir, I have heard of converts to the Catholic church being baptized over again. What is the meaning of that?"

"They are only baptized conditionally, in case there has been any informality in the former ceremony. This precaution is exceedingly necessary, owing to the careless way in which many Protestant clergymen perform the rite. It frequently happens in parish churches, when several infants are baptized together, that some of them are not touched by a drop of water, while others receive too little to render their baptism valid."

"And is not that a dreadful thing, your Reverence; since Christ has said that unless we are born again of water, we shall not enter into the kingdom of God?"

"It is indeed, John; and now that you see the awful importance of it, I hope you will always inculcate on your friends and neighbours the necessity of getting their children properly baptized."

"That I will, Sir," answered Blount; "and now that it strikes me, I'll tell your Reverence a strange thing. When I was in Ireland with the regiment, I was quartered in the house of a Catholic. The man's wife took ill, and was delivered of a child, which was so weakly that it did not seem like to live many hours. They sent for the priest to baptize it; but, in the meantime, it grew worse and worse, so that the father, thinking his Reverence would not arrive in time to find it alive, baptized the infant himself Was not that great presumption, Sir?"

"Not at all, John; because in cases of necessity, such as that which you mention, where a priest cannot be had in time, any one may baptize. This is the rule of the Catholic church, though a person in orders —such as a deacon—is preferable to a layman, a man to a woman, and a Catholic to a heretic. In any case, persons acquainted with this fact would be guilty of great sin if they permitted a child to die before their eyes unbaptized."

"I'll remember that, Sir," said Blount; "it is a knowledge that may come in useful some day. And now, your Reverence, I'll ask you another question. Suppose a person were most anxious for baptism, and meaning to receive it the very first opportunity—if death carried him off unawares, would he never get to heaven?"

"Catholic theologians have written on the point," said the rector; "that if a person can in no way procure the administration of baptism, but has an earnest desireof it, with a perfect love of God and true sorrow for his sins, it is the baptism of the Holy Ghost, and therefore he could get to heaven and see God. There is another case also I may mention. If a person heartily desiring baptism were put to death for faith in Christ before receiving it, being a martyr, he would be baptized in his own blood."

"Well, Sir, I am much obliged to you for your instructions, and now I think I have a pretty clear idea of what Catholics believe about baptism. They have very good scripture reason for what they say; but there is one thing yet which goes rather against my old fashioned notions. If I recollect right, in the first talk we had together about it, you said it procured the forgiveness of sins; and indeed for that matter I can quote a text to the same effect myself. 'Repent and be baptized, every one of you, in the name of Jesus Christ for the remission of sins.' (Acts. ii. 38.) Still, Sir, I should like to know what is the use of the blood of Christ for washing away sins if baptism does it?"

"Baptism only washes away sin in virtue of the sufferings and death of Jesus Christ, and by His precious blood which it applies to our souls. Once for all, I repeat John, that Catholics hold it impossible to obtain any grace or favour from God whatsoever, except through the merits of the death of Christ, and that baptism as well as the other sacraments are only made use of, because our Saviour ordained them as the means by which we should reap the benefit of His death on the cross."

"I am glad to hear your Reverence say so," replied Blount, "for it struck me more than once that you made too much of the sacraments; but this indeed is keeping them in their proper place. I'll ask another question now, if you won't think me impertinent, for I like to know the outs and ins of things. If a man having reason to fear that he had never been baptized, were to go to a Catholic priest and ask for it, is there any preparation he would need to make, or might he receive it immediately?"

"It would," answered the rector, "be the priest's duty to see in the first place that he was well instructed in the Catholic religion, and firmly believed all its articles; that he was sorry for his sins, resolved to lead a good life henceforward, and was willing to make restitution where he had injured any one."

"But suppose," rejoined Blount, "that the man cheated the priest, and either did not believe Catholic doctrines, or was not truly sorry for his sins, what would be the consequence then?"

"He would incur great guilt by telling a lie to the Holy Ghost," replied Mr. Feversham, "besides awfully increasing henceforward his own responsibility, from the new obligations he took upon himself. At the same time he would not receive the grace of the sacrament for the remission of his sins, which could never be obtained unless by a sincere repentance he renounced them."

CHAPTER XIV.

"That strain again; it had a dying fall;
O, it came o'er my ear like the sweet south,
That breathes upon a bank of violets,
Stealing and giving odour." SHAKSPEARE.

"All minstrels yet that e'er I saw,
Are full of game and glee,
But thou art sad and woe begone,
I marvel whence it be." *The Hermit of Warkworth.*

IT was a beautiful forenoon when Mary and Mrs. Egremond again set out on their charitable mission. On reaching the habitation of the two old women whom they had previously visited, the death-like stillness somewhat astonished them, and on knocking at the dilapidated door no one answered. They tried to open it, but it was fastened. At last one of the neighbours ascended the stair-case, and informed them that the apartment had now been empty more than a week. The bedridden sufferer had died within two or tnree days of their last visit, and her cousin after seeing her buried, set off for Liverpool to join her son.

This woman notwithstanding a little infirmity of temper, had acted with heroic charity, supporting her ungracious relative by the labour of her hands, even while she herself was suffering from illness ; stinting herself of her necessary food, in order to procure her the small luxuries for which she craved; at the same time daily receiving an amount of impertinence and abuse, the tenth part of which would have made a more ordinary character give up the good work in disgust. The rich are daily waxing colder and more selfish, and with a few bright exceptions, daily shutting closer their hearts and their purses against the poor. The seat of charity, of that benevolence which denies itself in order to alleviate the sufferings of others, is not amongst the wealthy and affluent, not amongst the rich and great of England, not amongst the titled and honoured; where then must we seek it? In the simple cottages of the poor. Where the rich man grudges giving away the hundredth part of his weekly income, the poor labourer has often been known to support a distressed comrade, though to do so, he had to share with him his daily earnings. No one hears of this charity, no one praises it; but God knows it, God has written it in the book of life, and at the last day will give him who has bestowed even a cup of cold water on a disciple, a most rich reward. But how much greater, how much more glorious than the rest will be the crown of those, who, like the poor widow that cast two mites into the treasury, have given, not of their abundance but their all!

We have no intention of describing every house visited either by the two friends or by Mary alone. On the contrary, we shall merely relate scenes which have anything to do with Catholicity, the chief subject of our pages; frankly admitting, that what we do mention is rather something uncommon than a sample of the rest.

Mary and Mrs. Egremond were conducted one day by their little ragged friend, the grocer's errand boy, to the abode of a blind harper, whose story as already related by the neighbours had inspired their sympathy. The dwelling consisted of two rooms, one opening off the other, and situated at the top of a high house. The outer apartment was very clean and tidy; in it they found the harper's wife, a pretty good humoured looking woman, thinly clad in a gown which though neat was much patched. She was busily trying to pacify half a dozen small children who were making an aproar, the younger ones crying vociferously for bread, and complaining that they were very hungry.

"Hush, hush, dears! be quiet, or poor papa will get no sleep. You shall have your dinner as soon as it is ready," said the woman.

"But, mamma, you have given us no breakfast," shouted one of the insurgents.

The children became instantly peaceable as the ladies entered, who could not help admiring the order and cleanliness of every thing, notwithstanding the extreme poverty. They found the harper on his bed in a cheerful looking inner room, or more properly large closet; and his wife, after placing chairs for the ladies, which with the bed filled up nearly all the vacant space, respectfully withdrew, closing the door that they might not be disturbed by the noise of the children. The harper did not appear more than five-and-thirty; he was very little, much marked by the small-pox, and was now in the last stage of consumption, which was clearly denoted by his hurried breathing, the wasted appearance of his body and his ghastly paleness, only relieved by a bright red spot on each cheek. At their entrance he tried to sit up, but could not from weakness raise himself off his pillow.

"It is very kind of you, ladies," he said in a tone

and manner so superior, as to surprise his visitors, "it is indeed very kind of you, to visit the sick bed of a poor man like myself; I thought all the world had deserted me, but God is kind to raise up new friends to a wretch so undeserving."

Mrs. Egremond, who was greatly pleased with the man's address, turned the conversation on his illness, and after inquiring how long it had lasted, expressed her hopes of his recovery during the ensuing summer.

"No, madam, no," he replied, "recovery is not for me. My disease is deceitful, and flatters me now and then for a time; but I know too well that within my breast are the seeds of speedy dissolution. It is an awful thought, Madam: for I fear to die! Yes! I tremble to meet my God, for mine has been an ill-spent life! I shall tell you my history, ladies, if you have patience to listen. It is very short, and there is nothing extraordinary or romantic in it; but it may serve as a warning, for you to repeat to others. My father was a respectable farmer in one of the counties bordering on Wales; his character stood high, and his circumstances were affluent for his station. I was the youngest of a numerous family, and lost my sight from small-pox before I remember anything. My father spared nothing in procuring me all the education suitable to the blind, and after I was twelve, was at the expense for several years of paying a young man to read aloud to me some hours every day, on subjects of general literature, suggested by the clergyman of the parish. I had a very retentive memory, and seldom forgot anything I had once heard. My chief ability lay in music, and my father, though much prejudiced against the profession of a fiddler, as he called it, was at last persuaded to allow me to learn the harp, chiefly induced to do so by the solicitations of the neighbouring gentry, who promised when I should make sufficient progress, to do all in their power to bring me forward in London. In a lucky, or perhaps I should rather say an unlucky hour, I was despatched to a musical seminary, where in a short time my masters said that I distanced all competitors. There is my harp, ladies, in that case at the corner of the room; your chair touches it, Madam, it is behind you," said he, turning his face to where Mary sat. "I have been offered a handsome price for it; enough to support us for nine months if I would sell it; but I won't, Ma'am, for I love it better than wife or children, or friends; I love it too well, though it has been my ruin! Besides I am not cruel; for though my children are starving, yet if I sell the harp to get them bread, when I recover I shall have nothing wherewith to support them. No, no! I am not cruel; though my wife thinks so; I must keep the harp!"

"But you said just now," said Mary gravely, "that there is no chance of your recovery!"

"Oh, Ma'am, Ma'am! how can you speak that way! It is true, reason tells me of the probability that I shall die, but I am not prepared! I am afraid! My sins have been dreadful! I cannot die, Madam! There never was anything yet which I could not do when once my strong determination *willed* it. I *willed* to reach eminence in my profession, to attain fashion and affluence; and I succeeded because I had so *willed!* Nothing ever failed with me when my strong will grappled against its difficulties; except indeed at present;—one thing! I would get better! but, alas, I cannot! If I got better now I could earn riches for my children, and procure them a station in society; for I would reform and amend, and no longer waste in debauchery the money that fortune used to pour into my lap, almost without seeking for it. I would be an altered man, ladies; you would see it, if Providence chose to spare me; for I cannot, will not, die at present!——I say, Madam," continued he in a hoarse voice struggling with agitation, and seizing hold of Mary's arm, who chanced to be nearest him, "I say, Madam, I will tell you a secret," and he lowered his voice till it was hardly audible.—"I was once as ill as this before, with the same complaint—consumption; and a skilful physician cured me, giving me to understand, that if I led a regular life my health would continue; but that a return to my old disorderly course would be ruination. Well, as long as I was in danger, I was penitent, just as I am now, vowing to God to lead a good life as soon as I got better, and to lay in a store of wealth both for my own old age and for my children; just exactly as I do at present! Well, God heard me, for I was in a dreadful fright, and there never was such a penitent! So I got better and went about again. I kept my good resolutions for two months, and then I fell into bad company and spoiled all! Now what I say is, that God will not trust me a second time, and that I am doomed to hell!"

The poor fellow here sank back quite exhausted, for in his excitement he had momentarily raised himself from the pillow; a violent fit of coughing now seized him, during which he spat so much blood, that Mary in alarm ran for his wife.

"He will soon be better, Ma'am," she said, as she entered, "all he wants is a little quietness now; something about old times has agitated him I suppose."

The two ladies immediately took their leave, promising to return soon again, and giving some silver to the poor woman, who though she blushed deeply, thanked them with gratitude and respect.

"It strikes me," said Mrs. Egremond thoughtfully, as they were returning towards her house, "it strikes me that I have met this poor fellow before in very different circumstances. You know that since my husband's death twelve years ago I have renounced the gay world; circumstances, however, compelled me to visit London about seven years since, and while there, the relations with whom I resided, could talk of nothing but the extraordinary genius of a blind harp player, Powell by name, who had lately raised himself into notice. This man had adopted quite a different style from that of the foreign artistes who are so much admired now-a-days. Although gifted with wonderful execution and command of the instrument, he seemed to disdain those tricks of the art, (perhaps I should call it that mechanical though brilliant sleight of hand,) by which his rivals sought to surprise us. His forte lay in appealing to the feelings and the passions, and he chiefly effected this by the dexterous use he made of his own national music. At times his bold and martial notes would present the most vivid idea of a battle, and you could fancy that you heard the trumpet clanging and the war-horse neighing; then his mood would change into strains of melting tenderness, and he has often made strong men weep like very girls at his piteous music. In short, I was told that there never had been anything like it in London before. Though not in the habit of going to public places as you may suppose, I did for once break through my rule and attended a concert which he gave. Whether it was the effect of his music, or that I was overpowered by finding myself for the first time since my widowhood in a gay and crowded assembly, I know not; certainly I was most painfully agitated; and in the midst of a pathetic adagio, whilst the company were actually holding their breath lest they should lose a sound, I fainted away and was carried out. I cannot be sure that this is the same man, but it seems to me very likely, particularly as I remember now, having heard that Powell was dreadfully dissipated, and though at that time he was turning the heads of half London, yet more than one person prophesied that from his habit of drinking to excess, he would not retain his popularity long. Yet I don't know how to account for the excessive poverty in which the family are now, and still less for what brings them to Overbury. We must inquire into it, for I really feel curious."

"So do I," said Mary, "and I can't help thinking that you are right in conjecturing that this is Powell; for notwithstanding genius, dissipated habits such as you describe, are quite sufficient to account for the misery in which we now find him."

As Mary had agreed to spend two or three days with Mrs. Egremond, they gladly embraced the opportunity of paying the harper a visit on the following morning.

They found the poor man a great deal better, and his faded countenance lighted up with a gleam of pleasure as he heard their approach.

"I was thinking, ladies," he said, "that if I am as much better next time you honour me with a visit, as I am to-day, I might almost play something for you on the harp! The very idea has raised my spirits; for I should like to give you some pleasure in return for your kindness."

"Oh! William! William!" exclaimed his wife, who had not yet left the room, "one would think you raving mad! The very last time, ladies," continued she, addressing her husband's visitors, "that he touched his harp, he got so excited, that after a while he fell back, and I found the floor all covered with his blood! Since that day he has never left his bed! So for pity's sake, ladies, don't ask him to play! He becomes wild or mad when he touches his instrument; I used often to think that he was out of his senses when he played! As to the sounds that he would bring out of it, they frightened you or they made you cry, just as he pleased! His harp used to be meat and drink to him when he was well, but now to touch it is death. No, no, ladies! don't ask him!"

"You may be sure we shall not," replied Mrs. Egremond; "for however great the treat would be to hear such a musician, it would be both cruel and unpardonable did we permit him to indulge us at the expense of his health."

"Very well, Alice!" said her husband, "since these ladies think it would be wrong I won't speak of it again. It was a little vanity on my part, for I wished to show them what I could do, that they might not think me a novice in my profession."

"I could never suppose you such," replied Mrs. Egremond, "for the remembrance of your music which I heard seven years ago in London, is still fresh upon my ears!"

"Of my music! You heard me in London!" cried the poor man, and covered his face with his hands. "Then you have contrasted my former state with the present! You see now to what wretchedness misconduct has reduced me! Well, well, I am humbled! And you will go home and say, 'Poor Powell! So this is the end of his vanity and of the haughty airs he gave himself! He thought in his pride that he should be the founder of a new school in the musical world; and he did not rate himself too highly either, if he had kept sober. But he was a drunkard, a filthy grovelling drunkard! And, alas! drunkenness was not his worst fault!' Oh! my God, have pity on me!......Now you know me, ladies—you despise me; do you not?"

"So far from despising you," replied Mary, "your candour in accusing yourself makes us respect you; for a fault acknowledged is half amended. We know what the temptations of genius must be. And to find oneself so courted and caressed was enough to render the strongest head somewhat giddy."

"Oh, Madam, you have said the truth!" replied the harper. "I had neither principle nor steadiness of character to keep me right. After my father's friends sent me up to London, my success was most extraordinary; when I gave concerts they were crowded to excess, and the nobility paid large sums for an hour of my playing at their private parties. But it was not that, ladies, it was the clubs, and the gentlemen's dinners, and suppers, and night-frolics, that were my ruin. I could not keep within bounds, and once I overstept the limits of propriety, I ran headlong forwards till I outstript all my competitors in vice. I was very merry, and had an answer for every one; they said I was most amusing when I was tipsy; and that beyond all comparison I then played best; so the gay young men used to divert themselves with urging me to drink, and unfortunately I was only too ready to comply. On first going to London I had married the daughter of an organist, in whose house I lodged. Her influence might have restrained me, for I was really attached to her, had it not been that unfortunately a meddling friend whispered to me a few months after our union, that my wife was pining from disappointment, having all along been attached to another; the threats of her father, who considered me a rising young man, having alone forced her to marry me! This story had some small foundation in truth, though not to the extent which I was led to suppose. As it was, my vanity was hurt, and my temper embittered; and instead of trying henceforward to conciliate my wife's affections, which I might easily have done, for a more kind, amiable, and conscientious creature never existed, I gloried in insulting her, and boasting of my misconduct. Meanwhile my popularity went on increasing, and probably was at its height at the time you mention having seen me in London. After that it fell off a good deal owing to my own bad habits; and latterly the female nobility altogether ceased to patronise me, on account of the disgraceful state of intoxication in which I was sometimes mad enough to appear, when they had engaged me for their private concerts. Still the gentlemen took notice of me, and one way or another I received a good deal of money; but I did not get rich, for I squandered it as fast as I made it. At last, about eighteen months ago, after complaining all the winter of a severe cold, which nevertheless had in no way checked my career of dissipation, I suddenly found myself very ill, and sent for a physician. To my great surprise he pronounced me far gone in consumption, and said there was but small chance of saving my life. Then, as I told you, ladies, came the time of penitence, for I was afraid to die; I sent for a clergyman, and made those around me read pious books aloud; I formed many good resolutions, and learned to pray; I also vowed to God that if He would spare me a little while longer, I would lead a new life, and make amends by my sobriety and good conduct henceforth, for the scandal I had already given. My good wife has since told me that during this period she was very happy, for I showed her then a degree of tenderness to which she had been a stranger for years. Well, I recovered, ladies, as I think I told you, and for some few months was an altered man; but as I grew stronger, my good resolutions became weaker: at last, one unfortunate day, I met some of my old companions, who mentioned having been enquiring for me in vain at my former haunts. I refused at first to accompany them, for I knew my weakness; but in the end after repeated solicitations, they prevailed. That night, or rather next morning, I returned home intoxicated! The whole of the next day I was ill and out of spirits, dissatisfied with myself and inclined to quarrel with all the world. In the evening I sallied forth in hopes of getting rid of my blue devils, and again met my tempters.

"It is needless to go into particulars, ladies; suffice it to say I was soon involved worse than ever in the vortex of dissipation. Still I had one virtue left, I was honest, never having been tempted to the contrary vice.

"During my illness, which was of long continuance, I had got into difficulties, having previously laid by nothing. Instead of trying to pay off my debts, which I might have done in a very short time, I now went on increasing my expenditure, forgetting likewise that I no longer made so much money as formerly, since my delicate health necessarily curtailed my labours. About four months ago, one of my elder brothers, with his wife and child, came to London; he had lately disposed of the lease of his farm very advantageously, and sold his stock preparatory to settling in America. I know not what demon tempted me, but on some pretext I got his money into my hands, as though only for a few days. The same evening when half intoxicated, I laid a wager with a noble lord who shall be nameless, but who has since retired to the continent on account of a swindling transaction on the turf, in which he was implicated. I staked all my brother's money and lost! People say I was not fairly dealt by; be that as it may, I was a ruined man! Had my health continued, I might have soon regained the sum to pay my injured relative; but the shock was so great when I realised what I had done, that I burst a blood-vessel and was rendered useless. I know not how my wife tried to appease him; she did all she could, for she gave him the greatest part of the profits from the sale of our furniture; we then retired to miserable lodgings, and I believe he has now returned home to his friends. Alas! I am much in debt to him still, and he regards me as the cause of his ruined prospects!

"You now know most of my story, ladies, and can imagine the rest; how we sunk lower and lower, and became poorer and poorer. My former friends refused to assist me, saying that they could not in conscience bestow money on a person who had in his day wasted so much, and whom it was impossible to reform.

"For the last six weeks we have been wandering about from place to place, in hopes that the change of air would alleviate my complaint. Whenever I felt a little stronger, I contrived to make an arrangement with some hotel-keeper to let me play in the travellers' room, and by that means managed to support myself and my family. And I have sometimes, when in extremity, even played in the street. Since the last ten days, my illness has so much increased as to incapacitate me for the least exertion. We have been very badly off, my poor children almost starving; and what is worse, there is little hope of better times coming round, for the physician whom my wife called in to see me, declares my condition hopeless, and that I must die. He says I may possibly linger a month or two, but that the resources of art to restore my health are entirely unavailing. I try to look calmly at the prospect, but it is in vain; I cannot face death without a shudder. How happy should I be, could I, like the beasts, lay down my head and die, never again to awaken! How I mourn the soul's immortality! Oh, for annihilation! I curse the hour of my birth! And if I dared, I would curse the God that made me, only to be miserable!"

"This is horrible!" whispered Mary to Mrs. Egremond. "Do come away, or else stop this language."

"You are wrong to despair thus," said Mrs. Egremond to Powell, who was leaning back exhausted. "God is merciful, and ready to hear you, if you return to Him."

"So I was told when I was last ill," replied he. "I believed it, and took advantage of it. I returned to Him, and I thought He had received me. He would have kept His promises doubtless, had I kept mine; but I mocked Him—I vowed, and did not perform! There was a pious minister used to visit me; my wife had persuaded him to come, though at first I had been unwilling to receive him. He told me that if I could feel a saving faith, an assurance of salvation and justification in Christ Jesus, I would have nothing to fear, for that this would be a sign that I was one of the elect. At last I did feel it, and said so to him; he replied, that in that case he was satisfied, for I was evidently a vessel of election. Now, ladies, this is what puzzles me; how was it that I had at that time this perfect assurance of faith, and yet was permitted by God to relapse afterwards into my iniquity, and become worse than before? How was it that God permitted me to fall into despair; so that, whether I was right or wrong in having at one time the full assurance of salvation, it seems now impossible for me to regain it, and I am doomed to perdition! I cannot get out of my head that, by breaking my good resolutions, I told that lie to the Holy Ghost which it is said in Scripture shall never be forgiven, neither in this world nor in the world to come...........My children are starving, my wife a beggar, my brother is ruined—all by my fault! I am my own murderer by my dissipation, and hell is yawning for me, for I have lied unto God!"

"No one should despair," said Mary. "The greatest saints mentioned in the Old Testament at times fell into sin, and yet on their repentance they were not rejected. Remember David. No man's sins could be greater than his, and yet God freely and fully forgave him."

"I know the Bible very well, Miss," said Powell; "and can repeat it by heart, so I have not forgotten a line of that to which you allude. I have often revolved that very story in my mind, in hopes of drawing some comfort from it, but I cannot; the circumstances are not similar. God did not freely and fully forgive David; he punished him well by the loss of his child, and by the dissensions in his family, particularly the rebellion of Absalom: all of which were threatened by the prophet Nathan. Now, if I were going to live a little while longer, God would have time to punish me in this world, so that there would be some chance of me escaping in the next. But, instead of that, he seems about to cut me off in my sins, before I have time to prove my sincerity by leading a new life. And in any case, ladies, I am not like David, for I never was a saint, but, on the contrary, a dreadful sinner; so I have no reason to hope God will show me the same favour as to His heretofore faithful servant."

"You are determined to make out a bad case for yourself," said Mrs. Egremond. "Trust in Christ, and pray earnestly, and you will yet be saved."

"Who is there to give me this assurance, Madam? No prophet like Nathan will come to tell me I am forgiven. Whom, then, can I believe? No one has authority to speak pardon to me. I have lost that assurance which the clergyman said was the pledge of salvation, and what can I do now? Nothing, but wait till hell is ready!"

"What a dreadful state of mind the poor man is in!" whispered Mary. "Would it not be well to propose sending a clergyman to him?"

Mrs. Egremond took the suggestion, and said to Powell, who, compressing his lips, was awaiting her answer with a forced calmness: "My good friend, neither this lady nor myself feel at all competent to answer you, although we know your arguments are wrong. Would you, therefore, let us bring a clergyman with us the next time we return, who, I hope, by his words of comfort may give peace to your soul."

"As you please, ladies," replied the harper. "After all your kindness, it would ill become me to refuse anything you propose; but, I tell you frankly, it is needless."

Mary and Mrs. Egremond now left the invalid to repose; and going into the outer apartment, entered into conversation with Mrs. Powell, whom they found an intelligent and pleasing person, though by no means gifted like her husband. Alluding to his present inquietude of mind, they asked if he had been subject all his life to similar fits of depression.

"On the whole, ladies, I think I may say no," replied Mrs. Powell; "his spirits, though generally high, were sometimes unequal, it is true; yet he never was in a state like the present before, unless, perhaps, very slightly, for a few days during his last illness. It is a dreadful thing to hear him sometimes; he gets into such despair, that he curses his Maker. This distress of mind is increasing his illness, and alas! no doctor can cure it."

Mrs. Egremond now told Mrs. Powell their proposal to bring a clergyman; the poor woman appeared grateful, but shook her head and said it would be of no use. The two friends soon after took their departure, slipping a trifle into the hands of one of the children, and promising next time they came, to bring Mrs. Powell a supply of needlework, which she informed them she was anxious to undertake.

"What clergyman do you propose bringing?" inquired Mary as they walked home.

"There is scarcely any choice in Overbury," replied Mrs. Egremond, "unless you get a dissenting minister, which, although they are often very estimable men, holding views on the subjects of grace and sanctification similar to my own, I would rather not do, since people have already accused me of leaning too much to sectarianism. There are only three Episcopalian clergymen here at present, for the rector of the parish is an absentee; and of these three one is old and very indifferent, the other is in bad health, which leaves Mr. Sharples as the only available person."

"What sort of a man is he?" asked Mary.

"A very clever and intelligent man, strongly evangelical, and who I am glad to see cultivates the acquaintance of all sects and parties, with one very proper exception, that of Catholics, against whom he has a sort of pious horror. This dislike, however, affords us much edification and instruction, as it renders him fond of controversial sermons, which I attend regularly along with numerous other people."

"And do you think he is the most likely person to do good to Powell? I should have preferred a plain practical Christian that could touch his heart by speaking from experience of the infinite love of God."

"Well, Mr. Sharples can doubtless do so if necessary; he is one of those who having been justified through the blood of Christ, and sanctified by the Spirit, have their hearts right with God."

"But how is it that you are able to speak so decidedly?" inquired Mary.

"Because the Spirit in Mr. Sharples bears witness to my spirit, and manifests to me that he has been born again."

"I don't quite understand," replied Mary.

"I dare say not," replied Mrs. Egremond; "until you are yourself converted and renewed by the Spirit, you must be unable to comprehend the things of the Spirit."

"But tell me, dear Mrs. Egremond, how does one become converted? I am anxious to be so. I do sincerely desire to please God and to serve Him; and yet I don't know what I must do in order to be converted in the mode you speak of."

"Do nothing, Mary; you do far too much; and it is that regard for works, which is your bane."

"And yet, Mrs. Egremond, I do not in reality trust to my works. I trust only in the merits of Jesus Christ; but I think that if for His sake I give even a cup of cold water, I shall receive a reward through God's mercy, though in truth I deserve nothing."

"Mary, Mary, don't you know that by faith alone we are saved?"

"Of that I am well aware," replied Mary, "and never thought of contradicting it; at the same time I think that a living faith manifests itself by outward fruits."

Though the discussion between the ladies continued for some time, yet in mercy to our readers, we shall spare them the conclusion, only remarking that after many arguments on both sides, they each retained their own opinion.

CHAPTER XV.

"And by the poor man's dying bed the holy pastor stood,
To fortify the parting soul with that celestial food;
And in the mortal agony, the priest ye might behold,
Commending to his Father's hands, a sheep of His own fold."

NEALE.

"WELL, my friend," said Mr. Sharples to the harper, after a long preliminary conversation. "Mrs. Egremond has been giving me a sad account of you. How is it that you despair of God's mercy? Do you not not know promise, that though your sins be as scarlet, they shall be made as white as snow? And do you forget that Christ came, not to call the just, but sinners to repentance?"

"I know all that, Sir, but it seems to me that I have told that lie to the Holy Ghost, which can never be forgiven, at least not by an ordinary man."

"Of course not," replied Mr. Sharples, "no man can forgive sins; you must go to Christ alone."

"That may be very true, Sir," said Powell, "but as I can neither see nor hear Christ, I cannot tell whether I am forgiven or not by Him, and my uncertainty, not to say my despair, still remains."

"Then you are very foolish," replied Mr. Sharples, "you must just take the gospel as other Christians take it. Since Christ left the world, no one has had authority to say, 'Thy sins are forgiven thee;' and it is ridiculous in you to expect or desire the privilege of a verbal assurance of forgiveness, from which the faithful since our Saviour's days have been debarred."

"I beg your pardon, Sir," said the harper; "had I lived in the Apostles' time, I should at least have had my wish; they had power to forgive sins."

"No one ever had power to forgive sins but God alone," replied Mr. Sharples.

"And yet, Sir," rejoined Powell, "Christ said to the disciples, 'Whose soever sins ye remit, they are remitted unto them, and whose soever sins ye retain, they are retained.' (John xx. 23.) If I had lived in the times of Peter or John, they would soon have set me all to rights, for they had received from Christ power to forgive sin."

"Oh, ho! I see the thing now!" replied Mr. Sharples, "Romish nonsense! Take care of your hand, my good friend, for you are on the brink of a precipice. You are ignorant, I suppose, that this is one of the very arguments made use of by the idolatrous church of Rome in support of the doctrine of auricular confession. We shall, however, not dispute as to what power apostles had, or what they had not; we don't live in their times, so have nothing to do with them."

"Still, Sir, it strikes me sometimes, that there might be some holy men in existence, as much favoured by God as the prophets and apostles were, who had received the power from Him to forgive sins in Christ's name."

"As to that," said Mr. Sharples, "any one may promise you forgiveness of sins in Christ's name, if you truly repent and amend."

"But I would not believe any one," replied Powell. "I want some one having special authority."

At this moment a messenger arrived in a great hurry, to say that Mr. Sharples was particularly wanted at home; so, taking a hurried leave, that gentleman departed.

In the evening he happened to meet Mrs. Egremond and Mary, who eagerly inquired what he thought of their protegé.

"I think him intelligent, but pig-headed, with some wrong notions in his brain which it is next to impossible to drive out. He was quite calm and reasonable when I saw him; not at all so violent in his despair as you had led me to expect."

Two days after this, a neatly-written billet was left at Mr. Sharples's door; it was from Mrs. Powell, begging that gentleman to honour them once more with a visit, as her husband declared himself quite uneasy till he should see him again. The clergyman was not sorry to return, in hopes of finding the man in better disposition for receiving profit: and here we must do him the justice to acknowledge that on no occasion was he ever known to neglect a sick call, except in cases of infectious disorders, when duty to his family kept him at home.

"You are looking better since I last saw you," were his first words to Powell, on entering his humble apartment.

"Yes, Sir, I feel greatly better," replied the latter; for a new idea has struck me, which fills me with unspeakable comfort."

"And what is that?" asked Mr. Sharples.

"We shall do, Sir, as is enjoined in the Common Prayer-book of the church of England, at the part called the Visitation of the Sick. I shall make what is termed there 'a special confession' of my sins; after which you will absolve me, as is there enjoined, saying, 'By his (Christ's) authority committed to me, I absolve thee from all thy sins,' &c., &c. I did not know till yesterday, Sir, when my wife read aloud to me the Visitation of the Sick, that clergymen of the church of England had that power; but now that I see they claim it, it is all I want."

Mr. Sharples stood aghast!

"And is it come to this?" he said. "My poor friend, you are indeed very far gone in delusion! Did I not warn you the other day that these were Romish ideas? This hint should be enough to an Englishman and a Protestant; for, as a general rule, all that is practised and believed by that false church is wrong, and the slightest approach to her doctrines should be avoided like the trail of a serpent."

"I never thought of the church of Rome, Sir, in what I said," replied the harper. "I only meant to adhere closely to the rules of the church of England. If I am wrong in doing so, will you have the kindness to explain why all this is written in the Visitation of the Sick?"

"Because at the time the Prayer-book was compiled, the church of England was not sufficiently purified from Romish error. Since those days, praise be to God, much has fallen into disuse, according as our eyes gradually became opened to the danger of adhering to popish practices."

"And may I ask you, Sir," continued the harper, "are all the clergy of the establishment of the same opinion on these points with yourself?"

"Unfortunately I cannot say they are," replied Mr. Sharples. "In Oxford, particularly of late years, there are many divines who would wish to revive the practices of confession and absolution. Still, I am glad to think they are but a few, and cannot be looked upon as representing the sentiments of the great English body."

"Then, is confession practised, and absolution given universally in the Catholic church, just as mentioned in the prayer-book?"

"It is," said Mr. Sharples. "We look upon it now as one of her most dangerous errors, and one of the great causes of that spiritual domination, which, thanks to her devilish wiles, she has contrived to exercise over the minds of men for so many centuries."

The harper did not reply, being seized almost immediately with one of his frequent fits of coughing, which lasted so long, and was so violent, that in the end his visitor left him, seeing he was far too exhausted to continue the subject.

About an hour after Mr. Sharples's departure, Powell called his wife. "Do me the favour, Alice," he said, "to put on your bonnet and shawl, and go make enquiry where the Catholic priest resides. See him yourself, if possible, and say that a poor dying man desires to speak with him at his earliest convenience. Perhaps he would even come to-night, or to-morrow morning."

Mrs. Powell was surprised; but, being too much accustomed to implicit obedience to question the command of her somewhat arbitrary husband, she silently departed. She had but little difficulty in finding the house where both the Catholic clergymen resided, for they were well known to a large proportion of the manufacturing population. In about an hour she returned, bringing one of them back with her. Over this portion of the story we must now draw a veil; as were we to describe all that ensued between the priest and the harper, it would necessarily involve much repetition of previous subjects: since, before the former could hear Powell's confession, and give him the benefit of absolution, it was necessary to instruct him in Catholic doctrine, after which, if he were firmly convinced of its truth, he must be received into the church by conditional baptism, before anything else could be done. All we shall at present mention is, that shortly afterwards, the harper, with his whole family, changed their lodgings; and that neither Mrs. Egremond, Mary, nor Mr. Sharples were, for a long time, able to trace them.

We shall now return to Farmer Blount, whose business had not lately called him to Overbury, where alone he could meet Mr. Sharples, so that in his conversations with the rector he showed plainly that he was not at present under extraneous influence, and seemed much more anxious to gain information than to find objections.

"I am mighty anxious, your Reverence," commenced he at their next meeting, "to hear some more about the seven sacraments. I have had great satisfaction in thinking over what you said of baptism, because now I have a clear notion of it and I see its use. I have just been saying to myself, that if you will learn me to understand other religious points as clearly, so that I may know what I am about, and not be groping my way in a mist, or like blind Harry, be always a stumbling with a handkerchief tied over my eyes, why then I'll have pleasure in religion, and take to it in my old days. I've had a wish for some time back, to set about trying to please God in earnest, but I've never yet begun, seeing I did not understand right what to do, and the preachers I have heard I could not make much of. They gave pretty enough discourses, but I seldom could tell after I went home what it was all about; or if I did know what they were after, ten to one it was something different from what I had gathered from another clergyman. But I beg your Reverence's pardon for speaking so much; will you please to let us hear something about the next sacrament?"

"Confirmation is the name of the second sacrament," replied the rector, "which can only be given after baptism: the outward and visible sign consists in the imposition of the bishop's hands along with prayer, and anointing the forehead with chrism; while the inward and spiritual grace is the receiving the Holy Spirit. The Catholic church holds confirmation to be a sacrament ordained by Christ, because as such it has come down to us from the days of the apostles; this I could prove from a countless number of quotations from the fathers, but they are not in your line, John."

"That's true, your Reverence; however, I would like to hear scripture for it, if you please. Is there any mention made, for instance, of the apostles giving confirmation?"

"Peter and John," replied the rector, "confirmed the Samaritans after they had been baptized; as you will find in Acts viii. 14—17. After praying for them that they might receive the Spirit, 'Then laid they their hands on them and they received the Holy Ghost.' Also in Acts xix. 6, we find St. Paul confirming the Ephesians, 'And when Paul had laid his hands upon them, the Holy Ghost came on them.' St. Paul again refers to confirmation, when he speaks 'of the doctrine of baptism, and of laying on of hands,' in Heb. vi. 2."

"Thank your Reverence," said Blount; "I find you have good scripture for it, but let me see if I understand it clearly. The outward part is the laying on of hands, the inward part is the receiving of the Holy Ghost, and the whole has been ordained by Christ, or the Apostles would not have given it; but what is the meaning of the chrism you spoke of, Sir?"

"Chrism," said Mr. Feversham, "is consecrated oil, which is used in many ceremonies of the Catholic church according to ancient usage. The church of England also retains the use of oil in one instance at least, the ceremony of the royal coronation."

"There is another question I should like to ask," continued the farmer; "may any body give confirmation the way one may give baptism, if the person wishing it be in danger of death?"

"No," replied the rector, "confirmation is very different from baptism. Without being baptized we cannot enter heaven, but there is nothing of the kind said with regard to confirmation. As in scripture we only find the Apostles administering it, so their successors, the bishops of the Catholic church alone have power to give it. An ordinary Catholic priest has not authority to do so, and those of his congregation who desire it, must wait the visitation of the bishop of the diocese; just in the same way as the Samaritans of whom we were speaking, could not receive the Holy

Ghost from those who converted them, but had to wait the arrival of persons in authority over the other clergy, such as Peter and John."

"Then I suppose," said the farmer, "that Peter and John were what you call bishops."

"Yes," replied the rector, "and the subject of episcopal authority is one I am anxious to explain to you, but which it is better to defer till we touch upon the sacrament of Holy Orders."

"As your Reverence pleases," said Blount; "and now I should like to know, Sir, what is the meaning of the name confirmation?"

"It means that those who receive it are confirmed and strengthened in the true faith. They are henceforth considered soldiers of Christ, being *confirmed* in strength to fight against their spiritual enemies. This sacrament is the great means of deriving fortitude, and of this you may see an example in the history of the Apostles. Before they received the Holy Spirit, they were weak and cowardly men, and with the exception of St. John, too fearful to remain near our Saviour during His crucifixion; but after the feast of Pentecost, when God Himself confirmed them by sending the Holy Ghost in the form of fire, their natural dispositions seem to have been totally changed, and they became bold and fearless in preaching Jesus crucified, not only willingly but joyfully, suffering pains, torments, and even death for His sake."

"But, Sir, if I remember right, the gift of the Holy Ghost was a very different thing in the Apostles' times from what confirmation can possibly be now-a-days. Those who received the Holy Ghost could work miracles, and speak strange languages."

"Very true, John; because, at that time, the Christians were comparatively few in number, living among pagans, whom God purposed to convert; and in order to prove the divine mission of those who first preached the Gospel, miraculous powers were very frequently bestowed from on high, but they were not then, any more than they are now, the unfailing accompaniment of the gift of the Holy Spirit."

"Still, Catholics believe in miracles," said the farmer. "I have heard strange tales of that. Your Reverence need not go for to deny it."

"Certainly not," replied the rector, "and I shall do just as you please; either explain to you now the Catholic belief with regard to miracles, which you will find very far from the ridiculous thing you suppose—or, which I would rather do, defer entering upon it till we have finished our present subject, the seven sacraments."

"Well, Sir, as you please; I like regularity, and see the advantage of taking as good a method in choosing the religious points to be first discussed by my thick head, as in choosing the seed to be first sown in an obstinate clayey soil, drained for the first time. I often compare your Reverence to a good strong subsoil plough, cutting up the deep prejudice roots, and letting the narrow-mindedness run off. And now, Sir, since it is settled that we are to go on with confirmation, will you tell me how often it may be received, and what preparation one must make for it?"

"It can only be received once," replied the rector; "for, like baptism, it imprints a character upon the soul which can never be effaced: for this reason people should take care how they receive it, seeing they can only have the one opportunity of obtaining such a great grace, which is lost if they approach it unworthily."

"What do you mean by unworthily?" asked Blount,

"Receiving the sacrament ignorantly, without being properly instructed as to its nature; or, what is still worse, receiving it in the state of mortal sin, for the Holy Spirit will not enter into a soul thus defiled."

"Well now, your Reverence, tell me how Catholics set about preparing themselves for confirmation. I ask because who knows what I may do myself some day."

"Supposing you already baptized, you must examine your conscience, and make a good confession, praying fervently to God to prepare your soul for receiving His Spirit."

"I suppose a Protestant could not receive confirmation from a Catholic bishop," rejoined Blount, musing. "If they could, I'd go myself to get it. I've a great notion of the sacraments, Sir. As I saw in a little book I was reading lately, they are means appointed by Christ for receiving grace or divine assistance. Now, God knows, we poor mortals need it badly! I would take all the means I could to get help from God to become a good man; and, since there are seven sacraments, if I turn Catholic, I'll receive them all in God's name!"

"Don't be so fast, my good friend," said the rector, rather inclined to smile. "In your state of life it would be impossible for you to receive them all, even were you a Catholic; seeing one is holy orders, the sacrament by which candidates for the priesthood are ordained! Besides, another of them, extreme unction, can only be received on a death-bed!"

"Well, at any rate, your Reverence, I am mighty anxious to hear them all explained, and I take it very kind of your Reverence, that you tell the meaning of things so willingly. If Catholic priests were all like you, Sir, people would not have to find fault with them for keeping their flocks in ignorance!"

"There, John, is one of your prejudices, which, when you know a little more of the Catholic priesthood, you will learn to correct. It is one of the first duties of a priest to communicate the most full and ample instruction on religious points to those under his charge. Nothing is kept back, nothing is concealed: on the contrary, you will find all the information I have already given you, and much more, in a variety of cheap and popular books of devotion which Catholics everywhere have in their hands."

"We'll see! We'll see, Sir," replied Blount. "I believe your word before any man; still, your Reverence, when I'm in Overbury, at any rate, I'll have a talk with some of those Irish folks, that go about the Catholic chapel, and take a look into their books."

"You cannot do better," said the rector; "but I must send you away, for I have an engagement at this hour. Come back as soon as you like, John, and in our next conversation I shall say a little more to you about the Blessed Sacrament."

As the farmer proceeded homewards, he was overtaken on his path by that worthy, Jacob Hogg. "Fine afternoon, Sir!" exclaimed the latter. "Oh! it's wonderful! wonderful! how the Lord pours the dew of His blessings on the far-quarters and back corners of the earth! You have heard the news, Farmer, I suppose?"

"No," replied Blount, "what news? I've heard nothing lately!"

"Not heard," exclaimed Jacob, "how the Lord has stretched out His arm, and girded His loins like a mighty man! Well, I'll tell you! In the South Seas, where coral islands spring up like mushrooms, there is a cluster, whose name I forget, where God has been pleased to convert the Queen of the country to our connection! Ah! it is wonderful how the Spirit has been poured out on her heart, and how the sins of the black woman have become white as snow! She has already set about translating the Scriptures into her native tongue, for she knows English, having often boarded British vessels with a boat-load of vegetables! Then she has given each of the missionaries a fine lot of the richest and finest meadow-land, besides promising as much more to as many ministers as like to come and settle! The mission has likewise got the monopoly of the entire trade of the islands, which when we consider the cocoa-nut oil, cotton, tobacco, &c., is no bad thing! Oh! it is beautiful thus to see the light of the gospel dawning on the heathen! If any thing occurred here to make me leave my shop, it would be no bad spec settling there! However, I need not speak of such a thing, since the shop is flourishing more and more every day! By the way, Farmer, when are you and I going to arrange that little matter I spoke of—the loan at seven per cent. interest?"

"Never, Jacob, never. I'll have nothing to do with trade, or usury either; they are not in my line."

"Say ten per cent. then, Farmer," continued Hogg. "I know of a most profitable investment for these same Islands I spoke of. Not that I am in want of ready money for my shop—far from it; but it is a down-right pity and crying sin to lose such a golden opportunity of turning a penny, as the Ethiopian Queen's conversion; they say she has a perfect rage for gilding and glass buttons; now, as I doubt not she is well supplied already with both articles by the zeal of the missionaries, in order to succeed, we must strike out a new idea! What I propose is, to get a supply of lackered metal and painted glass jewellery, comprising all sorts of female ornaments, with pious words and texts of Scripture engraved upon them; that would be highly scriptural, you know; witness the phylacteries of the pharisees!"

"Whatever you may think, Jacob Hogg, I am not to be taken in with your cock-and-a-bull story of the Ethiope or cannibal queen! All the world has a notion that the credit of your shop is not to be reckoned on: and I never lend where I don't expect to be paid: so good morning, Jacob."

"Old blackguard! I'll be even with you yet!" exclaimed Mr. Hogg, shaking his fist at the farmer as the latter strode down the lane.

CHAPTER XVI.

"And yet there is a very great difference between the ark of the covenant with its relics, and thy most pure body, with its unspeakable virtues; between those sacrifices of the law, which were figures of things to come, and the true sacrifice of thy body, which is the accomplishing of all those ancient sacrifices." (Thomas à Kempis.

"You were to tell me this time, if I remember right," said the Farmer to Mr. Feversham, "about the Sacrament of the Last Supper. But I would rather, Sir, that you explained to me another thing; and that is, what popish priests mean, by offering sacrifice. I was in Overbury rather later than my usual time yesterday, and found a crowd going into the church where Mr. Sharples preaches, to hear what he calls his Wednesday evening lecture against popery. So I went in too, and heard him; he spoke with great spirit, Sir, and what he chiefly attacked was the idolatrous sacrifice of the mass! That is a thing I cannot exactly understand, nor see the reason for."

"I am glad you have mentioned the subject just at this time, John; for it relates to the topic we had intended discussing to-day. I mean, the Blessed Eucharist. It is now some time since I pointed out to you the scripture texts in which Christ so plainly declares 'This is my body,' and 'this is my blood.' If you have been thinking on the subject at all, I should like to hear your opinion now?"

Blount scratched his head, and after some hesitation said, "It is not for me to pronounce an opinion, your Reverence; but my own private notion is, that it is wisest, safest, and most natural to take our Saviour's words to the letter; and the more I think on it, the more I am convinced. Though to own the truth, it is not a thing I would acknowledge yet to every one, for *it is* an extraordinary doctrine, and I should like to consider it a little more. However, Sir, you may take for granted I believe it, since I have no doubt the time will come when I'll defend it sturdily!"

"Well, John, that is quite enough, so I shall proceed with my subject. In the mass, from which our communion service is taken, the bread and wine are consecrated in the words of our Saviour, by the hands of the priest, and thus become the body and blood of Christ!"

"I understand that," replied Blount. "But why do you call it a sacrifice?"

"Before I answer you, let me explain what a sacrifice means," replied Mr. Feversham. "A sacrifice is something real and tangible offered to God by His minister, in which the sovereign power of the Almighty is acknowledged by the destruction or change of the thing offered. We call the mass a sacrifice because the bread and wine are changed at the moment of the consecration, and though still retaining their natural appearance, become the body and blood of our Lord, which are offered to God by the priest, and of which he and the other communicants afterwards partake. The clergy offer this sacrifice in virtue of divine authority; for Christ said, 'This do in remembrance of me.' At the consecration, the priest repeats the very words used by our Lord when He took the elements of bread and wine and consecrated them at the Last Supper."

"Well, Sir, I'll not dispute whether this is right or wrong; though I think it must be right as long as Catholics stick to Christ's words, and have the communion service or mass in remembrance of Him. But I must say, that it is neither prudent nor scriptural to call it a sacrifice, because we all know that sacrifices were to cease when Christ came."

"There I disagree with you," answered the rector; "the bloody sacrifices of the old law, which were mere figures of the sacrifice of Christ, were indeed to cease when the reality took their place; but since the bread and wine in their consecration actually become the body and blood of Christ, there is no reason why *they* should not continue to be offered to God according to our Lord's command, 'This do in remembrance of me.' The sacrifice of the mass was predicted many hundred years before our Saviour's time by the prophet Malachi, ch. i. v. 11. '......My name shall be great among the Gentiles; and in every place incense shall be offered unto my name and a pure offering......' Or, as in the Catholic Bible, which is much more faithful to the original, "In every place is sacrificed and offered to my name a clean oblation.'"*

"That's very curious, your Reverence," interrupted Blount.

"Sacrifice," continued the rector, "is an essential part of religion, and was always considered so by Christian as well as pagan nations, until Protestantism abrogated its use. From the days of Christ the Catholic Church offered sacrifice, as can be proved from the most ancient liturgies, the testimony of the early fathers,† and what (could you read the

* This text, according to the Catholic version, as well as Genesis xiv. and Psalm xc. are urged in proof of the Eucharistic sacrifice by the fathers of the second age, St. Justin, (in Dialog. cum Tryp. hone.) and St. Irenæus, (l. 4. c. 32.) Also by the fathers in the fourth age, St. Chrysostom, (in psal. 92.) and St. Augustine, (l. 18. de Civitate Dei, c. 35, &c.) and many others of equal authority.

† See the liturgies of the Latins, Greeks, Nestorians, Arminians, Ethiopians, Cophtes, Goths, &c. In the third century, St. Cyprian calls the Blessed Eucharist "a true and full sacrifice," (Epist. 63.) and in the fourth century, St. Augustine calls it "a true and sovereign sacrifice," (l. 10. de Civ. Dei. c. 20.) On this subject see also St. Chrysostom, (hom. 35. in Gen.) Epiphanius, (Hær. 55.) St. Jerome, (Epist. 126. ad Evag.) St. Augustine, (Conc. 1. ps. 33. l. 15. de Civ. Dei. c. 22. l. 18. c. 35. &c.) St. Cyril, Alex. (l. 2. Glaphyr.) Theodoret, (Qu. 24. in Gen.)

original Greek) would be to you the most satisfactory evidence of all, the Acts of the Apostles."

"How that, Sir?" asked the farmer.

"Because the Apostles are spoken of there as sacrificing! In the Acts, c. xiii. v. 2, you read in the Protestant Bible, 'as they ministered to the Lord and fasted;' in the Greek original it is, 'As they were *sacrificing* (litourgounton) to the Lord and fasting, the Holy Ghost said, Separate me Barnabas and Paul for the work whereunto I have called them.' This word, which I have rendered in English sacrificing, is, strange to say, the very one used by the Greeks to this day to express the sacrifice of the mass."

"Bless me!" exclaimed the farmer, "it's a bad look out for the Protestants, if their Bibles are so incorrect! I'll have Mr. Sharples told that; of course he'll own it, if it is true!"

"There are other striking passages to which I shall call your attention," continued the rector. "In the 110th psalm, 4th verse, we are told that Christ should be a priest for ever after the order of Melchisedech. When David wrote, as well as now-a-days, the office of a priest was to offer sacrifice. Let us see then what sort of sacrifice Melchisedech offered; for this will guide us as to what our Saviour was to continue doing. 'And Melchisedech, king of Salem, brought forth bread and wine; and (or according to the original Hebrew word, *vaw for*) he was the priest of the most High God.' Gen. xiv. 18. Melchisedech is a most clear type of our Saviour, as you will find demonstrated in Hebrews, and like Christ at His Last Supper, he offered an unbloody sacrifice or oblation to God."

"All that is very striking, your Reverence," replied Blount, "but the argument I'd count most on in this case, is the use of the whole Church since the beginning. If the ancient bishops that followed the Apostles called it a sacrifice, and if every body since their time till the Protestants began did the same, I think it likely they should know best, particularly as they seem to have scripture for it: I would not reckon on the opinion of these old folks, if it went against scripture, but in as far as it goes along with it, it is good in my eyes. You would have no objection, I suppose, Sir, to show the testimony of these fathers to any wise and learned Protestant clergyman that could read Latin and Greek?"

"None whatever, John," replied Mr. Feversham smiling, "you can have a list of them any day you like, to show Mr. Sharples."

"Well, that is all fair," said Blount; "but now I do think of it, I wrote down some texts Mr. Sharples quoted against it, which I'll let you hear if you please. 'Who needeth not daily as those high priests to offer up sacrifice, first for his own sins, and then for the people's; for this he did once when he offered up himself.' Heb. vii. 27."

"You should read the whole of the context, John," replied the rector, "and then you would see the drift of the passage you quote. A comparison is made throughout the chapter, between the Levitical priesthood and Melchisedech, and Christ is pronounced to be of the order of the latter; while, in the verse to which you allude, the difference is most strikingly pointed out between our Saviour and the before-mentioned priesthood; since He needed only once, and this was upon the cross, to offer a bloody sacrifice such as theirs! The words you quoted do not present any reason against our Lord's continuing the functions of a priest for ever after the order of Melchisedech."

"That's very well answered, Sir," said Blount; "but I'll try your Reverence now with more texts. There are a whole lot of them in the tenth chapter of Hebrews. 'By the which will, we are sanctified through the offering of the body of Jesus Christ once for all.'"

"Stop, stop, John!" exclaimed the rector, "the words '*for all*' are not to be found in the original."

"At any rate there is enough, your Reverence, to puzzle a clever Roman in what follows," continued Blount. "It says, that after Christ had offered *one sacrifice* for sins, 'He for ever sat down on the right hand of God;' and then at the 14th verse we are told, 'For by *one* offering He hath perfected for ever them that are sanctified.'"

"As far as I see," replied the rector, "you hold these texts to mean that we are sanctified and perfected by the one offering or sacrifice of our Lord Jesus Christ. Now I believe the very same thing, and so do all Catholics. The sacrifice on the cross is that by which the world was redeemed, and by which we are perfected for ever. All other means of sanctification or salvation which Christ has appointed, derive their efficacy from this one offering. But in the same way as this *one offering* is no ways depreciated by the constant intercession for us, which Christ as man makes to His Father, (see Heb. vii. 25.) neither is it injured nor made of none effect by the representing the same offering to God in the sacrifice of the altar."

"But there is another text yet, Sir, I have got marked, 'Nor yet that he should offer himself often,' &c. Heb. ix. 25."

"The apostle," answered the rector, "speaks here of the bloody sacrifice on the cross, which was only to be offered once; yet the fruit of it is to be constantly applied to Christians by the means appointed by Christ, which are the sacraments and the sacrifice of the altar."

"Well, Sir, I see that Mr. Sharples can't battle scripture with you any way; so we'll leave that if you please, and I'll ask you some questions of my own. If the sacrifice on the cross is so perfect, what is the good of other sacrifices?"

"Catholics offer no other sacrifices," replied the

rector, "it is the same sacrifice. As Christ offered Himself once upon the cross, so He now offers Himself upon the altar; in the former He really died, in the latter He dies mystically, in as far as His death is represented by the consecrating apart bread and wine to denote the shedding of His sacred blood from His body."

"But I don't just see the need of it," continued the farmer, "since we are redeemed by His death on Mount Calvary."

"In the sacrifice of the altar we have a standing memorial of our Saviour's death," replied the rector; "and by it the fruits of it are applied to our soul. I wonder that you find so much difficulty on this subject, because if you believe the words of our Saviour, that the blessed sacrament is His real body and blood, you can scarcely refuse to allow the reality of the sacrifice; otherwise, why have you the victim ready on the altar?"

"Mr. Sharples said, too, Sir," continued the farmer, who knew not what to answer, "that the mass is offered for the remission of sins."

"The sacrifice of the altar," replied the rector, "applies to us the fruits of the sacrifice of the cross: thus obtaining the remission of sin. We have truly upon the altar, as I trust you believe, the same blood of Christ which He shed; and our Saviour has already explained, in Matt. xxvi. 28, for what purpose it is there—'*for the remission of sins.*'"

"I am sure," continued the farmer, "I am much obliged to your Reverence for taking so much pains to explain things to me. As long as I keep in mind the prophecy of Malachi, and the type of Melchisedech, and how the Apostles sacrificed, I think I have no right to make objections; but would you just tell me a short and good answer to give Mr. Sharples, should he ever attack me about it?"

"You may say, John, that if what the Church of England catechism teaches be true, that 'the body and blood of Christ are *verily and indeed* taken and received by the faithful in the Lord's Supper,' surely, when the priest offers them to God on the altar, they must be an acceptable oblation or sacrifice: for how can our Lord be displeasing to His Father, or how can the fruits of His passion be more efficaciously applied than by His own dear self?"

"Supposing he were to say to me," rejoined Blount, "that, as Christ is now at the right hand of God, His body and blood cannot be on the altar—what should I answer?"

"Reply," said the rector, "that the body and blood of Christ are as much there as 'they are verily and indeed taken and received by the faithful in the Lord's Supper.' If he believe his own catechism he cannot well gainsay you."

"I think not," said the farmer, laughing. "And now, Sir, before I go, I should like well if your Reverence would read me the opinion of some of the big-wigs that lived long ago on this point—some of those you call the Fathers, Sir."

"Willingly, John; and it so happens that I have got St. Chrysostom at hand, whose name, I think, you already know from the short collect in the prayer-book. You shall hear what he says. 'We always offer the same Christ. Therefore the sacrifice is the same. Are there many Christs, because He is offered in many places? No, Christ is everywhere the same. He is entire here, and entire there, and has but one body. As, therefore, his body is the same, though offered up in different places, so the sacrifice is the same. He is our High Priest, who offered that victim which cleanses us. We now offer the same which was offered then, and which cannot be consumed.'" (Hom. 17. in Epist. ad Heb.)

"When did St. Chrysostom live, Sir? I would like to hear what those said who just followed the Apostles?"

"He lived during the end of the fourth, and beginning of the fifth century," answered the rector. "I shall now tell you what St. Justin says, who, in his youth, was contemporary with St. John the Evangelist. 'Christ instituted the sacrifice in bread and wine which Christians offer up in every place.' He then quotes the text of Malachi which you know. (Dialog. cum Tryphon.) St. Irenæus also, whose master, St. Polycarp, was the disciple of St. John, writes as follows: 'Christ, in consecrating bread and wine, has instituted the sacrifice of the new law, which the Church received from the Apostles, according to the prophecy of Malachi.'" (L. iv. 32.)*

"Thank you, thank you, Sir," interrupted Blount. "I'll do now; that is enough. I can't stand much learning, Sir, no more than my cows can stand much clover!"

The farmer now left the rectory; and on his road home was so absorbed in meditation, or, rather, in what is vulgarly called a brown study, that he did not observe Mrs. Benson, who, as he came up, stepped to the door of her house, and called to him. The good lady had to repeat her words several times before he became aware of her presence.

"Bless me, farmer!" she exclaimed, "if you had been of our connexion, I'd have said for sure that you were wrapt in prayer just now. As it is, I suppose you was calculating profit and loss, and thinking how to make friends of the mammon of unrighteousness in the true style of a carnal man."

The farmer shrugged his shoulders, and making no answer to this absurdity, was going to pass on, when she continued:

"You may as well step in, and get little Neddy; he has been idling his time here this half-hour, for his mother sent him a message to me. I've been tutoring him to show respect for the ministry; and to

* See first note page 172.

call me 'Your Reverence' henceforth, now that I am an unworthy preacher of the word."

The farmer entered, and biting his lips to repress a smile, advanced to take Neddy by the hand.

"One would think, Blount, that you were possessed by a dumb devil. Sit, down, I beg of you, while we hold sweet converse together for a little space. I wonder now, brother-in-law, that you don't begin to look after the concerns of your salvation. You are not so young as you have been; and you will find some day, to your cost, that your house will come toppling down about your ears, for it is built on sand."

"I know better nor that myself!" cried Neddy. "There's not as much sand as would sand a floor for a mile round. Mother sends me on the donkey for it."

"Be quiet, Neddy," said his father. "And what would you have me do in the case, Mrs. Benson?"

"Why, as to that there are different opinions. My advice is to wrestle unceasingly with the Spirit; but Jacob Hogg, for whose opinion I have a very high reverence, and Mr. Longab to boot, both say, that a sinner should wait for Christ, and be still; that he should not receive communion, nor use private prayer, nor read the Scriptures, nor do temporal good—at least for a while; because if he does these things, he will trust to them: whereas, by faith alone we are saved."*

"By their account then," answered the farmer, briskly, "I have been in the right way these many years: for I have literally done nothing—neither frequented the church, received the sacrament, nor prayed. The only thing I did was to read the Bible."

"And you trusted to that! I knew it!" exclaimed Mrs. Benson. "Come, come, farmer, I speak for your good. Go to the meeting-house next Sunday;

* Wesley mentions many of this Society holding these opinions. See his Journal December 31st, 1739.

I am to hold forth again; and in my sermon I shall make such particular allusion to your case, that, perhaps, your heart will be touched. It will be very easy for me to bring you in, seeing I am going to lecture on the clean and unclean beasts, and it will all be one subject."

"I have other occupations for Sunday than to attend the meeting-house," answered Blount, drily, "so you may spare yourself the trouble of mentioning me, since I won't be there to hear. Come along, Neddy; it is dinner-time, and more, so haste thee home."

"Unfortunate man!" exclaimed Mrs. Benson, as she gazed after them, throwing herself into the theatrical attitude which she now frequently practised, thinking it would be useful in the pulpit—"Unfortunate man! spiritually a leper and full of sores! To remove from thee the scales of prejudice, gladly would I become a potsherd for the Lord's work, didst thou but know, like Job, how to use me! As it is, thou art fit for nothing but to point a moral and adorn a tale!"

CHAPTER XVII.

> "Dootless there are some texts in the Bible that savour o' popery.—It was a pity when the man that made the English Bible was at it, that he didna fling a wheen mair chapters into the Apocrypha, jist to shut the Papist's mouths." *My old Nurse.*

So you have managed to persuade your father to let you invite Mrs. Egremond here," exclaimed

Lady Harriet to her daughter, "without ever consulting me on the matter! But a poor, ill-used, suffering invalid has no right to expect consideration! Because I am nervous, your father and yourself regard me as a cipher. But I won't stand it—no I won't!"

"Dearest mamma," replied Mary, "I asked papa's consent first, because I thought I knew already that you wished it. Did not you say only yesterday that you were dying of ennui, and that you would give worlds for a rational companion? So I consulted with papa, and we both thought it a good plan, if you approved of it, to invite Mrs. Egremond."

"Yes, I see it all," rejoined Lady Harriet. "It is a conspiracy to rob me of my peace! Last summer, when Mrs. Egremond was here, she was all sympathy and consideration for me at first; but you and the rector worked upon her, and in the end she absolutely took the liberty of saying that more air and exercise would benefit my complaint, and that I should begin by rising earlier, and coming down, at least, to the afternoon meals. As if anything would do me good! I know my own complaint best; and more care, with less contradiction from my friends, is my only chance of recovery."

"Dear Mamma, I wish to do every thing to make you happy!"

"It is likely you do, child, when you always take your father's part, and pretend to be of his opinion! When he doled out so unwillingly the money to pay the upholsterer's bill, you looked quite as aghast as himself at the amount! That shows consideration for my feelings, indeed!"

"I was vexed, dear Mamma, because Papa said we were living above our income."

"There now, who puts such stuff in your head? However, don't speak of it; I hate the subject! Talk of something else. And then my soup and my jellies, constantly so abominable; it is only by the greatest victory over my temper and regard for the Sevres china, which I cannot easily get replaced, that I don't throw every thing into the fire after the first mouthful."

"I am afraid, dear Mamma, that it is owing to your want of appetite that every thing appears so bad; when the weather gets a little warmer and you are able to walk in the flower-garden before dinner it will be different."

"So you say!" replied the discontented lady. "If I were living in town I should be quite well, but it is this odious country air which is killing me!"

Mary was going to answer, but her mother interrupted her saying, "Don't reply! Don't say a word! I know the sermon you would preach by heart already! Go make yourself useful if you can do nothing else. See Fanchette washed! I can't trust a maid to do it alone; servants can wash a dog sometimes, but certainly not dry him properly unless closely watched! And come back when you have done and let me know if he bit any body, or screamed much when he felt the water!"

"Yes, Mamma, I shall," answered Mary, who departed accompanied by her mother's very ill-natured pet. She had scarcely got to the top of the staircase, when Lady Harriet called her back to inquire, "Does Mrs. Egremond play piquet or whist?"

"I believe she does both occasionally," answered Mary.

"Then you may invite her," said Lady Harriet, "but the whole task of entertaining her must be yours; for, unless to play cards with me, I cannot stand the presence of a woman like her without nerves, who reads pious books and never employs a doctor!"

"Thank you, Mamma, very much!" cried Mary, running to kiss her.

Mrs. Egremond was invited accordingly, and gladly accepted the invitation, for she was very fond of Mary; and besides enjoyed the conversation of the rector, who, though he had always differed in opinion from her on some points, yet liked her company because her manners were pleasant and agreeable. She had even some influence with Lady Harriet, for they had been old school-fellows. The morning after her arrival, as she, Mary, and the rector were lingering at the breakfast-table, the conversation turned upon the Bible.

"How much do we owe to the reformers," exclaimed Mrs. Egremond, "for their exertions in drawing that blessed book from the obscurity in which it lay buried during the dark ages! For raising it again to its high pre-eminence! For teaching us to know it, to value it, and to appreciate it! For giving us the Bible, the whole Bible, and nothing but the Bible as the rule of our faith!"

"I beg your pardon," answered the rector, "so far from valuing it and appreciating it as it deserves, some of the greatest among them showed contempt for many portions of it; and instead of giving us the whole Bible according to our common version, would, if they had been allowed, have omitted some of the principal books!"

"I understand you," replied Mrs. Egremond, "you allude to Luther's doubts as to the authenticity of the Epistle of James!"

"He not only discredited the Epistle of James, but denied the authenticity of *three* out of the four gospels; saying that the gospel of St. John is the only true one!" said the rector.

"I was not aware of this," continued Mrs. Egremond, "but allowance must be made for Luther's warm enthusiastic character and naturally strong passions, which I dare say in the heat of argument, often betrayed him into expressions of which in his sober moments he would have disapproved."

"If a few warm and inconsiderate expressions occurred in a man's writings, completely at variance both with his general character and the usual tone of his compositions, I grant your argument would be good; but if you had ever studied Luther's life and writings, you would find them all of a piece. You cannot well admire his reverence for the Bible, when he writes such passages as the following. "I will not receive* Moses with his law; for he is the enemy of Christ."† "Moses is the master of all hangmen."‡ "The ten commandments belong not to Christians." "Let the ten commandments be altogether rejected, and all heresy will presently cease; for the ten commandments are, as it were, the fountain from whence all heresies spring."§

"Papa! I never was more surprised in my life!" exclaimed Mary. "And did Luther actually teach such a thing?"

"He did indeed," replied Mr. Feversham, "and he also wrote that the book of Job was, 'as it were the argument of a fable!'‖ But what can you expect better from those reformers who expunged from the Bible the books which they term apocryphal, though they had hitherto been received by the Church! If they were not to blame in doing so, neither could they be to blame for criticising or rejecting parts of that portion of the Scriptures which is handed down to us!"

"You don't surely recognise the Apocrypha as inspired?" said Mrs. Egremond. "In my opinion the Apocrypha may very well be rejected without injury to the rest of the Bible."

"And yet," continued the rector, "the Apocrypha comes to us resting on the same authority as the New Testament! We have no means of knowing that

* In coloc. Mensal. c. de Lege and Evan.

† Ibid. fol. 118. ‡ Serm. de Mose.

§ In convival. collog. cited by Auri Jaber, cap. de Lege.

‖ In Serm. convival. Tit. de patriarch and prophet; and Tit. de Libris Vet. et Nov. Test.

either is inspired, and the word of God, unless by the decision of the Church and the voice of antiquity."

"But," rejoined Mrs. Egremond, "I have heard that some of the ancient fathers did not receive the Apocrypha."

"That was before the Church had decided upon it; after which there was no appeal. If you are unwilling to receive any books that were ever doubted, in like manner you should reject the last chapter of St. Mark's gospel.* Also parts of the 22nd of St. Luke,† and the 8th of St. John;‡ the Epistle to the Hebrews,§ and the Epistles of St. James, St. Jude, the second of St. Peter, the second and third of St. John and the book of Revelations;|| for some ancient writers disputed all these!"

"But, if I mistake not," rejoined Mrs. Egremond, "one of the Articles fixed those books alone as canonical, of whose authority there never was any doubt in the Church."

"Most true," replied the rector, "the 6th of the Thirty-nine Articles does so: but in this the Church of England is inconsistent. If she reject those books not publicly declared canonical, though never generally doubted by the primitive Church, she ought along with the Apocrypha to deny the authenticity of a great many more. If, however, she will abide by the decision of the Church so early as in the fourth century, the third council of Carthage, at which St. Augustin was present, reckons the same books as canonical which the Roman Catholic Church now receives!"

"I must say," rejoined Mrs. Egremond, "that this appears to me an idle and unprofitable specula-

* See St. Hierom, epist. ad Hed. q. 3.

† St. Hila, l. 10. de Trin. and Hierom. l. 2. contr. Pelagian.

‡ Euseb. H. l. 3. c. 39.

§ Id. l. 3. c. 3.

|| Et. c. 25, 28. Hierom divinis Illust. in P. Jac. Jud. Pet. and Joan. and Ep. ad Dardon.

tion; what need have we to go by the decisions of the ancient church when the Scriptures bear evidence for themselves, to their being the word of God! Who that reads them can doubt their being inspired?"

"And yet," said the rector, "it would be only natural to doubt the inspiration of some parts of the Old Testament, where blood-thirstiness, cruelty, and other things which we now regard as crimes, are tolerated; nay, commanded to certain individuals! We might also doubt the inspiration of those portions of the New Testament which seem at first sight to contradict each other! Believe me, dear Mrs. Egremond, it is not every one to whom it is given to see clearly from internal evidence, that all the Bible is God's word: if the Bible was written for all, the learned and the unlearned, the spiritual and the gross, the wise and the simple, then it should come to them recommended by more authority than the witness it bears itself."

"And pray," said Mrs. Egremond, sarcastically, "on whose authority would you receive the Scriptures?"

"On the authority of the Catholic Church," answered the rector, "which in the first place pronounced what books were inspired, and rejected such as were not; and in the second place faithfully transmitted to us the important trust."

"I am not fond of the term Catholic Church," said Mrs. Egremond, "it always reminds me of the Romanists."

"In the fourth century, when the Catholic Church decided in council which books were canonical, you surely allow she was the true Church," said Mr. Feversham, without noticing the interruption.

"I suppose so," said Mrs. Egremond thoughtfully. "There certainly were no better churches at the time."

"And you will surely grant the Catholic Church,

(or Roman as you call it,) the merit of faithfully transmitting to us what she then received. Luther himself says, 'We are obliged to yield many things to the Papists—that with them is the word of God, which we received from them; otherwise we should have known nothing at all about it.'" (Comment. on John 16.)

"There I disagree with him," said the lady, "for to me the internal evidence of scripture is enough. However, we have wandered from the point where we started; you said that the first reformers did not show much respect for scripture; what other proofs have you for this bold assertion?"

"Many proofs could be given," answered the rector, "but a few will perhaps content you. Calvin affirms, that 'Peter added to the schism of the Church, to the endangering of christian liberty and the overthrow of the grace of Christ.' He also reprehends Peter and Barnabas, &c.* Castalio commanded the Song of Solomon to be taken out of the canon.† Zuinglius and other reformers affirm that all things in St. Paul's epistles are not sacred, and that in sundry things he erred."‡

"I am sorry to hear all this, papa," said Mary. "When such able and learned men as the first reformers attack the Scriptures, it makes one tremble! Poor human reason, how fallible it is!"

"And for my part," said Mrs. Egremond, "I am only sorry that the rector should attach such importance to a few isolated examples!"

"They are far from isolated, Madam," replied the rector, "I could tire your patience with their catalogue;§ and it is only in mercy to my listeners that I stop."

* Calvin in Galat. c. 2. v. 14. p. 511.

† Vid. Beza in vita Calvini.

‡ Tom. 2, Eleuch. f. 10. Magdeburg. Cent. 1. L. 2. c. 10. Col. 580.

§ See a work reprinted by R. Coyne, Dublin, in 1807, entitled "Errata to the Protestant Bible, or the truth of their English translations examined." Pages 3. 14. 17. 18. 35, 36, &c.

"I grieve that you have occasion to say so," said Mrs. Egremond, "but these are old stories which it is most unprofitable to rake up. Rather let us employ our time in studying and meditating upon the sacred volume, which, in spite of all you allege, still, by God's providence, remains to us!"

"I quite agree with you, dear Madam," said the rector, "in regarding it as the best thing you can do. If searched in an humble and unprejudiced spirit, much truth, now little regarded by the Protestant body, would be brought to light. No one can reverence the divine volume more highly than I, as it stands in the original; but you must forgive me for blaming our English translation for many wilful corruptions! They who transcribed it, were so anxious to avoid what they termed the errors of popery, that they sometimes perverted the text to suit their purpose."

"You are in a strange carping humour this morning, Mr. Feversham—pardon me for saying so; I cannot make out your motive," said Mrs. Egremond, "but as we are all, I trust, inquirers after truth, let us hear a few of these corruptions."

"I shall mention them with pleasure, since you wish it," said the rector. "Afraid of encouraging belief in the Catholic doctrine of purgatory, the translators of the Bible have wilfully mis-rendered the word *inferos*, which means a place for departed spirits, into which, as you find in the apostles' creed, our Saviour descended. This abode used to be termed hell in our language, though very different from the hell of the damned; but as it is now convenient to deny the existence of such a place altogether, *inferos* is generally rendered in the Protestant Bible by the term '*grave.*' They have, however, rightly translated the word in one instance at least, where David says, 'Because thou wilt not leave my soul in hell!' (Acts ii. 27.) Had they followed their usual plan, they should have called it 'in the grave!' "

"But does it matter much, Papa?" asked Mary.

"It does, indeed, make a great difference; to quote only one example out of many—by their mistranslation they hide from Protestant readers the fact, that the patriarch Jacob three several times bears witness to the existence of this third place for souls!*

"Let us hear some more of these mistranslations if you please," said Mrs. Egremond, "for it appears to me that the sooner we get to the end of the subject the better."

"The translators of the Bible, unlike the Oxford party now-a-days," said Mr. Feversham, "had no high idea of the dignity of sacred orders, or the advantages of ordination, so they in general, if not always, translate the word 'presbyteros,' which means priests, by the term '*elders!*' For example, in the original of St. James v. 14. the sick are not enjoined to send for the elders of the church to pray over them and anoint them, but they are to send for the *priests!* And in Acts 14 and 23, the original text does not say like our version, that the Apostles ordained elders, but that they ordained *priests!* In another place they translate the word bishops (episcopos) *overseers!* Acts xx. 28. They also frequently pervert the text, when a passage occurs that appears to favour the reverence paid in the Catholic Church to images. They sometimes do the same with what relates to the celibacy of the clergy, and to what is termed in the ancient Church the sacrifice of the mass! Where St. Peter says, 'Give diligence to make your calling and election sure,' they miss out what follows in the original, '*by good works!*' (2 Pet. i. 10.) However, we must not blame our translators too much, seeing that they were much more con-

* See Genesis xxxvii. 35. Gen. xlii. 38. and Gen. xliv. 29. 31. where the word *inferos* is translated grave instead of hell.

scientious than their predecessors. They did not, like Calvin, reject the words, 'many are called but few are chosen.' Neither did they, like Luther, omit in their translation, 'But if ye do not forgive, neither will your Father which is in heaven forgive your trespasses. (Mark xi. 26.) Nor did they, like him, expunge from their text the glorious verse where St. John in his first epistle bears witness to the Trinity and unity of God. 'For there are three that bear record in heaven, the Father, the Word, and the Holy Ghost, and these three are one!"

"So Luther did all this!" exclaimed Mary.

"He did," replied the rector, "and a great deal more. And now, if Mrs. Egremond and you have any curiosity to pursue the subject, I shall be most happy to lend you a work which gives authority for most of what I have stated, besides furnishing a great deal of curious information on the same topic: it is called, 'Errata to the Protestant Bible, or the Truths of their English Translations examined.'"

"And does not it show most strikingly," said Mrs. Egremond, "the candour which distinguishes Protestantism, that such a work should ever have been published?"

"I beg your pardon," said Mr. Feversham, drily; "the book in question is a Catholic publication; but the authorities given are perfectly unexceptionable, and generally such as few Protestants would object to."

"What comes from an impure source is seldom pure," replied Mrs. Egremond. "And you must excuse me for saying that, since it is published by Catholics, I have no desire to see the book."

"I should like to read it, papa," said Mary, timidly; but Mrs. Egremond, rising to leave the room, heard no more.

We shall now change the scene to a neat little cottage parlour, where Mrs. Benson and Jacob

Hogg are sitting together, engaged in earnest conversation.

"It is not a wide enough field, Jacob. No, it is not, this here village," said Mrs. Benson to Mr. Hogg, who had called to enjoy an hour of what he termed *spirituous* conversation with her, on the things appertaining to salvation. "Yes, Jacob, my heart pants for a grander and more glorious sphere! My powers are great, and my lungs are good; why, then, should not my voice be heard even unto the Indies, and other places in the bowels of the earth? Could I but get my little property sold!"

"What have you to sell, servant of the Lord?" enquired Mr. Hogg, with a strong snivel.

"I have the cottage in which I live, valued at a hundred pounds; the small house Adams has taken, worth a hundred and fifty more; besides the field at the end of the village, which brings as much profit as all the rest put together," said Mrs. Benson.

"A very pretty property," replied Jacob; "and a very snug thing to turn to account by investing it, so as to lay up treasure in heaven. I've no manner of doubt that you will like the thing, too, in a pleasurable point of view most amazingly, Ma'am. The queen, by all accounts, is a woman quite after your own heart—an energetic, strong-minded, intellectual piece of goods. I know she is energetic, for she seized all the property of the heathen idols, besides that of the false priests, for her own use; then, she is strong-minded, for she saw the advantage to herself in giving our missioners pretty little estates which she confiscated express from her own people for them. And better than all, like yourself she has intellects, being a living specimen of the feast of reason and the flow of soul! You and she might run in a curricle together, Ma'am. Besides, your assistance will be invaluable in the arduous task she has undertaken of translating the Book of Life. Though she will, doubtless, be a crack hand at translating the text, yet I should think she would be the better of getting you to write the commentaries, and add a practical exposition of the prophecies."

"Glorious task!" exclaimed Mrs. Benson. "But, after all, I could not leave my children."

"No occasion, Ma'am," said Hogg; "by all means take them with you. The society of the intellectual crowned heads before mentioned, can scarcely fail to be beneficial to them. Besides, who knows what influence you may gain at court by your virtues and resignation, not to speak of the girls' white faces being sure to be at a premium out there; so, if you play your cards well, you may get them royal matches!"

"To do good to the soul of her Royal Highness, the black queen, would be all I should desire," answered Mrs. Benson, trying to repress a smile of satisfaction at the idea of connexion with royalty. "What, then, Jacob Hogg, would you advise me to do? Lo! I am willing!"

"Sell your property, if you can get a purchaser, which I do not doubt. Put the money received into my hands, with the exception of a small sum for present subsistence. Be joyful, and trust in the Lord, till I secure you a passage to the Pickmanbone Islands, where I shall invest your money to the best advantage, so that you may have a snug farm, with a comfortable parlour and maid of all work, waiting you on your arrival. I shall get a friend in London to write to the queen before you sail, who, I have no doubt, will see a supply of tea, sugar, soap, &c., laid in for you, and the beds well aired before your arrival."

"What a dear, comfortable angel her Royal Highness must be! I long to press her to my agitated bosom!" said Mrs. Benson. "After all, it is a queer thing! To think of me, like another Paul, traversing the salt sea-foam to preach unto the heathen; or, like Solomon, going to return the visit of the queen of Sheba! And, then, my two girls! Thank God, I shall advance their prospects while I labour in His vineyard! But the voyage, Jacob! How many months' sail did you say it was?"

"I told you," said Jacob, "that I did not know exactly. A good lot of months, I guess! But what matter! Will not the time appear short, occupied as you will doubtless be in prayer and praise?"

"Very true, Jacob; but the sickness! the sickness terrifies me! One cannot be singing hosannah with one's head over the side of the vessel!"

"You are right, Ma'am," replied Jacob, "but as wherever I can, I try to find a parallel in scripture, for the edification of those with whom I hold converse, we shall see what the Bible says to that. Now in the sacred volume I find that after three days and three nights, spent doubtless in great upheaving and agitation of the stomach, the whale at last vomited forth Jonas out of her mouth!"

"But that does not apply to me!" interrupted Mrs. Benson.

"You are wrong," said Jacob, "it applies mightily to your case. The whale, like yourself, was a chosen vessel of the Lord. It ploughed the mighty deep as you yourself will do. It was grievously sick for three days, at least so is my pious belief; you will probably be so also. At the end of that time it got quit of what clogged its stomach, and, God willing, you will do the same; at least my prayers and those of the brethren will not be wanting to that effect! Now as I follow scripture in every thing, and as there is no more mention made of any further attack of sickness befalling the whale, let us in humble faith hope the same for you, leaving the rest to Providence!"

"Many thanks, Jacob," said Mrs. Benson, holding out her hand to him, while the tears filled her eyes, "many thanks for your beautiful exposition of scripture! Dear me! a talk with you would encourage one to face a lion in his den, not to speak of the monsters in the mighty deep! When you write next to London, Jacob, try to get some of the brethren there to convey a message from me to her Royal Highness. Give her my most warm love and dutiful affection, and humbly beg her, when she can spare a moment from her important task of translating the Scriptures, to say a prayer, and drop a tear, for a venturesome widow-woman, about to skim across the waters to her, like Noah's dove, bringing the olive branch of gospel tidings in her mouth!"

"I will, I will," said Jacob Hogg, evidently much affected, for he was wiping his eyes with his handkerchief. "Say nought about it to any one till you see me again, and God bless you for the present." So saying, and wringing her hand, the pious haberdasher hurried away.

CHAPTER XVIII.

"For what other nation is there so honoured as the Christian people? Or what creature under heaven so beloved as a devout soul, into whom God cometh that He may feed her with His glorious flesh? O unspeakable grace, O wonderful condescension."

THOMAS à KEMPIS.

"MR. SHARPLES is uncommonly anxious to find out how I get information, Sir, and for what reason I come to him, when I have clergymen so much nearer home," said Blount, one day to the rector. "Somebody has been telling him too, that I often go to see you; and altogether he is in a fine puzzle! I didn't much like his arguments, and I thought at one time of giving up going to him, but on the whole it is best to continue to hear both sides of the question. He said to me the day before yesterday, 'What makes you come to me at all? You are getting more papistical every day, and farther removed from Gospel truth! One clergyman should be enough to solve your doubts, and why don't you stick to Mr. Feversham!"

"What did you then reply?" asked the rector.

"I said, Sir, that there was such a difference between your way of speaking and his, that it was worth my while to hear both. So then he began asking me who the Catholic is that tries to pervert me; but he could not worm that out of me with all his speaking. After that we had some talk about transubstantiation, and I defended it through thick and thin. At the last he called me an obstinate old fool; for you must know, Sir, I had forgotten most of your good arguments, and I stuck to one, the best of them all, which I answered over and over again to every objection Mr. Sharples made, till I dare say I provoked him. I said, your Reverence, Either you, Mr. Sharples, are wrong, or Jesus Christ told an untruth! He said plainly of the sacrament, 'this is my body,' and 'this is my blood,' and I tell you once for all, I'll believe Him to the last!"

"An excellent answer, John; and I am very glad to find that your conviction is now so strong of the real presence of Jesus Christ in the blessed sacrament!"

"I believe that it His is real body and blood," said the farmer, "but I am not so sure that He is present in a living manner, precisely as He was on earth."

"And yet how can you doubt it, John; as our Saviour was only to die once, so, since His glorious resurrection, His body, soul, and divinity have never been separated. Where His body is, there He himself must truly be; so in receiving the blessed Sacrament our Saviour actually enters into the heart of the communicant, ready, if worthily received, to bestow upon him all graces and blessings; to heal his spiritual diseases, to cleanse him of his imperfections, to strengthen him to overcome his weaknesses, to inspire him with new vigour in pressing forward to the goal set before him, and more than all, by thus uniting Himself closely and intimately with him, to give him a foretaste of eternal life!"

"And this is the privilege of Catholics in receiving the communion!" said the farmer very thoughtfully. "When I am convinced of the truth of the other Catholic doctrines, the sooner I receive the body and the blood of my Lord, the happier I shall be; though, indeed, I am unworthy of it! If all the points in the Catholic religion are as true as this, I'll be a happy man. This is a doctrine worth dying for, Sir! I can't think how any Catholic in his senses can turn Protestant, even though his Church should be full of corruption, to lose such a glorious privilege! Protestants have nothing to compare to it!"

"That is most true, John," said the rector. "I have often thought lately, how poor and meagre Protestantism must appear to a reflective mind. If Protestants are right, then are Christians much worse off than those under the Jewish dispensation; for, as I have mentioned before, during the old law God manifested Himself in an extraordinary manner, in the Holy of Holies; and by means of the Urim and Thummim we even find Him personally consulted. Protestants have no privileges so great as these! It would even appear from their belief that God had withdrawn, instead of approaching Himself nearer to the faithful since the coming of Christ. But how different with Catholics! They have their Lord and their God always among them under the form of the Blessed Sacrament! The poor, the sick, the lonely, the miserable, have only to enter the Church of God, there to find all they can desire! The bereaved have here a father, friend, and brother, to supply the place of those loved ones they have lost; the poverty-stricken who are despised and trampled on by the world, will here be graciously received by the King of kings, who will deign to listen to their prayers, and bestow riches upon them not of this world; and above all, the guilty wretch, the weight of whose crimes crushes him to the earth—who dares not even look up lest he meet the glance of an offended God—even he will be welcomed, and his sins, though they be like scarlet, made as white as snow, if he but come to the long suffering and lowly Jesus, who tarries for him in the sacrament of the altar, and in his presence, humbly weeping for his sins, ask, 'Lord, what must I do to be saved?' "

"God grant that I may be heard when I also make that prayer," said the good farmer; "henceforth I shall repeat as often as I can remember, the words, 'Lord, what must I do to be saved!'—until it please God to set all my doubts and difficulties at rest by conducting me into the true Church, when I trust I shall no more be in a mist, neither knowing what to do, nor what to think!"

"Do so, John, and without doubt God will listen to you; an humble and fervent, even though short ejaculation, is sure to wing its way to the throne on high. And now that I think of it, is there any particular subject that you would wish discussed to-day?"

"Indeed, there is your Reverence," said the farmer, "and one that has given me some uneasiness, and staggered me a deal lately. Why do Catholics, Sir, refuse the wine in giving communion? Why do they half the sacrament? It seems indeed, very strange, that believing what they do about it, they should give the body and not the blood of our Saviour to communicants."

"Such a thing would be impossible," answered the rector. "When our Lord ascended into heaven, He was no more to die; in other words, His body and blood, soul and divinity, were never again to be separated from each other. Therefore, he who receives any portion of the blessed sacrament, receives our Lord Himself whole and entire. It is vain to say that because the Catholic communicant does not partake of the sacramental cup, he does not receive the blood of his Saviour; for when the body of Jesus is given to him, the blood is along with it and connected inseparably with it, since it is not a dead, but a living body."

"You give a reasonable explanation, Sir," said Blount; "and yet reasoning does not satisfy me. I would rather you could reconcile it with Scripture, which I fear goes mightily against it. Did not Christ say when He consecrated the bread, 'this is my body,' and of the wine, 'this is my blood?' Surely, this looks as if He meant to keep them distinct."

"To answer you, John, I must go back to the same argument as before. Did Christ mean a dead or a living body and blood? If the latter, they cannot be separated from each other, otherwise you would make them out to be dead and inanimate. Besides, if you believe in the real presence of our Saviour, your difficulty would lead you into an absurdity."

"What your Reverence says is all very reasonable, but does it not interfere with the command of Christ? for did He not at the last supper, take the cup, and say to His apostles, 'drink ye *all* of this?' Matthew relates it if I mistake not."

"You are right, John, and what is more, St. Mark likewise writes, that they all drank of it."

"Well now, your Reverence, did not I say so?"

"Nevertheless, John, it is no argument in your favour. Observe, who were they to whom Christ gave this injunction? Those who were present at the last supper, the twelve Apostles! Now many things were enjoined to them which were not commanded to the laity. They were commissioned to preach and baptize, (St. Mat. xxxviii. 19, 20.) to absolve sinners, (St. John xx. 22.) and upon this very occasion to do as Jesus Christ had been doing, that is, to consecrate and to administer the blessed sacrament in commemoration of Him. Therefore ordinary persons are no more commanded to partake of the cup because the apostles were so enjoined, than they are commanded to perform priestly functions, such as consecrating the divine sacrament, &c."

"But," replied Blount, "I do not see why Christ ordered the apostles to drink of the cup, since if doing the same is not necessary for ordinary people, it should not be necessary either, for apostles and priests."

"You remember," said Mr. Feversham, "how I explained to you, that the blessed eucharist is a sacrifice as well as a sacrament. The apostles and their successors, the bishops and priests of the one only true church, were appointed by Christ to offer this sacrifice, it being done in commemoration of His death; and in order to represent more clearly the separation of His blood from His sacred body, the elements are consecrated separately, and for the same reason the priest who offers the sacrifice partakes of them separately."

"But suppose," rejoined the farmer, "that a stranger priest should come into the church, and want to receive communion like any other person, would the priest who was performing the service give him to drink from the cup?"

"No, John, he would not; because it is only necessary for the priest who offers the sacrifice to partake of both kinds."

"Well, I am glad at all events," said Blount, "that a priest not officiating would be just treated like the rest. That's fair. But I have an objection now to make. Does not Christ say, 'Except ye eat the flesh of the Son of Man, and drink His blood, ye have no life in you?' And does not this mean that we all should do both?"

"Certainly, John; but in receiving the blessed sacrament in either species you most assuredly partake both of His body and blood, because, in either case, it is your living Saviour who enters into your heart, and there can be no dividing Him. On this subject, St. Paul's words are remarkable: 'Therefore, whosoever shall eat this bread, *or* drink this cup of the Lord unworthily, shall be guilty of the body and blood of the Lord.'" (1 Cor. ii. 27.)

"Oh, your Reverenc ." exclaimed the farmer. "Well, if I ben't surprised! I've caught you napping at last. It is not 'eat this bread, *or* drink this cup,' in my Bible, but it is '*and* drink this cup,' which makes all the difference. The way your Reverence quotes it, one would think that St. Paul meant, though you only received part of the sacrament, you might be guilty both of the body and blood of our Lord. Now, Paul speaks of a person receiving both the bread and the wine."

"You are both right and wrong, John," replied the rector. "The Protestant Bible is certainly as you quote, thanks to the translators, who wilfully corrupted and altered the text, substituting *and* instead of *or* to favour their own preconceived opinions. However, do not take my word alone for it, but ask any one conversant with the original, whether or not I am right."

"No occasion, Sir; I would take your word before any man's," said Blount, who, after pausing for a moment, continued, "Your Reverence has proved to me that communion in both kinds is not necessary; but that is not to say that it is forbidden, so why does the Catholic Church make such a work about it?"

"One of the reasons which induce the Catholic Church at present to give communion only in one kind to the laity, is the great danger there would be of spilling the blood of Christ were all to receive of the cup. This discipline has also been confirmed by general council, in opposition to some heretics who contemned the practice of the whole Church."

"What does your Reverence mean by saying *at present?* Did the Catholic Church ever allow communion in both kinds?"

"Yes; and she holds that she may do so again whenever she pleases, having absolute authority in all matters of discipline."

"So, indeed!" cried Blount; "then I've got a new light to-day. I thought the Catholic Church never changed. But I find I have been wrong."

"The Catholic Church is immutable and unchangeable in all matters of faith or points of belief, but she has a right to do as she pleases with regard to all external customs or forms of acting. For example, she has always held that, receiving the blessed sacrament in either species we receive the entire body and blood of Christ; but she has, at different periods, permitted the faithful to receive it under both forms, and sometimes only under one."

"Is it not odd, Sir, that all Protestants disapprove of it? There must be some strong objection to it, when so many good and learned men of different persuasions have left their testimony against it."

"All Protestants do not do so; on the contrary, some distinguished English dignitaries have sided with the Catholic Church in this matter. Even the French Protestants, who generally give their communion in both kinds, decreed, in a synod held at Poitiers in 1560, 'that the bread of our Lord's Supper ought to be given to those who cannot drink wine.' Luther himself declared, 'that if a council should either appoint or permit communion in both kinds, he would, in spite of that council, receive it in one kind, or not at all.'"*

"Did the first Christians ever receive it under one kind only?" asked Blount.

* Hist. de Variar, C. 2. § 10.

"Yes," replied Mr. Feversham, "in the communion of infants, who were allowed to drink of the cup without receiving the second consecrated element, or host, as it is termed by Catholics.* Also in domestic communions, for, during the persecutions, the faithful were permitted to carry home the consecrated host, which they might receive in private when they durst not meet in public to celebrate mass.† And, besides, one kind was used in administering to the sick."‡

"Well, if all that be true, your Reverence, about the first Christians, it shows me at least that it is not a new-fangled notion of the Romish Church. Still, Sir, I cannot get out of my head the words of Christ: 'Except ye eat the flesh of the Son of Man, and drink His blood, ye have no life in you.'" (John vi. 53.)

"And certainly," replied the rector, "in receiving the blessed sacrament under one species, Catholics do both; for, as I said before, the blood cannot be separated from the living body. As if to recognize this great truth, our Saviour, no less than four times in the very chapter you have quoted, promises eternal life to eating alone. 'This is the bread which cometh down from heaven, that a man may eat thereof and not die.' (50th verse.) Again, in the next verse, 'If any man eat of this bread, he shall live for ever.' In the 57th verse, 'So he that eateth me, even he shall live by me.' And in the 58th verse, 'He that eateth of this bread shall live for ever.'"

"I see I must give up the argument for the present at least, Sir," said Blount. "All you say is very good, and ten to one you are right. Still, I can't believe everything you prove to me at a minute's warning; I require time, your Reverence, to get accustomed to the notion, particularly if it goes against my grain in the first place. I am like my

* Cypr. de Lapsis, 2.

† Tert. l. 2. ad Ilorem c. 5. St. Cypr. L. de Lapsis.

‡ St. Denys of Alex. apud Euseb. l. 6. Hist. c. 44.

own cows—I require to ruminate, and chew the cud of reflection; only they, poor beasts! finish off a matter far faster than I can do, for it will take me a month at least to stomach this."

CHAPTER XIX.

"There was an ancient house, not far away,
Renown'd throughout the world for sacred lore,
And pure unspotted life; so well, they say,
It governed was, and guided evermore.
* * * * * * *
This holy rule was unto me radde,
And expounde in full notable wyse,
By vertuous men, relygious and sadde,
Full well expert, dyscrete, prudent and wyse,
And observantes of many gootly emprise.
* * * * * * *
'How much,' said he, 'more happie is the state,
In which ye, father, here do dwell at ease,
Leading a life so free and fortunate,
From all the tempests of these worldly seas,
Which toss the rest in daungerous disease;
Where warres, and wreckes, and wicked enmitie,
Doe them afflict—which no man can appease." SPENCER.

IT was about this time that a new visiter arrived at the rectory, a niece of Lady Harriet, a Miss Jane Beauclerk, who was about the same age as Mary. She was very good-natured and lively; though ignorant, she was not more so than many other young ladies, who, like her, had received an expensive education. She had a reputation for cleverness, which, in reality, was but flippancy; and was generally allowed to be amusing, from an engaging habit she had of never thinking before she spoke. It was to amuse her and Mrs. Egremond, that the rector one fine afternoon proposed an excursion to visit some ruins a few miles distant.

"What dear romantic creatures these monks must have been!" cried Miss Beauclerk, while the party were gazing in admiration at the old moss-grown walls. "So this was a convent—was it?"

"They certainly chose most beautiful sites in general for their buildings," rejoined Mrs. Egremond. "We must at least allow them the praise of good taste. What a pity they were such drones, wasting their time in idleness and ignorance, when they might have been performing their duties as good husbands and fathers in the Christian community."

"That is just what I think," exclaimed Miss Beauclerk. "A set of crusty old bachelors!"

"Do you not allow," asked the rector, "that each individual has a right to choose the state of life to which he is best fitted, and which is most agreeable to him; and since St. Paul recommends celibacy more than marriage, why should it not be adopted by those who please?"

"Paul had his prejudices as well as his neighbours," said the young lady; "and the example of our own established clergy, who generally are family men, shows very well what is thought now-a-days of such antiquated notions."

"Well, Miss Beauclerk, we shall not discuss at present the advantages or disadvantages of celibacy: but you will at least allow that a free-born Englishman has a right to remain single, if he does not choose to take a wife."

"Ah, I see what you are driving at," replied she. "After all, when one considers the enormous families of some of the English curates, the sickly wife, and the squalling children, the noise in the nursery, and the quantities of bread and butter used weekly, I'd rather be a monk myself than undergo it. Come, now, Mr. Feversham, do tell us what it was that made so many enter the cloister in ancient days. I shall be serious for once, for I suppose they had higher motives than I gave them credit for just now."

"I shall take your promise," said the rector, smiling; "so, if you can be attentive for ten minutes, sit down on the grass, and I shall reply to you. The monastic was a Christian life according to the precepts and counsels of Christ; and convents were instituted that in them might be practised the community of goods, the simplicity of life, and the ardent piety of the first Christians. Those who wished to do these things in perfection, and to fly from the temptations and turmoils of the world, entered a convent."

"I listen to you, Mr. Feversham," said Mrs. Egremond, "in sad astonishment. How can you speak of Christian perfection where gospel truth was unknown? However, go on, pray, go on. I am curious to hear what more you will say."

"And I am curious too," cried Miss Beauclerk. "'Community of goods' would be a pleasant thing when one had rich neighbours; and 'simplicity of life,' I suppose, means keeping cows, and enjoying country pleasures."

"The monastic life," continued the rector, regardless of the interruption, "implied poverty, or the renouncement of personal possessions."

"Then, if each individual was poor," interrupted Mrs. Egremond, "what use did they make, pray, of the enormous wealth which, we are told, the monasteries possessed before the glorious Reformation?"

"They expended it in various ways. Every monastery was, in fact, a great hospital; and most of them were obliged to relieve a number of poor people every day. They were likewise houses of entertainment for almost all travellers, and in ancient times supplied the place of inns. They were schools of learning, and each convent had one or more persons appointed to teach, while all the neighbours that desired it might have their children taught grammar and church-music free of expense. In the nunneries, likewise, young women were taught needlework and reading, and even Latin sometimes. So that not only the lower rank of people, but even noblemen and gentlemen's daughters were educated in those places."

"Now, will you stop a moment, rector?" said Mrs. Egremond. "I should like to know on what authority you make these assertions. We shall take each topic separately, and begin with monastic ignorance. All the world knows that the times when the monastic system flourished most, are called by common consent the *dark ages.*"

"Yes, indeed," rejoined Miss Beauclerk, for the moment adopting Mrs. Egremond's phraseology; "we all know, for example, that Robin Hood's Friar Tuck had but very so-so views of gospel truth."

"You ask, in the first place, for my authorities, Mrs. Egremond," said the clergyman. "I can refer you for what I have just said to the writings of the Protestant Bishop Tanner, who held the see of St. Asaph in George the Second's reign, as quoted in the Fourth Letter of Cobbett's Protestant Reformation. And now, if you like, I will read you a few extracts from a volume relating to this very subject, which I put into my pocket, thinking it might be useful, before we came out. 'The early monks did not disdain the ancient learning, for we know that the missionaries of St. Gregory brought a Homer with them to England; and Raban Mauer, commemorated as having first brought Greek literature to the Germans*...........All the greater houses contained men of eminent learning, down to the latest times, when the Benedictine Order gave to the republic of letters

* F. Cornelii Monach, Breviar Fuldense Historicum.

Ménard, Mabillon, Montfauçon, D'Acheri, Gallois, Delfau, Massuet, Bulteau, Gerberon, Gesvres, Lami, Garnier, Roussel, and Ruinart. The mendicant orders produced also men of most profound erudition. Joseph Scaliger, writing to Isaac Casaubon, tells him to search in the king's library for some notes of a Dominican friar on the Alcoran, which will greatly assist his studies, and without which he will find obscurities that will be inexplicable. The English Franciscans were especially learned towards the end of the thirteenth century. Then shone Rodulph Coleburg, Roger Bacon, Henry Willot, Thomas Dorking of Norfolk, Richard Rufus, Adam de Marisco, William of Ware, John Walleis, John of London............Robert Crusins, and Richard Middleton,' &c."

"Is not this torrent of erudition positively awful?" cried Miss Beauclerk. "Pray what is the name of the little book from which it pours forth? Some Popish Breviary, doubtless!"

"It is the tenth volume of Mores Catholici, or the Ages of Faith; and if Mrs. Egremond cares to take the trouble to read the ninth chapter, she will no longer venture, I suspect, to accuse the monks, as a body, of ignorance!"

"The assertion of one Catholic writer in favour of monkish learning, is no authority when compared to the mass of protestant testimony to the contrary," said Mrs. Egremond.

"I beg your pardon," replied the rector. "Protestant writers on this subject rarely trouble themselves with quoting ancient authors to support their bold assertions; while on the contrary, this more unassuming volume gives hundreds of references to ancient writings, composed during the very times of which they narrate the history."

"The monks had splendid libraries too, had they not?" asked Miss Beauclerk. "They wrote their books instead of printing them, which I think was foolish, as it must have given far more trouble."

The rector smiled and continued, "Yes, Bishop Tanner informs us, that they not only wrote the missals and other books used in divine service, but were generally employed on other works also, such as the Fathers, Classics, Histories, &c. Sometimes they even got lands given for the purpose of maintaining copyists."

"How tiresome that must have been!" interrupted Miss Beauclerk, "for my part, I would rather write two new books than copy half-a-one!"

"This very feeling," replied the rector, "shows you how much obliged we ought to be to the monks who, by their patient labours, prevented literature becoming extinct. These good monks were also great historians; the same author relates, that in all the greater abbeys there were persons appointed to take notice of the principal occurrences of the kingdom, and at the end of every year to digest them into annals. They also kept registers of births, deaths, and marriages; while state papers, charters, constitutions, acts of parliament, &c., used to be sent to them for preservation. For example, a copy of the famous Magna Charta was sent to every abbey in the country."

"That must have been a great bore too!" said Miss Beauclerk, "for I know myself the trouble of keeping quantities of papers, memorandums, and accounts; I burn mine once a-year, for it is the only way of keeping my drawers tidy! By the way, had they circulating libraries in those days? I don't know how I should exist without them."

"Books were too expensive," replied the rector, "to be lent indiscriminately; but, as a compensation, the monkish libraries were open to every one, while rare and valuable books were often more accessible to the public than they are now, as you will find described in the same chapter of Mores Catholici I quoted before."

"I wish you would tell us something now about the way they treated the poor," said Mary.

"I shall read you what is said in my little volume here," replied the rector. "Their intercourse with the poor is characterized by a manner which no one can mistake or misinterpret. For, see how they receive the rustic group before their gates; kissing the white hairs of the old men, caressing the children, catechizing the barefooted stripling, with as much care and tenderness as if he were the son of a prince; giving the dowry for the maid, paying the debts of the indigent, sending provision to the house of the infirm and filling the hearts of all with gladness."—(Mores Catholici, 10th v. 609 p.)

"Mere poetical descriptions are no proof," said Mrs. Egremond.

"Certainly not," replied the rector, "but the extraordinary amount of Catholic charity particularly as dispensed by convents, is a thing so well known, I scarcely thought you would have required proof from me. However, I shall refer you to a very entertaining work, 'Cobbett's Protestant Reformation;' where you will find what I say, and much more, tolerably authenticated. There you will see how Poor Laws were unknown until the supporters of the poor, the generous monks of the olden time, were chased from the land of their ancestors; the frightful destitution and famine which followed, and drove the indigent to desperate rebellion; the heart-rending cruelty with which the poor were treated by the new protestant government, and their lamentations over the exile of those who were indeed their fathers!"

"It was to be expected," said Mrs. Egremond, "that a set of ignorant people who knew no better, should deplore the fall of their old superstitions; and as I have heard that the monks supported many idle individuals, it was but natural that at their fall, their former dependents should be discontented."

"The whole realm was in commotion, as you will see by Cobbett, so much so that foreign troops had to be called in to quell the disturbances!" said the rector.

"Well, after all, I do think it would have been better to let the people keep their old religion if they liked," said Miss Beauclerk. "It must have been more agreeable to get relief from those that made it a pride and a pleasure to give alms, as my grandfather, who travelled in Spain before the revolution, used to tell me of the monks there, than to be shut up in one of those great staring union workhouses! Besides, when ignorance is bliss 'tis folly to be wise! For which reason I thank God every night for making me an enlightened protestant!"

"You are not very clear, Jane, in your way of speaking," said Mary, laughing.

"I mean that I am satisfied with the religion I was born in, and so were the papists long ago. Three-fourths of protestants, and myself among the number, profess our belief simply because our fathers brought us up in it, none of us knowing either the why or the wherefore! Therefore the saying, 'when ignorance is bliss,' applies to us, as much as to our Catholic ancestors!"

"There is plenty of ignorance, but very little bliss now-a-days," said Mary.

"Speak for yourselves, young ladies," said Mrs. Egremond. "They whose hearts are not right with God, cannot discern the things of the Spirit, and therefore it is not wonderful that they should plead guilty to carnal ignorance."

"Come now, dear Mr. Feversham," cried Miss Beauclerk, who was always in a hurry to change the subject when Mrs. Egremond talked in a religious strain, "tell me, was it only people sick of the world, grand, byronic, blasé creatures that entered convents; men like Rembrandt's pictures, with gloomy, searching expressions, long beards, mysterious eyes, noble foreheads and flowing garments? Or were all sorts of every-day characters admitted?"

"All were welcomed," said the rector, "of whatever character they might have been, who appeared actuated by the sincere desire of advancing in christian perfection; the convent was suited to no particular rank, age, or disposition more than to another, and accordingly the greatest diversity of character and history might be met with there. Doubtless great sinners frequently retired to the cloister in order to do penance, but the ranks of the monks were perhaps more frequently reinforced by

.........'Men for contemplation framed,
Shy and unpractised in the strife of phrase,
Meek men, whose very souls perhaps would sink
Beneath them, summoned to such intercourse;
Theirs is the language of the heavens, the power;
The thought, the image, and the silent joy.'

What an asylum do monasteries furnish to young men of this character, shrinking from the gaze of cold worldly wisdom, inexperienced in its calculations, unsullied by the tarnish of its vulgar wants, sick of its formalities and anxious to cast off the mean restrictions it imposes, which bind so firmly by their number, though singly so contemptible!" (Mores Catholici, vol. 10. p. 51.)

"You quote well on this subject," said Mrs. Egremond, "but not in a very protestant strain. Were I to shut my eyes, I could fancy myself talking to a popish priest."

"And yet," said the rector, "I am not singular in my ideas; for your great protestant moralist, Johnson, has also acknowledged some of the advantages of the cloister. 'For some,' he remarks, 'have little power to do good and have likewise little strength to resist evil. Many are weary of their conflicts with adversity, and are willing to eject those passions which have long busied them in vain; and many are dismissed by age and diseases from the more laborious duties of society. In monasteries the weak and timorous may be happily sheltered, the weary may repose, and the penitent may meditate. Those retreats of prayer and contemplation have something so congenial to the mind of man, that perhaps there is scarcely one who does not purpose to close his life in pious abstraction, with a few associates serious as himself.' "

"Poor Johnson! He was all for legality and good works! Living the while in sad ignorance of the saving power of Jesus," said Mrs. Egremond.

"Bless me!" cried Miss Beauclerk, "a man with a wig like what we see in his pictures, could not have been ignorant of any thing! He was our English Solomon, Mrs. Egremond! Talking of Johnson puts me in mind of the lady that was so fond of reading his dictionary, because she said, it presented such an enchanting variety of subjects! But apropos of monks and monasteries, did you ever hear of our famous abbot's apple? An apple-tree which grows in my father's orchard, said to have been planted by the monks ages ago! It bears finer fruit and in greater quantity than any other tree in the county! The gardener says that the monks knew some secrets about the management of fruit-trees which we have lost now-a-days! So you see, Mrs. Egremond, they were not entirely good for nothing!"

"You are right, Miss Beauclerk," said Mr. Feversham. "They excelled in all sorts of manual labour, and were, in fact, the great agriculturists of the middle ages. Slaudenmauer informs us that, 'In the fifth and sixth centuries the monks who were not employed in preaching, tilled the ground, and converted deserts into fruitful fields. Where there had been only wastes and barbarous pagans, men saw gardens, meadows, and corn-lands, as if a new created world, and also great towns. Posterity,' he adds, 'has ungratefully repaid them, having no eyes for that which can be accomplished by a life that is spent in prayer, labour, and contemplation.' Rubichon also relates that, 'the monks were founders of cities, and true fathers of their respective countries. They built beautiful edifices and bridges, hospitals and colleges; they made roads, plantations, drainages, and above all, they made a happy people.' "

"Thank you, thank you, Mr. Feversham, we shall not dispute this point with you," said Mrs. Egremond; "I see from what you say that the monks knew how to employ their day-labourers; however they might have been lazy enough themselves for all that! A few evangelical preachers would have been worth a million of clod-hoppers!"

"And who but the monks evangelized Europe?" exclaimed the rector. "Through that benighted region the light of faith was spread in the seventh century, by the Benedictines! Amongst others, by Augustin, Wilfrid, and Cuthbert, in England, and Boniface in Germany, not to speak of the missionaries in Spain and Gaul, Denmark and Poland! Surely, we ought to feel some little gratitude to the men who converted our ancestors from cruel and debasing superstition, and taught them, Mrs. Egremond, to call upon the name of Jesus!"

"In those days," replied that lady, "the Church of Rome was less corrupt than it is now; so we can, in some degree, account for the zeal with which they pursued their missionary labours."

"I beg your pardon, Mrs. Egremond," said the rector, "the same zeal continues to this day, influenced doubtless by the same causes; witness the oriental missions undertaken in later times by the mendicant orders, the astonishing conversion of millions of souls in India by one man, the Jesuit, Francis Xavier, so late as since the reformation! And what is still more striking to us, the herculean labours of the Catholic clergy, regulars as well as others, at the present day in China, where scarcely a month elapses without bringing tidings of the martyrdom—yes, the *bloody* martyrdom of one or more devoted missionaries! These are the men who do not, like some protestant missionaries I know of, content themselves with remaining in a comfortable house great part of the year, and now and then in the fine season, making a pleasant excursion round the Chinese coast, sending here and there a few bibles and tracts on shore! These soldiers of Christ penetrate into the interior, supplied with no luxuries, often without necessaries, regardless of the burning sun and torrents of rain which at the different seasons alternate, and braving the rage of a hostile government which pursues and hunts them to the death. And yet I do not say all—for it is not death alone—but death preceded by the most cruel torments Chinese ingenuity can invent! These things are but little known among protestants, nevertheless they take place in our own times—in this practical age of utility, when young ladies regret that heroism is extinct, and that the common-place reigns triumphant!"*

"We have wandered somewhat from the subject, I think," said Mrs. Egremond. "The modern achievements of the Roman missionaries, who in China succeed in substituting one kind of popular superstition for another, have surely little to do with the state of monasteries in the middle ages. Notwithstanding all you have said, I still suspect they must have been a great drag on the rest of the community, and by no means popular."

"And yet," replied the rector, "they fulfilled all the conditions which now-a-days would ensure popularity. Almost all the great works which in modern times would be termed national, were formerly under-

* See the Annals of the Propagation of the Faith.

taken by the monks, and hence many of them were styled by the people the fathers of their country.* For example, the abbots of Croyland used to preserve the embankments in the fens, from charity to their neighbours, and for safety to the country.† The English Saxons blessed the monastery of Durham, at whose expense a prodigious work was undertaken, a solid road of wood and sand laid through the vast morass and forest of Depyny.‡ A vast number of parish churches in Somerset were rebuilt or repaired by the abbot of Glastonbury in the fifteenth century, whose initials may still be seen on the walls. A poor monk of Einsiedlin was the architect of what was afterwards called for its boldness and ingenuity the Devil's bridge.§ The abbot of Cork was the first to erect a salmon weir in that country. The monasteries also filled the place of agricultural societies, both for instructing the peasantry and making experiments in cultivation. They succeeded in raising rich vineyards and producing excellent wines, in many places where now-a-days there are none; and in others, such as near the Abbey of St. Gall, since the time of the monks the wine has deteriorated. They were easy landlords, asking low rents and giving long leases, so that under them, Hume says, 'the farmers regarded themselves as a species of proprietors.'"

"I am quite tired of this," cried Miss Beauclerk. "Tell us something romantic about them. Were not some of the famous old painters monks?"

"Yes," said the rector, "in comparatively later days Fra Bartolomeo and the blessed Angelico of Fiesoli have shed immortal honour on the cloister; and, during the so-called dark ages, many monks were famous for their devotion to the pursuit of paint-

* Sicilia Sacra ii. 1080.

† Hist. Croylandensis, Rer. Ang. Script. 1.

‡ Id.

§ Chronique d' Einsid, 27.

ing, as well as to the kindred arts of music and poetry. To use the words of the famous Lacordaire: 'In entering under the sweet shade of the cloister, the Christian offered to God whatever peculiar talent he had received from Him. Before the altar all the brethren resembled each other by prayer; but, on returning to their cells, the prism was decomposed, and each expressed after his own manner a ray of the divine beauty.' And now, if you wish more information, you must peruse for yourselves this little volume of 'Mores Catholici,' from which I have been plagiarizing during the last half-hour."

"Oh dear, I have had enough!" cried Miss Beauclerk; "and as for poor Mrs. Egremond, I quite pity her for the infliction you have made her undergo so mercilessly. She has been looking sad and sorrowful, like another Niobe, while you were talking.........Or, like an owl in an ivy bush," she continued, as she looked round, and observed that Mrs. Egremond had slipped away as she began to speak, and was now examining the ruins at a little distance, "there must be something the matter with her, I fear. She was gazing at you with such a tearful expression during your harangue. She begins to think, I suspect, that your notions of the gospel are getting misty. And for my part I don't wonder, for I believe in my heart that you are a Jesuit in disguise!"

CHAPTER XX.

"The Papists are terrible rogues,
The Pope is a thundering thief,
On a Friday he laughs in his sleeve,
As he dines on his mutton and beef.
"You may steal, you may murder, or swear,
Absolutions are always to buy,
Upon my life it's true,
Now, what'll you lay it's a lie?" *Orangeman's Song.*

It was Wednesday evening, the day of Mr. Sharples's weekly lecture on the errors of popery. Blount having been later than usual in Overbury, took the opportunity of going to hear him. Confession and absolution were the subjects on which he spoke, and which he handled in a masterly way. He enlarged on the encouragement given to sin by the Catholic faith, as no crime was too bad to be absolved by the priest. He particularly instanced Ireland, where it was well known every sin had its price. A man, on the payment of half-a-guinea to the parish priest, would receive absolution for committing murder. Absolution for setting a house on fire might be had for seven and sixpence; and for the smaller offence of theft the price varied from sixpence to half-a-crown, or even five shillings, according to the article stolen. In harvest, when labour was better paid, and the temptations to crime less frequent, the prices always rose. In very bad seasons they were somewhat cheaper, but all was regulated in the pastoral of the bishop of the diocese, and in his private instructions to each clergyman. The priests were very stiff in standing on their rights; so much so, that it often happened that poor wretches left the tribunal of confession with their sins but half-told. One in particular was overheard by a godly Protestant saying to the confessor with a laugh, "Please your Reverence, I'll keep this same here mistake I made in knocking a man down and leaving him lifeless, till my next Easter confession, when I'll have got more of the rhino!" "Such, my friends," continued Mr. Sharples, "is but a small specimen of the practical working of that great master-piece of Satan—popery. Not only can the forgiveness for crimes committed, be purchased for filthy lucre, but sins can even be pardoned in advance through the medium of indulgences! This, of course, is a more expensive mode of managing the fell transaction, and chiefly suited for the rich, as the poor can rarely afford to purchase permission to commit sin beforehand. These facts in some degree account for the vast wealth of the Catholic clergy in ancient times, and also, perhaps, for the great attachment evinced by Catholics even to this day for their religion. By no other do they think they could purchase heaven so easily; and at the same time, with so much impunity, enjoy all the luxuries, vanities, and sinful pleasures of this life." A great deal more was said to the same effect, but Farmer Blount, getting sleepy, slipped away, disbelieving most of what he had heard, but yet determined to enquire into it by and by.

About a quarter of an hour afterwards there followed along the same road a middle-aged couple, the woman gesticulating with great energy, and her companion, a sleek, well-complexioned, oily-looking man, gazing at her with mingled respect and admiration, now and then relating some circumstance to her, which only seemed to increase her animation.

"Proud shall I be," said the gentleman, whom our readers perhaps already recognize as Jacob Hogg, "to supply your highly-gifted mind with as many facts as you like, that you may preach a spirit-stirring sermon to supply the vacuum left in the discourse of Mr. Sharples."

"I want something original—something quite new," exclaimed Mrs. Benson. "I hate walking in the beaten track. I wish to probe to the bottom the ulcers of popery, and tell what has never been told in the pulpit before."

"It won't be easy," replied Jacob, "to discover anything more effective in the disgusting or tragic style, than has already caused a sensation when uttered by our poets in Exeter Hall!"

"*Poets* do you call them! I thought they were generally ministers that spoke there," said Mrs. Benson.

"So they are doubtless," replied Jacob; "but I call them poets too, because as how they draw largely on their imagination for facts, which I take to be the only way to stir the people of England into admiring a popular preacher."

"The imagination, doubtless, is a great gift of God," responded Mrs. Benson, with a sigh. "May He that reigns above grant, that we may all make as good a use of it in His service to expose the deformities of popery, as do the poets and prophets of Exeter Hall. But now for the facts, good Jacob—original, if possible, and never before presented to the public."

"Did you ever hear," said Jacob, "of the favourite penance given by Catholic priests, to walk for so many miles with peas in the shoes?"

"Oh, that's an old story! vulgar, quite vulgar!" cried Mrs. Benson. "Something more original, if you please."

"Why, I don't pretend to have any imagination," said Jacob. "I'd rather stick to truth, which is the best policy in the long run. Did you ever hear of the way they do penance in Rome? I've heard tell that there are churches in Rome, where crowds of sinners go in the dead of the night; they all stand in a circle, and each man bastes his neighbour before him with all his might."

"That's common-place," said Mrs. Benson, tossing her head.

"Well, really now," said Jacob, "I don't know what to say. Did you ever hear why monks were made? They are men that wear long robes that cover their entire body all but their eyes and a small bit of their nose, for the purpose of ventilation. No man knows either their father or their mother, or, indeed, how they came into the world, for they are strongly suspected to be lusus naturæ!"

"What's that?" exclaimed Mrs. Benson.

"It means much the same as habeas corpus!" said Jacob, with learned gravity. "Well, as I was saying, they sit in boxes called confessionals all day long (I got the information from a Swiss valet that had travelled); and on the lid being taken off, up they start suddenly, ready to hear all the unspeakable sins which the Romans do not dare to tell ordinary priests."

"Bless me, how awful!" cried Mrs. Benson, with a shudder. "A monk in a box is assuredly the abomination of desolation in high places. But, gracious me, there's a light! What can it be? They are not surely burning furze at this time of night."

"It's an odd sort of light, too," said Jacob, gazing in the direction to which Mrs. Benson was pointing. "We'll see what it is more clearly when we pass this shady part of the road."

"It's a light that's come at a very suitable time," rejoined Mrs. Benson, "just when we were talking of the papists. It seems to me to be a memento mori sent by the Lord to recall to our understandings popish persecution, in the days when wicked priests put godly ministers into tar-barrels before setting them on fire, thus making gospel Christians into flambeaus and chandeliers, clearly putting them to a use which their Maker had never intended."

"What a wonderful woman you are, Mrs. Benson!" exclaimed Jacob, with enthusiasm. "You may believe me or not as you like, but you talk more like a printed book, stereotyped and published in London, than any female I ever heard tell of, past, present, future, or pluperfect."

"And I may return you the compliment, Jacob," said the lady, "for you have a most marvellous and spirit-stirring choice of words, that overpowers me with an all-overishness at certain seasons."

"Powers be here," cried Jacob, darting forward and nearly overturning his astonished companion; "I'm done for, if the village is not on fire!"

Mr. Hogg had some reason for his exclamation; they had just passed the trees, when they beheld a bright sheet of flame suddenly rise from a mass of smoke about half a mile distant.

"Run, run for your life, Jacob," exclaimed Mrs. Benson; "My children, Oh! my children; I am Rachel weeping for her babes! Save them, Jacob, or they will be hot cinders! Oh! play a good leg, man, I could run faster myself. To think of the three children in the fiery furnace being acted over on my hearth! God be merciful to us!"

Happily for the poor woman, she and Jacob had not run very far, before they discovered that the fire was at some distance from their possessions. It was farmer Blount's homestead that was blazing; on discovering which, Jacob in great glee exclaimed, "God be thanked! the Lord knows the difference between the elect and the reprobate!"

Mrs. Benson on the contrary, remained scarcely less agitated than before, and besought Jacob to hasten onwards and render some assistance.

"My help cannot be much wanted," replied he coolly, "there seems lots of people there already, more's the pity," he continued in an under tone;

and then turning to Mrs. Benson, "don't you think, Madam," said he, "that it is an interfering with Providence putting out a fire? It would be more Christian-like for farmer Blount to sit still with his hands in his pockets watching the fire run its course, to the tune of 'Thy will be done, Hallelujah,' than to be making all that stramash there."

"We are weak mortals, Mr. Hogg," said Mrs. Benson; "few, indeed, are purified gold of Ophir like yourself. Therefore, I say, go assist them. You may at least help to save the furniture."

"That's true," cried Jacob, running off as a new idea seemed to strike him. "Who knows what I may find?" added he to himself.

Farmer Blount, on his return from Overbury, had been the first to discover a fire on his own premises. It had evidently been smouldering for some time, and no sooner were the doors opened to discover the seat of the mischief, than it burst forth with great vehemence. The neighbours were quickly alarmed, and did all in their power to render assistance; but, notwithstanding their efforts, nearly the whole of last year's valuable crops were destroyed in the barns. Luckily, the dwelling-house and furniture were saved, though not without some damage to the latter; for the neighbours, at the suggestion of Jacob, while the farmer was busy in another direction, tossed the most of it out at the windows, to save it from the raging element, which, the haberdasher observed, being a minister of the Lord's vengeance, was sure to attack the house. Jacob was likewise very busy in rummaging through all odd corners, "to save valuables," as he said; in which occupation he was closely followed and assisted by little Neddy, who gazed at him in mingled astonishment and awe, while ransacking all the cupboards and boxes which he from his babyhood had been forbidden to touch.

All this time Dame Blount was in a neighbouring cottage in violent hysterics; Mrs. Benson was in vain trying to pacify her, and calm her agitation, the fright having put her nearly out of her mind. Her screams were indeed awful: "Save the blessed rubrick at any risk!" she exclaimed. "Smother it in wet blankets! Never mind my chairs and tables, but toss the thirty-nine articles out of the windows first. Lord, have mercy upon all bishops and curates! Keep them dry, with their top-sides upmost!"

"Hush, my dear," said Mrs. Benson, soothingly; "the fire is nearly out now."

"From battle, murder, and sudden death, from fire and hail, snow and vapour, may church and state, the royal and the phœnix insurance offices be delivered!"

"Poor creature!" exclaimed Mrs. Benson; "the fire has touched her head, never strong at the best! She must be put to bed as fast as possible."

"I was not surprised at the fire; no, not at all!" cried the dame, struggling in her sister's arms. "I knew the judgment would come! Was it not mentioned in the next precedent paragraph of the rubric? Was it not the ordinary, to wit, Parson Feversham, proceeding against the offending person, John Blount, according to the canon?"

At last the fire was entirely extinguished, and the farmer, who was scarcely recognizable from dust and smoke, had time to rest from his labours, and contemplate the devastation. It was with a sad heart that he beheld the fruits of last year's industry totally destroyed; and yet he felt thankful; for his wife and child at least had been preserved to him.

"This is a sad blow you have met with, my poor friend," said the rector, who came down early next morning as soon as he heard of the accident. "If I can in any way be of service to you, you may command me."

"Thank your Reverence very kindly," said the farmer; "but indeed the mischief will be easier borne than you would think. The savings I told your Reverence a good while ago that I had in the bank will cover the damage. To be sure, it will take all, and not a farthing over, which will destroy my fine schemes about Neddy. I had meant, Sir, to make a gentleman of him, by giving him a fine education; but I see now that it is God's will it should not be so."

"And yet, my friend," said the rector, "if, as you say, your savings will cover all the damage done, you should still, having no debts, be able to save enough from your future income to give him an excellent plain education."

"Very true, your Reverence; but, you see, old men will be foolish; and I thought I might have laid by sufficient, when the time came; to send him to Oxford or Cambridge. But I am content, as it has happened," continued the farmer, with a sigh. "He might have spent his time badly, and got his head turned from stepping out of his station."

"That is all true, Blount," said the rector; "though I should hope better things from your son. However, I don't think you need give up your plans all at once; the boy is a mere child still; and as it will be a dozen years nearly before he could be fit for a university, you have ample time before you to save."

"I beg your honour's pardon," said Blount. "If things were as they were, half the time would do me; but as it is, rents are high, and prices low: so that I have had enough to do the last two years to pay his lordship's agent, without laying by a farthing. God be thanked! I have just enough in the bank to repair the mischief done by the fire, or I'd have been a ruined man this day!"

The rector sighed. "I am glad at least, Blount," said he, "that you bear your loss with such philosophy, or, to speak more properly, in such a Christian spirit."

"I deserve no credit," said Blount. "I see I can't

help myself, so it is needless complaining. I only wish I could make out who set the barn on fire."

"It was not insured, I suppose," said the rector.

"No, Sir, unluckily it was not," replied the farmer. "My landlord's agent used to get everything insured for me, but latterly there was some mistake; the money I sent to him not being sufficient both to pay it and a fine that was due: yesterday only, to my great surprise, I learned that I was owing three weeks' insurance. So you see, your Reverence, the insurance office cannot be expected to make any compensation."

CHAPTER XXI.

"Show me bitter tears, that I may mingle mine with yours. Impart your trouble to the priest as to your father, he will be touched with a sense of your misery. Show to him what is concealed without blushing; open the secrets of your soul as if you were showing to a physician a hidden disorder; he will take care of your honour and of your cure." St. Gregory of Nyssa.

It was only two days after the fire, that the unfortunate farmer, somewhat to the rector's surprise, was shown into the study.

"I've walked up this fine evening to see your Reverence," said he, "after working busily all day to repair some of the damage."

"I never expected you, John, in present circumstances, and I should have thought you were too busy to resume our conversations for months to come," said the rector.

"And so I ought to be," said the farmer, with a sigh. "But, somehow or other, I am in such low spirits I find it impossible to rest in my mind; so, after fatiguing myself with hard work all day, I just came up to get a little comfort from you, Sir."

"I wish I could impart any, my good friend; but you have not told me how the dame is getting on; is she bearing the misfortune well?"

"Just so-so," replied the farmer. "It was partly to escape from her and her visitors that I came here just now. Her sister Benson, and her son-in-law Jacob, (whom God forgive me for disliking,) are with her, and trying to persuade her that the fire was a just punishment for my sins. Jacob was asking as many questions about the burning, and what had been lost, as if he were the insurance office in flesh bodily. My corruption rose against the man, so I took my hat and walked out. And now, Sir, you'll excuse me for asking, but if you would begin your instructions again, it would do me good, and be a divertisement to my thoughts. You were on the sacraments, if I remember well, your Reverence."

"Yes, you are right, John," said the rector; "we had finished baptism, confirmation, and the blessed eucharist; and now we shall go to the sacrament of penance."

"I never heard of that sacrament," said the farmer.

"I suspect you have," said the rector, "but you do not recognize it by that name. Did we not talk some time ago of confession and absolution?"

"To be sure we did," said Blount; "and that minds me it was the very thing I wanted to ask your honour about. Mr. Sharples said in a sermon that the forgiveness of any sin could be got by paying for it; and in Ireland, for example, absolution for murder might be had for half-a-guinea."

"This assertion is totally false," said the rector; "a priest dare not, under pain of the most severe penalties, receive money for giving absolution. The thing is never heard of among Catholics, and is a pure invention of Protestants, who, as often as the assertion is disproved, return unblushingly to the charge. They sometimes ground this allegation on a little book called "Taxa Cancellariæ Romanæ," which gives a list of crimes and their prices; it has repeatedly been published by the Protestants of Germany and France, and as often been condemned by Rome: but it has always been the custom of the enemies of Catholicity to seek for her doctrines in the books published by her foes, while they will not take the trouble of searching the expositions of her doctrine in works authorized by herself."

"That is scarcely fair, I opine," said the farmer; "but will your Reverence tell me now the true doctrine about it? Can a priest give absolution to any one he likes?"

"Not unless the penitent perform his part," replied Mr. Feversham. "He must make a full and entire confession of all the sins he can remember, with sincere sorrow for the past, and a firm resolution, by the grace of God, never more to offend."

"But suppose he should cheat the priest, and not tell all his sins, or even suppose he should say every thing, but pretend to be sorry when he was not, and be intending to do the same sins over again, what would be the consequence?"

"The priest, if he detected any of these things, would refuse to give him absolution; and if, on the contrary, being deceived, (which might happen,) he should pronounce the words of absolution, the person thus lying in the sight of God would receive no benefit from it, but would incur tremendous guilt."

"Do you think the priests are often deceived?" asked Blount.

"Sometimes they must be," said Mr. Feversham; "but, in general, bad Catholics prefer staying away from confession altogether, to desecrating the sacrament; for, in acknowledging their faults to the priest, they are taught to look upon Jesus Christ in his person, who, seeing into their hearts, knows whether to give or to withhold forgiveness of sin. The priest may be deceived, but God cannot."

"Then, if it be God in the end who forgives sin, what is the use of going to the priest at all for it?"

"Because," replied the rector, "confession and absolution are the means appointed by God for the forgiveness of sins committed after baptism. We all know that the Almighty can forgive when and how he pleases; but if he appoint a certain method for so doing, we must keep to it."

"Yes, I remember," said the farmer, "how Christ said to the Apostles, 'Whose soever sins ye remit, they are remitted unto them; and whose soever sins ye retain, they are retained.' (John xx. 23.) And, 'Whatsoever ye shall bind on earth, shall be bound in heaven; and whatsoever ye shall loose on earth shall be loosed in heaven.' (Matt. xviii. 18.) And you showed me too, Sir, that if the Apostles had that power, it must continue with their successors, for Christ promised to be with them always even unto the end of the world. (Mat. xxviii. 20.) That's all clear enough, and I won't gainsay it. It's scriptural, and that's every thing. But it is an odd thing, Sir, that Catholic priests are the only people to claim the power."

"Not the only people to claim authority to forgive sins; you forget what I showed you some time since in the Common Prayer Book," replied the rector. "There confession and absolution are clearly authorized."

"But, Sir, if the Church of England does not

practise these things, it makes little difference whether the prayer-book be right or wrong."

"Some English clergymen," said the rector, "have begun within the last few years to revive this doctrine, as well as many other ancient usages long exploded."

"That's all very well, Sir," continued the farmer, "but I thinks more of the Church where every priest without exception maintains his right coming down from the Apostles to give absolution, than of the English Church, where some of the ministers think it altogether sinful, others are ashamed to confess they believe in it, and those that maintain it boldly must be at loggerheads, I should think, with the rest of their brethren."

The rector sighed; and after pausing a little, in hopes of a reply, the farmer went on to say, "I'd like much to hear from your Reverence how people set about making a confession."

"The first thing to be done is, to pray earnestly to God to assist us in this most important work," said Mr. Feversham. "We must then carefully examine our conscience to discover what sins we have committed, and how often. We must try to feel a sincere sorrow for our transgressions, and make firm resolutions, with God's grace helping us, never more to offend Him."

"It would be next to impossible for me," said Blount, "to remember all the sins I had committed during my life. It would be needless trying, for they are past counting."

"It is sufficient," said the rector, "for you to tell all you remember, for God does not require us to do impossibilities. However, the mode in which people are taught to examine themselves must bring to light much more than at first sight might be expected. The ordinary Catholic prayer-books give ample light on the subject. After explaining the nature and obligations of each of the ten commandments, the penitent is furnished with a list of questions, teaching him how to examine himself in what points he has transgressed them. The seven deadly sins, the roots or springs from which our evil-doings arise, are also explained, and he is taught to examine himself on them, as well as on his duties as a Christian and in the state of life to which he has been called by God. Another excellent preparation for a general confession, is to divide one's life into so many parts—the season of childhood, of youth before entering the world, or the period at school; the time spent in different countries, or in different situations; the manner in which we have performed our duties under each different superior we have had through life, and so on. The more minutely we search into different circumstances, and thus divide our history, the more likely we are to make a good examination."

"Very true, your honour; but suppose, after all your trouble, you forgot something very important, what would be the consequence?"

"Nothing more than that you would be obliged to return to confess it, if you remembered it before receiving communion, or, if after that, at your next confession."

"I think you said, Sir, that you don't get true absolution unless you are sorry for your sins; now, suppose, Sir, I was going to confess, and anxious to do well, but for the life of me could not feel the sorrow I ought, what should I do?"

"In that case you must pray to God to soften your heart, and give you true contrition. He has said, 'Ask, and you shall receive; seek, and you shall find.' The great thing is to make preparation for some time beforehand, by prayer, meditation, and reading pious books. If you thus strive to prepare your mind for making a good confession, doubtless God will do the rest."

"It often strikes me," said the farmer, "that God can't be much pleased with some folk's sorrow. I've seen sinners on their death-bed as greatly vexed as they could be for their sinful life, but it was as evident as possible that it was all because they were frightened for hell-fire, and not because they grieved to offend God. I wonder if their sorrow gets much reward."

"It is a good thing, John, to be sorry for our sins on any motive whatsoever, if it help us to amend; but the slavish and cowardly sorrow of which you speak, cannot be so acceptable to God as that more noble affliction which grieves because God has been offended, who is so good, and who loved us enough to send His dear Son to die for us. However, John, the best way to test your own sorrow, is to see if it lead to amendment of life—for, if so, it is good."

"If I don't mistake, Sir, the Catholic priest, after giving absolution, orders a penance to be done—what is the use of it?"

"The Church holds that sin is remitted by sacramental confession and absolution, as to its guilt and eternal punishment in hell. Nevertheless, the sinner must suffer for his sins, that the justice of God may be appeased. For example: the prophet Nathan said to David, 'The Lord also hath put away thy sin.' However, in the verse following, he adds that he is still to be punished by the death of his child. In like manner Moses was punished temporally for his sins, by being excluded from the promised land. Sin is always followed by suffering; and the favourites of God are punished in this world, that they may be spared in the world to come. Supposing always that the guilt of sin is remitted by absolution, yet, if some punishment for it be not suffered here, it must be suffered in purgatory."

"So, if we have sinned at all, we must suffer, forgiveness or not: that's main hard!" said the farmer. "But what has that to do with the penance the priest gives?"

"A great deal," replied the rector. "The priest

for his penance gives some good work to be performed, or prayer to be said, which, if we do in a right spirit, offering it to God in satisfaction for our sins, will doubtless be accepted by Him in lieu of part of the punishment due to them."

"I can't say that I think that scriptural," said the farmer, shaking his head.

"Why not?" asked the rector. "Do we not frequently read in the Bible of the wrath of God being turned aside by prayer, fasting, &c.? and what is that but making satisfaction, or doing penance? Did not God decree that Nineveh for its sins should be overthrown; and did he not remit that temporal punishment when they put on sackcloth, fasted, and cried for mercy?"

"That is a case in point, I allow," said Blount; "and I'll think of it at home. I am no hand to-day at arguefying, Sir; some days I like to battle with your Reverence, feeling, as I do, mortal pugnacious and game-cockish! but at this minute I am down-hearted and meek as a lamb, all with thinking on this plaguy fire. However, it is unmanly to take on so, therefore I'll show fight, and ask another question. What do Catholics mean by getting an indulgence to commit sin?"

"There are such things as indulgences," replied Mr. Feversham, "but there never was one giving leave to commit sin; nor yet was there ever an indulgence remitting the eternal punishment of past sin: for sins committed after baptism can only be forgiven through the sacrament of penance, and by contrition."

"What is an indulgence at all, then?" asked Blount.

"It is a release of temporal punishment due to sins repented of, confessed, and already pardoned as to the guilt. Bossuet gives the following account of an indulgence: 'When the Church imposes upon sinners painful and laborious works, and they undergo them with humility, this is called satisfaction. And when regarding the favour of the penitents, or some other good works which she has prescribed them, she pardons some part of the pain due to them, this is called an indulgence.' "

"But there never was an indulgence mentioned in the Bible," said Blount.

"I will give you an instance of one," said the rector. "St. Paul, in 1 Cor. v., speaking of an incestuous Corinthian who had taken his father's wife, says, that in the name of the Lord Jesus Christ he had judged 'to deliver such an one unto Satan for the destruction of the flesh, that the spirit may be saved in the day of the Lord Jesus.' This, you will allow, is giving temporal punishment in order that the soul may be saved. The Apostle also, in the last verse of the chapter, directs the wicked person to be put out from among them, in other words, excommunicated. Well, in the 2nd chapter of the Second Epistle, St. Paul, speaking of the same person that had caused so much sorrow among them, says that his punishment is now sufficient, and that he forgives him in the person of Christ. This remission of his temporal punishment, his excommunication, &c. was an indulgence."

"I understand this explanation very well," said Blount, "as far as it goes; but there's more in these things that is incomprehensible to me. I've heard speak of indulgences for twenty days, or a year, or seven years, and so on. You'll not make that clear, or I'm mistaken, your Reverence."

"In the times of the first Christians," said Mr. Feversham, "penances were much more severe than in our days. For example—three, seven, and ten years of penance used to be imposed for sins of impurity, perjury, &c. It often happened that the penitent, by his edifying life, showed such symptoms of sincere amendment, that it was judged by his spiritual superiors unnecessary that he should make out the time of penance at first appointed. In some cases he was forgiven at once, as in the Corinthian already alluded to; in others a commutation was made, and some good work appointed, which should hold good for the twenty days, the year, or whatever time had been appointed for penance. When you read, therefore, of a seven years' indulgence, for example, you will take notice that it is never given for nothing: some good work is always stated as the condition for obtaining it, which good work is as a commutation for seven years' penance for past sin already forgiven by God, but the temporal punishment of which had still to be suffered."

"I begin to have a notion of it," said Blount. "Suppose a father had a son that behaved very ill. In his absence he left a person to act in his name, and forgive his son when he should be penitent. The son comes and asks pardon of that person, who gives it in the father's name. But the father, who is God, has ordered that the son, though forgiven and made friends with, should still suffer something for his faults. The church, or person appointed, gives him this something to do, which is his penance; and afterwards, seeing him really amended, excuses him in his father's name from finishing it, which is an indulgence."

"Very well, indeed, John," said the rector;" you have got a pretty clear notion of it. And when, as in the instance you give, *all* the temporal punishment due for past sin is remitted, it is called a plenary or full indulgence."

"Suppose, Sir, that the penitent, having performed all the outward conditions for gaining this full indulgence, should not be right with God in heart, neither be sorry enough for his sins, nor love Him sufficiently, would he in reality get it?"

"Assuredly he would not, John."

"So, after all," said the farmer, "notwithstanding all the helps of outward things, all the forms, ceremonies, and sacraments in the Catholic Church, you will be none the better unless your heart is right, and you are sincere. What a big lie it is in Protestants to say that outward forms are all that is thought of among Catholics!"

CHAPTER XXII.

"Show me thy faith without thy works, and I will show thee my faith by my works." ST. JAMES, ii. 18. Protestant Bible.

"Do come here, Mr. Feversham," cried Miss Beauclerk to the rector, whom she saw passing the drawing-room window, at which the ladies were sitting during the forenoon. "Do come here and settle a dispute. Fancy me turned theologian, and arguing with Mrs. Egremond on works, election, and faith made sure, and a great many other puzzling things, till I have almost persuaded her I am an infidel, or at least a papist. She says that good works are unnecessary; so I reply that, in that case, I may do just what I chuse, be the veriest butterfly of fashion, waste my time, and do nothing to please God, and be as sure of heaven as Wesley, Whitfield, or any of her saints in the end. A very comfortable doctrine for us idlers! Is not it?"

"You misinterpret me a little," said Mrs. Egremond.

"Ah! now, Mrs. Egremond," cried the young

lady, "don't explain; we all know what you mean. Let us rather hear what the rector says on the subject."

"Don't ask Mr. Feversham," said Mrs. Egremond, "he is becoming more and more Popish daily, and will only put you wrong. Depend upon it, like the Romanists, he trusts altogether to works and nothing to Jesus."

"That is just what I want to hear!" said Miss Beauclerk, "I'd give any thing to know a little more about Catholicism! — that dear, delightful, old-fashioned church, with fine cathedrals, rich vestments, swinging censers, mysterious confessions, and awful revelations!"

"Excuse me, Jane! But what a deal of nonsense you do talk!" interrupted Mary. "Here is papa patiently waiting. What do you wish to ask him?"

"I wish to ask him the Romish doctrine about works and merits," said Miss Beauclerk, with more gravity. "By so doing I shall find out his own sentiments, for I think Mr. Feversham, like the modern Puseyite school, generally sides with the Romanists. Besides, I am actuated by the charitable motive of enlightening Mrs. Egremond, who I suspect gives the unfortunate Catholics credit for a great deal of nonsense that they do not really believe."

"I shall be happy to tell you the Catholic doctrine on this subject," said the rector, "and I will, as nearly as possible, give you the words of an enlightened Catholic priest whom I heard explain it."

"Enlightened!" ejaculated Mrs. Egremond, with a deep sigh.

"No man can be justified," continued the rector, "but by the grace of God through Jesus Christ; and only those are justified to whom the merits of his passion are communicated. Sin is forgiven us by the pure mercy of God through Jesus Christ, without any merit or desert on our side."

"I agree with all that," said Mrs. Egremond,

"but you don't pretend to say that Papists believe it?"

"Indeed I do," said the rector, "and what I have repeated is nearly word for word taken from an old Catholic book, given me by the same worthy priest I mentioned, called, 'A plain and rational account of the Catholic faith,' &c: I shall go on quoting from it if you please; 'none of the acts which in the conversion of a sinner precede his justification, whether they be faith or good works, can merit this grace. Good works after justification are not equal to the reward of future happiness.'"

"They are not equal to it indeed," interrupted Mrs. Egremond, "nor do they deserve it in the slightest degree!"

"Well," said the rector, "my little book agrees with you so far as to say, they are not acceptable to God, but as they proceed from the grace and derive their value from the merits of Jesus Christ. It also teaches us that we can do nothing of ourselves in order to salvation, not even have a good thought."

"With your last sentence I fully agree," said Mrs. Egremond.

"And I do not;" said Miss Beauclerk, "for very good ideas come into my head, capital thoughts in short, and no one puts them in!"

Mary could not help smiling, but the rector went on. "Catholics believe that there is no merit but what is a gift of God through Jesus Christ, and of which no man can glory. Whence it follows, (as the Council of Trent speaks with St. Augustin,) that when God crowns our merits he only crowns his own gifts."

"It is most true," said Mrs. Egremond, "that God only rewards his own gifts—but it is incorrect in my opinion to call them by the name of our merits; we have no merits!"

"At any rate," said Miss Beauclerk, "if we don't get according to our merits, we at least get according to our deserts, so I really would not quarrel about words—it all means the same thing!"

"Catholics believe," continued the rector, "that God has promised eternal life as a reward to those who serve Him faithfully in this life: according to these words of St. James, (i. 12.) 'Blessed is the man that endureth temptation; for when he is tried he shall receive the crown of life which the Lord hath promised to them that love him.' This promise contains a covenant or bargain between God and man, whereby it is stipulated that man must perform certain conditions in order to get eternal life. All that the Catholic Church means by the word merits, is that the fulfilment of these conditions gives us, in virtue of God's promise, a title to the reward."

"But," said Mrs. Egremond, "why do you say that we *merit* the reward when you must confess that our works can never be equal to it?"

"I allow that our works in themselves are nothing," said the rector. "Still, if God has promised to reward them, then, purely in virtue of that promise, they are entitled to the reward, or *merit* it, if you will."

"I never can believe that God in any circumstances will reward works," said Mrs. Egremond, "as long as I remember the text, 'If by grace, then is it no more of works; otherwise grace is no more grace!'" (Rom. ii. 6.)

"It is not a quotation in point," said the rector, "for the Apostle's object in saying this, was to convince the converted Jews at Rome, that their election to the faith of Christ was not owing to their preceding good works under the law, but purely to the grace of our Lord Jesus. You surely would not gather from these words that after their conversion they might give up good works as being unnecessary? Did St. Paul mean this, he would contradict Jesus Christ, who said, (Matt. xix. 17,) 'If thou wilt enter into life, keep the commandments.'"

"Come now, rector! don't preach up works!" cried Miss Beauclerk. "It is such a comfortable pleasant doctrine that of getting to heaven by doing nothing! It would just suit me if I could only forget the story of the poor fellow in the parable, that got into a scrape by sitting still and burying his talent in a napkin!"

"Remember the text, Mr. Feversham," said Mrs. Egremond, in a solemn voice, "'Not by works of righteousness which we have done, but according to his mercy he saved us!'" (Tit. iii. 5.)

"Go on, and finish the quotation, when you will see the meaning," replied the rector. "'Not by works of righteousness which we have done, but according to his mercy he saved us, *by the washing of regeneration* and *renewing of the Holy Ghost.* Which he shed on us abundantly through Jesus Christ our Saviour.' In this St. Paul speaks of the first grace of justification by baptism, which no one can possibly merit. However, to avoid being misunderstood, I shall repeat again, that Catholics hold we are saved entirely by the grace of Jesus Christ, which alone can make our works conducive to salvation."

"And you hold the same belief, doubtless," said Mrs. Egremond, "that works are conducive to salvation! Ah! my good friend, remember the text, 'When ye shall have done all those things which are commanded you, say, We are unprofitable servants, we have done that which was our duty to do.'"

"Were you to say so to a Catholic priest," replied the rector, "rely upon it, he would promise to take your advice, for he would know that we are wholly unprofitable to God, who neither derives profit from our services nor stands in need of them. Nevertheless we are his servants, and have in so far a title to wages, because He has graciously pleased to promise them to us. He will also assuredly keep this engagement, for He has said that 'He shall reward every man according to his works.'" (Matt. xvi. 27.)

"Do you know," cried Miss Beauclerk, "that it is a rich treat to hear you two disputing! You both realize so forcibly the lines,

'He that's convinced against his will,
Is of the same opinion still!'

Now I can't stand this much longer! Such a quantity of Bible texts brought in array by the combatants! And I so susceptible and impressionable! A little more of the same conversation would metamorphose me into an incarnation of Cruden's Concordance! Mary, I wish you and I were two great volumes of some old family Bible, lying on a shelf, with nothing to do but to be dusted twice a week—then we should be sure of heaven, for being too heavy to move we should have nothing to do with works, which, as Mrs. Egremond said before the rector came in, are a snare to withdraw one from salvation! I am going to take a walk, good people, so adieu! Mr. Feversham, will you come and open the garden-door for me?"

The rector accompanied the lively young lady, who no sooner left the room, than Mrs. Egremond, turning to Mary, thus addressed her:

"My dear child, I grieve to see that your father is becoming more of a Romanist in his views every day. I am incompetent to argue with him; but I wish with all my heart that Mr. Harvey were here."

"Your wish will soon be accomplished," replied Mary, with a smile. "I have just received a letter saying Harvey will arrive here to-morrow."

And Harvey did arrive late in the evening of the next day, to Mrs. Egremond's great delight, who told Mary she was most anxious, the first opportunity, to have a private conversation with him. The next day all the family, except Lady Harriet, assembled at breakfast; and Harvey amused and interested them with his account of Oxford and Oxford men. The rector alone did not appear to enjoy the subject, and tried to change it as often as the names of Pusey and Newman, &c., were introduced.

"Are you acquainted with a young man of the name of Pulteney, who entered a year or two since at your college? He is the son of a very old friend of mine, and in consequence I am interested in his success," said Mrs. Egremond.

"I know him well," replied Mr. Harvey, "and a fine fellow he is. During the first eighteen months he was rather wild, and took up with a very disorderly set. However, they fleeced him pretty well, and got him into a scrape or two. After that he took ill, and remained some time in a precarious state. During his convalescence, my reverend friend, Mr. Camden, visited him frequently, and had the satisfaction of seeing his views gradually change: his mind became sobered and his ideas enlarged, and now, in conduct and deportment, he is as exemplary as his friends could wish. He is at present studying for the Church; and from his talent and piety great things are expected. He sets an example to all our young men; it is quite edifying to behold the austerity with which he fasts, and his punctuality in frequenting confession."

"Frequenting confession! What do you mean?" exclaimed Mrs. Egremond.

"I mean that he goes once a week, in common with several others, to confess to Mr. Camden," replied Mr. Harvey, as coolly as though he had said nothing unusual.

"Good heavens!" cried Miss Beauclerk. "Has he turned Catholic? Do, like a good creature, Mr. Harvey, try to put a stop to his being a priest. He has such a fine property, and used to flirt with me so!"

"He is a Catholic, indeed, Miss Beauclerk," replied Harvey; "but not in the sense you suppose. "A Roman Catholic and an Anglo-Catholic are very different. We English Catholics belong to the great Apostolic body, while Roman Catholics, in England at least, where they interfere in our established dioceses, are schismatic."

"Ah, well—that's all right!" said Miss Beauclerk. "No matter what he calls himself, so long as he explains it away, and does not take a vow of celibacy."

"But, pray explain yourself, Mr. Harvey," said Mrs. Egremond. "Is it really true that some Oxford men practise confession? On what plea do they justify themselves?"

"We regard it," replied Harvey, "as authorized and practised by the Church, though fallen of late, like many other old and venerable customs, into disuse. The very prayer-book teaches it, in the visitation of the sick, when, if the sufferer have anything on his conscience, he is to be moved to make a special confession of his sins, and the minister is to give him absolution."

"And a sad remnant of popery it is," said Mrs. Egremond. "I wonder it has not long since been expunged from the prayer-book."

"Why should it?" said Harvey, "when in perfect accordance with the voice of antiquity, and with the whole beautiful system of the Anglican Church?"

"I was just reading lately in the work of an English bishop," said Mrs. Egremond, "that private confession was never thought of as a command of God for nine hundred years after Christ, nor determined to be such till after one thousand two hundred."

"I must make bold to differ with his lordship," said Harvey, smiling; "for Tertullian, who lived in the age succeeding the Apostles, writes as follows: 'If you withdraw from confession, think of hell-fire.'* Origen, who wrote soon after, advises the sinner 'to look carefully about him in choosing the person to whom he is to confess his sins.'† And in

* Lib. de Pœnit. † Hom. 2. in Ps. 37.

the fourth century, St. Basil writes:* 'It is necessary to disclose our sins to those to whom the dispensation of the divine mysteries is committed.' "

"I have no faith in what the fathers say," replied Mrs. Egremond; "for there never was a Romish doctrine which some of them did not favour."

"Nay, don't speak so disrespectfully of the fathers," said Miss Beauclerk. "I have loved and venerated them ever since Mrs. Hemans's beautiful song of 'The Pilgrim Fathers' was sung to me by my mother. Think of the dear old creatures—how 'Amidst the storm they sang! And the stars heard and the sea!' —But I forget the rest."

Here Miss Beauclerk was interrupted by a shout of laughter, in which even Mrs. Egremond and the rector joined.

"Well, I can't see what is to laugh at in my quoting one of mamma's songs," said Miss Beauclerk. "To be sure, it was published rather before my day; but that makes it all the more suitable to your antiquated conversation. And why I should not quote from the Fathers as well as Mr. Harvey I don't see."

"Mrs. Hemans was alluding to the Puritans, my dear young lady," said the rector, with difficulty composing himself, "when she wrote the lines you quoted."

"The puritans," exclaimed Miss Beauclerk, "that is very odd! but how was I to know? The name Fathers being the same accounts for the mistake. Do tell us now some more of confession, Mr. Harvey. And does Mr. Pulteney really go to con-

* Rule 229. St. Paulinus, the disciple of St. Ambrose, relates that he used to weep over the penitents whose confessions he heard, but never disclosed their sins to any one but to God alone, (in Vit. Ambros.) St. Augustine writes, "Our merciful God wills us to confess in this world, that we may not be confounded in the other," (Hom. 20.) And in another place he says, "Let no one say to himself, I do penance to God in private." Is it then in vain that Christ has said, "Whatsoever you loose on earth, shall be loosed in heaven? Is it in vain that the keys have been given to the church?" (Hom. 49.)

fession? What a droll thing it must be! How I should like to hear his confession! Would his confessor, Mr. Camden, repeat over again what he told him?"

"Of course not," replied Harvey, "that would be against ecclesiastical rule; the Church of England has made a canon requiring her ministers not to reveal confessions. (See Canones Eccles. A. 1693. n. 113.)

"What would the great reformers Luther and Calvin have said," ejaculated Mrs. Egremond, "could they have foreseen these abuses?"

"Luther would have considered it all right," said the rector, now beginning to speak; "for, in his Catechism, he expressly declares, that he believes the forgiveness of the priest to be the forgiveness of God." (In Catech. Parv.)

"And as for Calvin," said Harvey, "for whom, by the way, I have no great respect, we read in Fuller's Church History that Bancroft, the then bishop of London, in a conference with James the First, assured his majesty that the Geneva reformer approved of both general and private confession and absolution. But, indeed, in the Church of England, confession is no new thing. Heylin tells us, that Archbishop Laud endeavoured to enforce auricular confession, and was himself confessor to the duke of Buckingham. In his History of his own times, he also informs us that bishop Morley was confessor to the duchess of York while she was a protestant."

The conversation was here interrupted by the entrance of a servant, who, presenting Lady Harriet's compliments, begged the ladies to come and sit an hour in her dressing-room. They accordingly rose, and, in leaving the room, Mrs. Egremond pressed Mary's hand, who, on looking at her, observed that her eyes were filled with tears.

CHAPTER XXIII.

"Another had charge sick persons to attend,
And comfort those in point of death which lay,
For them most needed comfort in the end,
When sin, and hell, and death, doe most dismay
The feeble soule, departing hence away." SPENCER.

"How are you coming on, my good friend?" said Mr. Feversham to the farmer, who called upon him in the evening after the preceding scene. "I hope you are gradually getting the] place made comfortable."

"Pretty well, your Reverence," said Blount. "I've been making a sight of purchases since I saw your honour last, for the farm-stock, as I told you, was almost altogether destroyed. To-day I have been working hard, stowing away the things and superintending the workmen. I see plainly all my little savings will be expended before I get things right, and to look as they have done. Howsomever, I'll do very well, and so will the dame and Neddy, if God tries us no farther; but I could not stand any more calls on me for money, 'cause as why, I have no more wherewith to pay. I have just enough, and barely so, to get on from this day."

"And indeed, notwithstanding your heavy loss, John, you ought to be very thankful that God during the time of your prosperity put it into your mind to save for the evil day, otherwise you would have been ruined by this accident."

"That is true, your honour: I've barely saved my

distance just now, so as to keep free of debt. And I humbly say that I'll thank Providence to try me no farther in the way of mishaps, for I have no more money in my pocket to pay for them. I've very little time now-a-days to come up to speak with your Reverence, so I hope you don't take it amiss me asking for you in the evening when my work is done. Will your Reverence finish the other sacraments now? Since the fire I've been more anxious than ever to talk to you, and hear how to save my soul. It has come into my head continually that it was only God's mercy kept me from being burned alive in the flames."

"I am very glad to find you in these dispositions, John," replied the rector. We have now discussed the four first sacraments, and the next we come to is Extreme Unction."

"That is the anointing the sick with oil, is not it?" said Blount, "but why do you call it a sacrament? It always comes strange to me the calling anything a sacrament except Baptism and the Lord's Supper!"

"I have already explained," replied Mr. Feversham, "that a sacrament is an outward and visible sign of an inward and spiritual grace ordained by Christ—let us see, from the words of the Apostle St. James, if Extreme Unction fulfils these conditions. 'Is any sick among you? Let him call for the elders, (in the original version, *priests*,) of the Church; and let them pray over him, anointing him with oil in the name of the Lord. And the prayer of faith shall save the sick, and the Lord shall raise him up, and if he have committed sins they shall be forgiven him.' Now the anointing with oil, and the praying over the sick man, form the outward sign of the sacrament; and St. James explains the inward grace when he says, 'The prayer of faith shall save the sick......... And if he have committed sins, they shall be forgiven him.'"

"But how do you make it out to be ordained by Christ?" asked the farmer.

"Because the Apostles were sent to preach what Christ had taught them, and were besides filled with the Holy Ghost; our Saviour spoke through their lips, and in obeying one of the twelve we obey Him."

"It is not mentioned in the Gospels though; I can vouch for that!" said the farmer.

"It was taught the Apostles nevertheless, or St. James would not have written it," replied the rector. "We know that Jesus was seen of his disciples forty days after his passion, during which he spoke to them 'of the things pertaining to the kingdom of God.' Are these things all expressly written? No—but the Apostles were sent to teach them. St. John himself declares that if all were written respecting Jesus, the world itself would not contain the books!—what idle folly it is then to suppose that the Gospels contain the whole!"

"I spoke without thinking," said the farmer. "Certainly it would be showing great disrespect to an Apostle, to suppose he could invent a sacrament without being authorized by his master. I wonder why the Church of England, that holds to Scripture so much, should have given it up, for, as you say, and I see from the Bible also, it is an outward sign and an inward spiritual grace, which is all that is required for a sacrament, by their own catechism! Perhaps, your Reverence, it was not practised in old days, and as Episcopalians don't like new things, they have thrown it away!"

"So far from that," said the rector, "to borrow the words of Milner in his End of Religious Controversy, 'Origen, who was born in the age next to that of the Apostles, after speaking of an humble confession of sins as a means of obtaining pardon, adds to it *the anointing with oil prescribed by St. James.*'*

* Hom. 2. in Levit.

St. Chrysostom, who lived in the fourth century, speaking of the power of the priests in remitting sins, says, they exert it when they are called in to perform the rite mentioned by St. James.'* Milner also alludes to Innocent I. Cyril of Alexandria, Victor of Antioch, St. Gregory the Great, and the Venerable Bede bearing the same testimony."

"Howsomedever that's nought to me," replied the farmer, "seeing I know not any of these old folks even by name, except St. Chrysostom. And now I'll ask your Reverence a few questions; may any one get Extreme Unction?"

"Only those who being come to the use of reason, are in danger of death by sickness. It is neither given to children under the age of reason, nor to persons under sentence of death."

"Do Catholics go to confession before receiving it?"

"Yes," replied the rector, "the sacrament of penance must be received before every other sacrament, except that of baptism, in order to purify the soul and enable her to receive worthily the grace of God communicated sacramentally."

"Tell me some of the good effects of Extreme Unction, if you please, Sir," said Blount.

"It heals the soul of her weakness and infirmity, and also of propensity to sin, besides removing somewhat of the debt of punishment. It strengthens her to bear bodily illness and to resist spiritual enemies. In short, it enables her to die well. But now that you have got on so far, John, I would recommend you to read some Catholic book of instruction which will give you more particular information than I have time to do."

"Thank your Reverence kindly for the advice," said the farmer; "but at present, Sir, I have no time for reading at home. Besides, unless your Reve-

* De Sacerd. L. 3.

rence is mortal tired of me, it is a deal pleasanter getting instruction from you than out of a book; for I generally fall asleep over black and white."

"Indeed I am not tired of you, John; on the contrary, it gives me pleasure to be of service to you," said the rector.

"Well, if that is the case, Sir," rejoined Blount, "now that we have finished Extreme Unction, suppose your Reverence tell me a little more about Purgatory; you did not say much about it when you spoke of it a good while since. Do all Catholics go there?"

"No," replied the rector, "those whose stains of sin are entirely washed away in the blood of the Lamb, go straight to heaven; alas! I fear, their number is but few. Those who die in the guilt of deadly sin, such as the rich man mentioned in the parable in the gospel, go to hell; while there is a third description of christians, who when they die are neither so perfectly pure and clean as to be exempt from the least spot or stain, nor yet so unhappy as to die under the guilt of unrepented deadly sin, such as these the Church believes to go for a time to a middle state which is called purgatory, where they can be benefitted by our prayers. But did I not tell you this before?"

"I dare say you did, Sir," replied the farmer, "but a thick head like mine, is the better of hearing a good thing twice over. The souls get to heaven afterwards, don't they, when they are purified?"

"Yes," answered the rector, "and our prayers can shorten the period of their probation."

"But I don't see," rejoined the farmer, "why christians who are going to heaven in the long run at any rate, should not get in at once without shilly-shallying on the road in an out of the way place like purgatory! Can your Reverence give more scripture texts for your opinion, besides those you mentioned before about fire, (1 Cor. iii.) and the spirits in prison that Peter speaks of?"

"In the last verse of the twenty-first chapter of Revelations, we are told," replied the rector, "that there shall in no wise enter into heaven anything that defileth; now, as we can scarcely expect to be found pure from all sin at death, this text would seem to exclude us altogether from heaven, unless a third state existed where we could be purified. Again, we are told in the twelfth chapter of Matthew that we must render an account of every idle word we have spoken—must we go to hell if we have not received absolution for such trifling faults? Certainly not; and there must therefore be another place of punishment for such little transgressions."

"You told me also, I remember, Sir," rejoined the farmer, "that sin must always be punished with suffering, even those sins which have been pardoned in the sacrament of penance, and that if we don't suffer affliction in this world, we must do it in the next. And now I want to ask your Reverence on what authority you pray for the dead?"

"Catholics pray for those souls who are in purgatory, that their punishment may be remitted, on the authority of the Church, whose practice it has been from the beginning, as the early fathers testify.* Even the Jews were in the habit of praying for the

* Tertullian, in his book of the "Soldier's Crown," chapter third, written about a hundred years after the death of the Apostles, reckons oblations for the dead upon their anniversary days amongst the immemorial traditions observed by all Christians; and in his book, "De Monogaimia," chapter tenth, he affirms it to be the duty of a Christian widow to pray for the soul of her husband, and to beg refreshment for him, and to keep his anniversaries. See St. Cyprian Epist. 66. Arnobius, l. 4. Eusebius, l. 4. de Vita Constantini, c. 71. St. Cyril of Jerusalem, Catech. Mystag. 5. St. Gregory Nazianzen, Orat. 10, &c. Hence St. John Chrysostome, Hom. 3. upon the Epistle to the Philippians, tells us that it was ordained by the Apostles, that the dead should be commemorated in the sacred mysteries; and St. Aug. Serm. 32. de Verbis Apost. sec. 2. that it was a practice received from the fathers, and observed by the universal church. And it appears from St. Epiphanius, Hær. 75. that Arius was ranked amongst the heretics by the church in the fourth century, for denying that the prayers of the living did the dead any good.

dead. We find in the second book of Maccabees, 12th chapter, that prayers and sacrifices were offered for the sins of the departed. But really, John, I must send you away now; for I must no longer neglect the friends who are staying with me."

The farmer accordingly took his hat and departed. In passing through the village, Mr. Hogg looked out of his shop and called after him to stop.

"I am going your way," cried he, running after him breathless, "and would gladly, Providence willing, have a little pious and sedative conversation with you, farmer."

"I can't hinder you going my way," replied Blount, rather gruffly; "but as for the pious conversation, we'll dispense with it if you please."

"A chip off the old block I see!" said Hogg, with an insinuating smile. "Still humorous, pleasant, and funny as ever! I like your bluff frankness, farmer; its after my own heart! I can't bear deceitful dispositions; so when a man is sea-sick as it were, at the very mention of my pious conversation, I respect and venerate him when he shows openly his disgust at me! These are my ingenuous feelings, farmer; but there's few that know me! There's nothing like humility after all, father-in-law! Now I know I am a great sinner, with nothing but filthy rags to cover me; I know my back slidings have been wonderful in a general way; I know I have broken the ten commandments dozens of times, though I defy any of our connexion to prove particulars! I know I am a reptile, a mere glow-worm set up in a perspicuous situation to lead others into the narrow path by my example! But the connexion of the faithful in this parish does not know all that. They think a mighty deal of me, and they praise me to my face! Now I, knowing I am but a varmint prowling about the Lord's vineyard, am vexed at this! The good report of men acts as a vesicating Spanish-fly blister on my tender conscience. The modesty rises in lumps, I am in great pain, and continue anguished, until I meet with some plain-spoken man like you, farmer, who speaking truth to me like a two-edged sword, cuts the blister up and lets my natural modesty pour forth as at this moment."

"And well do you deserve to be cut up," replied the farmer, "the only pity is that you never feel it! You are the most brazen-faced hypocrite I ever met with! Your modesty indeed!"

"That's right, farmer! That's right!" whined Jacob. "Pitch it into me, for I deserve it!"

The farmer though somewhat inclined to be angry, could not help laughing heartily.

"It does one good to see you merry," said Jacob, "the Lord delighteth in a cheerful countenance! Talking of that, my wife and I had an amiable dispute this morning; all for relaxation with no venom or hydrophobia in it! Says she to me, Jacob, it is a mortal shame in you to grudge me a new gown, seeing I brought you a princely dowery of two hundred pounds! No Sarah, says I, be correct, for probity is the soul of domestic life: you only fetched me one hundred and ninety-nine pounds, two-and-sixpence, the odd shillings went to pay expenses. With that she began to cry, 'cause, she said, I called her a liar, and the place for liars is hell-fire. So I told her not to be disheartened or cast down about it, for I'd go to you and ask which was right, in case you should have kept any of the papers relative to that 'ere transaction. The poor woman is taking on so about it, and says she can't get Ananias and Sapphira out of her head. She has a mighty tender conscience, has Sarah!"

"Apt to blister, I suppose," said the farmer.

"Come, come, farmer, no more nonsense I beg," said Jacob; "I'm in earnest now, in pity to the weaker vessel's feelings. Think of the wife of my bosom lying in bed, as she is to-day, tossing about in all the anguishful terrors of a hot conscience. So, farmer, tell us like a good man, have you any of the papers left relative to that business; or may be you lost them the night of the fire."

The farmer coloured at this remark.

"Oh, well never mind," continued Jacob, "look for them at your leisure, and let me know the particulars when you find them. I would not trouble you at all, only I am particular about my poor woman's feelings. We are taught to be so in the gospel; does not the Lord care for the meanest insect, and does He not in His mercy take charge of sparrows and other varmint? which, as I often think, is a lesson to us husbands to be compassionate to our wives. I'll say good day to you now farmer, but I'll call up next week, and see if you have looked out the papers."

"I thought as much," muttered Jacob, when the farmer was out of hearing; "I don't think there is another scrap of paper about it, beyond what I've got hold of."

The poor farmer, after spending an unquiet forenoon, returned on the evening of the following day to the rector.

"I am ashamed to show my face here," he said; "but truly, Sir, you are my only comfort. My rascally son-in-law has been making inquiry about the receipt for his wife's money; and if I can't find it, he will have it in his power to sue me at law for it. A power of things were lost the night of the fire, and though I have searched every where last night and this morning, I can't find this same paper."

"I should hope your son-in-law is incapable of taking a dishonest advantage of you, farmer," said the rector. "Besides, how is he to know you have lost it?"

"He can't know, your Reverence; and yet if he has not a suspicion, what makes him come and ask to see it? To be sure, he told me a long cock-and-a-bull story about his motives: but I don't believe a word of it. It's all a trick to get me into a scrape. He's shockingly in want of money, and will scruple at nothing to get it. However, your Reverence, it's no use talking and worrying one's self. Will your honour tell me a little more about religion, to take off my mind from these pains and griefs?"

"I will with pleasure, John," replied the rector. "If I mistake not, we had finished all the sacraments except holy orders and matrimony."

"So matrimony is a sacrament," exclaimed the farmer. "Well, I need not ask your Reverence much about that, seeing I know as much of it as any man, considering all my troubles and vexations with the dame. I have heard it called a holy estate—what's the meaning of that?"

"Our Lord," replied the rector, "showed that it is holy and not to be condemned, by having graciously pleased to honour it with his first miracle at Cana of Galilee. It was instituted by God himself, and is a mysterious symbol of the union of Christ with His Church."

"And what grace is received in this sacrament?" asked the farmer.

"The married couple thereby receive grace to love each other in God," replied the rector, "to bear with each other's weaknesses, and to bring up their children well."

"There's a plaguy sight of unhappy marriages," rejoined the farmer, "notwithstanding this grace. The dame and me got precious little when we were joined, or she would not have so many crotchets now. How do you account for that, your Reverence?"

"I have nothing to say about Protestant marriages, but I know that even Catholic ones are seldom entered into with proper dispositions," replied the rector; "the greater part are actuated by motives of inclination or worldly interest, never consulting God in their choice. Besides, those who are not already in a state of grace—I mean, free from mortal sin—cannot expect benefit from this sacrament."

"That's a bad look out for Protestants," exclaimed the farmer, "seeing they can't get to confession, and as you have proved to me, there is no other way after baptism for getting washed from sin. But there are many miserable Catholic marriages as well as Protestant. That I can tell your Reverence, for I've seen them."

"Of course there must be, John; for bad Christians unfortunately are far more common than good: and Catholics who neglect their many means of grace deserve to be more punished than those who have not had the same advantages."

The farmer was going to reply, but the rector, interrupting him, continued, "We have taken so long, John, to discuss the seven sacraments, that I should like, if possible, to finish them this evening: so, if you please, we will go now to the sacrament of holy orders."

"That's for making ministers and priests, is it not?" said the farmer. "But I don't see very clearly why it is called a sacrament, it seems to me a ceremony rather."

"Holy orders," replied the rector, "are a visible sign of an invisible grace instituted by Christ. The outward part is the laying on of the bishop's hands, accompanied with prayer. In this manner the seven deacons were ordained, 'whom they set before the Apostles: and when they had prayed, they laid their hands on them.' (Acts vi. 6.) So also were Paul and Barnabas...........'The Holy Ghost said, Separate me Barnabas and Saul for the work whereunto I have called them. And when they had fasted and prayed, and laid their hands on them, they sent them away.' (Acts xiii. 3.)"

"But are you sure, Sir," asked the farmer, "that there was a particular grace given by this laying on of hands?"

"St. Paul declares so," answered the rector, "when he says to Timothy, 'Stir up the gift of God which is in thee by the putting on of my hands.' (2 Tim. i. 6.) As for the functions of the clergy, our Saviour pointed them out when he told his Apostles to go and teach all nations, to baptize them, and to instruct them in all he had commanded; also when he ordered them to consecrate the blessed Eucharist, and partake of it in commemoration of him, and when he gave them power to remit or to retain sins, which power, of course, they could not know how to exercise without hearing the confession of sinners."

"I beg your honour's pardon for interrupting you," said the farmer. "But, if God's ministers ought to do these things, there are few of them right ones now-a-days. There may be Protestant ministers that think they can remit sin like the Apostles; but they are precious scarce, for they never came across me, and I have known a good many of them. As for consecrating the Blessed Eucharist, if you mean by that the real body and blood of Christ, it is not very likely *they* do it, when they don't believe it is in their communion. And as for teaching all that Christ commanded, they don't do that either, for I never heard from them, nor nobody else, a great deal you have proved to me from Scripture. I begin to believe, Sir, that they are not right ministers—our ordinary English ones."

"I agree with your conclusions, John," replied Mr. Feversham; "the clergymen of the Church of England are not true priests, and dissenters do not even lay claim to the title. You gather this, among other reasons, because they do not preach all you learn from Scripture; I, on the other hand, would be of the same opinion with regard to their not being priests, even were their doctrines perfectly pure and scriptural. To be a priest, a man must be ordained by the successors of the Apostles; the English Church lays claim to this, but I deny its title. However, this is not a question to interest you."

"Whom do you call the successors of the Apostles, if you please, Sir?" asked the farmer.

"The bishops of the One Holy Catholic and Apostolic Church," replied the rector. "They who in regular succession, without break or interruption, received from the Apostles, by the imposition of hands, the grace of God, and those functions and powers which our Saviour conferred upon the Apostles and their successors when he promised to send upon them the Spirit of truth, and to be with them always even unto the end of the world."

"Then it is a great thing to be ordained by a true bishop," said the farmer. "But now that I think of it, I have heard dissenting ministers say, that there were no bishops in old times, and that they are a late invention."

"That is indeed a bold assertion, seeing that bishops are repeatedly mentioned in the New Testament," replied the rector. "You have only to read the Epistles to Timothy and Titus to see this. We gather from Revelations that the angels of the Seven Churches, to whom St. John wrote, had jurisdiction over their sees—in other words were bishops. So also were Timothy and Titus, for their power to ordain may be learned from Scripture. We find from the early fathers that St. Peter was the first bishop of Rome, St. James was made bishop of Jerusalem by the Apostles, and St. Polycarp was made bishop of Smyrna by St. John."

"But why are Catholic bishops under the pope?" asked Blount. "There was no pope in the Apostles' time."

"Before answering you, I shall ask you some questions. Have you not remarked," said the rector, "that many masters are hard to obey, for they are apt to give different orders? Or, to give you a simile, would you have liked, when you were a soldier, and fighting in an enemy's country, that the colonel of each regiment had been independent, and not under the general? Or, to make it still worse, that the officers were independent of the colonel?"

The farmer laughed.

"As to that, Sir," replied he, "I can only say that if each regiment had been independent, and taken its own way, the men would soon have been scattered; the officers, having different opinions, one would have gone this way, another that way. The enemy would have taken advantage of the disorder, and soon have cut us up. I would not have been alive this day to talk to your Reverence. No, no, Sir! Commend me to subordination to officers, and all being under one head, or else there would be the devil to pay, and no mistake."

"Just the same way, said the rector, "if the clergy were not under the bishops, and if the bishops were not under one spiritual head, there would be diversity of opinion and difference in judgment; all order would give way, and an infinity of different sects, as has been seen since the Reformation, would start up. Now, our Saviour desired that the Church should be One, as He and His Father are One: to maintain this unity the bishops of the Catholic Church are all under the bishop of Rome."

"A very wise regulation, I doubt not," said the farmer, "but is it scriptural?"

"You believe," replied the rector, "that our Saviour desired unity in his Church, and you have allowed that unity cannot be maintained under different heads, therefore one must be over the others."

"I think so;" answered the farmer. "And yet, if it were necessary, why did not Christ put one over the other Apostles for the same reason?"

"So he did," said Mr. Feversham. "He distinguished St. Peter above all the others, and promised that upon him he should build his church, also to him alone among all the apostles did he give the keys of the kingdom of heaven." (Matt. xvi. 18, 19.)

"Is not it curious, your Reverence, that these promises to St. Peter never struck me before!" said the farmer. "And yet they are very remarkable! But what connexion has that with the Catholic priests and bishops being under the Bishop of Rome?"

"Because the Pope or Bishop of Rome is St. Peter's successor, the apostle having been the first Bishop of that See," replied the rector.

"Oh! I see the thing now!" said the farmer, "howsomedever we must not go too quick! Wait till I'm sure of Peter being the head of the apostles, and it will be time enough then to speak of successors! It strikes me that Peter denying his master, is a reason against his being put over the rest."

"It might have been so with men, but certainly not with God. The greatest saints, as we find in scripture, have fallen into grievous faults and yet have been pardoned and accepted. You might as well urge David's sin, as a reason why he should not have been the founder of a royal race and the ancestor of the Messiah, as say that St. Peter's denial of his Master, of which he most bitterly repented, should have prevented the fulfilment of our Lord's prophetic promises."

"Well, I'll not dispute on that just now," replied the farmer, "I must have a talk with Mr. Sharples about it, for it is good to hear two sides of a question; and though it is likely I may come to your opinion at last, rector, yet a good thing is none the worse of being attacked, if it stand the battle. Before I go, Sir, will you just tell me shortly all your scripture proofs for St. Peter being the chief apostle?"

"I will with pleasure," said Mr. Feversham. "Matthew in numbering the apostles, terms him 'the *first* Simon who is called Peter.' (Matt. x. 2.) The other evangelists also, always give the first place to Peter. In fact, as Bossuet observes, Peter was the first to confess his faith in Christ; (Matt. xvi. 16.) the first to whom Christ appeared after his resurrection; (Luke xxiv. 34.) the first to preach the belief of this to the people; (Acts ii. 14.) the first to convert the Jews; (Acts ii. 37.) and the first to receive the Gentiles. (Acts x. 47.) Surely some distinction is implied in St. Peter being called three times by our Lord to declare that he *loved him*, and at last to say that he *loved him more than the other apostles;* likewise in being enjoined each time to feed Christ's lambs, and afterwards to *feed his sheep also.* Was not this constituting him the pastor or shepherd of Christ's flock? It is also particularly inferred that he should be over the other pastors, from the words of Jesus Christ, (Luke xxii. 31, 32,) 'Simon, Simon, behold Satan hath desired to have you that he may sift you as wheat: but I have prayed for thee, that thy faith fail not: and when thou art converted, strengthen thy brethren.' May there not be some mysterious meaning in Jesus entering Simon's ship in preference to that of James and John, to *teach the people out of it;* in the miraculous draught of fishes which followed, together with Christ's prophecy to Simon, '*from henceforth thou shalt catch men?*' "

"It may be so, your Reverence," said Blount, "but these last examples may or may not, mean a great deal. They are not particularly convincing, however, to my mind."

"Wait a little, John, and I shall give you what will better satisfy you, I trust," said Mr. Feversham. "You remember at our Saviour's first interview with St. Peter, he said: 'Thou art Simon, the son of Jona: thou shalt be called Cephas, which is by interpretation, a stone.' (John i. 42.) Well, after St. Peter's confession of our Lord's divinity, Jesus explains why he was called a stone or rock, in the words, 'Thou art Peter, and upon this *rock I will build my church,* and the gates of hell shall not prevail against it.' "

"That clearly proves," said the farmer, "that Peter was to be the foundation-stone of the church, and if it were to continue till the end of time, the foundation-stone must last too, so Peter or his representative must be in his place still!"

"Just what I wish to prove, John," said the rector, "but you interrupted me in the middle of a quotation. Jesus goes on to say, 'And I will give unto thee the keys of the kingdom of heaven; and whatsoever thou shalt bind on earth shall be bound in heaven; and whatsoever thou shalt lose on earth shall be loosed in heaven.'" (Matt. xvi. 18, 19.)

"That is an awful power, Sir, and almost too great for man to comprehend; said Blount: "if Christ had said less it would have come home to me more."

The good man now took his leave and hastened homewards, for it was getting late; and the rector then rejoined the ladies.

"I am so glad you are come, Mr. Feversham!" cried Miss Beauclerk, as he entered. "We are having a lecture from Mr. Harvey on antiquity! He has been laying claim to it for the English Church, which surely is bad policy; for it strikes me that novelty was the great recommendation of all the reformation churches!"

"Yes," said Mrs. Egremond, "if we are to venerate antiquity, let us go to Rome at once; but don't let us claim to our Church what I rejoice to think does not belong to it."

"Pardon me, ladies," rejoined Harvey, "I certainly think you have not studied the subject, or you would be of a different opinion! If there be any Church now in the world, which truly reverences antiquity, and pays a proper regard to it, it is our Church! The Romanists talk of antiquity, while *we* observe and follow it."*

* See Catena Patrum, No. 3.

"I don't agree with you, Harvey, said the rector. "Surely the sixth article supersedes the traditions of antiquity, when it says, 'Holy Scripture containeth all things necessary to salvation.'"

"The sixth article is certainly so worded," replied Harvey, "but I deny that this supersedes antiquity; for a canon set forth in the year 1571, forbids any thing preached from the pulpit 'to be religiously observed and believed by the people, but that which is agreeable to the doctrine of the Old or New Testament, and collected out of the same doctrine by the Catholic Fathers and the Bishops of the Ancient Church.' Thus you see veneration for Holy Scripture and reverence for antiquity are exquisitely combined!"

"If we are only allowed to interpret Scripture as the ancient fathers have done," said Mrs. Egremond, "all private liberty of judgment would be at an end, and we might as well have had no reformation at all."

"You suppose that I go farther than I intended," replied Harvey. "Preachers are not forbidden to interpret particular texts differently from the Fathers so long as they keep within the analogy of the faith, and do not presume to raise any new doctrine; indeed they may say any thing new as long as it is offered as opinion only or inferior truth, and not pressed on the people."

"You explain the thing cleverly, Mr. Harvey," said Miss Beauclerk, "since you venerate antiquity by sticking close to the fathers, while at the same time you leave excellent loop-holes for differing from them."

"What I admire most in the first reformers," said Mrs. Egremond, "is the boldness with which they burst through the shackles of antiquity and cast them away! Mad indeed are those who would resume them!"

"I agree with you, Mrs. Egremond," said Miss

Beauclerk; "for if Mr. Harvey is right, originality should generally be avoided as dangerous, and if the reformers had cast that aside, I fear the protestant religion would never have been established."

"The reformers may well say," replied Harvey, "'defend us from our friends!' No greater injury could be done them than to assert that they originated the religion they maintained!"

"Yes," rejoined the rector, "without either giving praise or blame to the reformers, there can be no doubt that the sure sign of a heretic is to originate the faith he maintains; for truth is one and cannot change; either truth must at one period have left the world, which cannot be the case consistently with Christ's promises, or it must bear the stamp of unchanging antiquity."

CHAPTER XXIV.

"I am joined in communion with your holiness, that is, with the chair of Peter. Upon that rock I know the Church is built, whoever eats the Lamb out of this house is profane, whosoever is not in (this) ark, shall perish in the deluge." St. Jerome.

"Mr. Sharples is inclined to think, your Reverence," said Blount to Mr. Feversham at their next meeting, "that Christ never intended any of the apostles to be over the rest; for He gave them no encouragement, when they contended which should be the greatest."

"Our Lord said," replied Mr. Feversham, "'If any man desire to be first, the same shall be last of all and servant of all;' but in these words he recommends humility in superiors, not equality of authority."

"At any rate," said Blount, "I know one text that preaches up equality: St. Paul says, 'In nothing am I behind the very chiefest Apostles, though I be nothing.'"

"You may see by the context," replied the rector, "that St. Paul is speaking here of his labours, doctrine, and miracles, which have nothing to do with the question if St. Peter had superior jurisdiction."

"Well, at any rate," said Blount, "Mr. Sharples pointed out to me how Paul withstood Peter to his face at Antioch, which does not look as if he thought him his superior."

"St. Peter in this case was to blame," said the rector, "because he withdrew himself from the table of the Gentiles for fear of offending the Jews, thereby giving scandal. But this does not take away from his superiority, for there are some occasions in which a superior committing a fault may be blamed by an inferior. In short, the arguments you adduce are all as nothing, when weighed in the balance with the clear promises of Christ, that on Peter he would build His church, and give him the keys of the kingdom of heaven."

"That may be true, Sir," said Blount, "and yet it is a satisfaction to hear objections answered. Mr. Sharples, Sir, always sets up Paul in opposition to Peter."

"That avails him little," said the rector; "he ought to remember that the bishop of Rome is the successor both of St. Peter and of St. Paul. Both honoured Rome by their preaching and their death."

"But are you sure, Sir," rejoined the farmer, "that the bishop of Rome has always been looked upon as the head of the rest? Did the first Christians think so?"

"Most undoubtedly," replied the rector, "the Church has never acknowledged any other as her chief pastor, and no other has ever claimed the title as St. Peter's successor. The disciple of the Apostles, St. Ignatius, in his Epistle to the Romans, calls the Church of Rome the presiding Church. St. Irenæus, who lived in the second century, calls the same,* 'The greatest and most ancient Church, founded by the two most glorious Apostles, Peter and Paul;' adding that all sectaries are confounded by the Roman tradition. 'For to this Church, by reason of its *more powerful principality*, it is necessary that every Church resort, in which the apostolical tradition has always been preserved by those that are in every place.' St. Cyprian, in the third century, writing to Pope Cornelius, calls Rome 'the chair of St. Peter, and the principal church from which the unity of priesthood is arisen.'"†

* L. 3. C. 3.

† St. Cyprian's 55th Epistle to Pope Cornelius. In further proof of the supremacy of the bishop of Rome, see also St. Optatus bishop of Milevis, in his second book against Parmenianus the Donatist bishop of Carthage, where he thus addresses himself to his adversary: "You cannot pretend to be ignorant that Peter held first the bishop's chair in the city of Rome, in which Peter as head of all the Apostles sat—in which single chair unity might be maintained by all, lest the rest of the Apostles should each one claim his own separate chair. So that he is now a schismatic and an offender, who against this single chair erects any other. In this one chair, which is the first of the properties of the Church, Peter first sat; to him succeeded Linus, to him Clement, &c. Give you now an account of the origin of your chair, you who claim to yourselves the holy Church." And St. Jerom, writing to Pope Damasus, Epist. 57. tells him, "I am joined in communion with your holiness, that is, with the chair of Peter; upon that rock I know the Church is built; whoever eats the lamb out of this house is profane; whosoever is not in this ark, shall perish in the deluge," &c. St. Augustin, in his psalm against the Donatists, thus addresses them, "Come, brethren, if you have a mind to be ingrafted in the vine. It is a pity to see you lie lopped off in this manner from the stock. Reckon up the prelates in the very see of Peter, and in that order of fathers, see which has succeeded him. This is the rock over which the proud gates of hell prevail not." And in his 162nd epistle, he tells the Donatists, "That in the see of Rome the principality of the apostolic chair was ever acknowledged."

St. Prosper, in his dogmatic poem against the enemies of grace, calls

"Thank you, rector," said the farmer; "I'll take it on your word that the Church has always considered the Roman Bishop as the head, for your word is as good to me as that of these old folks. And now I should like to know what is the good of spending so much time in talking over the Bishop of Rome? It seems to me there are other things more necessary."

"There can be nothing more necessary, John,"

Rome "The see of St. Peter, which being made to the world the head of pastoral dignity, rules by religion all that she possesses, not by her arms." And to the same effect St. Leo the great, in his first sermon upon St. Peter and St. Paul, thus addresses himself to Rome, "These are they who have advanced thee to this glory, that being made the head of the world, by being St. Peter's see, thou hast a wider extent of religious empire than of earthly dominion. For though by thy many victories thou hast extended thy dominions far and near by sea and land, yet that which has been subdued by the labour of thy arms, is not so much as that which has been made subject to thee by Christian peace." All these fathers whom we have quoted, lived within four hundred years after the passion of Christ. The supremacy of Rome has been acknowledged by many general councils, as by that of Ephesus in the sentence of deposition against Nestorius, anno 431; the general council of Chalcedon in the epistle of St. Leo, anno 451; the general council of Constantinople, anno 680, in the epistle to Pope Agatho; not to mention many general councils of later date. Though as Pope Gelasius in the council of Rome of seventy bishops, anno 494, has declared, "The Roman see hath not its pre-eminence over other churches from any ordinances of councils, but from the words of our Lord and Saviour in the gospel, Thou art Peter, and upon this rock I will build my church, &c." The bishop of Rome has in every age since the days of the apostles exercised supremacy over other churches. Pope Victor in the second century, threatened to excommunicate bishops who kept Easter at undue time, (Eusebius L. 5. Histor. Eccl. c. 24.) Though he relented at the remonstrance of St. Irenæus and others, yet he was never charged with usurping authority which did not belong to him. In the third century, St. Cyprian, (Epist. 67.) wrote to Pope Stephen, desiring him to despatch letters to the people of Arles, authorizing them to depose Marcianus their bishop, and substitute another in his place. In the fourth century, Pope Julius cited St. Athanasius bishop of Alexandria, the second patriarch of the Church to his council at Rome, to answer the accusations of his adversaries, who accordingly did appear and was cleared. (See St. Athanasius's apology against the Arians.) The same pope restored by his authority to their sees from whence they had been deposed by the Eusebians, St. Paul bishop of Constantinople, St. Lucius bishop of Adrianople, Marcellus bishop of Ancyra in Galatia, and Asclepas bishop of Gaza in Palestine, as Sozomenus (L. 3. C. 8.) words it, "because by reason of the dignity of his see the care of all belonged to him." In the fifth century, Pope Celestine deputed St. Cyril patriarch of Alexandria, as his delegate to excommunicate Nestorius patriarch of Constantinople. (Tom. 3. Concil. Labbe, p. 349.) In the same century, St. John Chrysostome and St. Flavian, both patriarchs of Constantinople, unjustly deposed by councils in the East appealed from their judgment, the one to Pope Innocent the first, the other to Pope Leo the Great. Not to mention many other instances in all these centuries.

replied the rector. "Christ prayed that his Church might be one as he and his Father are one; to preserve this unity, he appointed St. Peter and his successors to be its head. From St. Peter, on whom the Church was founded, all authority must flow; they therefore who refuse to acknowledge the Bishop of Rome as supreme head, break that unity desired by our Lord, and become schismatics."

The farmer considered a few minutes and then observed, "For the life of me, I can't feel the interest you take in the Bishop of Rome, and I would rather talk now, if your Reverence please, of another thing. I was a puzzling myself yesterday about something I saw in the communion service of the Common Prayer-Book. It says in the creed there, 'I believe One Catholic and Apostolic Church.' Now I want to know why they say they believe in the Catholic Church when they don't belong to it?"

"They say they do belong to it, John, though in reality they do not," replied the rector. "However, this is a subject into which we ought to enter more closely, and I am glad you have proposed it: particularly as it is connected with the topic we have just been discussing. The true Church is One, Catholic, and Apostolic, as is proved by the creed you have quoted. Let us now see if the Church of England fulfils these conditions."

"The creed saying it, Sir, is not enough for me, I should like first to get Scripture to prove that the Church must be One, Catholic, and Apostolic—and after that we might see if the Protestant churches come up to what is required."

"Certainly, John," said the rector. "We shall therefore begin with the unity of the Church. Christ says, (John x. 16,) 'And other sheep I have which are not of this fold; them also I must bring, and they shall hear my voice, and there shall be *one* fold and *one* Shepherd.' St. Paul likewise writes, 'So we being many are *one body* in Christ, and every one members one of another.' (Romans xii. 5.) 'There is one body and one spirit, even as ye are called in one hope of your calling; one Lord, one faith, one baptism.' (Ephesians iv. 4, 5.) And Christ prays not for his apostles alone, 'but for them also which shall believe on me through their word, that they all *may be one.*' (John xvii. 20. &c.) Without unity the Church or kingdom of Christ could not long subsist, as you allowed in some measure the other day; for, 'Every kingdom divided against itself is brought to desolation, and every city or house divided against itself shall not stand.' " (Matt. xii. 25.)

"All these texts prove, if I understand you rightly," said the farmer, "that Christ desired there should be only one Church instead of many."

"Yes," replied the rector, "where unity is wanting, the Church of Christ cannot exist."

"Then, if we believe our Saviour," continued Blount, "Episcopalians, Presbyterians, Methodists, Independents, besides dozens of more sects whom I can't name, must have but a poor chance, since at the best only one of them can be right! Mr. Sharples wanted me to lump them all together and consider them in a bundle as the Church of Christ; but our Saviour could not possibly have intended such differences when He prayed that they all might *be one!*"

"I quite agree with you, John," said the rector, "and the more closely we investigate the subject, the more do we detect this want of unity. Not only are the different Protestant sects at variance with each other, but in each one the members disagree among themselves on the most important points. Take, for example, the English Church; what opposite opinions are held by her ministers according as they belong to the evangelical or high-church party! And yet all appear equally cherished within her bosom! The most conflicting doctrines are openly taught in different parishes, with regard to justification, election, and sanctification! One party in the English Church considers the Bible to be the only rule of faith; but this is denied as a principle by another, who assert that it is merely an opinion in the Church, though not universally received.* Some divines enforce the doctrine of episcopal authority, and enlarge much on the dignity of the priesthood; others leave it in the back ground, content not to avail themselves of it, perhaps because they disbelieve in it. Some of the clergy, such as the famous Archbishop Laud, have been considered by others of their own persuasion as little better than papists; and if Laud did not himself, some bishops of his time at least, treated with Rome to bring about a reconciliation; we will not say whether there may not be others at the present day who follow their example! Of the Evangelical party, on the other hand, there have always been many to admire the Geneva discipline and desire a greater simplicity of worship; were their principles carried out, the sacraments would be undervalued and episcopal ordination would be considered an empty name! But indeed I have said enough to show you that unity of opinion is not to be found in the Anglican Church."

"But, Sir," said the farmer, "though I regret as much as any one the differences of opinion among Christians, yet I think you are may-be too hard on people. No two human beings can agree on every point, and I think you look for a union of sentiment in the Church of England, which I doubt if you will find among Catholics, with all their boasting!"

"Jesus Christ taught all that is necessary to be believed," replied the rector, "and we peril our salvation if we differ from Him. Therefore in this matter we must give no play to human nature, as you call it, but submit our judgment to what has been revealed. The Catholic Church teaches what has

* See British Critic, p. 384.

been taught from the beginning since the days of the apostles; she has pronounced definitively on all points necessary to salvation, including the subjects disputed in the Church of England, which I mentioned just now. He that refuses to agree with her decisions is not a Catholic, and is thrust from the pale of her communion; those alone who implicitly believe what she teaches are Catholics, therefore surely I am right in affirming that among them there is unity."

"Yes, Sir," said the farmer, "of course you are; but I think it a very hard thing indeed that all Catholics must believe whatever the Church teaches; there ought to be some room left for private difference of opinion!"

"Well, John," said the rector, "although you do not think yourself obliged to believe whatever the Catholic Church teaches, yet, in spite of yourself, you have come round to her opinion in several very important matters. Supposing that we discuss all her doctrines in their turn, should you find in each that her opinion is the best, and most reasonable, according to your private judgment, then perhaps you may adopt the belief in her infallibility."

"Well, time will show," replied the farmer, laughing. "You gave me a hit on this same subject before, if I mind right. There is one thing at least in which I agree with your Reverence—that the words of Scripture must have a meaning, and were not intended to fall to the ground; however, I'll take my time and consider the matter. The words 'one fold,' 'one Shepherd,' 'one faith,' 'one body in Christ,' are all very striking, and most especially so is our Saviour's prayer that they all may be one."

The farmer rose to go away, and then, as if changing his mind, hesitated and said, "If your Reverence be'nt in a hurry, I could sit awhile yet and get some more instruction. Would you tell me, Sir, what is the meaning of Catholic, and why the Church must be Catholic?"

"Sit down again, John," replied Mr. Feversham, "I have plenty of time. The word Catholic means universal, which implies three different things; a *universality of time*, for the true Church must be the Church of all ages; a *universality of place*, because it must be the Church of all nations; and a *universality of truth*, because it must be for ever orthodox and teach all truth. The name of Catholic is that by which the true Church has been known since the very times of the apostles, and whenever heretics have arisen, introducing some new form of belief, they have been obliged to take another name, to distinguish themselves from the great body of believers. It is true that some Anglican divines usurp the term Catholic for their own party; but it is easy for an unprejudiced person to decide to which church the appellation really belongs. They are the true proprietors of the name, who always take it, are commonly known by it, and are even called it by their greatest enemies. They, on the contrary, have no right to the title who only claim it occasionally, to serve some purpose, and are known to the world by a different appellation. St. Jerome says, in his dialogue against the Luciferians, 'To tell you briefly and plainly the sentiments of my soul, we must live and die in that Church, which having been founded by the apostles subsists to this day. But if in any place you hear some that are called christians, taking a name not from our Lord Jesus Christ, but from some other, as Marcionites, Valentinians, Mountainers, Field-conventiclers, (Campenses,) know that such are no Church of Christ, but a synagogue of Antichrist............Nor let them flatter themselves that they quote the Scriptures for their tenets; since the devil also quoted Scripture, which consists not in the reading, but in the right understanding.' Instead of Marcionites, &c., we might perhaps substitute the names, Episcopalians, Presbyterians, Wesleyans, Calvinists, Lutherans, &c."

"I'll remember all this, Sir," interrupted the farmer, "whenever I hear that part of the creed, 'I believe in the holy Catholic Church'—and I'll just ask the Protestants, since they believe in it, why they don't get the name? And now, Sir, will you speechify a little about the three kinds of universality? I count this better than hearing your Reverence in the pulpit, for it is a great satisfaction to me, being able to give you a word back now and then!"

"The true Church," replied the rector, "must subsist during all ages, as we find from Scripture. 'In the days of these kings, shall the God of heaven set up a kingdom which never shall be destroyed: and the kingdom shall not be left to other people, but it shall break in pieces and consume all these kingdoms, and it shall stand for ever." (Dan. ii. 44.)

"If your honour please," said the farmer, "I can quote Scripture myself for it. Christ said to Peter that the gates of hell should not prevail against his Church; which I'm sure was as much as promising that it should always stand firm and true! And I'll tell you another text besides, rector, to show you that I don't forget your instructions; Christ said to his apostles, that is, to his Church, 'Lo I am with you alway even unto the end of the world!'"

"Very well indeed, John," replied Mr. Feversham.

"But I am not done yet, Sir, at all," continued Blount, "I've got an objection to my own texts. How can the Church have continued firm and true, when, as Mr. Sharples tells me, there have been what they call councils, always adding something new to her doctrines every now and then? That is a terrible thing against you, Sir!"

"In saying so, Blount, Mr. Sharples was guilty of a gross mis-statement. The Catholic Church never claimed authority to create new doctrines; on the contrary, the general councils were convoked in order to define what had been universally believed by the Church from the beginning, and thus to eradicate and cast away all approaches to novelty, which, as truth is unchangeable, must necessarily always be false. These general councils were the bulwarks of the Church against heresy; whenever a daring innovator arose to introduce novel theories or self-willed opinions, a convocation was summoned of the chief clergy and bishops throughout the whole christian world; they then, with the Pope at their head, proceeded to examine into the doctrines of the apparent innovator, to see how far they were in accordance with the faith handed down to them by their predecessors. In cases where the Church had not previously decided, they bore testimony to what had been always taught in their respective churches from the beginning. From these decisions there could be no appeal, and henceforth to teach a contrary doctrine was heresy. Thus you see that the councils so far from *creating new doctrines,* only put in a more definite light the universal and ancient tradition of the Catholic Church."

"Well, I'm glad you have explained it, Sir; for I'll tell Mr. Sharples about it next time I see him. And now I want to know why you say the Catholic Church is the Church of all nations?"

"Because she has in every age converted infidel nations by her missionaries to the faith of Christ, and to this day sends her clergy into every country for that end."

"Does it say in the Bible, Sir," interrupted the farmer, "that this is a mark of the true Church?"

"Yes," replied the rector, "you will find in Isaiah xlix. 22, 23: 'Thus saith the Lord God, Behold I will lift up mine hand to the Gentiles, and set up my standard to the people: and they shall bring thy sons in their arms, and thy daughters shall be carried upon their shoulders. And kings shall be thy nursing fathers, and queens thy nursing mothers,' &c. And in the 54th chapter, verse 3: 'For thou shalt break forth on the right hand and on the left: and thy seed shall inherit the Gentiles,' &c. Also 60th chapter, verse 3: 'And the Gentiles shall come to thy light, and kings to the brightness of thy rising;' and in the 11th and 12th verses: 'Therefore thy gates shall be open continually: they shall not be shut day nor night, that men may bring unto thee the forces of the Gentiles, and that their kings may be brought.' Isaiah and Micah also term the true Church the mountain of the house of the Lord, to which all nations are to flow. It was also signified in Daniel ii. 34, 35, by the stone hewn out of the mountain without hands, that 'became a great mountain and filled the whole earth;' or, as the prophet interpreted in the 44th verse, 'a kingdom which shall never be destroyed, and the kingdom shall not be left to other people, but it shall break in pieces and consume all these kingdoms, and it shall stand for ever.' You see from these texts, John, that the conversion of kings and nations is a certain mark by which to find out the true Church."

"That's all pretty clear," said Blount; "but now, if your Reverence pleases, we will go to facts: and so I ask what nations the Catholic Church has converted."

"See in the first age," replied the rector, "what the Apostles did, particularly St. Peter and St. Paul, the founders of the Church of Rome."

"I don't think it any particular glory to the Catholics what the Apostles did," muttered the farmer in a low voice; "since all Christian Churches, I doubt not, will lay claim to that merit."

"In the second century," continued the rector, unnoticing the interruption, "great conversions were wrought in Africa, Gaul, &c.; and king Lucius with his people were converted in Britain by missionaries from Rome. In the third age the Goths and other barbarous nations were brought to the true faith; and in the fourth age we find the Ethiopians, the Iberians,

&c., converted. Were you to repeat this to a Protestant, he might perhaps answer, that these things occurred when the faith of the Church was still uncorrupted, and ask, did these things continue in after-times. I reply, *yes;* the same blessing has continued with the holy Catholic and Apostolic Church from these remote ages, even unto this day. In the fifth century St. Palladius, sent from Rome by pope Celestine, converted the Scots.* St. Patrick, sent by the same pope, was the apostle of Ireland.† In the same century the French, with their king Clodovæus, were brought over to the kingdom of Christ by St. Remigius of Rhemes and St. Vedastus of Arras. In the sixth century St. Ninianus, a Briton, trained up at Rome in the Christian faith, converted the southern Picts to Christ.‡ St. Columba or Columkil brought over the northern Picts or Highlanders to the Christian religion, and, notwithstanding a mistake he fell into from want of information (not from contumacy) about the proper time of celebrating Easter, was a faithful member of the Church, and is honoured by her as a saint. In the same century St. Rupert converted the Bavarians; and St. Columbanus, and his disciple St. Gallus, converted Suabia.§ Towards the end of the same century St. Augustin the monk, sent by St. Gregory the Great, brought over Ethelbert, the most powerful of the English Saxon kings, with his people, to the faith of Christ."||

"Will your Reverence just stop a moment," in-

* See St. Prosper adversus Collat—and the Centuriators of Magdeburg, Centur. 5. Col. 18, &c.

† See the Centuriators, Centur. 5. 1426; and Centur. 6. Col. 754, 755. Where they acknowledge him to have been a man famous for sanctity and miracles, and to have even raised the dead to life, and yet charge him with Popery.

‡ Bede L. 3. Hist. c. 4.

§ See Heylin's Cosmography, p. 431., and the Atlas Geography, vol. 1. p. 438.

|| Bede's Ecclesiastical History, lib. 1. chap. 25, 26.

terrupted the farmer, with difficulty smothering a yawn, "can you give examples of the same kind for every hundred years down to the present time?"

"Yes," replied Mr. Feversham, "what about it?"

"Nothing particular, Sir," said Blount, whose face got red, "except indeed that I'm mortal tired, and would take the rest on your word, if so be as your honour would stop. And perhaps next day I come, you'll tell me what upshot you would draw from all these grand conversions?"

"Very well, John," said Mr. Feversham, "come back the first day you like, and I will answer any questions you choose to put."*

* "In the seventh century the light of the Gospel was further propagated among the English by St. Paulinus, who baptized Edwin, king of the Northumbrians; by St. Felix, who converted the East Angles; by St. Birinus, who converted the West Saxons; by St. Aidan, St. Chad, St. Wilfrid, &c.: so that, in a short space of time, the whole nation was gained over to Christ, and no people was more devoted than the English to the See Apostolic, from which they received the faith. In the same century St. Kilianus, first bishop of Wirtsbourg, an Irish monk sent by pope Conon, converted Gosbert, duke of Franconia, with his people. (Atlas Geog. p. 438.) And St. Willibrod, an Englishman, (ordained bishop, and sent by pope Sergius,) converted the Netherlands. (Atlas Geog. p. 438.) In the eighth century St. Wilfrid, an Englishman, commonly known by the name of Boniface, ordained and sent to preach by pope Gregory II., converted Hesse, Thuringia, Westphalia, and Saxony; and is usually esteemed the apostle of Germany. (Atlas Geog. p. 438.) In the ninth century St. Ansgarius, a monk of Corby, and the first archbishop of Hamburg and Bremen, general apostle of the northern nations, converted Holstein, and carried the light of the Gospel into Sweden. (Heylin's Cosmog. p. 484, 501.) In the same century, St. Cyril and St. Methodius, Greeks by nation, sent by pope Adrian II., converted the Sclavonians, Moravians, and Bohemians. (See Martinus Polonus, ad annum 859; Eneas Silvius. Hist. Boem. l. i. c. 13; Martinus Chronerus de Rebus Polon. l. iii.) It was St. Methodius that obtained leave from pope John VIII. to celebrate the liturgy in the Slavonic tongue................

"In the same century the Bulgarians also, with their king, were admitted into the pale of Christ's Church. See the answers of pope Nicholas I. to the queries of this prince and his people, newly converted to Christianity. Tom. viii. Concil. Labbe. In the tenth century the Danes were converted by St. Poppo, first bishop of Arthusen. (Heylin's Cosmog. p. 484.) The Goths in Sweden by St. Sigifrid, an Englishman, about the year 980. (Atlas Geog. vol. i. p. 208.) The Poles and Prussians, in part, by St. Adalbert, archbishop of Prague. (See the Atlas Geog. p. 229 and 248.) In the same age St. Bruno and St. Bonifacius, two apostolic preachers of the Roman communion, laboured with great fruit in the conversion of the Russians of Poland. And, about the same time, the Moscovites were brought over to Christ by the Greeks, Wolodinar, the first Christian czar, being baptized anno 988. (See Le Brun's Dissertations upon the

CHAPTER XXV.

"I hae been tellt that a popish priest maun sing a Latin bravura every day, an' sit on ashes every Wednesday an' Friday."

My Old Nurse.

MEANWHILE Mrs. Benson's sermons were received with great enthusiasm by the Methodists of the neighbourhood, and although Mr. Longab had returned, that gentleman, to gratify popular feeling, still permitted her occasionally to use his pulpit. It was on a Monday evening, after having held forth on the

Liturgies, t. ii. p. 412.) Nicholas II. was at that time patriarch of Constantinople, and in communion with the see of Rome.

"Le Brun informs us that though the Moscovites were converted by the Greeks, it was nearly four hundred years before they joined them in their schism. About the beginning of the eleventh century, the Hungarians were converted under their king, St. Stephen. (Atlas Geog. p. 1635.) And the Norwegians under Olaus III. anno 1055, the English assisting in the work, says Dr. Heylin; (Cosmog. p, 484.) who adds that they, relapsing for the most part to their former idolatry, were finally regained to Christianity by the means of pope Adrian IV. about the year 1156. The Islanders also were converted in this century by Olaus Erugger, the pious. (Atlas Geog. p. 145.) In the latter end of the twelfth century, Courland, Samogitia, and Livonia received the faith of Christ by the preaching of St. Meinardus, (Heylin, p. 524; Atlas Geog. p. 262, 263.) In the thirteenth century, pope Innocent IV. sent the Dominicans to preach to the Tartars. (Vincent, l. xxx.) In the fourteenth century Lithuania was brought over to the Christian faith under Wadislaus Jagello, about the year 1388. (Heylin's Cosmog. p. 524.) In the latter end of this century, and the beginning of the fifteenth, flourished St. Vincent Ferrerius, who, by his preaching and miracles, converted about twenty-five thousand Jews and Moors. (St. Antonin, 3 part. Hist. Tit. 23, c. viii.) In the fifteenth century were converted the inhabitants of the Canary Islands, &c. And the Portuguese preached the faith of Christ with great success in the kingdoms of Congo and Angola. (Heylin, Cosmog. p. 996, 998. So far of the times before the pretended Reformation, and of preachers certainly joined in communion with Rome. Nor has the hand of God been shortened in these latter ages; but it has in a great measure repaired the loss which the old religion had sustained by the unnatural rebellion of her children in Europe, by the conversion of many millions of infidels in all preceding day with her usual eloquence, that Mrs. Benson entered Jacob's shop as he was busily engaged folding up different articles, and putting every thing in order for the night. The weather was uncertain and showery, and a few minutes before her arrival, a gentleman, evidently a stranger, wrapped in a large cloak so that it was difficult to discern his features, had taken refuge from the rain, and after purchasing a trifle, patiently sat down to wait till the sky should become more clear.

"Good evening Mr. Hogg," exclaimed the lady as she advanced towards him. "How's your soul?"

"Dry, barren, and unfruitful as usual," sighed

other parts of the world. In the sixteenth century St. Francis Xavier carried the light of the Gospel to the coasts of Malabar, Travancor, and the Fishery in the East Indies, to the Molucca Islands, and the Islands Del Moro and Japan; converting by his miracles many hundred thousands of these barbarians to Christ. His followers and successors converted the kings of Bungo and Arima, &c.; so that the Church of Japan counted no less than six hundred thousand Christians; and stood for a long time the shock of the most violent persecutions, in which innumerable martyrs suffered with a piety and constancy not unworthy the primitive times; till all communication being cut off, and no means left of any priests coming amongst them, the public profession of the faith was at last extinguished. In the same age, the Spaniards having settled themselves in the Philippine Isles, preached Christ to the infidels there with such success that, according to the account in 'Lettres Edifiantes,' (Recueil xi. Let. 3.) there was at the time they were published ten hundred thousand Christians, some said two millions, in those islands. During the sixteenth and seventeenth centuries the missionaries also made great progress in diverse other parts of Asia; as in China, where there are great numbers of Christians spread through different provinces of that vast empire. In the kingdoms of Tonquin and Cochin China, where there are numerous churches in spite of persecution; in the kingdom of Madurè, and other provinces of India on this side the Ganges, where the number of Christians increases daily; in the kingdom of Thibet, and in the Marian islands, where the inhabitants now are all Christians. As to Africa, the conversions have chiefly been upon the coast of Zanguebar; in the great empire of Monomotapa; in the kingdom of Sierra Leon, where F. Bareira, the Jesuit, baptized the king, anno 1607, &c. In America, Martinus a Valentia, an apostolical preacher of the order of St. Francis, with twelve companions, converted so great a number of the Indians in the empire of Mexico, that, if we may believe Thomas a Jesu, (De Conversione Omnium Gentium, l. iv. c. 5.) there was not one of this number who had not baptized a hundred thousand between the years 1524 and 1531. In the same century St. Lewis Bertrand, a Dominican friar eminent for sanctity and miracles, preached the faith to several provinces of South America, and penetrated into the very heart of Peru, converting an innumerable multitude of barbarians. His labours have been seconded by those of others; so that now the inhabitants of Terra Firma, of New Granada, of New

Jacob, "but as I hope without any more dangerous ailment, unless it be a slight touch of dyspepsia, owing to the strong meat you give us in your sublime discourses. And how do you find your soul, Mrs. Benson? I should say from the way in which you hold forth, that it was in a fine healthy state, and thriving mightily."

"So-so, Jacob, only so-so; it is but poorly and in a weakly state," replied the lady. "My wings are clipped and my energies kept down by worldly cares. I have not been able yet, Jacob, to find a purchaser for my houses, at least not one that will offer me a fair price; for I am not a person to be content with less than the value of the thing I part with. This worries me, and truly I am filled with anxiety, and my heart burns within me when I depict to myself the desolate and lone condition of that poor Ethiope Queen, pining for my society and sighing for intellectual privy counsellors. Gladly would I fly to her at once, on the wings of a dove, or by rail-road or steam, or any other way it pleased Providence, so that it was not in a balloon, which certainly has to do with the

Andalusia, of Popazan, and of Peru, are in a manner all Christians. About the middle of the same century, the Portuguese Jesuits laid the foundation of a flourishing church in Brazil, which in a short time increased to such a degree as to take in no small part of the inhabitants of this vast country, who are at present zealous Christians. The religious of the same order also penetrated into the heart of Paraguay, and inviting the barbarians out of their woods and mountains, have both civilized them and made them Christians. The cross of Christ was also prosperously erected in the great kingdoms of Tucuman and Chili, where the bishop of Imperiali alone had, according to Collier's Historical Dictionary, fourscore thousand Indians under his care. In North America the most remarkable conversions were made in the seventeenth century in New Mexico and the adjoining parts, and in Canada, where the French omitted no care to bring over the Indians to the faith of Christ; not to speak of a settlement in California, and many other missions in all parts of the infidel world."

The preceding is taken nearly word for word from an old book—"Grounds of the Old Religion, by a Convert," chap. vi. published in 1742.

For the present flourishing state of Catholic missions throughout the world, we refer our readers to the seventh lecture, volume first, of "Lectures on the principal doctrines and practices of the Catholic Church," by the Right Rev. Dr. Wiseman; also to the "Annals of the Propagation of the Faith."

prince of the powers of the air; but you see, Jacob, as you say yourself, I must sell my little property first to pay my passage, and make a good figure at the Pickmanbone islands, besides, I ought to have some money to put in the investment you spoke of."

"Very true," replied Jacob, "nothing can be done without money. Make haste, sell your houses, put the proceeds into my hands, and I will purchase your outfit; so that you and your children may be equipped in a style befitting your rank to play a distinguished part at her majesty's court. But I say,"—and here Jacob lowered his voice to a whisper, so that the stranger who was in the shop could not possibly hear him—"I say, don't say a word of this either to Mr. Longab or to any other of the connexion. The truth is, *he* is jealous of you, jealous of your superior talents, your thrilling eloquence, and your appalling imagination. Besides, he has a young woman in his eye, with a good figure, and who is a powerful speaker like yourself, whom he has a mind to set up in opposition to you, and raise to be his wife. Did he know of this brilliant opening at her black majesty's court, he would not hesitate a moment to bespeak it for her."

"Goodness gracious, what can I do, Jacob," exclaimed Mrs. Benson. "My heart-strings, that were so near broken at the death of the dear departed late Gabriel Benson, would snap at once, did I meet with this new disappointment. What would you advise me to do? anything rather than that the Mrs. Longab that's to be, should get this appointment."

"Do," cried Jacob, "why *do* nothing, but sell your houses quickly, and don't haggle so about prices. Sacrifice a little for the sake of ready money, and above all things, keep your mouth close and your tongue tied, and don't let out the secret."

"I will, I will," said Mrs. Benson, "as soon as I get anything like a reasonable price."

"You'd better not shilly shally," cried Jacob;

"The black queen is a woman of ardent passions and strong affections; there's a vacancy in her heart at present, which if you don't occupy quickly, will be filled up.......Or at least," he continued, "if in expectation of you she should keep that treasure-store of loving affection which bubbles up continually in her glowing heart—if, I say, for your sake she should keep it pent up and confined, the consequences might be serious for her health, or what would be worse, (but perhaps more likely,) she'd take to dram-drinking! People of that strong intellectual cast, with volcano affections corked up as it were, always do."

Mrs. Benson walked up and down the shop for some minutes in great agitation, and unmindful of the presence of the stranger, who was now busily engaged in reading a small and thick bound volume which he had taken out of his pocket.

"Well, Jacob," at last she ejaculated, "I'll take into consideration what you have said. And now I'll ask your advice about another thing. What Romanistical subject shall I choose for my next sermon, and what little tit-bits of facts will you give me to put into it?"

"Why, I don't know," replied Jacob, "my mind is so taken up with that poor unfortunate black queen, that I can think of nothing. My imagination is not spirity enough this evening to invent facts."

"Come now, good Jacob," said the lady, "give us any little thing you remember, sure it is not necessary to invent, when popery with all its abominations lies invitingly before you."

"That is true," replied Jacob with a thoughtful air; "what say you then to the strange tongue, Latin I mean, in which the priests preach to the people?"

"And do all Romans understand Latin?" inquired the lady in amazement.

"Oh, no," answered Jacob, "and that is the beauty of the system, for the priests can say what monstrosities they like in their sermons, without fear of being understood. That is what makes popery so inviting to the ignorant, because all the things hard of belief are clothed in Latin. Besides, you know, 'out of the abundance of the heart the mouth speaketh,' and a priest's heart is so black, that if he were ever to speak in English, all men would be so horrified that they would flee before him like young canaries when a cat is coming, so no wonder he speaks Latin. They tell a strange story in London about the blackness of a priest's heart. It is said, that in a private museum belonging to a distinguished orator of Exeter Hall, there is a priest's heart preserved in a bottle of spirits, and that this heart is now, and always was, blacker than the darkest midnight. They say that a raven looks quite brown beside it, and that the owner of the largest dye-works in London has offered repeatedly a thousand guineas for leave to analyze that heart, in order to discover from it a new black dye, that might supersede all that has ever been known of corbean-mourning!"

"Wonderful, most wonderful," exclaimed Mrs. Benson; "have you any more facts as interesting, for these are what I delight in?"

"As many as you like," replied Jacob, warming with the subject. "You never heard perhaps of the atrocities practised while asking little infants their catechism; the poor innocents are questioned and must answer in Latin, which of course they don't understand; and whenever one of them gives a wrong answer, instead of the good old birch system which used to be in my young days, the master pricks him on the back with a lancet in the form of a cross, or else in the coldest day in winter puts him into a shower-bath of what they call holy water, which, as you perhaps know already, is at all seasons colder than ice."

"That is inhuman indeed," cried Mrs. Benson,

"and altogether beats hollow the cruel uncle, that murdered the robin-red-breasts in the wood."

"And if you are fond of historical subjects Madam," continued Jacob, "you may mention how in all ages the Church of Rome has been in the habit of butchering innocent Protestants, because they would not converse with each other in Latin, preferring to do so in their mother tongue, English. The truth is, that if it had not been for the glorious reformation, the English language would have been forgotten, and we should all have been reduced to speak by signs like the monkeys."

At this piece of information, a stifled laugh was heard from the corner where the stranger was sitting, but on Jacob looking round he appeared so absorbed in the study of his book that Mr. Hogg proceeded, thinking that he must have been mistaken. "Then every priest," he continued, "has a thing secured with seven patent locks that they call a Breviary. He carries this about with him wherever he goes; most people think it a book of prayer, but there they are mistaken. It is a box with a false binding made to look like a book, and it contains whips and things for twisting the joints; in short, it is a pocket edition of all that is necessary for a priest in the confessional, to inflict penance on his penitents before he gives them the forgiveness of their sins. The little Breviary-box also contains a code of secret instructions for the priest's guidance when he has to do with uproarious sinners; but of that I shall say nothing, for they are too dreadful for man to utter or woman either!"

"Did you ever see a breviary, Mr. Hogg?" asked the stranger, now for the first time speaking and advancing towards him; "for if, as I suppose from your utter ignorance of what it contains, you have not, I shall be happy to show you the one I now hold in my hand."

Mr. Hogg, who felt quite confused at this awkward

interruption, mechanically stretched out his hand for the volume. It was a small and neat though thick little book, bound in black leather. On opening it, it appeared closely printed, and here and there in red ink.

"Lord, have mercy on us!" cried Mrs. Benson, as she peered over Jacob's shoulder, "not one word can I understand. That's doubtless the unknown tongue, as spoken on the seven hills at the court of the old woman of Babylon!"

"And now, my good friends," continued the stranger, "you must allow me to give you a little information in my turn on the subjects you have just been discussing, which, as I am a Catholic priest myself, I ought to be fully competent to do."

At this Jacob started and seemed very uncomfortable, while Mrs. Benson drew herself up, and looked virtuously indignant.

"Catholics," the gentleman said, "have never put Protestants to death for not knowing Latin, the greater part of their own body being in the same predicament; neither are children catechised in that language, but, on the contrary, are instructed in religion in their mother tongue. The breviary, which is used daily by the clergy, is a collection of psalms and prayers; and high testimony has been borne to its excellence by many divines of the Church of England. It is not the custom for Catholic priests to preach to their congregations in Latin; on the contrary, they always in this country speak English, and do all in their power to simplify their subject, and make their listeners well acquainted with the articles of Catholic belief. On this matter, however, you ought to judge for yourselves, and go for one Sunday at least to the Catholic Church of St. Mary's at Overbury. As for you, Madam," he continued, addressing Mrs. Benson, "you seem to have such a laudable curiosity to enquire both into our belief and practice, that I would advise you to apply to the fountain-head at once, and get accurate information from the person best qualified to give it, a Catholic priest. I can answer for the Reverend Mr. Howard, at St. Mary's chapel-house, receiving you with politeness, and replying to all your queries any day you like to call upon him. And now, Sir," continued the gentleman, once more turning to Jacob, "allow me to give you a caution before I depart. Take care again how you invent falsehoods against any body of Christians; remember that there are such things as law prosecutions, and that some have undergone imprisonment, others paid heavy fines, for defamation of character."

With these words the stranger took his hat, and wishing them good night, left the shop.

"As sure as I'm a living man, that's Mr. Howard himself!" cried Jacob. "Who would have thought it! It was uncommon venturesome and bold in him to contradict me in my own shop. If it had not been your presence, Mrs. Benson, and our Lord's injunction to suffer contumely for His sake, big man as he is, I'd have castigated him on the spot."

"It's well you did not," said Mrs. Benson; "for though the Lord would doubtless have been on your side, yet the priest was big enough to put a little body like you in his pocket. But to think of his imperance, wanting me to call on him, and go to his chapel! Why, I'd sooner go to a playhouse on the Lord's day than there!"

We shall now change the scene, and transport our readers to the rectory, where, strange to say, Mr. Howard's name formed at this very moment the subject of conversation.

"I have always forgotten to ask," said Mr. Harvey, "if any of the present party are acquainted with Mr. Howard, the Catholic priest at Overbury. I chanced to meet him in the railway as I was coming down, and found him a most intelligent companion. Between ourselves, it was quite wonderful how many religious subjects there were on which we agreed."

"I don't know him," cried Miss Beauclerk; "but I should like his acquaintance above all things. Do, Mary love, help me to coax your father to ask him to dinner. A Catholic priest and an Italian bandit are the two beings on earth I should like best to know!"

"I am afraid Mr. Howard is far too grave and matter-of-fact not to fall far short of your romantic ideas," said Harvey.

"At any rate, Mr. Harvey, do tell us what you talked about. And, Mr. Feversham, I must positively insist upon your waiting to listen, instead of slipping away to your study, as I see you are meditating. Do for once join our circle round the fire."

The rector could scarcely refuse this request, so, laying down his book, he joined the party, though somewhat apprehensive of what was to follow.

"Mr. Howard and I," continued Harvey, "touched lightly upon a great variety of subjects; and perhaps, had we entered upon them more deeply, we should not have agreed together so well as we did. Among other things, we both deprecated the Reformation; the originators of which, in trying to cut away a gangrene, seriously mutilated the sound limbs."

"What sound limbs, may I ask?" said Mrs. Egremond, who was beginning to feel vexed: "I do not much care for your conversation with the priest; but tell us, I implore you, your own views on the subject."

"Willingly, Madam," replied Mr. Harvey. "There are so many sound parts which the Reformers rejected, that it is difficult to enumerate them all. However, I shall mention those which first occur to me. In our eagerness for liberty, and anxiety to escape from the despotism of Rome, we have in a great measure overturned episcopal authority. I will not deny that it still exists; but, practically, it is fearfully disregarded. One would think, from the way many of the clergy go on, that each was independent in his own parish.* Then, we do not realize sufficiently our happiness in belonging to the Apostolic Church;† we do not call to mind, as we ought, that our Church is the true one, and that salvation can be found in no other."

"I beg pardon," interrupted Miss Beauclerk, "but I thought that the Roman Catholic, and not the English, was the Apostolic Church."

"Hush, Jane! do not interrupt, like a good girl," whispered Mary.

"The very clergy have, in my opinion, since the Reformation almost universally fallen into a great mistake," continued Harvey, without noticing Miss Beauclerk. "They neither uphold their dignity nor their rights, as successors of the Apostles: on the contrary, they hide and try to keep back, as much as possible, whatever portions of our belief tend to inculcate the awful and important mystery of their calling. Church authority is so practically lost sight of, that the episcopal body no longer dares to wield ecclesiastical censures, and excommunicate incorrigible sinners or open apostates.‡ Then, since the Reformation, the church services have been curtailed, and though modern Christians find them still too long, they form but a small part of what was the ancient worship.§ Seven times a-day at the canonical hours, though frequently, I allow, these services were compressed into two, pious Christians could join together to worship God; but, now-a-days, few people desire it, nor could they if they would: for, with the excep-

* For this view of Episcopal authority, see Tracts for the Times, No. iii. p. 8.

† No. iv. p. 7.

‡ See Tracts for the Times, No. viii. p. 4.

§ See No. ix.

tion of a very few holidays, the services are in general only on Sundays. Since the Reformation we have lost (perhaps through inadvertence) the most beautiful and excellent book of devotions ever written—I mean the breviary;* which, alas! as a whole, is now only used by our antagonists the Romanists. Then, since the Reformation, we have gradually lost the apostolic custom of celebrating the Lord's Supper daily; and this is most truly a *sin of the Church.*† We do not even fast before receiving the sacrament; an apostolic custom in use before the Reformation, and for some time after.‡ An ancient liturgy has also been taken from us, and a modern one arranged in its place. This is a change by no means to the better; for perhaps, next to the Holy Scriptures, the ancient liturgies possess the greatest claim to our veneration and study.§ To use the words of an amiable friend, 'As a whole, the Catholic ritual was a precious possession, and if we, who have escaped from popery, have lost not only the possession but the sense of its value, it is a serious question, whether we are not like men who recover from some serious illness with the loss or injury of their sight or hearing; whether we are not like the Jews returned from captivity, who could never find the rod of Aaron or the ark of the covenant, which indeed had ever been hid from the world, but then was removed from the temple itself.' "‖

"What a beautiful quotation!" exclaimed Mary.

"As for me!" cried Miss Beauclerk, "I was not paying attention to the quotation at all; for I was thinking that if the English Church is so defective as you make out, I wonder you still continue to belong to her!"

"Very well said, Jane!" exclaimed Mrs. Egremond, who for once agreed with the young lady's sentiments.

* See 75th and following Tracts.

† See Tract No. vi. p. 4.

‡ Tract lxvi. p. 11.

§ See Tract lxiii.

‖ Tract No. xxxiv.

Harvey coloured as he replied, "Far be it from me to disparage the venerable church to which I belong, and which has every claim to my love and admiration. Let us only act up to what she inculcates, and carry out her views and intentions, then all will go well. What I regret is, that through laxity of discipline, through indifference, and through short-sighted ignorance, so many of her clergy neglect to penetrate into the depths of her meaning, so that her treasure-stores of knowledge, grace, and benediction, have been too long unexplored except by a few chosen souls. Believe me, my dear friends, (and in what I say I am sure Mr. Feversham will coincide,) that owing to the want of faith and the coldness of charity among her children, the Anglican Church has long deemed it prudent to imitate as it were the *disciplina arcani* of the primitive church. Thus they to whom the deposit of her faith was committed, withdrew from common use or left but slight indications of doctrines which had been recently, or might again be abused."*

"Give us examples, Mr. Harvey," said Mrs. Egremond.

"Such as," replied he, "her views of the spiritual benefits of absolution and confirmation, or the spiritual gifts in ordination, which though not dogmatically enunciated, the Anglican Church pre-supposes to be already known through the successive teaching of her ministers. To these I might add her doctrines with regard to the eucharistic sacrifice, the intermediate state, the grace received both in the sacraments, and in those other mystic rites which the Romanists add to their number; besides many things which I should tire your patience by enumerating."

"In short," said Mrs. Egremond, "those of your school would try to persuade us that we had been Catholics all our lives without knowing it. The next

* Tracts for the Times, Catena Patrum, No. iv.

step your party will take, will be to deny the Queen's supremacy and negociate with the Bishop of Rome!"

"We are far from that still," said Harvey, with a smile. "The Romanists know that we are their most formidable opponents, indeed the only body able to grapple with them at their own weapons, and appeal to antiquity and the testimony of the fathers against them."

"I never knew any good come from appealing to the fathers," said Mrs. Egremond; "those who have studied and relied upon them most, have generally ended in becoming papists!"

"If Mrs. Egremond will pardon me changing the subject," said the rector, "I should like much, Harvey, to hear what you believe with regard to the Eucharist; in other words, will you tell these ladies what the Anglican Church pre-supposes to be already known through the successive teaching of her ministers on this subject?"

"I shall do so willingly," said Harvey. "Our Church rejects the notion of transubstantiation, but does not the less hold a *real vital* presence of Christ in the sacrament.* Though she forbids to hold the doctrine of a *corporal* presence, yet she does not presume to overloook the strong words of Christ, 'this is my body, and this is my blood.' In short, as the catechism says, 'the body and blood of Christ are verily and indeed taken and received by the faithful in the Lord's Supper.'"

"I must say," interrupted Mrs. Egremond, "that so far from simplifying the matter, you make out a new mystery. How can the body and blood of Christ be really taken and received, if He be not corporeally present?"

"I am not going to let Harvey dispute the subject with you just now," said the rector, laughing, "such discussions would detain us too long, when we are all

* For similar views see p. 14 of Dr. Hampden's Inaugural Lecture on appointment to theological chair at Oxford in 1836.

anxious to hear something more of what has been concealed by this Disciplina Arcani, which I must confess is a very good idea!"

"You are right, Mr. Feversham," said Mrs. Egremond, "I want very much to hear what Mr. Harvey exactly means by the term eucharistic sacrifice!"

"I mean," replied Harvey, "that in the Eucharist,* an oblation or sacrifice is made by the Church to God, under the form of his creatures of bread and wine, according to our blessed Lord's holy institution, in memory of His cross and passion; we also believe it to be a commemorative and impetratory sacrifice, a benefit to the whole Church independently and over and above the benefit to the individual communicants. It even benefits that portion of the Church which has passed into the unseen world."

"What you say," interrupted the rector, "appears to be nearly the doctrine of the Church of Rome!"

"Not at all," replied Harvey. "The Romish Church has corrupted and marred the apostolic doctrine in two ways; by the error of transubstantiation, and by that of purgatory."

"If you do not believe in purgatory," said the rector, "what do you mean by saying that the eucharistic sacrifice benefits a portion of the Church in the unseen world?"

"I mean," said Harvey, "that their state, though higher and more purified than ours, is still necessarily imperfect until the consummation of all things, and so capable of increased spiritual joys."

"How do you account," asked the rector, "for so many of the fathers inculcating the doctrine of an intermediate place of suffering for the souls of the faithful departed?"

"The subject," answered Harvey, "is somewhat vague; it appears to me that different opinions were held in the primitive church with regard to it. Per-

* For Harvey's sentiments on this subject, see p. 4, &c. of No. iv. Catena Patrum.

haps all difficulties may be reconciled by adopting the belief of a general fire at the day of judgment, through which all souls must pass. However, I must confess, that neither my friends nor myself have quite made up our minds on the subject."

"And now you must let me take my turn in asking Mr. Harvey questions," said Miss Beauclerk. "What did you say about sacraments and mystic rites a while ago?"

"Rather than repeat what I said," replied Harvey, "I will explain what I meant; and first with regard to the two sacraments of baptism and the Lord's Supper. I hold that far too little stress is generally laid upon this awful dignity; and that few people are aware of the real doctrine of the Anglican Church with regard to the supernatural and stupendous graces they confer. I likewise hold that the five other rites termed sacraments by the Romanists, convey particular graces; and that of ordination in a most especial manner does so, and partakes in a remarkable degree of the nature of a sacrament. Indeed, to confess the truth, I should not hesitate muc about adopting the name of sacrament as applied to the whole seven; for the very catechism seems to favour the idea; it mentions two sacraments only as generally necessary for salvation, but by no means excludes the other five."

"These admissions are very well," said Mrs. Egremond, "they doubtless are very fine, and they sound very liberal; but believe me they are dangerous! You admit too much to stop where you are. Depend upon it, those gradual approaches to popish doctrine, and that romantic regret for the useless practices done away with at the reformation, will lead you on, by little and little, until you sigh for reunion with the Church of Rome!"

"And truly," cried Mr. Harvey, his face flushing with enthusiasm, "when one surveys the grandeur of their system, a sigh arises in the thoughtful mind to think that we should be separated from them!"*

"Is this your true opinion? Do you really think so?" exclaimed the rector, with unwonted pleasure gleaming in his countenance.

"It is a dream! a mere dream!" continued Harvey, calming down as he looked at the rector with surprise; "Alas! *Union is impossible!*"

CHAPTER XXVI.

"It is clear the Apostles did not deliver all things in writing, but many things without it; and these too deserve to be believed. Let us then give credit to the traditions of the Church. It is tradition; seek no further." *St. Chrysostom*, Hom. 4, in Ep. 2, ad Thess.

"Your Reverence was speaking last about the universality of the Church, if I remember right," said Blount, at his next visit to the rector.

"Yes, John," replied Mr. Feversham, "I tried to prove that the Catholic Church is the Church of all ages, of all nations, and of all truth; for Christ has said, 'All power is given unto me, in heaven and in earth. Go ye therefore and teach *all nations*, baptizing them in the name of the Father, and of the Son, and of the Holy Ghost; teaching them to observe *all things* whatsoever I have commanded you: and lo I am with you *alway* even unto the end of the

* Tracts for the Times, No. xx. p. 3.

world.' (Matt. xxviii. 18.) Thus you see that the perpetual presence and assistance of Christ was expressly promised to maintain this three-fold universality."

"Very true, your Reverence," said Blount. "The next thing to be done, is to see whether the Protestant Church or the Popish agrees best with the description. I have no doubt which side you'll make out has the best of it, Sir; I expect you'll smash the Protestant claims in a jiffy; I could a'most do it myself, though an ignorant man."

"It is very evident," said the rector, "that none of the modern reformed sects can be the Church *of all ages*, because not one of them had any being until fifteen hundred years after Christ; whereas the Old Communion which they forsook, had a visible being in all ages from Christ's time till this day. Again, not one of them has any possible claim to be considered the Church *of all nations;* whereas the Old Communion takes in great numbers in most nations in all parts of the world. And lastly, as to the teaching *of all truth,* though all sectaries claim it, none of them can produce such titles to justify their claim as the Catholic Church can do."

"Now, Sir, let me put in a word, if you please," said Blount. "You have not explained yet how the Catholic Church teaches all truth; and I opine that is the first thing to be done."

"You are right, John," said Mr. Feversham. "Christ promised that 'the Spirit of truth' should guide her 'into *all truth.*' (John xvi. 13.) Now the Catholic Church alone receives without exception, all parts of the Scripture which the holy fathers and ancient councils have received; she alone adheres to all ancient traditions, receives the decrees of all lawful general councils, &c. Whereas sectaries reject some part or other of the Scriptures,* and all of them

* See Chap. xxi.

despise apostolical traditions and the definitions of general councils; and consequently cannot be thought to maintain *all truths.*"

"Hilloah!" cried the farmer, starting. "I've caught you at last! Is not *tradition* the very word I've been wishing so long to hear from your Reverence's mouth; for Mr. Sharples has primed me with the best of arguments against it! The fact is, rector, I'm main glad you've mentioned it, for I was afraid I should forget my learning if you had put off much longer. What is the use of tradition at all, Sir, when we have the Holy Scriptures? I count it neither honour nor profit to the Catholic Church that it holds by tradition!"

"We have Scripture warrant for it, however," replied the rector. St. Paul says, 'Therefore, brethren, stand fast and hold the traditions which ye have been taught whether by *word* or *our epistle.*' (2 Thess. ii. 15.) Here St. Paul speaks plainly of unwritten traditions *taught by the Apostles,* and gives them the same weight and authority as to his own epistle."

"Well, Sir," replied Blount, "I don't want to gainsay Paul; nevertheless, I think it a wiser and safer thing to stick fast to Scripture alone, seeing that since Christ's time, believers have always done so."

"That is impossible," said the rector, "since it was not till a number of years after Christ's death, that the Scriptures were all written; during which time believers could only hold by the teaching of the Church, in other words by apostolic tradition. The Apostles meanwhile wrote on particular occasions to particular persons or congregations, without giving directions or providing means for communicating their epistles or gospels to all the christians in the world: so that long after the books in your Scriptures were written, they were not universally spread, and it was not until the end of the fourth century that they were all formally declared by the Church to be inspired."

"That beats everything!" said the farmer, "and how were they fixed then, Sir?"

"Tradition bearing testimony to their being the inspired word of God, they were pronounced such by the authority of the Church," replied the rector.

"It strikes me, Sir," said Blount, "that when the books in the New Testament were collected, the Church had, may-be, a better guide in the task than tradition. When those that did it, took the books written by the Apostles, depend upon it they were long-headed enough to know they could not go far wrong!"

"But they did not abide by what the Apostles wrote," said the rector, "for they also took the gospel of St. Mark and the Gospel and Acts written by St. Luke, and they even rejected an authentic work composed by him whom the college of Apostles proposed to be one of the twelve, a saint 'full of the Holy Ghost;' I mean St. Barnabas! Now if Protestants do not in spite of themselves, pay respect to tradition and Church authority, I ask them why they thus prefer the writings of St. Mark and St. Luke to those of the companion of St. Paul?"

"Indeed, that's what I can't answer," said the farmer thoughtfully; and after a pause, during which he seemed to be considering, he continued, "You speak, Sir, of a tradition we are bound to believe, and so does Paul in his Epistles; and you say that Scripture was even fixed by Church authority, guided by tradition; so now I'll tell your Reverence a bit of a secret, that though Mr. Sharples set me up to talk against tradition, I don't know rightly what you mean by the word."

"I am glad you have told me so, John," said the rector, "for there is nothing more absurd or more useless than to argue upon points when you do not understand the meaning of the terms used. Apostolic tradition is that species of tradition which we are bound to believe. Whatever is found one and the same throughout those Christian Churches which have any pretensions to antiquity, in the different parts of the world, can be no error; but must, on the contrary, be apostolic tradition: for it is impossible that many and distant Churches could all err *into one faith.* However, to make the matter simpler, I shall give you St. Augustine's definition: 'Whatever is found to have been held by the universal Church throughout the world, and not to have had its beginning from any ordinance of bishops or councils, but to have been prior to any such ordinance, that same is to be esteemed a tradition of those by whom the Church was first established—that is, of the Apostles of Christ.' "*

"That same is a very good rule," said the farmer; "but, as Mr. Sharples said, papists don't keep to it, for every general council invented something new, and stuck it on to the old belief. He says that the reformers went back to what was believed in the early times, and cast aside all the extra things that the pope had tacked on."

The rector sighed. "I see, John," said he, "that I shall have hard work with you, if you forget so quickly the things which you have learned. So far from the general councils inventing new articles of faith, (as indeed I explained to you the other day,) the bishops and prelates were only summoned to declare what had been always taught in their respective dioceses from the beginning—in other words, what had been handed down to them by their predecessors. A general council was always summoned when any novelty began to be taught in the Church; and by this means heresy was publicly protested against as soon as it was broached, and the unity of the faith thus gloriously preserved. I shall now put it to yourself,

* St. Augustine, L. 2, De Bapt. c. vii.; L. 4, c. xxiii.; L. 5, c. xxiii.

John, to decide whether Protestants have preserved the old belief. Do they believe in the real presence of Christ in the blessed Eucharist? Is mass said in their churches? Do they generally believe in the full efficacy of baptism? Have they not discarded extreme unction? In short, do they hold the greater part of what I have been lately teaching you?"

"Faith, Sir, they don't; and it requires no witch to answer that," said the farmer.

"And have I not," continued the rector, "proved to you the truth of the chief disputed points, either from Scripture or the authority of the Fathers, who were the most learned and greatest doctors of primitive times—generally, indeed, from both? And how can you then, parrot-like, repeat without thinking of the old accusation, that the reformers go back to the doctrines and practices of primitive times; and that the belief of Catholics is made up of comparatively modern inventions?"

"I ask pardon, Sir," said the farmer, "I own I did speak without thinking: for certainly, if what you have told me is true, the Catholics and the first Christians join together in believing differently from the Protestants. At the same time, Sir, you have not set me at rest on everything yet; I am satisfied with all I have heard, but we have not come to the end: so, may be something will come out on Mr. Sharples's side before the argumentations are finished; however, I mean no offence, Sir. But, now that I think of it again, your Reverence, why *will* you not stick to the Bible?"

"Catholics hold by the Bible far more strictly than Protestants do," replied Mr. Feversham; "as indeed I have been proving to you by my Bible quotations in favour of doctrines which Protestants reject, and which quotations they therefore virtually despise."

The farmer pondered a little over this reply, and then observed: "Well, Sir, I like to know things clearly and distinctly; and if you would just tell me, in a few words, what rule of faith Catholics hold by, then I could get to the bottom of the thing, and feel more satisfied."

"The Catholic rule of faith," replied the rector, "is the *word of God*, contained in the Scriptures and traditions of the Apostles, proposed and interpreted by the Church of God."

"Now," said the farmer, "stop a bit, I'll think over that. Catholics hold by 'the word of God;' that's all fair—as 'contained in Scripture;' that's right too—and in the 'traditions of the Apostles;' that's what I am more inclined to stumble at. However, as Paul commands us to hold by the 'traditions taught by word of mouth,' I suppose I must swallow that too; though, when I have time, I'll poke a little deeper into it, and tell you Mr. Sharples's objections. The next thing is, 'as interpreted by the Church of God;' and that's what I'm not fond of. For I think that every man with common sense should interpret things for himself."

"You think like a true Protestant," said the rector smiling; "for the Protestant rule of faith is the written word of God, as interpreted by every Christian for himself. Let us just see to what this has led. Has it not been the source of endless divisions and differences of opinion? Are there not countless sects among Protestants, and new ones arising daily? This comes from trusting to the private interpretation of individuals. On the other hand, look at the Catholics. They abide by the decision of the Church, with whom Christ promised that the Spirit of truth should abide for ever. They are all of one unchangeable opinion on the subjects which affect their salvation, for they rest their belief on that rock against which it was promised that the gates of hell should never prevail. Catholics alone maintain that unity which you yourself allowed to be one of the marks of the true Church; and they maintain it, by God's grace, in consequence of not permitting private interpretation."

"It's a fine thing, unity, Sir, I allow," replied the farmer. "At the same time, I question if we should go against Scripture to preserve it. Now, are we not told to 'search the Scriptures' for ourselves?"

"Yes," replied the rector; "Christ tells the Jews to 'search the Scriptures: for in them ye think ye have eternal life; and they are they which testify of me.' (John v. 39.) But it was the Old Testament of which He spoke, and He wished them to gather from its contents that He was the Son of God; so I don't think your quotation much to the point."

"Well, but does not Paul," continued the farmer, "write to Timothy that the Scriptures 'are able to make thee wise unto salvation, through faith which is in Christ Jesus?'"

"St. Paul," replied the rector, "here speaks of the Old Testament, the only one then extant: which certainly, along with the 'faith which is in Christ Jesus,' such as St. Paul and the other Apostles had taught, was sufficient to make him 'wise unto salvation.' In short, John, there is no text which can authorize a man to prefer his own private judgment to that of the Church of God."

"But let us come to facts, Sir, if you please. Is there any text against private judgment?"

"Yes," said Mr. Feversham. "St. Peter says, 'No prophecy of the Scripture is of any private interpretation.' (2 Peter i. 20.) And in another place the same Apostle points out the danger of individuals interpreting for themselves, when he says of St. Paul's epistles, 'In which are some things hard to be understood, which they that are unlearned and unstable wrest, as they do also the *other Scriptures*, unto their own destruction.' (2 Peter iii. 16.)"

"That is an awful warning, truly," said the farmer, pondering. "And now, Sir, I'll tell you over what I have gathered from all you have said, and you'll tell me if I'm right. That Apostolic tradition bore testimony to what was to be taken as God's word, and the authority of the Church decided and fixed it; so, if we show no respect to tradition and church authority, we may then throw the Scriptures overboard, for we would have no proofs that they are true."

"Extremely well, John," said the rector.

"But, Sir, I have more to say," continued Blount. "Now that I think of it, Mr. Sharples pointed out to me how Christ reproved the Pharisees for laying aside the commandment of God, and holding 'the tradition of men.'"

"Among the traditions prevalent in our Saviour's time, some were divine, such as the doctrines of the resurrection and the last judgment, &c.; and these our Saviour did not condemn, but, on the contrary, confirmed. Others were merely human and of late invention, such as the washing of pots and cups, &c.; these our Saviour rejected. Catholics also have divine traditions, such as the inspiration of the Gospels, the observation of the Sunday, and other things not contained in Scripture; it is to these that we appeal on the authority of the Catholic Church."

"Mr. Sharples, Sir, told me some very queer stories about saints," said Blount, "that he maintained were traditions held in the Catholic Church. Now, must all Catholics believe them?"

"In addition to divine tradition, which is chiefly included in the articles of faith defined by the Church," replied the rector, "there are historical and even fabulous traditions, of which we may judge as we think best. If these legends, which Mr. Sharples related, are supported by good historical proof, they deserve attention; if not, only ignorant or foolish people would pay regard to them."

"Will your Reverence, then, give me some good rule that I may know which traditions I am bound to believe, and which not; for how is a poor man like me to find out which are divine, and which human?"

"The Church, to which Christ promised to give the Spirit of truth, has already decided for you. You will find all that her children are bound to believe in her articles of faith, as explained in the abridgment of the Douai Catechism, which I shall now give you if you like."

The farmer thanked Mr. Feversham for the little book; and, after receiving it, he departed.

Meanwhile, all went on as usual in the rectory. Lady Harriet chiefly kept her room, complained of ill health, and read novels. Her daughter and visitors paid her frequent visits during the day, but she never liked them to remain long, as she said their talking excited her nerves. Mary often walked with Harvey, and had interesting conversations with him, in which he gradually unfolded to her many near approximations to Catholic truth. The rector also took every opportunity to draw him out, and appeared delighted whenever their views coincided. Harvey, likewise, was curious to hear Mr. Feversham's opinions on different topics; and though the latter gradually cast aside his reserve, and spoke more openly, it was amusing to observe how slow the younger clergyman was in discovering the truth: the rector's sentiments on many points being only what he had heard expressed before, and in no stronger language, by the ultra members of his own party. Though by no means going so far as some of these gentlemen, many of whom were his private friends, yet so liberal was Harvey in his notions, that the rector would have found it impossible to shock him by differing from him, as long as he kept off one delicate subject—namely, the necessity for leaving the Anglican party to enter into the One Holy Catholic and Apostolic Church.

It was some days before Blount returned to the

rectory, and when he did so, Mr. Feversham found that he had meanwhile been with Mr. Sharples.

"I want to ask your Reverence," said he, "if there might not be other ways of finding out that the Bible is the word of God, besides the Church having taught so? For instance, when people find that every word of the Bible is true, is not that proof sufficient?"

"Certainly not, John," replied the rector; "for there are many true narratives which are not divine."

"But," said the farmer, "we read in Scripture itself that it is the word of God; besides there is something not like other books in the whole way in which it is written that might give you a notion of the truth."

"You might say as much for the Alcoran of Mahomet," said the rector. "It also informs us that it is the word of God. Many parts in it are highly extraordinary, nay, even grand and sublime. Depend upon it, it is not the style that makes the word of God, any more than royal garments make a king. St. Augustine was of the Catholic opinion when he maintained to the Manichees that 'he would not believe the Gospels themselves unless the authority of the Church induced him to it.' (Contra Epist. Fund. c. iv.)"

"Another thing said by Mr. Sharples," continued Blount, "was that the Spirit of God in us will teach us all things, among the rest, that the Scriptures are the word of God."

"Enthusiasts are only too apt," said Mr. Feversham, "to fancy that they have the Spirit of God, and they make it a cloak for many extravagances. Before we follow the guidance of the Spirit, we must test it by a Scripture rule to discover if it be the right Spirit. St. John tells us, 'We (that is, the pastors of the Church) are of God: he that knoweth God heareth us; he that is not of God heareth not us. Hereby know we the Spirit of truth, and the Spirit of error.' (1 John iv. 6.) Now, those heretics who have gone against the universal teaching of the Catholic Church, and disobeyed their chief pastor, cannot expect the Spirit which moves them to be the true Spirit of God, and consequently cannot rely upon its testimony."

"But, Sir," replied Blount, "Mr. Sharples says, that when a person has the true Spirit of God, there is no mistaking it, he always knows it himself."

"If you are content to take private testimony," said the rector, "there are doubtless many who will tell you that they have the Spirit of God. So said the Anabaptists soon after the Reformation, when they ran naked about the streets, shouting for the subversion of governments, and committing many murders and excesses.* So said Johanna Southcote, when she pretended to be with child of the Messiah. So say the notorious Mormonites; and so also said those Methodists quoted in terms of reprehension by Fletcher, Wesley's successor, when they wrote such words as these: 'Though I blame those who say, Let us sin that grace may abound; yet adultery, incest, and murder shall, upon the whole, make me holier upon earth and merrier in heaven.'"†

The farmer scratched his head, and said, "Well, well, I'll give up the Spirit, unless so far as it will stand the Scripture test you gave; for I see there is no end to the hobbles the doctrine of a private Holy Spirit in each person might get me into. So now we have given that up, I'll ask another question. You have been giving me Scripture texts for most of what you have been teaching me, so what is the use, your Reverence, of lugging in tradition and Church authority at the tail of the day, when the battle is more than half fought."

"Because, as I told you," replied the rector, "the Catholic rule of faith is the word of God, contained

* See Milner's End of Controversy, Letter vi. which gives this and many other examples.

† See Milner's End of Controversy, Letter vi.

not in the Scriptures alone, but also in Apostolic tradition, both being interpreted by the Church of God. To satisfy your Protestant mind, I have hitherto tried to take most of my arguments from Scripture only; and although I shall, as heretofore, quote Scripture, and go along with it, it is time now to learn you to pay some respect also to tradition and Church authority."

"Well, Sir," said Blount, "go on speechifying if you please, and explain a little more; I am only anxious to get to the bottom of my difficulties."

"The Scriptures, as I told you," continued the rector, "are not the whole rule of faith; neither are the Scriptures and apostolic tradition taken together; for if we had no more we should infallibly go wrong, since each person would interpret them differently according to his private judgment, influenced by his peculiar disposition and natural prejudices. Jesus Christ, however, has given us a guide in the teaching of the One, Holy, Catholic and Apostolic Church, to which he has promised the Spirit of truth to abide with her for ever. Her explanation of Scripture and apostolic tradition, renders the Catholic rule of faith complete. And now, John, to make the thing very clear to you, I shall give you some other reasons why the Bible cannot be the whole rule of faith, and why we must also rely on tradition and Church authority. The Bible no where gives us a catalogue of the canonical books; and Protestants are therefore, in spite of themselves, obliged to take their inspired writings on the authority of Church tradition. Secondly, unless they, like Catholics, rely upon this authority, they cannot tell whether the books of Scripture they now have, are the same as those written by the inspired penmen."

"You are a cunning man, rector," interrupted the farmer, "driving Protestants, in spite of themselves, either to give up their religion, or to feel obliged to tradition and Church authority!"

"The Scripture," continued the rector, "cannot be the whole rule of faith; because the Protestant sects that hold it to be so, differ among themselves as to its explanation; something else is therefore necessary to make it a complete and sure rule. Again, in all controversies about religion, Scripture itself is the subject debated; another judge is therefore required. A judge ought to hear both sides and decide the question; Scripture alone never decided any controversy; for unfortunately it can be pulled about to favour all sides. There are also some things not fixed in Scripture, which yet are generally held by christians. On what authority do Protestants keep Sunday, instead of Saturday, the Jewish sabbath? They ought either to give it up, or confess the truth that they keep it solely on the authority of tradition, for it is not commanded in the Bible to keep holy the first day of the week!"

"What a pity," exclaimed the farmer, "that I had not known that, when our regiment was quartered in Scotland during my young days! I never saw sourer folks than these Scotch Presbyterians about keeping the sabbath holy. What a joke it would have been had I known that nothing was said in the Bible about keeping the first day of the week in that way! How I'd have floored them if I had known it!"

"But you must not go too far the other way, John," said the rector; "we are obliged to abstain from work and to spend part of the Sunday at least in prayer and devotional exercises; we are taught to do so by apostolical tradition and by the command of the Church. It is the Lord's day and must be kept holy, though not in the puritanical and severe manner which is still so prevalent in Scotland. And now, John, I shall tell you some more things very important to christians, which yet cannot be made out from the Bible. In baptism, for instance, how do we know that sprinkling with water is sufficient; for most assuredly immersion or dipping was practised by the

Apostles? Could we gather from Scripture whether laymen can lawfully baptize or consecrate? If christians may make war, swear before a magistrate, or go to law?"*

"Now I'm getting a notion of things," said the farmer. "We must learn all this from apostolical tradition as explained by that Church to which Christ promised the Spirit of truth."

"Another thing which you must remark," continued the rector, "is that the unwritten word of Christ preached by the pastors of his Church, was the rule of faith before the New Testament was written. When did this rule lose its authority, or where is it mentioned that it did so? St. Paul commands the faithful to stand fast and hold the traditions taught by word as well as by writing. (2 Thess. ii. 15.) He also pronounces anathema against those that would alter it. (Galatians i. 8, 9.) Again, the apostle does not say that faith comes by reading but 'by hearing.' (Rom. x. 17.) It is not said in Scripture or tradition that our Lord commanded his disciples to write, but we are told that they were commanded *to preach*; and surely the apostles could not have believed the Scriptures to be the whole rule of faith, or they would have procured them to be written in the vulgar tongues of all the people that they converted. Besides, John, you may find from Scripture itself that many important things were not written. Does not St. John say, 'And there are also many other things which Jesus did, the which if they should be written every one, I suppose that even the world itself could not contain the books that should be written?' (John xxi. 25.)"

"Don't you think, Sir, however," said Blount, "that Scripture is most honoured by those who take it as the only rule of faith?"

"Not at all," replied the rector; "by so doing they

* Great part of what the rector says on this subject is copied from "Grounds of the Old Religion."

set it at the mercy of any enthusiast who likes to interpret it, and hence, as I gave you examples, the most blasphemous nonsense is occasionally uttered. Suppose, John, that, in this country when people disputed about property or right, there were no judges to go to, no arbitrators to whom one could appeal, do you think that the books of the law as each one might interpret them for himself, would be sufficient to maintain order and arrange differences?"

The farmer laughed: "I fear, Sir," said he, "that each party would twist the law to his own side. We should not be able to get along at all without a judge."

"And if so in temporal affairs," continued the rector, "how much more must be necessary a judge or court of appeal in spiritual matters affecting our everlasting salvation. God is too good to leave us in hopeless darkness and misery, He wills that all men should 'come unto the knowledge of the truth.' (1st Tim. ii. 4.) and that they all should be one. Now this is impossible without a living guide and judge to whom we can appeal when unity is endangered by differences of opinion. This judge must be divinely recommended and assisted, all must be able to hear and understand his voice, on him the most unlearned may securely rely, to him the most learned must be obliged to submit; his sentence must be clear and decisive, and from it there must be no appeal. Where can we find this judge, if not in the ever-living Church of God?"

"Have you nearly finished about tradition, and the Bible, and church authority?" asked Blount.

"If you are satisfied on the necessity of believing apostolic tradition, and on interpreting both it and the Scriptures according to the voice of the Church, then I have finished," replied the rector, "but if not, I could still say some more which might perhaps influence your opinion."

"To say the truth, rector, I am nearly convinced at

present," said Blount, "but may be after a day or two I may forget some of your arguments, and require a hitch up again. If your Reverence please we'll stop now, for though I like to hear your instruction, yet I often get sleepy before you are done. So if you please, we'll put off the rest you have to say till next day I come." So saying, the farmer took his hat and departed, stretching himself and giving a loud yawn as soon as he closed the door of the library.

CHAPTER XXVII.

"Our minister was a great stickler for haudin by Scriptur', but he didna muckle like whan his wife ae windy day refused to tak' a mote out o' his e'e, sayin' she wad staun by Matthew seventh and third."

My old Nurse.

"HERE I am back again," said Farmer Blount, the very next day after the preceding conversation, as he re-entered the library of the rectory. "I hope your Reverence be'nt sorry to see me. I come so often that I'm ashamed; but your Reverence does not know how anxious I am to find the true Church, and get into it as soon as I know it: I am not comfortable at present; and I think that God sent the fire to my house, which destroyed so much of my property, as a sort of warning to me like, not to put my heart any longer in making money, but to give it to Him. And Jacob Hogg too, Sir, has been keeping me in hot water, giving me continual hints about the receipts for his wife's money, which he always asks me to show him, but which I cannot find. So you see, Sir, I have really no comfort except in talking with you about religion, for it's no use setting my heart on worldly consolations, seeing Providence gives me but a poor share of them."

The good man sighed, while the rector did his best to encourage and raise his spirits.

"It is no use talking, Sir," he continued. "I have a presentiment that something evil is going to happen. I'm in the power of a bad man, Sir; and there is little doubt that he'll use his power to ruin me, since it will be to his own advantage."

"You say that you have lost Jacob's acknowledgment for the receipt of his wife's fortune," said the rector; "but were there no witnesses to the transaction?"

"There were two most respectable witnesses present," replied the farmer; "but, unfortunately, one of them is dead, and the other went some years ago to Canada: his friends have heard nothing of him since, so it is supposed he was lost on the passage out."

It would be useless to enter into all the details of the conversation which followed; we shall, therefore, proceed at once to the conclusion of the subject discussed in the preceding chapter.

An hour had struck, when the farmer, starting, exclaimed, "I wish your Reverence would finish what was left last day, that I may have something to occupy my mind with when I go home. The Protestants were finely done for last day, when you showed that they had no authority for keeping the Sunday, if they would not take it on the warrant of the Catholic Church."

"The truth is, John," replied the rector, "that nothing is more dangerous than to say that you will only believe what is proved in Scripture; apostolic tradition is absolutely necessary besides, in order to supply what is wanting; and Church authority is likewise indispensable to interpret both it and the Bible."

"I ask your pardon, Sir," said the farmer, "but I can't bear to hear you say that Apostolic tradition is necessary to supply what is wanting in the Bible. Surely, Sir, the Bible is complete."

"The Bible is part of the word of God, but not the whole," answered Mr. Feversham; "for, as I have told you, there are allusions in Scripture to the unwritten word. I shall now give you an example of an important doctrine held by Protestants, and not clearly defined in Scripture — the existence of the Blessed Trinity. If you wish to prove that Christ is God, and equal with Him, does not the text, 'My Father is greater than I,' seem to go against it? And, again, where is it said in Scripture that the Father, the Son, and the Holy Ghost are all three one God, and yet distinct in person? Protestants are obliged to accept the doctrine of the Trinity on the authority of the Church or Apostolic tradition. Should they refuse to do this, then, to be consistent, they ought, like the Socinians, to reject it altogether, for they cannot prove it from Scripture."

"Well, that *is* a scrape that you make Protestants get into when they take for their motto, 'The Bible, and nothing but the Bible,'" said the farmer, laughing.

"There are many commands in the Bible besides," continued the rector, "to which Protestants do not adhere."

"But I think we ought to keep strictly to all that is commanded in the New Testament," interrupted Blount.

"Some of the commands would prove very inconvenient," replied Mr. Feversham; "and though Catholics know which are obligatory and which are not, on the authority of the Church, yet Protestants, who will allow no authority but the Bible, ought certainly to obey them literally."

"Clearly so," said the farmer; "but what are the commands you speak of?"

"Does not St. Paul," said the rector, "in the 15th chapter of Acts, forbid to eat things strangled or blood? Do Protestants keep this command when they eat blood puddings, or gravy, or fowls which have their necks twisted?"

"That beats everything!" cried the farmer; "but I'll take care again how I eat them."

"Few Protestants would be so scrupulous," said the rector. "We are also told by Christ, 'Swear not at all;' (Matt. v. 34.) 'Call no man father upon earth,' &c.; (Matt. xxiii. 9.) 'Give to every man that asketh of thee; and of him that taketh away thy goods ask them not again;' (Luke vi. 30.) 'When thou makest a dinner or a supper, call not thy friends nor thy brethren,' &c. (xiv. 12.) Do Protestants keep these commands literally? They ought to do so, when they say, 'The Bible, the whole Bible, and nothing but the Bible.'"

"Indeed," replied the farmer, "your Reverence knows as well as I do, that they don't. But do Catholics?"

"No, they do not," said the rector; "but Catholics act consistently, for they follow, with regard to these matters, Apostolic tradition, as explained by the Church: whereas Protestants to be consistent, having no authority but the Bible, ought to follow it implicitly."

"There is another command which Protestants don't follow," said the farmer, "that I have often wondered at myself; and that is washing each others' feet. Surely, that is clearly commanded."

"It is certainly more striking than any of the examples I have given," said the rector; "and it proves still more clearly how inconsistent the Protestants are in not following what is so explicitly laid down in their only rule of faith. There are hundreds of other examples which might be given, which, as well as some of those I have quoted, have been occasionally put in practice by an isolated sect, thus becoming occasions of disunion and contention for those wranglers among themselves who adopt the Bible alone as their guide."

"Well, Sir, I am much obliged to you for all you have told me," said the farmer; "but, before I go, would you repeat any texts of Scripture you remember that refer to tradition, just to strengthen me a little, if you please. I know that Paul bids us stand fast, and hold the traditions we have been taught; but is there any thing else?"

"Yes," replied the rector; "St. Paul also desires us to 'keep the ordinances as I delivered them to you.' (1 Cor. xi. 2.) He likewise commands us to withdraw ourselves 'from every brother that walketh disorderly and not after the tradition which he received of us.' (2 Thess. iii. 6.) He said to Timothy, 'Hold fast the form of sound words which thou hast heard of me.' (2 Tim. i. 13.) 'And the things that thou hast heard of me among many witnesses, the same commit thou to faithful men, who shall be able to teach others also.' (2 Tim. ii. 2.) 'But continue thou in the things which thou hast learned, and hast been assured of, knowing of whom thou hast learned them.' (2 Tim. iii. 14.)

"Now," said the farmer, "I am beginning to have a notion of things; your Reverence would make out that the Catholic Church has done what Timothy was commanded to do—that is, continued in the things she has learned, and been assured of, knowing of whom she has learned them."

The rector assented, and John continued: "Before we stop, Sir, I'd like to hear what the old folks say about tradition; I mean the great doctors that lived long ago, soon after Christ—the Fathers you call them, I believe."

"It would be endless indeed repeating all they say on the subject," replied Mr. Feversham; "however, I shall quote the sentiments of one or two, since you ask me. St. Irenæus, in the second century, writes: 'Suppose the Apostles had left us no Scriptures, ought we not to have followed the rule of tradition which they delivered to those to whose care they committed the churches?' (L. iii. c. 3.) 'It is Apostolical,' says St. Basil, 'to hold even unwritten tradition.' (L. de Sp. 8. c. xxiv.) 'Tradition, too, is necessary,' says St. Epiphanius, 'for all things cannot be had from the Scripture. Therefore the blessed Apostles left us some things in writing, and others by tradition.' (Hær. lxi.) St. Chrysostom agrees in the same doctrine: 'It is clear,' he says, 'the Apostles did not deliver all things in writing, but many things without it, and these too deserve to be believed. Let us, then, give credit to the traditions of the Church. It is tradition: seek no further,' (Hom. iv. Ep. 2. ad Thess.)"

CHAPTER XXVIII.

> "A list of the possessions in art and science which we inherit from the middle ages, would certainly startle any one who has never heard of them excepting from modern historians of philosophy."
>
> *Mores Catholici.*

"THERE is something I want you to explain," said Mary one day to Harvey, as all the party with the exception of the rector were sitting together in the drawing-room. "I was reading in the newspapers this morning a lamentation over the increase of popery, which it appears has made great progress during the last few years. Now it seems to me incomprehensible how the religion which is said to have been in a great measure the cause of the superstition and the ignorance of the dark ages, should be so far suited to the enlightenment of the present day as to spread in our country."

"I must differ from your first assertion," said Harvey smiling, "for I can in no way admit that Romanism was the cause of ignorance; on the contrary, the Roman Catholic Church has ever been favourable to learning."

"But were they not stupid and ignorant during the dark ages, when popery had most power?" asked Miss Beauclerk; "I always understood that the knights, though brave and handsome, were great dunces."

"Yes," said Mary, "what a sad account the historian Robertson gives of the want of all learning during the middle ages."

"Robertson," replied Mr. Harvey, "has lately been most triumphantly refuted by a clergyman of whom the Anglican Church may be proud, Mr. Maitland, librarian to the Archbishop of Canterbury, in his 'Essays on the Dark Ages.' He proves that Robertson, in all probability, had never seen the writings which he quotes, so falsely and partially are they stated. Indeed, the very writers to whose works he refers, bear triumphant testimony against him in other parts of their writings. Among other things which Robertson asserts is, that many clergymen, particularly from the seventh to the eleventh centuries, did not understand their breviary, and some even could scarcely read it. Now the fact is, as Maitland proves, that during these ages, the examination which candidates for holy orders had to undergo before being admitted to the priesthood, was far more severe and more difficult than what is common among the different bodies of Protestants now-a-days; indeed, it is a great chance if Robertson, with all his learning, would have been able to pass through it. However, you ought to read Maitland's work for yourself, to show you the excessive dishonesty, nay, rascality, of the standard Protestant historians."

"You use strong language, Mr. Harvey," said Mrs. Egremond; "to hear you speak with such contempt of *Protestant* historians, one would think that you were not a Protestant yourself."

"And neither am I," replied Harvey; "I consider the term Protestant, as one only fit for heretics; and I grieve to hear it applied to the Anglican Catholic Church."

"Bless me," cried Miss Beauclerk, "if you are no Protestant, what are you? You don't mean to call yourself a nondescript."

"I am a Catholic," replied Harvey gravely, "*not* a Roman Catholic, but an Anglican Catholic; I belong to a branch of that Church which exists throughout the whole world; were I to term myself Protestant, it would be restricting myself to communion with a narrow sect or party."

"What a pity I am such a stupid creature," exclaimed Miss Beauclerk, "these distinctions are far above my limited comprehension. However, there is one thing I like, the originality of the idea, for a clergyman of the Church of England to declare he is no Protestant."

Miss Beauclerk laughed, and Mrs. Egremond looked very grave, while Mary hastened to change the subject, which she feared might become disagreeable. "Even allowing, Mr. Harvey," she began, "that the middle ages are unjustly accused of ignorance in some respects, on what plea can you extenuate their neglect of the Scriptures? the account which Milner gives of Luther discovering the Bible is very striking."

"Yes," said Mrs. Egremond with a sigh, "I too have just been reading a very beautiful book, D'Aubigne's Reformation, which gives the whole account of it. The great reformer had been studying hard several years, and was twenty years of age, when one day turning over volumes in the library, he happened to find a Bible; this precious book was new to him, for he had hitherto always believed, that the small portions of the epistles and gospels read occasionally in the Church, formed the whole of God's word; imagine then his sensations!"

"Excuse me interrupting you, Mrs. Egremond," said Harvey, "but pray read what Maitland says on this very subject. He proves your author's information to be most incorrect. The assertion that Luther discovered the Bible after several years' study, bears the stamp of falsehood. No less than twenty editions of the Latin Bible had been *printed* in Germany before Luther was born. Nay, previous to his birth, it had been printed at Rome, Florence, and Placenza, not to speak of Venice, where it had passed through eleven editions. Now how absurd to say that a young man who had received a liberal education, and by all accounts made very great progress in his studies at Magdeburg, Eisenach, and Erfurt, actually did not know what a Bible was, because, as it is mentioned with great simplicity, 'the Bible was unknown in these days.' It is really extraordinary with what monstrous lies the English public are gulled."

Mrs. Egremond looked exceedingly ill-pleased, and Mary hastened to start a new topic.

"Now, Mr. Harvey," she began, "you have done nothing this forenoon but wound the pride of those who, like Mrs. Egremond and myself, consider themselves enlightened Protestants; do therefore say something in praise of your countrymen, and tell us how superior we are in point of education and enlightenment, or what is better in true piety, to Romanists abroad. Do now," she continued, as she saw he hesitated, "I wish to see Mrs. Egremond pleased with you again."

"I wish with all my heart that I could!" replied Harvey, laughing, "but unfortunately your requests only tend to plunge me into deeper disgrace with Mrs. Egremond; for of course if I answer at all, I must do so truly. I believe that the lower classes in many Catholic countries, are far better instructed than they are with us; and as for the piety of England, the less we say of it the better! Perhaps, Mrs. Egremond, you may not have seen an interesting work published lately by Mr. Ward,* an Oxford clergyman, 'The Ideal of a Christian Church?' In some letters at the end of it there are passages so apposite to the present topic, that I shall quote them, coinciding as they do with my own observation and experience. Speaking of Catholic countries, the writer says, 'That the poor are ignorant, is, I believe, an entire misapprehension; I never talked to any who were so; I should say they are far, very far, better instructed in religious knowledge than our own people of the same class, and their attention to their religious duties, is to my mind, quite affecting. I have seen in large manufacturing towns, hundreds upon hundreds of workmen in their working dress, at mass at five o'clock in the morning, before going into the factories, with their books, and joining heartily in the service; and I need scarcely add what a contrast this forms to the habits of the same class of persons in this country. I have visited also many Catholic schools abroad, chiefly those under the superintendence of the Christian Brothers, and my opinion is, that we have nothing to compare with them, either as to the regularity and order of the schools, the extent of the secular education, the carefulness with which religious instruction is conveyed, or the number and

* At the time this was written, Mr. Ward was still a member of the Anglican Church.

character of the teachers. Upon the whole, my last impression, on returning from a foreign country (Belgium) to our own, was, that I was coming out of a religious country into one of indifference; the open churches of the former, the frequent services, the constant worshippers, the solemn ceremonial, the collected air of the clergy in their ministrations, the indubitable devotion and reverence of the people, their unhesitating confidence in their Church, has nothing approaching a counterpart with us; I know nothing more disheartening (I speak of the effect produced upon myself) than a return to England after some time spent in Catholic countries; everything seems so careless, so irreverent, so dead; with all my heart I wish, especially for my children's sake, that I could see in this country, some approximation to the solemnity, reverence, devotion, and earnestness which I have witnessed abroad.' "

"As it seems, Mr. Harvey," said Mrs. Egremond, in a cold tone, "that you agree with the sentiments of the writer you have quoted, pray have the goodness to inform us, how you account for this startling fact, if fact it be, the inferiority of England in point of piety."

"The coldness and indifference towards religion among our countrymen," replied Harvey, "is, alas! easily accounted for. The mass of Episcopalians are ignorant, or forget, that they belong to the *one only true Church;* the Church which is *holy, Catholic and Apostolic!* Hence they are unaware of their own privileges, and neglect the means of grace held out within her pale! Let the Anglican clergy preach their high vocation, inculcate church authority, and no longer fear to bring to light those dearest parts of our religion so long kept in the back ground! Even the people, encouraged by the example of their pastors, will love their religion, will glory in it, and will press forward with such rapid steps in the paths of holiness, as to set an example to Europe!"

"Well done, Mr. Harvey," cried Miss Beauclerk. "And when all this happens, (as the author of John Gilpin says,) 'May I be there to see!' "

"But, Mr. Harvey," said Mary, "it makes me sad to think that continental Catholics, people of a false persuasion, should excel us in true piety, or in attention to the mental culture of the poor."

"Say not, I beg you, of a false persuasion," replied Harvey. "The truth is, the Anglican Church is more nearly allied to the Catholic Church abroad, than to any other denomination of Christians. The Anglican is a branch of the Catholic Church scattered throughout the world. The praise bestowed upon Catholics in the letter I quoted, is in some sort a praise to ourselves, because it is praise of the great body of which we are members."

"You ought to speak for yourself, Mr. Harvey," said Mrs. Egremond. "Thank heaven, the evangelical party in the Church of England, protests loudly and strongly against such sentiments as yours, which if carried out, would revive once more the golden days of popery!"

"I beg your pardon, Madam," replied Harvey, bitterly, "there is little fear of our becoming Papists; for, to use the words of a late writer in 'The Churchman,' 'Since the Romanists in this country not only keep aloof, but unanimously and bitterly repel us, it does appear like an intimation of Providence, that the Anglican Church, if she is to develope herself in a Catholic sense, shall not be beholden to any other Church, but owe it entirely to the working of Christ's Holy Spirit within herself.' "

After this speech of Mr. Harvey's, the whole party were silent for a few minutes, and even Miss Beauclerk appeared graver than usual. At last Mrs. Egremond said, "This new Anglican party appears to me to resemble the Romanists in so many particulars, that it defies my poor head to detect much difference! Could you enlighten me, Mr. Harvey?"

"Some of our divines," replied he, "certainly approach more nearly to Romanist views than do others; still there must always be a wide and impassable chasm between the churches, as long as the Romanist gives to the existing Church the ultimate and infallible decision in matters of faith, while the Anglican abides by *antiquity*."

"But I thought antiquity had been papistical!" interrupted Miss Beauclerk.

"If you mean by papistical," replied Harvey, "holding allegiance to the Pope, I must beg entirely to differ from you. Many members of our party are doing their best (and with considerable success) to prove that submission to the Pope as supreme head, was by no means absolutely required by the Church in days of yore."

The conversation was now interrupted by the entrance of visitors, and Harvey shortly afterwards withdrew to the library, to prepare his sermon for the ensuing Sunday; one of a course which he had already commenced developing High-church Anglican views, which, though perhaps above the comprehension of the poorer parishioners, might yet he hoped effect some good among the neighbouring gentry. His words, however, on the two preceding Sundays had not entirely fallen to the ground among the less educated portion of the community, as will be gathered from a conversation at which we shall permit our readers to be present, between Dame Blount and her sister.

"So your letters are addressed now-a-days to the Reverend Deborah Benson, I hear tell!" were the first words uttered by the dame, as she seated herself in her sister's comfortable parlour. "Bless me! who would ha' thought it would ever have come to that! Many's the deep sigh I've drawn for you, sister Benson, since the last three weeks, ever since the new Pusey-man is come down—Mr. Harvey I mean! He has given me a kick forward on the road that leads to the march of intellect! The schoolmaster is now abroad, and is going about like a roaring lion to see what ignoramuses he can devour! I have got clear notions now of what a schismatic and a dissenter are, and I can tell you, sister, you are in a dangerous state, unless you will take my advice."

"The prophet Jonah took a hint from the worm that eat his gourd," replied Mrs. Benson, in extraordinary good humour, and with a condescending smile, "so I don't see why I should not follow his example and hear what you have got to say; whether I take the advice or not, is another thing!"

"You see, sister," continued the dame, "you have got the fame of being a fine preacher, and though I was against the thing at first, yet I am more conciliated to it now; because it brings honour to our family, and I always said something great would come out of us. Besides your name is Deborah, and you take after your namesake among the prophets! Well, as I was saying, it is a pity that a woman of your rhetoric and arrogance, not to speak of your other fine parts, should be out of the right way! I am not against your being the primmy Donny in any meeting-house, but I wish you were properly authorized to preach, which you are not. Mr. Harvey says that unlawful pastors are sheep in lamb's clothing, and that nobody has no right to preach without apostolic succession to back them! Now, what I want you to do, Deborah Benson, is to stir heaven and earth to get it! The ministers of the Church of England, Mr. Harvey says, all have it, but many forget they have it, and their people don't know it!"

"Whew!" cried Mrs. Benson, "the new papistical notions are preaching here, I see! Me have any thing to do with *apostolic succession!* It is all humbug as far as your Church is concerned, dame! It is a good joke stealing these fine things from the Papists! Take care of your hands, sister, or you'll be a Catholic before you know."

"So I am a Catholic," replied the dame. "Mr. Harvey says we all are! I did not like the name at first, but since I remembered it was a word in the Creed, and that I know that Catholic means our own Church and State, I am well content and proud to be it."

"What stuff!" exclaimed Mrs. Benson. "How can anybody say that Catholic means Church and State! Sure it is the *State* that keeps down Catholics, and used to fine them and put them in prison! Many's the good laugh I've had with the late Gabriel Benson when he used to tell me the funny stories of how his grandfather, an Irish orangeman and spy in the government employ, used to hunt out the Catholics! Depend on it, dame, Church and State hate them, or used to do it."

"It would be well if we practised Scripture more than we do!" said the dame, tossing her head; "unless we fulfil it, we cannot expect a blessing! I am sure it is heavy on my conscience the way in which I have neglected the beautiful command, 'Cast not your pearls before swine!' However, next time I hold conversation with you, sister, I shall mind better."

"Come now, dame, don't be flustry," said her sister, who began to think she might get some available information from her, upon which to enlarge in her next sermon, "tell us what more you have learned from Mr. Harvey; for, like Solomon, I wish to get all sorts of knowledge, and if I could, would study from the Leviathan upwards, down to the meanest mite on a papist's cheese!"

Somewhat mollified by this magnanimous speech, the dame proceeded. "Well, sister, to begin at the beginning, the thing I like most that I have heard tell of lately, are the beautiful new names and dictionary words to adorn conversation with, that are coming into fashion. It would thrill through bone and marrow, not to speak of tearing your heart-strings, to hear Mr. Harvey preach about cornices, effigies, tapers, curfew, penance, belfries, and all the other things that he calls minor rites!"

"But what is the meaning of these words? some of them I am not accustomed to hear," asked Mrs. Benson.

"There's the beauty of them!" replied the dame chuckling. "I like a man like Mr. Harvey, that appeals to our higher faculties, and towers like a spread-eagle above our comprehension! A man like that, with dictionary words, elevates the intellectuals!"

"But miner rights!" exclaimed Mrs. Benson, "has any one attacked the miners, that they stand to their rights?"

"You are a fool, Deborah, though I say it, and though you are a wonderful preacher!" replied the dame. "Do you not know that all I have been saying, applies to the new model 'church and state' that the Puseys are getting up! If such things as these are above your comprehension, what will you say to 'sedilia,' 'panels,' 'altar-plate,' 'baptismal fonts,' and how will your eye be able to soar to hairy spires rising to heaven, not to speak of gothic arches and fret-work!"

"It would *fret* a saint to hear you gabble such nonsense! Before I'd use long words, I'd know the meaning of them!" interrupted Mrs. Benson.

"I'll tell you what, sister," replied the dame, "you meddle with what is neither your nor my business! As long as the Pusey ministers know what they themselves mean in using these long words, it is all right; for I assure you it is impossible for their congregation to know what they would be at, and neither is it expedient that they should do so; since, as I tell you, it is the highest compliment a church dignitary can pay to his flock, when he treats them to a little learning, something that he has bought and paid for at Hoxford or Cambridge, which would not be worth a snuff if they could tell what it meant !................. There is one thing, however," added the dame heaving a sigh, "that I should like to know the meaning of. Last Sunday, Mr. Harvey spoke of the chancel in a church; now that does not puzzle me, for I think it has something to do with the Chancellor of the Exchequer; but immediately afterwards he began to speak of a crypt below a nave! Now, by his account, there is a knave in every church, which seemed to me a most dreadful account to give of the English clergy. However, my mind is more at ease about it to-day, than it was, for I begin to think that the knave must be the clerk who reads the responses!"

At these words the dame was startled by a loud shout of laughter: "I ask your pardon, dame!" said Farmer Blount, who now stepped forward, "I am sure I meant no offence; but for the life of me I could not help laughing; just a fit of good humour comes over one sometimes, that one can't help, sister Benson! You'll know it yourself, by your own feelings, doubtless!"

So saying, the good farmer hurried his wife away to give him his supper.

CHAPTER XXIX.

"Let no one exclude himself from the number of those who fast, in which all men of every age, of whatever rank and dignity, are comprised. Angels draw up the list of them that fast. Take care then that your angel put down your name; desert not the standard of your religion." ST. BASIL.

"HERE I am back again, your Reverence," said the farmer, as he again entered the library. I've just been thinking, Sir, that we have missed something; for it says in the creed, 'I believe in One Holy Catholic and Apostolic Church.' Now you showed me the need of unity, also that the true Church must be Catholic; but as you said not a word about her being holy, I began to smell a rat; and thinks I, his Reverence has been too cunning to speak of what he knows the Romans can't pretend to more than their neighbours."

"You have judged too hastily, John," replied the rector; "holiness is one of the marks of the true Church; and if I have purposely deferred the subject, it was only that you might be previously instructed in some points necessary for appreciating the merits of the case. However, since you are in a hurry, we shall begin immediately. The Apostles' Creed, as you say, teaches that the true Church must be holy... ...."

"But how can any Church be holy, composed of men?" interrupted the farmer. "Go where you like, there will always be sinners in a congregation, for human nature is still human nature, and there is no such thing as washing an Ethiope white, or keeping a sow from growing bristles on its back!"

"Very true, John," replied the rector. "There will always be a mixture of good and evil men in the Church of God upon earth. We find so in Scripture, when it is likened to a floor where chaff is mingled with wheat, to a net in which there is bad fish as well as good, and to ten virgins, five of whom were wise and five foolish. In short, if the Church consisted exclusively of good men, it would not answer the description given in the Gospel."

"You'll be a clever man, rector," replied the farmer, "if, after allowing all that, you can make out that the true Church is holy."

"We shall see, John," replied Mr. Feversham. "In the first place, the Church is holy with regard to its founder, Jesus Christ, the author and fountain of sanctity; it is also holy from its calling, all its members being called to sanctity; its doctrine has ever been pure and holy, teaching the practice of all holiness; and its seven sacraments are so many sources of grace, always flowing and ever open for the sanctification of souls; not to speak of the Eucharistic sacrifice daily celebrated, by which the merits of the passion of Christ are applied to us. Another argument, which, as you learn more of Catholicity, will probably strike you, is the great sanctity of many of the members of the Catholic Church, and the glorious saints she has produced in all ages."

"Do you not think," said the farmer, hesitating, "that the Protestants could lay claim to some of these kinds of holiness?"

"Very possibly," replied the rector; "but let us see whether Protestants or Catholics substantiate the *best* claim. Both pretend to have Christ for their founder and head, but with this difference—that the one derives a visible succession, in the same communion, from His Apostles, and most certainly had its beginning from Him; while the other can show no such succession, and had its beginning fifteen hundred years after."

"You'll except, Sir, the new Pusey-folks, won't you?" interrupted the farmer. "They count up to the Apostles, as clean and neat as possible."

"We shall not dispute their claims at present," replied the rector, laughing. "It is enough that I am correct with regard to the mass of Protestants generally, including the evangelical party of the Church of England, who certainly would claim no greater antiquity than I am disposed to allow them. But, to go on with our subject; the Catholic doctrine is built on the infallible promises of God, that He would be with His Church always even unto the end of the world, that He would send unto her the Spirit of truth to guide her into all truth, and that the gates of hell should not prevail against her, &c. &c.; while the Protestant doctrine gives the lie to all these promises, and consequently must be wrong. We shall now examine which religion affords its members the greatest means of attaining sanctity. The old Church has the advantage in daily celebrating the Eucharistic sacrifice which Protestants have discarded, in a much more frequent participation of the blessed sacrament, in the confession of sins and priestly absolution, in more frequent prayer and fasting."

"Ah! stop a bit, if you please, Sir," interrupted the farmer. "I don't like to hear you mention as an advantage in the Catholic Church a thing in which I can't see any good. How can a man that wants his dinner be more pleasing to God than one that, like me, makes a hearty meal, and says his grace after?"

The rector smiled and replied: "It would depend altogether upon the spirit in which the thing was done, whether the man that wanted his dinner or the man that took it pleased God best. However, if we begin the subject of fasting, we must put off finishing the holiness of the Church for a little."

"I'd rather go on about fasting, if your Reverence pleases, to get my mind set at ease upon it; for a thing that comes between a man and his meat is no joke, I can assure you. What is the good of it at all?"

"To chastise ourselves, and do penance for our sins, that, like the inhabitants of Nineveh, we may obtain mercy from God; to curb and restrain our passions and appetites, and to bring the flesh into subjection to the Spirit; and, lastly, to be enabled by fasting to raise our souls more easily to God, and offer him purer prayer."

"So, so; I begin now to be better up to it," said the farmer. "I remember you telling me that, even after our sins are forgiven as to their guilt and the eternal punishment of hell-fire, we must still suffer something to satisfy God's justice; and I suppose that, if a man punish himself by fasting God will take it, instead of making him pay out the debt in purgatory. Now I see the thing a little more clearly; the Ninevites fasted, and God spared their city; and David fasted after he went wrong, and God forgave him."

"Quite right, John," said the rector; "still, you must remember that David's fasting, though it helped, was not altogether sufficient to appease God's justice, for He sent the royal penitent some heavy afflictions besides. Fasting, therefore, is only one means among many others for making satisfaction, or in other words for receiving the temporal punishment due to our sins after their guilt has been washed away by the blood of Christ."

"Then do you think, Sir, that if we punish ourselves enough, God will not punish us?"

"Clearly so," replied the rector; "but few people indeed succeed in cancelling altogether the debt of suffering due for their sins."

"But, Sir," interrupted Blount, "if they die without balancing their debt, what becomes of them?

They won't go to hell, I think you said, if they had made a good confession, received absolution, felt truly sorry, and done all else that they could to become friends with God."

"Your memory is bad, John," answered the rector. "Have you forgotten how I told you that they make out the remainder of their debt in purgatory, where their souls are purified, and which is a prison whence they shall not come out till they have 'paid the uttermost farthing?'"

"I do remember now," said the farmer; "but there is a question I want to ask: Do those souls that have made out their debt while living on earth, pass through purgatory at all?"

"They do not," said the rector.

"Howsomever," continued Blount, "I would rather put off the doing penance, and satisfying for my sins, until I went to purgatory; for a man that works hard, and has a roaring appetite at meal-times like me, would rather pass through purgatory three times than want his dinner."

"But the sufferings in purgatory are believed infinitely to exceed anything we have an idea of in this life," replied Mr. Feversham; "indeed, they are considered by many divines to equal hell-fire in intensity, though not in duration; so I think we should try, if possible, to escape them. Besides, if we suffer to please God while in this world, we shall be proportionally rewarded for it in heaven by a greater degree of happiness and glory; while, by undergoing pain in purgatory, we merely satisfy God's justice, and gain no further increase of joy in heaven."

"What other ways are there for making satisfaction to God's justice besides fasting?" asked Blount, with a deep sigh.

"The chief means," answered the rector, "are prayer, mortification of our senses, good works, such as alms-deeds, or assisting the sick, &c., gaining indulgences, and suffering whatever illness or sorrow

God pleases to send us with resignation; but, indeed, we can make our whole lives acceptable to God and meritorious, either for cancelling our debt or acquiring higher degrees of glory in heaven, by offering to our heavenly Father, every action, word, and thought, doing, thinking, and saying all with the intention of pleasing Him, and for His greater honour and glory. In this manner we may sanctify our everyday labours, nay, our very amusements."

"I should like to gain merit," said the farmer, "in any other way than by fasting. May be you know the proverb, Sir, that 'a hungry man is an angry man.' I never was like the 'geese,' as they say in Scotland, 'that liked their play better than their meat.' However, Sir, if I like to do other good works instead of fasting, would not that suit?"

"The Church," replied the rector, "has appointed certain penitential seasons, such as Advent and Lent, for fasting and doing penance, which are obligatory on all Catholics, unless for particular reasons they are dispensed."

"Well, Sir," said Blount, "you have learned me to know that the Church must be obeyed, for Christ says, 'If a man will not hear the Church, let him be unto thee as an heathen man and a publican;' so I had better gainsay fasting no further, that is, if you'll make out that it agrees with Scripture."

"That is easily done," replied Mr. Feversham. "The prophetess Anna is praised for serving God with fastings and prayers night and day. (Luke ii. 37.) The Ninevites by fasting obtained mercy. (Jonah iii. 5.) Daniel joined fasting with prayer, (Dan. ix. 3,) and by fasting was disposed for heavenly visions. (Dan. x. 3, &c.) David humbled his soul with fasting. (Ps. xxxv. 13.) Ezra and Nehemiah found aid from God by fasting. (Ezra viii. 23, and Nehemiah i. 4.) God called upon his people by the prophet Joel, 'Turn ye even to me with all your heart and with fasting, and with weeping, and with mourning.' " (Joel ii. 12.)

"But, Sir," interrupted the farmer, "a great many things were done away with in the Old Testament, and might not fasting be amongst them?"

"Certainly not," replied the rector, "for Christ gave us an example of fasting forty days, (Matt. iv. 2.) and prescribed lessons for fasting, (Matt. vi. 16,) besides affirming that when the bridegroom should be taken away, that is, after His death and ascension, His children should fast. (Matt. ix. 15. Mark ii. 20. Luke v. 35.) The first christians at Antioch fasted. (Acts. xiii. 21.) Paul and Barnabas were ordained with prayer and fasting, (verse 3.) Priests, or as they are improperly termed in the Protestant Bible, elders, were ordained by them in every church with prayer and fasting; (Acts xiv. 23,) the apostles approving themselves as the ministers of God in fasting, &c. (2 Cor. vi. 5.)"

"I wonder too, Sir," said the farmer, "that when Protestants hold by the Bible and nothing but the Bible, they should have given up fasting!"

"That is not the only thing to be wondered at," said the rector, "considering their pretence of keeping strictly to Scripture, they need some effrontery to deny the real presence of our Saviour in the Blessed Eucharist, a thing more clearly expressed than almost any other Scriptural dogma, not to speak of their discarding Extreme Unction, commanded by the Apostle St. James, &c., &c."

"I've seen a great deal of that same sort of thing in the world," said the farmer. "Them as does not do the thing gets credit for it; and them as does gets none! It beats everything, how the Protestants that pay no attention to a deal in Scripture, get credit for holding by it, while the poor Catholics that take it to the letter so much more, get laughed at for their pains, and are told to their face that they despise Scripture! But we forget that we have not done with fasting yet, Sir; is it true that Catholics always fast on Fridays?"

"No," replied Mr. Feversham, "they only abstain from animal food, but as the quantity is unrestricted, they cannot be said to fast."

"Yes, I remember now," said the farmer, "they take fish or eggs on Fridays instead of butcher-meat. No mention is made in the Bible, though, of not eating flesh on Fridays!"

"True, John; but it is a command of the Church, whose authority is sufficient for us to abstain from flesh not only on Fridays but on Fast-days in general. Thus she teaches us to mortify our appetites; and certainly we shall be better able to resist temptation, and refrain from unlawful gratifications, if we are sometimes in the habit of denying ourselves what is otherwise lawful."

"That is very true, your Reverence," replied the farmer, pondering. "Have we any example in Scripture of abstaining without mention being made of fasting?"

"Yes," said Mr. Feversham, "St. John the Baptist was commanded to abstain from wine and strong drink. (Luke i. 15.) In the desert he afterwards kept abstinence, his food being locusts and wild honey. The Nazarites among the Jews considered that they made themselves more acceptable to God by abstaining from wine and strong drink, &c. And Daniel........."

"Well, Sir," interrupted the farmer, "don't mind going on, for I am sure I am content; the Church has ordered it, and I allow that she had a wise motive in doing so; for a man accustomed to deny himself in little things, will be less likely to yield when he is tempted to do ill. But, Sir, you have not told me the way we are to fast. Do people take no meat all day on a fast-day?"

"That would be very hard," replied the rector, "and in many cases dangerous for the health. One full meal is allowed on fasting-days, but it must not be taken before mid-day, while custom has introduced a small collation at night. In former times, during the first twelve hundred years, fasting was more strict, particularly during Lent, when Christians did not eat before the evening."

"At any rate, Sir, it is not so bad as I thought," said the farmer, "for if I may get my dinner, as much as I can eat, at twelve o'clock even on a fast-day, I'll manage very well. Now, Sir, I'd like to know if fasting is obligatory on every body, or if delicate atomies are excepted?"

"Children under age, sick or old people, persons obliged to labour hard, and women in a state of pregnancy or while nursing their children, are excepted: and besides, when the health of an individual suffers from fasting, he can obtain a dispensation from his pastor."

"That's all right," said the farmer, "but I have a case to put to your Reverence. Would God count a fast meritorious if you were sinning in other ways all the time?"

"Certainly not," said the rector. "God would not accept the fasts of the Jews, because on their fast-days they were following their self-will, and oppressing their neighbours. The first condition to render our fasts acceptable to God, is to renounce our sins; the second is to let them be accompanied with alms-deeds and prayer, of which we find an example in the book of Tobit."

"That's not in my Bible," interrupted the farmer.

"The third condition," continued the rector, unnoticing the interruption, "is to perform our fasts in a penitential spirit."

"Ah! well," sighed the farmer, "I must pray hard to God to help me to fast as I should do, if I become a Catholic. So now, Sir, will you tell me what are the principal Fasts?"

"The fast of Lent," answered Mr. Feversham,

"is the longest and most severe. It is an apostolical institution, since it has always from time immemorial been observed by the Church. It lasts forty days, the time our Saviour fasted in the wilderness, and thus we consecrate a tithe of the year more particularly to God by prayer and fasting. During this time we ought to do penance for the sins of the whole year, examine more narrowly the state of our souls, try to repair our spiritual strength, and provide remedies, as far as we can, for our habitual failings. By fasting during Lent we also celebrate more appropriately the passion of Christ, commemorated at that season, and prepare for Easter and for making our Paschal Communion. The other fasts of the Church are the Wednesdays, Fridays, and Saturdays in the four Ember weeks, the eves of certain great festivals, and the Wednesdays and Fridays in Advent."

"When are the Ember weeks, and what is meant by the name?" asked Blount.

"They are the weeks during which the Church gives holy orders to the candidates for the priesthood," replied the rector. "The first week in Lent, Whitsun week, the third week in September, and the third week in Advent. The name is derived from the custom of our forefathers to fast at those times in sackcloth and ashes, eating nothing but cakes baked on the *embers*, hence called *ember* bread."

"And what is Advent?" asked the farmer.

"Advent means *coming*," answered the rector. "The term is applied to the weeks before Christmas, during which we prepare for the coming of our Lord. And now, John, you really must go; for my time is precious and I cannot stay with you longer."

"Only answer me one question, Sir, and then I will go," said Blount. "Why is Friday chosen of all the days in the week for abstaining?"

"Because our Lord suffered death on that day," replied the rector, rising to leave the room. "Come back again, Blount, as soon as you like, and we shall finish the subject we first commenced, the sanctity or holiness of the Catholic Church."

The very next day Blount returned, which pleased Mr. Feversham, as it showed the interest he took in the subject. "I want to know, Sir," was his first inquiry, "if there is any other means of holiness in the Catholic Church, beside what you mentioned, that is not in the Protestant?"

"To answer you fully," replied the rector, "would take a long time, so many things might be mentioned. However, I have already told you the most remarkable means of holiness, with one exception; and that is, I have not yet spoken of religious orders. Suppose a person were anxious to devote himself entirely to God, to have no other object, aim, or end, than to serve Him and please Him; suppose that he wished to devote his whole time to prayer and deeds of charity, nay, to give up his whole substance, like many of the first christians, to alleviate the wants of the poor; whether do you think that person would be best able to put such good wishes into execution, by remaining in the world, taking a wife, and having children, or by giving up the world and associating himself with other individuals actuated by the same motives as himself?"

"Oh! the last, certainly!" replied the farmer; "besides, I don't think a man would be in his duty at all, who had a wife and children, were he to devote himself entirely to prayer and give away all his money in charity."

"Neither do I," said the rector; "at the same time the person who wished to lead the holy life I described, would do well not to marry!"

"Hilloah there!" cried the farmer, "a good husband and father is the most respectable member of society that I know."

"Do you not think," said the rector, "that there might be a case even more admirable, that of one who would follow to the letter the counsel of our Saviour,

'If thou wilt be perfect, go and sell that thou hast, and give to the poor, and thou shalt have treasure in heaven.'" (Matt. xix. 21.)

"It would be a hard thing indeed, to follow that!" said the farmer, looking alarmed. "You don't mean to say that all should do so?"

"Far from it," replied Mr. Feversham; "it is a counsel and not a command, therefore suitable only to a few and not obligatory on all. In the Protestant Church there is little or no facility for putting it into execution; while in the Catholic the way is open, for the various religious orders have practised it since the commencement of Christianity."

"You got me to allow, Sir," said Blount, "that they who wished to do all that, would be better to have neither wives nor children; but now I think of it, the first christians gave up their goods, and yet kept their wives, if I don't mistake."

"Some led a holy married life in the way I described," said the rector, "and others dedicated themselves to God in a life of celibacy. However, common sense will show you that it would be impossible now-a-days to follow the counsel which Christ gave to the young man, and at the same time do one's duty to a wife and family."

"Very true," said the farmer; "but there is a thing I'd like to ask; whether do you think that amongst the first christians who had all things in common, the married ones or those in a state of celibacy pleased God best?"

"No man can judge another," said Mr. Feversham, "there might be individuals amongst the married who were more acceptable to God than those who practised celibacy; nevertheless, there is no doubt that celibacy is in itself a higher state, and that in it there are greater means of perfection."

"How does your Reverence make that out?" asked the farmer, looking doubtful.

"St. Paul is certainly of my opinion," replied the

rector, "when he says, 'He that is unmarried careth for the things that belong to the Lord, how he may please the Lord: but he that is married careth for the things that are of the world, how he may please his wife.' (1 Cor. vii.) Which, by the way, is an unanswerable argument in favour of the celibacy of the Catholic clergy. St. Paul also adds, 'He that gives her (his virgin) in marriage doeth well; but he that giveth her not in marriage doeth better.' But indeed if you will take the trouble to read it, the whole of this chapter favours my argument."

"Doubtless," said Blount, "I remember it well; but I have only one objection; if everybody were of St. Paul's opinion, the race of men would die out, and surely that is not what God intends!"

"No fear of that!" said the rector. "The commands of God are for all; His counsels only for a few; and Christ Himself admits, while speaking of refraining from marriage, 'all men cannot receive this saying.'"

"And pray, Sir," continued the farmer, "is this all that makes a monk or a nun, to give their goods away, and to lead a single life?"

"No," replied the rector, "besides the vows of poverty and chastity, a religious takes a third, that of obedience."

"That's the worst of them all now!" exclaimed the farmer. "I'd rather do anything than swear to obey any man! How do you make out that it is agreeable to God?"

"Because," replied the rector, "obedience is better than sacrifice, since by obedience we give up to God and for God, that which is naturally most dear to us, our liberty; and that which stands most in the way of our soul's welfare, our own will and self-love. Besides, if the members of a religious community did not bind themselves to obey their superiors, no order could be maintained, and the institution in consequence would not be permanent: when you recollect the necessity of obedience in the army, you must admit its utility in a religious house."

"I dare say your honour is right," said Blount; "and yet it strikes me with wonder to think how women, that are naturally such contumacious creatures, (witness my dame,) can ever be brought to take a vow of obedience, or, what is worse, to keep it."

"Women, however," replied Mr. Feversham, "appear to find no difficulty in taking the vow of obedience to their husbands. Now, obedience to an ecclesiastical superior must in most cases be as easy, in many perhaps easier; for religious men and women in obeying those above them, know that they are obeying God in their persons, and that they are gaining incalculable merit, which will win them a proportional increase of joy in heaven; whereas, the commands of a husband are not always so holy nor so certain to be conformable with the will of God."

"It may be your Reverence is right," said Blount. "And now I want to know if all Catholic priests take the three vows of poverty, chastity, and obedience?"

"No," replied the rector, "they only take the vow of celibacy, that they may have more freedom and leisure to care 'for the things that belong to the Lord, and also that they may lead purer lives, befitting those counted worthy to offer the stupendous Eucharistic sacrifice.'"

"Well, I do admire the celibacy of the clergy," said the farmer; "and, above all, I think the monastic orders a fine thing. It must be a beautiful sight to see people giving up all to follow Christ. In respect of giving opportunities for that, the Catholic Church is certainly holier than the Protestant."

"The Catholic Church is indeed illustrious in this respect," continued the rector. "Many kings, queens, princes, and great personages in her communion have left all to follow Christ, not to speak of the millions of common persons who have embraced the rigours of a monastic or eremitical life, whereas the whole reformation will scarcely furnish an instance of the kind."

"You are great upon the subject of holiness, rector," replied the farmer; "but what I would like best to know is, not so much which church has the greatest means for acquiring holiness, as which in reality practises it most."

"We find among the members of the more ancient Church a greater faith, even to the working of miracles and casting out devils," replied the rector.

"Miracles!" exclaimed the farmer, aside. "I must remember that, and have a fling at them."

"And a far greater zeal," continued Mr. Feversham, "than has ever been found among sectaries in propagating the faith. There must also be a stronger hope for the joys of another world, or thousands in every age would not have quitted the honours, riches, and pleasures of this life, in order to merit them; a greater love of God in those who, despising all things else, enjoy in solitude the sweets of His heavenly conversation; a greater charity towards our neighbour, proved by more frequent and ample endowments for the benefit of the poor, institutions for redeeming captives, confraternities for the help of the sick, sisters of charity, brothers of mercy, &c."

"You speak of particular people amongst Catholics," said the farmer; "but do you really think, Sir, that there is more religion generally amongst them than amongst us?"

"Undoubtedly I do," replied the rector. "Witness the canonical hours of prayer observed by clergy and religious, many of them rising at midnight to recite the praises of God; the exercises of morning and evening devotion used by the generality of the Catholic laity, the solemnity and reverence with which the worship of God is performed in their churches, so different from Protestant places of worship; and, more than all, the infinitely greater frequentation of the sacraments. Humility must flourish among them, since it is so well cultivated by those who practise obedience. I have already alluded to the self-denial and mortifications enjoined among Catholics, and to the state of virginity, so much prized by the early Christians, which is held in honour by them. I must by and bye lend you some of the lives of their Saints, which will give you a few new ideas, and fill your mind with astonishment at their sublime practice of virtue."

CHAPTER XXX.

"To think o' the impidence o' thae papists, to set up sae mony saints; when John Knox and blessed W. Andrew Peden, had ower muckle humility ever to try to become saints." *My old Nurse.*

"WHY have Protestants no saints of their own, Mr. Feversham?" asked Miss Beauclerk one day, as she was sitting next the rector at breakfast. "It seems to me so ridiculous to name churches after old-fashioned saints. Instead of St. John's or St. Matthew's, it would be but fair play to call a church now and then St. Luther's or St. Calvin's."

"But what if the lives of these men would not justify any one in giving them the appellation of Saint?" replied the rector.

"You don't mean to say so! Pray explain for my benefit and that of Mrs. Egremond, who, I see, is listening across the table."

"In the first place, Luther was a monk, and broke his vows by marrying a nun," said the rector.

"How deliciously romantic!" exclaimed Miss Beauclerk; while Harvey, the Anglican clergyman, looked very grave.

"I shall not speak of the Life of Luther, which, by his own account, after he left the Church of Rome, was far from edifying; but can any one term a saint a man who could write as follows: 'That where the Scripture commands the doing of a good work, it is to be understood in this sense, that it forbids you to do a good work because you cannot do it.'* That to teach with Catholics, 'that God's commands are to be kept, is directly to deny Christ, and abolish faith.'† In some of his writings he sanctions the most gross immorality;‡ and it is well known how he gave permission to Philip, Landgrave of Hesse, to have two wives at once. Then, what do you think of a man that could write such nonsense as that 'every woman or child may absolve, in the absence of a priest, in virtue of the words of Christ, 'Whatsoever you shall loose upon earth,' &c.§ And that the immortality of the soul is amongst the doctrines which he calls 'monsters bred in the dunghill of Rome.'"‖

"Men of genius are always eccentric," said Miss Beauclerk. "But what do you say now to St. Calvin?"

"That he was a madman," replied the rector, "if not worse. He is charged with crimes of the blackest dye by both Lutherans and Catholics; and he wrote, 'That God has created the greatest part of mankind on purpose to damn them, without any foresight of their sins or prevarications.'¶ 'That the true faithful

* De Lib. Christ, T. 2. Fol. 4. 2. 2.
† T. 5. Fol. 311. 2. 4.
‡ See T. 5. Fol. 119. 1, and also T. 5. Fol. 123. 1. 17.
§ T. 2. Fol. 103. 2. 10.
‖ T. 2. Fol. 107. 2.
¶ See Collier's Dictionary of Calvinism.

cannot fall from justice, though they were to commit the most enormous sins.' "*

"Oh, Mr. Harvey," exclaimed Miss Beauclerk, "I beg of you to stop Mr. Feversham. Come forward like a true knight, and defend the reformers."

"I beg your pardon, Miss Beauclerk," replied Harvey; "I wish to have nothing to do with the reformers. The longer I live the worse I think of them. As Froude said, 'The Reformation is a limb badly set; it must be broken again in order to be righted.' "

"As to the foreign reformers," said Mary, "thank heaven, we may let them stand or fall, having our own glorious English Reformation of which to feel proud."

"On the contrary," said Harvey, "to use the words of Mr. Ward, in his 'Ideal of a Christian Church,' 'I know no single movement in the Church, except Arianism in the fourth century, which seems to me so wholly destitute of all claims on our sympathy and regard as the English Reformation.' "

"If you think so," said Miss Beauclerk, bluntly, "I ask you again, as I once did before, why do you stay in the English Church?"

"Your question," replied Harvey, "has nothing to do with what we are discussing, for the Church of England has retained her excellencies derived from antiquity, in spite of the desolating havoc wrought by the reformers."

"I very much dislike," said Mrs. Egremond, "to hear the reformers, to whom we owe so much, abused. However, I am glad to find that Mr. Harvey allows the excellency of the Church of England, though I would rather he had not ascribed it to antiquity, since it is the duty of Christians to hold by the Bible, and nothing but the Bible."

"I beg your pardon," said Harvey, "Paul did not

* L. 3. Inst. c. 2. n. 16. &c., c. 24, &c. &c.

recommend that to Timothy. (2 Tim. i. 14.) Besides, we all know that tradition preceded Scripture, and attested its canon."*

"I myself have heard English clergymen say," interrupted Miss Beauclerk, "that the Bible was the only rule of faith."

"It is certainly an opinion *in* the Church," replied Harvey; "but by no means universally received, much less a principle."†

"I am sorry to find," said Mrs. Egremond, "that there are Protestants willing to give up the good old motto, 'the Bible and nothing but the Bible.'"

"Doubtless Protestants keep the old watch-cry still," said Harvey. "I, however, am no Protestant, but an Anglican Catholic, and a member of that Church, which, in her twentieth article, claims 'authority in controversies of faith.'"

"Yes," interposed the rector, "and the same article forbids the Church to *enforce* anything besides what is contained in Scripture. Now, as we are all at liberty to judge whether the Church in her decrees coincides with Scripture or not, it follows that the Church may decree what we cannot reconcile with the Bible, and therefore be in the ridiculous position of decreeing what she has not power to enforce."

"At any rate," said Miss Beauclerk, "if the English Church, as Mr. Harvey and the 20th article say, really has 'authority in controversies of faith,' why does she not decide between Evangelicals like Mrs. Egremond and Anglican Catholics such as Mr. Harvey? Who can respect an authority that the possessors are too timid or too indolent to use?"

"She will one day pronounce decision, I trust in God," replied Harvey sadly.

"And now," said Mrs. Egremond, "excuse me for

* Sermon by Rev. John. Keble, M. A., entitled "Primitive Tradition recognized in Holy Scripture.

† British Critic, No. 40. p. 384.

changing the subject so abruptly, but I should like much to ask Mr. Harvey how he can call himself a Catholic, when the word means universal, and our Church only exists in a very small portion of the world?"

"Because the Anglican is a part of the Catholic Church," replied Harvey, "a national independent branch of it. Though individually she may err, yet through her we belong to that whole Church all over the world, which will never agree in teaching and enforcing what is not true."*

"I never liked the term Catholic even in the creed," said Mrs. Egremond; "it is so apt to mislead ignorant people, and make them think of the Church of Rome. And I do not think it any advantage to fraternize with foreign churches, some of which we know to be idolatrous, by way of making up that whole which you fondly assert cannot err."

"God forbid," said Harvey, "that we should be separated and cut off, as you seem to wish, from the great body of Christians throughout the world! Then, indeed, we should be schismatics in the full sense of of the word."

"Do you know," said Miss Beauclerk, "it strikes me there is a want of proper spirit in the Oxford party. They claim kindred with the Catholic Church, although the Catholic Church (I mean the Church which all the world calls Catholic) will have nothing to do with them."

"Foreign Catholics," said Harvey, "I have reason to hope, feel and act very differently on this subject from English ones. Besides, what need we care for the opinions of English Roman Catholics, knowing, as we do, that they 'are very justly charged with schism;' since the Church of England claims the spiritual allegiance of the people, to the exclusion of all rival claims."†

* See No. 40. British Critic, p. 380.

† See No. 40. British Critic. p. 435.

"Then do you mean that foreign Catholics are not schismatics?" asked Mary.

"Certainly I do," replied Harvey; "but the French Protestants may be termed so, because they do not join with the branch of the Catholic Church established in their country."

"Then, if you were settling on the continent, Mr. Harvey," said Miss Beauclerk, "do you think you ought to join the Roman Catholics abroad, though you repudiate them at home?"

"Your question is just, Miss Beauclerk," replied Harvey, "and would at least furnish matter for grave consideration."

"You are charmingly original, Mr. Harvey," said the young lady. "I delight in questioning you. What do you think of celibacy? Does it not throw a mysterious grandeur round the Catholic clergy? And would you become a monk if you lived at Munich, for example?"

Harvey made no reply, and Miss Beauclerk rattled on. "I saw the Beguines at Ghent, (talking of celibacy,) they did look so comfortable. I half thought of joining them. Indeed, perhaps I may when I come to their age—that is to say, if I don't make a good match beforehand. They were most of them so fat and fair, it was a pleasure to look at them. Between ourselves I hate a skinny old maid; that is my great objection to celibacy."

"And pray, Miss Beauclerk," said the rector, entering into her humour, though he could scarcely keep from laughing, "if that is your only objection, perhaps you would kindly point out its advantages."

"Why, I would make all the 'detrimentals'—the younger sons, I mean—take priest's orders; and then the mothers of England would be delivered from them, and have their minds kept easy; and all unmarried women past the age of five and twenty should take the veil. A nun's dress, too, is so becoming! The band across the forehead hides all wrinkles. I saw one at a fancy ball. She looked so pensive—wrapped in adoration! Fancy free! Pale Luna's meekest votary!"

"You do not quote very correctly, Miss Beauclerk," said Harvey, laughing.

"Well, at any rate," replied the young lady, "I am glad to have made you laugh, which was what I wished to do. You all look so desperately gloomy when you begin to talk about the Church, it makes me quite miserable to see you. Mary and Mrs. Egremond look like victims, the rector has an awful visage like that of a grand inquisitor, and Mr. Harvey has such strange amphibious opinions, that at times I think his mind (could we see it) must be a moral monster, shaped like the frightful creatures that lived in chaos. However, I must not speak ill of such respectable monsters, since Oxford and Cambridge turn out so many of them; I only pity them for hesitating whether to offer allegiance to queen or pope..............Come away, Mary," continued she, taking the arm of the latter, and rising to leave the room, which Mrs. Egremond had just quitted; "let us leave the gentlemen to their solemn conversation."

We shall now take a peep at Farmer Blount's household, which it is a long time since we have visited.

"Well, farmer," said the dame, laying down her spectacles, and raising her eyes from the book over which she had been poring—a catechism of natural history that had been left by a student, formerly a lodger in the house. "Well, farmer, I am mighty glad I can classify you now. You belong to the genus vertebrata; to which all caterpillars, reptiles, bees, and wasps appertain."

"How do you make that out, dame?" asked Blount, laughing.

"'Cause you are a book-worm, and only fit for a church-yard, since you dwell among the *tomes* that the rector lends you. I am glad to have learned that word *tome*—for it is the genteelest name for book of any that I ever heard; however, you had need to be cautious, farmer, for it is mentioned in the Gospels how a possessed person, who afterwards got his devil cast out, dwelt among the tomes. But, as I was saying, you belong to the genus vertebrata, which, I am sorry to find, are a class below my cows, which are reckoned (poor beasts!) among the mammalia, the highest of all next to the angels."

At this speech the farmer did not know whether to laugh or be angry; when he was relieved from his dilemma by the approach of visitors, Mrs. Benson and Jacob Hogg. The lady appeared highly excited, and scarcely able to control herself sufficiently to reply to the ordinary salutation of her relatives, whilst her companion wore an air of imperturbable calm, and every now and then cast his eyes up to heaven and sighed in a sanctimonious manner.

"Brother-in-law," exclaimed Mrs. Benson, as soon as she could sufficiently compose herself to speak, "are you acquainted with a pious minister of the Gospel in the town of Overbury, named Mr. Sharples?"

"I have seen him," said the farmer drily, his face getting red. "What about it?"

"O nothing! nothing!" replied Mrs. Benson, with forced calmness. "Only Mr. Longab was told by Mr. Hodgkinson, the pious attorney, that holds so many mortgages, and always acts for publicans, sinners, poachers, and housebreakers; and he again was told by his wife, who, good woman! was told by her dressmaker, that had it from Mrs. Sharples's lady's-maid, that had it from her mistress, who was told in confidence by her husband, that Farmer Blount of this parish was going to become a Roman Catholic! Is that true, or is it not, John Blount?"

"That is a question which you have no business to ask, and I have no need to answer," replied Blount.

"Then I take it for granted," said Mrs. Benson,

with great emotion. "Oh, Blount, Blount, that I should live to see this day! However, there is no need lamenting so soon, considering that no step has yet been taken; and you, with all your faults, are a reasonable man, and may yet be open to conviction. Jacob and I have just come down express to let you hear all the abominations of the Church of Rome. Begin, Jacob," she continued, turning to her neighbour, who had taken a seat opposite the farmer. The latter listened with an imperturbable countenance, while Mr. Hogg commenced:

"The papists worship stocks and stones, and pray to images and pictures," said he.

"Not to speak of burning incense and candles, and ringing bells," interposed the lady.

"They make a god of St. Peter, and a goddess of the Virgin," said Jacob.

"And they honour old rags and bits of bones, and keep the relics of saints in glass cases," said Mrs. Benson.

"Blessings on us!" said Dame Blount. "Is that the way in which they treat the widows of the saints? Thank goodness, even though John should turn out a papist, which I hope he has too much hedication ever to do, there is not much fear for me, seeing all the popes in Rome, and scarlet ladies into the bargain, could not turn him into a saint: so I am safe in that respect any way."

"I am not speaking of widows, but of popish relics," said Mrs. Benson, gruffly. "They say that they worship every Sunday in Overbury chapel a bit of Eve's apple; and on high days and holidays they bring out for adoration a golden phial containing some of the guano with which Adam manured the garden of Eden! No, no, sister, I'd not quarrel with them so much, if they did show the same respect for widows."

"Then they bring up people in ignorance," continued Jacob, "preaching to them in Latin or Greek, and instructing them in unknown tongues. There is not a papist in the world but what, if he had half-an-hour's conversation with a Protestant minister, would be converted, get the scales removed from his eyes, and see henceforth as though he had the best optician spectacles!"

"Then to think how they deluge children and sick people with holy water," continued Mrs. Benson, "causing the death of a great many through catarrh and rheumatism, not to speak of swallowing holy oil, and exorcising the devil."

"A deal better it would be," interrupted Dame Blount, "to take regular exercise on foot or horse-back, than to exercise the devil."

"Then they work miracles, and lay ghosts," said Jacob; "thus doing things beyond the power of nature, with which they have no business to meddle."

"I wish some of mother's hens would lay ghosts!" cried the farmer's little son, who had been sitting unnoticed in the corner.

"They would sooner commit murder than eat flesh on a fast-day," said Mrs. Benson; "though we all know that Paul forbids abstaining from meats."

"Yes," said Jacob, "praise be to God, I have always fulfilled that command of Paul; for I never would abstain from any meat I had a mind to, even when I've been ill and the doctor ordered me!"

"You can buy leave to commit any sin you like! Absolutions are dog-cheap! and in a fine season you can lay in as many of them as you please for next to nothing!" said Mrs. Benson. "Then they have a fine place called purgatory, in which any one can bespeak a seat by getting a ticket from the Pope! That saves them from going to hell, which they leave to the Protestants, forsooth!"

"It was them that invented gunpowder," said Jacob, "for Guy Fawkes' plot; not to speak of other fire-arms; for they had canons and Papal ordnance even in the dark ages—nay, in the course of my reading, I have found that every cathedral was provided with a number of canons that lay in stalls and appeared in processions."

"There is nothing too bad for Papists," sighed Mrs. Benson. "They call the devil old Harry, after our good reformation king, Henry VIII. and have unfortunately taught Protestants to do the same."

"You know the Pope deposed that same king," said Jacob, "which is the reason he wears a triple crown to correspond with Rome, Great Britain and Ireland!"

"None of your nonsense, Jacob," interrupted Dame Blount. "I have too good a hedication to swallow that. Old Harry was the father of our glorious English Reformation, and lived and died every inch a king; instead of the Pope taking crowns from him, he took power from the Pope and made himself into head of the Church! besides cutting off the heads of ever so many wives, and being the original of that fine, romantic, and illustrious character, Blue Beard!"

"Well, well," said Mrs. Benson, "let us leave history alone, though it is filled with solemn warnings, and go to facts. They take false oaths and leave out the second commandment, which is as much as to say that if they dared they would leave out the whole ten. But the worst and cruellest thing about them to my mind is, that when a person is dying, before the breath is out of his body, they dip him in holy oil, which they call extreme unction, and stifle him to death; upon which they embalm him with their incense and turn him into a papist mummy!"

"Very true," said Jacob. "And they pretend that extreme unction is performed in honour of the Apostle John, who was boiled alive in a cauldron of oil!"

"If you are done now," said the farmer, "I should like to go, having a great many things to look after about the homestead. You may be sure that I shall pay all the attention to your information which it deserves. So with many thanks to you, Mrs. Benson, and to you, Jacob, for your obliging interference, of which I have got quite enough, I wish you good day. I'll open the garden-gate for you if you like, it will be a short cut home." So saying, the farmer showed his visitors to the door.

CHAPTER XXXI.

"And how shall they preach except they be sent?" *Romans* x. 15.

"I'D like," said the farmer, the next day he called at the rectory, "to hear how the true Church is apostolic, now that you have shown me that it must be *one*, holy, and Catholic."

"The apostolic succession implied in the words of the creed," replied the rector, "denotes four things; a descent without interruption from the first society established by the apostles—a succession of doctrine derived from them, through an uninterrupted channel—a succession of holy orders in direct line from those ordained by them, and a succession of lawful commission or spiritual jurisdiction and authority to preach, administer sacraments, &c., such as Christ gave to His apostles, and which they imparted to their followers."

"Yes," said the farmer, "that was when Christ said to the apostles, 'Go ye therefore and teach all nations, baptizing them in the name of the Father, and of the Son, and of the Holy Ghost. Teaching them to observe all things whatsoever I have commanded you: and lo I am with you alway even unto the end of the world.' " (Matt. xxviii. 19, 20.)

"Very well indeed, John," replied the rector. "You might also have quoted from the 20th of John, 'as my Father hath sent me so send I you. Receive ye the Holy Ghost. Whose soever sins ye remit they are remitted unto them; and whose soever sins ye retain, they are retained.' You see from these texts, how Christ gave the apostles commission to teach; now even though clergymen be lawfully ordained, if they are not sent and commissioned by those who alone have power to send them, I mean, by the successors of the apostles, they cannot perform their functions lawfully. So even supposing the ministers of the Church of England to be true priests, which is most doubtful, they yet have no authority to act as such; because not empowered by the head of that Church which has subsisted without interruption from the times of the apostles. However, we shall say no more about that at present, but go through the three other conditions of apostolicity. The true Church must stand and flourish till time itself shall end, since Christ promised (Matt. xvi. 18.) that the gates of hell should not prevail against it; and that he should remain with it always even unto the end of the world; (Matt. xxviii. 20.) of his kingdom there should be no end; (Luke i. 33.) and the Comforter should abide with it (his apostolic Church) for ever." (John xiv. 16.)

"All true, Sir," replied the farmer. "I knew these texts before, and they prove that there must be no break between the true Church at the present day, and the true Church when the apostles lived."

"The same texts," continued the rector, "prove that since our Saviour and the Holy Spirit were to remain with the Church for ever, her doctrine must always be true and never could vary. Upon examination we find this to be the case in the Catholic

Church, for the Scriptures as well as the ancient fathers I have so frequently quoted, bear testimony to the truth and antiquity of her doctrines."

"That they do, Sir," replied the farmer, "as far as I have seen."

"Well, John," continued the rector, "I shall leave you to quote the texts for the third mark of apostolicity, which is a succession of pastors lawfully ordained from apostolic times. What powers did our Saviour give the clergy which could only be transmitted by regular ordination?"

"Christ said," answered Blount, "'Receive ye the Holy Ghost. Whose soever sins ye remit, they are remitted unto them; and whose soever sins ye retain they are retained.' Also the text at the end of Matthew, which I repeated just now, about teaching and baptizing all nations."

"Very well, John," said Mr. Feversham. "I must now show you how those alone whom Christ sent, have authority to do these things. Our Saviour says, 'As my Father hath sent me, even so send I you.' (John xx. 21.) Not to speak of the three verses at the end of St. Matthew's gospel, to which we have so often referred, giving such a glorious commission to the apostles and their successors, in virtue of the power given to Christ in heaven and in earth! What I now wish to prove is, that they who have not been authorized and commissioned by the apostles and successors to fulfil their apostolic functions, must be looked upon as usurpers, thieves and robbers. St. Paul writes, 'And how shall they preach except they be sent?' (Romans x. 15.) 'And no man taketh this honour unto himself, but he that is called of God, as was Aaron.' (Heb. v. 4.) And our Saviour himself says, 'Verily, verily, I say unto you, He that entereth not by the door into the sheep-fold but climbeth up some other way, the same is a thief and a robber.'" (John x. 1.)

"These same texts are a bad look out for dissenting ministers," said Blount.

"Yes, John," rejoined the rector, "and for all those not empowered by the present visible head of Christ's apostolic Church."

"I wonder," said the farmer, "that any Protestants have the face to repeat the words of the creed about believing in an apostolic Church, when the Protestant Church had not begun to exist four hundred years since, let alone when the apostles lived! Besides, so many sects have no holy orders at all, but let any layman preach, as the Methodists do! And some even cannot be called christians, for, like the Quakers, who don't baptize, they have never been made members of Christ's Church!" The farmer paused, and after a moment or two of reflection, continued, "Do you know, Sir, I think it will end in me becoming a papist! All that I've heard about the Catholic Church pleases me! She seems right in everything I have asked about, and it does not seem to me nearly so unreasonable as it did, to believe that she is infallible in the doctrine she teaches! If I am only required to believe what I find in that little Douai Catechism, then indeed it is not difficult; far less so than I had supposed! But does not your Reverence think of showing me the example? It is not for a poor hard-working man like me, to set up for to go before your Reverence! I never, Sir, all my life, was inclined to put myself equal to, far less to go before my betters!"

The rector appeared very uncomfortable at the close of this speech, and did not reply directly to the proposal so bluntly made.

"It appears to me," said he, "that you are somewhat premature; I am certain that all your difficulties have not yet been cleared up. Are you satisfied with regard to miracles, images, relics,..........."

"O stop, Sir, I beg!" interrupted the farmer. "Now I think of it, I have not near finished the list of things I made out to ask you about. And though I am pretty sure in the end of turning out a rank papist, yet it is as well to be cautious, and get all the difficulties finished off before doing anything. What does the Catholic Church believe about miracles?"

"The Catholic Church," replied the rector, "obliges her children to believe in the reality of the miracles recorded in the Old and New Testaments, and in the power always inherent in the Church to work miracles."

"But Catholics," said the farmer, "believe in many miracles not mentioned in Scripture."

"Do you believe," replied Mr. Feversham, "that such people as Queen Elizabeth, Mahomet, or Luther, ever did in reality exist?"

"To be sure I do," said Blount, "but what has that to do with the subject?"

"A great deal," said the rector. "You never saw these personages; but you believe that they once existed; because they are mentioned in all the histories of their times. Now, there are many miracles quite as well attested, which are mentioned by numerous authors, and ratified by the asseverations of a great number of eye-witnesses, examined by authority and legally recorded. If you believe well authenticated history you must believe in them."

"But I have been told of miracles for which there was but very little proof indeed; and yet some pious Catholics believed them," said Blount.

"That was their own affair," replied Mr. Feversham. "You need not follow their example."

"But after all," continued the farmer, "I don't think you should put miracles on a level with ordinary historical facts; since the one kind goes beyond nature and the other does not. It does not require so much faith to believe that Queen Elizabeth lived, as that the Church worked some great miracle."

"Very true, John; but the question is, can the Church, or can she not, work miracles; if she can, it is but reasonable to believe in any individual miracle which may be well substantiated by historical proof, as were those mentioned by St. Augustine and St. Jerome, or those worked in later times in India by the glorious St. Francis Xavier!"

"Well, Sir, let it be so;" said Blount, "give me good reason for the Church being as able to work miracles now as in the days of the apostles, and I'll give in."

"During the time of the old law," said the rector, "God honoured his servants in working miracles by their hands; is God's arm shortened now? Or is the new dispensation less glorious than the old? Besides, have we not the promise of Christ, 'He that believeth on me, the works that I do shall he do also, and greater works than these shall he do.'" (John xiv. 12.)

"Very true, Sir," said Blount. "It is but reasonable to suppose that the Christian Church should have more privileges than the Jewish one, and be at least as glorious in the way of working miracles. But are not some of the miracles which are best authenticated in the Catholic Church very ridiculous?"

"I am not aware of it," said the rector; "however to those that look out for the ludicrous there are few things that could not be turned into occasion for mockery. The miracles of the Old Testament would be an excellent subject of buffoonery—such as Balaam and his ass, Sampson and his jaw-bone, Joshua commanding the sun to stand still, &c."

"No doubt, Sir," replied Blount; "however, I am pretty well satisfied with what you have said, so, if you please, I'll ask about the next thing on my list, and that is relics. I've heard people tell, though I did not believe them, how Papists adore bones and rags, and affirm they can work miracles, because they had belonged to some of the saints!"

"Catholics," said the rector, "hold in great respect the bodies of departed saints, and indeed anything that ever belonged to them; nevertheless it is but an inferior honour, such as the Jews showed to the ark, to the tables of the law, or to Moses' rod. In like manner they honour the Church, because it is the house of God, and holy men and priests, because they are God's servants. Now the relics of saints also merit veneration, because they belonged to the favourites of God, and are memorials of those who are now with Christ in glory."

"I can very well understand all that," said the farmer. "It is but natural to keep with respect anything that has been used by a great or a good man. There is a cousin of mine, for example, that keeps locked fast in a drawer one of the curls of the great man's wig that wrote the dictionary, Dr. Johnson I mean. Her grandmother was sister to his servant-maid, and got it from her. And there was a private too, in your own regiment, Sir, that had got hold of one of the buttons of the coat Sir John Moore wore when he was killed. He thought as much of it as I do of our family Bible, and may-be more!"

"Well, John," said the rector, "these examples only show you how natural it is to preserve relics and to honour them. And if there was no harm in the soldier valuing the relic of Sir John Moore, still less could there be in a Catholic venerating the relic of a special servant and favourite of the Almighty."

"But surely, Sir," continued Blount, "Catholics maintain that miracles are sometimes worked by means of relics."

"Catholics maintain no more than Scripture does on this point," said Mr. Feversham. "Did not Moses' rod work many miracles? So did the mantle of Elijah, (2 Kings ii. 14,) also Elisha's bones when a dead body was let down into his sepulchre, 'And when the man was let down and touched the bones of Elisha, he revived, and stood up on his feet.'" (2 Kings xiii. 21.)

"Well, after that, Sir," said Blount, "I think

Protestants ought not to wonder at Catholics thinking much of the bones of saints; however, I have heard of none like Elisha since the gospel was written, and unless people worked miracles during their lives, I should not expect that their bones could do much."

"You have never read the lives of Catholic Saints, or you would confess that God's servants have been as glorious even in modern times as during antiquity. By and by, I shall lend you the life of a man who lived in the time of the Reformation, the apostle of India, St. Francis Xavier, whose wonderful miracles are attested by numerous contemporary writers."

"I should like well to see it, Sir," replied Blount, "as soon as I get a little more time for reading. But before we give over talking about relics, would your Reverence tell me if there is any example in Scripture of the clothes of saints working miracles?"

"Yes," replied the rector; "do you not remember how the woman was healed by touching the hem of our Saviour's garment? (Matt. ix. 22,) and how the handkerchiefs and aprons that had touched the body of St. Paul cured diseases and cast out devils?" (Acts xix. 12.)

"Well, Sir, before we leave the subject, will you tell me if the old doctors and fathers say any thing about honouring relics?"

"Indeed they do," replied the rector. "Eusebius says that after the martyrdom of St. Polycarp, whose body was burnt in 166, 'the Christians carried away his bones, which they valued more than gold and precious stones.'* St. Jerom writes against the heretic Vigilantius, 'Vigilantius fights with an unclean spirit against the Spirit of Christ, by asserting that the tombs of martyrs are not to be reverenced.' And in another place, 'The devils with which Vigilantius is possessed, roar at the relics, and confess they cannot

* Apud Euseb. L. 4. Hist. c. 15. p. 134.

bear the presence of the martyrs.' He also tells him, 'that all the bishops in the world were against him.'* And in his 53rd Epistle he writes, 'You tell me that Vigilantius vomits once more his poison against the relics of martyrs, calling us deists, worshippers, and idolaters, for reverencing dead men's bones. O unhappy man, who can never be sufficiently lamented!'"

"These quotations come in very pat, Sir," said the farmer; "however, I am beginning to think that I have had enough of them; for, no offence to your Reverence, I am getting very tired, and would rather come back another day."

CHAPTER XXXII.

"Nae wonder the kirk o' Scotland wad hae naething to say to Bishops, they'r the invention o' the pope, an' the spawn o' the deevil."

My old Nurse.

"I THINK it very bad policy," said Mrs. Egremond to Harvey, who had been descanting at great length upon Anglican orders—"I think it very bad policy indeed, to enlarge so much upon the necessity of apostolic orders, since thereby you throw discredit upon nearly all the reformed churches."

"Yes," said the rector, "the reformers cared but little for episcopal authority. Luther, though he

* L. contra Vigil.

never was a bishop, thought himself as good as one, since he invested his friend Armsdorf with the crosier.* Calvin established the presbyterian discipline, to exclude bishops for ever. Melancthon, Zuinglius, Ecolampadius, Bucer, &c., took care to have no bishops wherever they had power; and Knox drove them out of Scotland."

"I consider the Anglican Church," said Harvey, "as a thing totally distinct and different from other reformed churches. The latter introduced novelties and cast aside much valuable truth; while we Anglicans on the contrary retained all, or at least nearly all, that was venerable in the Church of Rome, merely cutting off a few excrescences, but preserving the Apostolic Church as founded by Christ intact. The apostolic succession of the Anglican clergy is their highest boast, and the key-stone as it were of the establishment."

"Strange, however, is it not," interrupted the rector, "that some of the first Anglican bishops, such as Cranmer and Barlowe, who had a great deal to do with the moulding and regulation of the establishment, should have made no secret of their contempt for holy orders and episcopal succession?"

"They were very right," said Mrs. Egremond; "apostolic ordination could only be derived by the English clergy through the idolatrous Church of Rome; and certainly that would not be anything to boast of. No; I would have nothing to do with the pope in any shape."

"Quite right, Mrs. Egremond," said Miss Beauclerk. "Were I an Anglican clergyman, I should think myself bound in loyalty to derive my orders from the queen."

"And quite as good they would be, in my opinion," said Mrs. Egremond, "as those derived from a pope."

"I do think," said the rector, "that it might be

* See Bossuet Histoire des Variations, L. 1. n. 27.

wiser for the English Church to say less about the dignity of her orders as derived from the Apostles, since some of the links of the chain appear to be wanting."

"What do you mean?" said Harvey, indignantly.

"I mean," replied the rector, "that for many years it was currently believed that Matthew Parker, from whom the English hierarchy was derived, was consecrated at the Nag's Head at Cheapside, by John Scory laying the Bible on his head with these words: 'Take thou authority to preach the word of God sincerely.'"*

"That is the old hackneyed story," said Harvey, with a sneer. "The Lambeth Register tells a very different tale."

"Very true," replied the rector. "The Lambeth Register, however, is strongly suspected of forgery; and, even allowing it to be true, it only plunges you into a new difficulty: for Barlowe, who is said there to have consecrated Parker according to King Edward's Ordinal, ('Take the Holy Ghost,') was probably not a bishop himself. Stevens, a Protestant minister, in his 'Great Question' writes: 'It is a wonderful thing by what chance or providence it happened that Barlowe's consecration, who was the principal actor in this, should nowhere appear, nor any positive proof of it be found, in more than fourscore years since it was first questioned, by all the search that could be made by so many learned and curious persons; as Mr. Mason, employed by the archbishop, and all the assistants he had in his time, whose book was printed in 1613, and again, with additions, in 1625 and 1638. Bishop Bramhall, and all the assistance he could procure in his time, about the year 1657; Dr. Burnet, &c., &c.'"

"Bishop Godwin of Hereford," replied Harvey,

* For proofs of this assertion, see "The Grounds of the Old Religion," by a convert, printed at Augusta in 1742.

somewhat nettled, "says he was consecrated on the 22nd of February, 1535."

"He gives us no proof, however," rejoined the rector.

"What is the good of proof?" interrupted Miss Beauclerk. "What matter whether the chain of succession is broken or not? The Anglican bishops are able enough to support their dignity without tracing their ordination through popes and cardinals, up to the Apostles. Dear me, why should we look beyond their actual position, which gives them so many claims to our respect? Luxurious palaces, handsome equipages, so many thousands a-year, seats in the house of lords, and so many livings in their gift to provide for poor relations! Bless me! they ought to be contented, and leave Apostolic succession to the papists!"

Harvey bit his lips; but he made it a general rule not to reply to Miss Beauclerk's flippant observations, unless absolutely obliged by politeness: for, though she sometimes by accident said a clever thing, it was impossible to argue with her.

"I am very glad, Mr. Feversham," said Mrs. Egremond, after a pause, "that you for once have adopted my side of the question."

"We at least agree together in thinking," said the rector, "that it would be wiser for the Anglican Church to boast as little as possible of her holy orders; and the Protestant controvertists of Queen Elizabeth's days are quite of our opinion. Whittaker says: 'I would not have you think that we make such reckoning of your orders, as to hold our own vocation unlawful without them; and therefore keep your orders to yourselves.'* Fulk and Sutcliffe also"........

"Oh, my dear rector, pray do not quote any more," interrupted Miss Beauclerk. "There can be nothing more tiresome than that habit of making long quota-

* Whittaker contra Duræum, p. 821.

tions from authorities for everything you say. Believe me, none of the fashionable authors or men of genius ever do."

"I cannot understand, Mr. Feversham," said Harvey, once more beginning to speak, "how, as a clergyman of the Anglo-Catholic Church, you can conscientiously attack the validity of her orders."

"It is not as a clergyman that I speak," replied the rector, colouring, "but as a lover of truth. Even though I were to give up the point, and admit that Barlowe and Parker had been made bishops according to the ritual of the Church of England, I should still think nothing of their dignity, and I deny their power to give orders to the rest of the Anglican clergy."

"How so?" said Harvey, looking very grave.

"The whole form," replied the rector, "for making bishops in the Ordinal of King Edward, which is pronounced by the consecrating bishop at the time of the imposition of hands, is this: 'Take the Holy Ghost, and remember that thou stir up the grace of God which is in thee by the imposition of hands; for God hath not given us the spirit of fear, but of power, and love, and soberness.' Now, I hold that only those words are sufficient to make a priest or a bishop which express the power of the order to be conferred; and these words would be quite as suitable at the confirmation of a child as at the making of a bishop. The very argument I use was urged by Erastus Senior in 1662, and the convocation then sitting changed the form to one somewhat better; but this alteration came a hundred years too late, their bishops not being validly consecrated during all that time, and hence unable to consecrate others even with the most orthodox ritual."

"It is a great pity," said Harvey, "to discuss questions like the present before ladies; I should prefer talking it over with you in private."

"And I beg you will not," said Miss Beauclerk.

"We all enjoy discussions so much; particularly, as in the present instance, when all parties are in the right."

"Allowing even," continued the rector, too much excited to notice the interruption, "that the form was valid by which Parker was consecrated, still it was uncanonical, being made without the consent of his metropolitan the Pope; it was also done in opposition to the other bishops of his province, and to all other bishops of the Church: in short, his ordination appears to me to have been schismatical."

"As I said before," replied Harvey, with constrained calmness, "this is not the place to enter upon learned discussions; when you have leisure however, rector, to spare me a few hours in the library, we shall look over together the very learned works of our divines upon the validity and dignity of Anglican orders, in which I trust you will find sufficient refutation of the calumnies which the enemies of the Anglican Church have heaped upon her."

During all this time Mary had been listening with great attention, and appeared very much distressed at the difference of opinion between her father and Harvey. She now went to the window and looked out, to conceal the tears which she could hardly repress.

"It is such a nice thing," said Miss Beauclerk, "to be up to both sides of an argument. People think you so uncommonly clever if you are a Puseyite one day, and a nondescript, like the rector, the next. Depend upon it, gentlemen, I shall make good use of the learning I have picked up in this house, when I next pay a visit to my uncle the bishop. How I shall make him stare when I tell him that his consecration is invalid, and that he must make a pretence of a picnic party to Rome, to get it done over again by the Pope! Or, perhaps, if I wish to put him into very good humour indeed, I shall take Mr. Harvey's method, and talk of the dignity of his episcopal office, and the disciplina arcani of the English Church; perhaps I shall even offer to go to confession to him, and if he be very kind indeed, I shall propose to sketch baptisteries, offertories, and cathedrals for him—all in the Gothic style, according to the Camden Society. ....But, dear me, Mary, what is the matter with you?" continued she, for the first time observing her cousin's agitation.

Mary hastily left the room, and Miss Beauclerk followed, for she really had a kind heart. Mrs. Egremond also rose, and quitted the apartment, so that the gentlemen were left alone.

"Good God, Feversham!" said Harvey, "what is the meaning of all this? I cannot tell you how distressed I feel when I hear you advocating opinions so unworthy of an Anglican clergyman. And Mary, too, you see how she suffers."

The rector did not reply, for his heart was swelling; but he made a desperate effort to be calm, in which he entirely succeeded, for his countenance was as immoveable as though it had been marble.

"Let us go to the library as I proposed," said Harvey, "and finish this disagreeable discussion on the validity of Anglican orders."

"As you please," said the rector, taking his young friend's arm, and leaving the room. "It is a question, however, of little importance to me, as even though I did admit the validity of your orders, I should still say that you had no power to act."

"Why so?" enquired Harvey, sharply, as they both entered the library.

"Because the Catholic Church," replied the rector, "from which the Anglican Church claims to derive her orders, considered both the ordainer and the ordained excommunicated heretics; and, therefore, never gave them jurisdiction or spiritual power in the Church of Christ."

"And do you then mean to say," responded Harvey, "that, even though it were proved to your satisfaction that the Anglican Catholic Church possessed holy orders, she has, nevertheless, no legal power to use them? Truly, this is strange doctrine coming from an English clergyman!"

"Yes," replied the rector, "I am of opinion that, even were Anglican holy orders indisputable, still the chief essential, that of Apostolic *mission*, is wanting —I mean, such mission and authority as was given by Christ to His Apostles, and derived in an uninterrupted channel from them, for preaching the word, administering the sacraments," &c.

"It appears to me," said Harvey, "to be perfectly sufficient if the Anglican Church can trace their bishops in uninterrupted succession up to the Apostles, as I am prepared to prove she can do. Does not St. Augustine say, 'A succession of bishops, descending from the see of St. Peter to the present episcopacy, holds me in the Catholic Church?'"

"The succession of bishops to which St. Augustine alluded," replied the rector, "all held the same doctrine as their predecessors; whereas the Anglican bishops differ from those from whom they pretend to derive their ordination, in the number of their sacraments, in their doctrine, and in their practice. Nothing can be more ridiculous than to suppose that they received from them commission and authority to act."

"I disagree with you," replied Harvey; "once the Anglican clergy received valid ordination, it could never be taken from them; and therefore the Church to which they belong is now, and will remain for ever, Apostolic and Catholic."

"For a Church to be Apostolic," replied the rector, "it is not sufficient that its clergy be regularly ordained, nor yet that they hold the episcopal see of their predecessors, they must also be members of the same Church and communion with those whose successors they pretend to be. The heretical Arian and Donatist bishops had quite as much right to call themselves true and Apostolic as the Anglican bishops have. Their ordination was most certainly valid, and they filled the sees of the Catholic bishops, their predecessors. Believe me, if you wish to make out that your Church is Apostolic, by all means make common cause with the Arians, for your position with regard to the Catholic Church, supposing even your ordination valid, is much on a par with theirs."

Harvey at this speech looked at first very angry; then he stared at the rector, and seemed bewildered. "For God's sake, explain yourself!" he exclaimed at last. "Are you going to leave the Church of England? You surely cannot hold these sentiments, and continue in her ministry!"

"You are right, Harvey," replied the rector; "it would indeed be base, unmanly, and ungenerous any longer to continue in a Church which I believe to be wrong. I must give up my living, and I am about to write to the bishop to say so; but God knows what is to become of my family!"

CHAPTER XXXIII.

"Much she discourses, and of various points,
All unconnected, void of limbs and joints;
She rails, persuades, explains, and moves the will,
By fierce bold words, and strong mechanic skill." CRABBE.

MEANWHILE Mrs. Benson got her little property sold, and placed the greater part of the proceeds in the hands of Jacob, who was to invest it in various kinds of merchandise, such as were likely to find a ready market in the Pickmanbone Islands. The good lady herself prepared for departure, and announced her intention of delivering a farewell address to the beloved flock over whose spiritual interests she had so faithfully watched under the superintendance and guidance of Mr. Longab. The latter gentleman was not sorry that she was about to leave, as most of his congregation preferred the originality of her style, to his own more common-place and long-winded discourses, which of course detracted much from his usefulness.

The sorrowful day at last drew near, on which she was to leave her native village and set off for London with her three daughters; preparatory to her embarkation in the little missionary vessel, which was to convey her and a few other pious passengers, on evangelizing speculations bent, to the Pickmanbone islands, she wished much to make her last solemn farewell in the meeting-house, and on a Sunday, but from this she was dissuaded by Mr. Longab, who was perhaps actuated by a slight feeling of jealousy.

Mrs. Benson, however, consoled herself by inviting her friends and admirers to a solemn banquet on the eve of the day fixed for her departure. After tea was finished, she cleared her throat and commenced her address. Much of what she said was couched in scriptural language, and she spoke in familiar terms of the most abstruse theological mysteries; we are, therefore, obliged to omit such parts in transcribing her discourse, otherwise we might incur the charge of writing blasphemy.

"My dear brethren," she began, "as this is not to be a sermon, I fear that a verse from Scripture would be inappropriate; I must, however, preface my discourse with something on which to hang my subject, and shall therefore quote part of that beautiful poem whose author unfortunately is unknown, but the merit of which lies between Homer and John Wesley—I mean,

'Fare ye well, and if for ever,
Then for ever, fare ye well.'

I know very well, my brethren, that I am but a she-apostle, and as such will not be much missed by those who have men to instruct them; nevertheless, I hope you will sometimes drop a tear over my many good qualities, when you remember that, like Noah's dove, I have flown away to the far quarters of the earth, with no less than three olive branches in my mouth—I mean my three daughters, the pledges of affection which the late Gabriel Benson left me in pawn. Like the harbinger of Spring, the cuckoo of the gospel, I am about to visit the Pickmanbone Islands, to carry there the light of truth. 'Fare ye well, and if for ever!' At least, let me beg from you the assistance of your prayers and spiritual wrestlings, particularly for my safe passage across the billowy main; for, alas! I have both the Atlantic and the Pacific to traverse, and though I place my confidence in God, yet I am awfully afraid of the sea monsters, particularly of the icebergs, that I hear go rampaging about the ocean, giving knocks right and left, like so many steam engines gone mad. However, I am not altogether down-hearted, for I hear that there are many pleasant and profitable sights to be met with on shipboard. For example, in crossing the Atlantic, I shall perhaps get a sight of that magnificent vessel, 'the ship of the desert,' sailing past in all her glory, recalling the days of Nimrod and Ishmael, for I have heard tell that she existed as far back. Then who knows but that somewhere in the Pacific ocean I may catch a sight of Horeb and Mount Sinai, not to speak of Mount Ararat, where the ark rested. I expect to find a sphere of active usefulness on shipboard, and my first object will be to make all the seamen converted characters; among other expedients for this end, I shall lay in one or two harpoons in case of meeting with whales, for I have no doubt in such a case, by dexterously alluding to the prophet Jonas, I may improve the occasion for the spiritual benefit of the sailors. I also look forward to much pleasant recreation from the British right of search into all slave vessels and suspected ships. You may be sure, beloved brethren, that I shall be among the most active in rescuing the poor negroes and other black cattle from the hands of their persecutors. But all this time I am forgetting my text, 'Fare ye well, and if for ever, then for ever, fare ye well.' You may now be curious to know what sort of outfit I am taking with me. I carry with me a few changes of raiment, for I cannot expect Providence to clothe me and my daughters like the lillies of the field, but I have taken nothing superfluous, for I am told that ready-made shirts grow on the trees in these favoured islands, and may be had for nothing. I have also laid in but a moderate stock of provisions, for I have little doubt that should they be exhausted during the passage, it will please God to send a supply of quails, as He did for the children of Israel in the wilderness. 'Fare ye well,' again my brethren, as the sublime penman hath it. There is now another thing which I may mention, as it may interest you, the advice coming as it does from a pious sailor; instead of an ordinary trunk for my clothes, as soon as I get to London, I mean to purchase that most approved seaman's chest Davy's Locker, which I am told is the safest of all coffers, never letting out anything it once gets in. And now, my dear brethren, broken-hearted I must bid you adieu; when I look upon your weeping countenances, and see the many snow white pocket handkerchiefs which are now being flourished, my spirit sinks within me. Alas! my next audience which I suppose will assemble beneath the equator, will probably consist of brutish kangaroos and ourang-outangs—creatures of feelings by no means so susceptible as yours, beings never known to weep. When I look at these white pocket handkerchiefs, Alas, alas, my feelings overpower me; I know I see them for the last time, for how can I expect ourang-outangs to know how to use them! However, as modern philosophers now assert, we are all descended originally from ourang-outangs, and when I reflect how civilization has gradually done away with the tails of our ancestors, I am consoled. They are creatures that may doubtless be made very useful to the missionaries, particularly when taught to read the Scriptures in their mother tongue! It is an idea of my own, that the woolly heads of these descendants of Ham may yet supply us with excellent broad-cloth; that, however, is for after consideration. Now, dear brethren, 'fare ye well' again, 'and if for ever, fare ye well!' I stand much in need of your prayers, for I hear that the islands in the Pacific are overrun with a most dreadful scourge, in consequence of being built on coral rocks; I allude to those awful vermin the coral insects, worse far than the ten plagues of Egypt, attacking man, woman, and beast. But a spiritual plague infinitely more dreadful than corporal miseries, requires also your prayers. You perhaps may not be aware that French missionaries sent by the Pope, have made settlements in the Pickmanbone islands; luckily the gallant Queen is determined to root them out with fire and sword, and to put into the stocks or the pillory all who may join them. She may as well let them alone however, for I have a plan worth two of that. Their object is to introduce the old woman of Babylon, and set her down in the very face of the missionaries on her seven hills. Now, I say, *let them!* By all means permit the scarlet woman to sit, and make herself as comfortable as can be on her seven pinnacles. Wait a bit, we'll bide our time; the judgment of the Lord will assuredly come; some day, when no one expects, she will whirr up into the air like a shot, and her bones be scattered to the four winds of heaven. For, my dear brethren—and here I shall let out the secret—one of the seven hills in the Pickmanbone Islands is a volcanoe."

At this announcement, Mrs. Benson's guests clapped their hands, drummed with their feet, and shouted "glory, glory." During the uproar, the eloquent speaker sank back overpowered by the violence of her feelings, and Mr. Longab and her other friends thought it expedient to break up the party.

Bidding adieu therefore at present to this heroic female missionary, we shall leave her to set off on her voyage, hoping it may be prosperous. And now let us return to farmer Blount, who having been present at the pathetic farewell uttered by his sister-in-law, nearly laughed himself into a fit. He did, however, feel very much concerned for the poor woman's infatuation, and though he did not at all like her proposed Quixotic expedition, what annoyed him most, was her implicit trust in Jacob Hogg, and folly in putting so much of her little fortune into his hands. Several times he had attempted to dissuade her, but his remonstrances were of no avail, except to render her more decided in the part she had taken. The next day Blount walked over to the rectory and inquired for Mr. Feversham, but to his great disappointment he was told that he was too unwell to see him. A few days afterwards he called again, and once more received the same answer. The truth was, that since the discovery of the rector's sentiments, Harvey had given him no rest, seizing every opportunity of attacking him when alone. Their discussions were most fatiguing and wearing out, neither party making a convert of the other; while poor Mary, who was now let into the secret, looked wretched and miserable beyond description. The distress of mind caused by the painful position in which the rector found himself, preyed upon his health, and it was almost a relief to him when over-persuaded by Harvey to delay a few weeks longer before tendering his resignation to his diocesan.

Another week passed away, and Blount began to feel exceedingly uncomfortable; naturally of an impatient temper, he fretted very much at being obliged to defer his inquiries; and the oftener he was disappointed, the more anxious he felt to get his perplexities solved and his uneasy mind set at rest. The next market-day that he was at Overbury, instead of going home directly when his business was finished, he took a walk in the direction of the Catholic chapel. There was nothing particular in its appearance outside, for the congregation was poor and able to give nothing for superfluous embellishment. Nevertheless, Blount's heart warmed as he approached it, and he thought to himself, "how happy should I now be, had I always frequented the house of God and practised good old Father Lefevre's instructions!" And then it came into his head how he had been told that the blessed sacrament was always kept within these consecrated walls, and that consequently Jesus himself was both spiritually and corporeally present there; and this thought filled him with awe and reverence. Had it not been for shame, lest he should be observed by the passers-by, poor Blount would have knelt down in the porch, for he did not venture to go in; and on his knees would have implored his living and present Saviour to forgive him the sins of his past life and receive him, a penitent sinner, into his fold. As it was, the only thing he did, was to lean against the railing which inclosed the chapel, and gaze wistfully at the door. He had not been there long, when a little group approached and arrested his attention, for they seemed about to enter. A pale and delicate though pretty woman, neatly but scantily and poorly clad, was supporting and guiding the steps of a blind man, evidently enfeebled by disease, and scarcely able to drag his steps along. Two little children followed hand-in-hand, but their steps were sad and slow, showing none of the glee which might have been expected at their age. Perhaps the poor little creatures were hungry—at any rate they were cold; the farmer mentally compared them with his own chubby little Neddy, and he felt compassion for them. As they did not seem to be asking charity, he did not like to offer anything, though he would have wished to do so. In ascending the steps, the blind man, who appeared exceedingly weak, stumbled and nearly fell; upon which Blount ran forward, and luckily was in time to catch him. The woman thanked him respectfully, and the man seemed about to do so also, but was seized with a violent fit of coughing, which apparently gave him great pain, and obliged him to lean against the wall for support. When at last it subsided, the woman, who seemed to be his wife, observed to Blount, that it was a thousand pities he had come out that day, the doctor who attended him having forbid him to leave the house; but he had felt so much better in the morning, he had over-persuaded her to let him go, for he was anxious once more to visit the Blessed Sacrament. "Yes," said the blind man, never doubting that

Blount was a Catholic, "my Lord came once into my house, to visit me at a time when I was too ill to leave my bed, and when the priest gave me holy communion for the first time; and now that I am able to walk, the first use that I must make of returning strength, is to visit His sacred altar and return Him thanks for all He has done unto me; perhaps it may be for the last time."

"Have you been long ill?" asked the farmer.

"Yes, Sir, a very long time," replied the poor man, "and now I am weary of life and would be glad to depart, if it pleased God to take me away."

"Oh! William, do not talk so!" said his wife, sobbing. "What will become of us when you die!"

"God will provide," he replied. "He has promised to be the husband of the widow and the father of the fatherless, and in His hands I leave you. Besides, you have a kind mother that will always watch over and take care of you, 'the hope of christians and the refuge of sinners.' Surely, my dear wife, you may trust in Mary, after she has done so much for your poor husband. I was plunged in the depths of despair," continued he, turning to Blount, "I had no hope; for I felt the load of my sins sinking me down—down into the deepest hell! It was all useless telling me of Jesus' love, and God's mercy! At last I went to the priest, made my confession, and got absolution. That comforted me, and I knew I was pardoned. However, a short time after, my old despair came back again. It was like a madness, Sir. At last the good priest who attended me, told me it was altogether a temptation of the devil, and that I must invoke the great and powerful name of Mary to deliver me from the assaults of the fiend. I did so, Sir, and since then, I have felt ineffably comforted. When Jesus Christ gave the apostle John to his mother to be her son, he gave me also, and you, Sir, and the whole human race. We are all her children, and if we will only love her, and call to her, and fly to her in all our difficulties, as simple little children do to their mother on earth, she will act a mother's part to us, and get us all we ask. I am so convinced of it, that I am not frightened to leave my wife and my children to her. She will take better care of them than ever I could have done; for no one ever trusted her in vain."

"Come into the chapel now, dear William, and rest yourself," interrupted his wife. "You will suffer, I fear, for this exertion."

"Gladly will I enter the house of God," continued the blind man, his face beaming with enthusiasm; "for *her* dear Son is calling to me now, 'Come unto me all ye that labour and are heavy laden, and I will give you rest.'"

The farmer looked at the poor sufferer with admiration, nay, with envy; and as the humble group entered the chapel he followed them. They knelt as they entered, and so did he; after a moment they rose, and the poor woman conducted her husband to a seat; but the farmer still continued kneeling at the foot of the chapel; his whole frame shook, and while he prayed to God to touch his heart and give him the faith of the poor blind dying man, he wept very bitterly. At last he was startled by feeling something touch his hand. It was the youngest of the children, who, looking up in his face, said, "Don't cry and take on so. I know God will pardon all your sins and comfort you, the way he has done papa; and then Mary will be your mother."

The farmer took the little fellow up in his arms and kissed him; he felt as though God had spoken to him through the mouth of the innocent child. "When you say your prayers to-night," at last he said, "will you ask God to do all this for me?"

"Oh! yes," replied the little fellow, "if you will ask our mother Mary for coals to warm us, and something to eat, for we are very cold and hungry."

"That I will," said the farmer, smiling. "And

now I shall give you something that she sends already." So saying, he felt in his pocket and took out a sovereign, which he could but ill afford to part with since his late severe losses, and bestowing it upon the child, hastily left the chapel, before the boy had time to show it to his parents, or they to thank him.

In the evening after his return home, Blount walked once more up to the rectory, and on asking for Mr. Feversham, was told that he had been confined to bed for some days, but was now a little better and able to see Mr. Harvey, with whom he was engaged at the moment the farmer called. The latter turned away very much disappointed. "I wonder if his Reverence would be vexed," said he to himself, "were I to go to a priest at once! Some folks would not like it, and think I was using them ill; but the rector is another guess sort of man! I'll try it any way, for I cannot help thinking it would please Mr. Feversham mightily, next time I came to see him, could I tell him that I had been at the priest and was now as good as a born Papist!"

Ere another week had elapsed, Blount set off to put his resolution in practice. He felt a little nervous as he turned down the street towards the priest's house, and as he passed the chapel he involuntarily looked round; perhaps it was to see if the blind man and his family were near the door; or perhaps to look if any of the passers-by recognized him, for he felt a good deal ashamed. But this was a sensation of which he determined to get rid; so drawing himself up, and assuming as unconcerned an air as possible, he boldly marched up to the entrance and rang the bell. No one answered at first; and a little tempter whispered, "You had better go away, for nobody is in; and at any rate you are not welcome. Priests have no time to attend to such intruders."

"Try once more!" urged the farmer's good angel. He did so, and at last an elderly female made her appearance, apologizing for keeping him so long waiting. The farmer hesitated, for he did not know for whom to ask.

"Which of the priests do you wish to see?" said the woman, divining his errand.

"Whichever you like," replied the farmer, in confusion, his face becoming red.

"Very well," said the servant, smiling, "I'll tell the one that is first disengaged; for they are both busy hearing confessions just now."

"Don't let me trouble them," rejoined the farmer, glad of an excuse for escape, his courage beginning to fail him. "I can easily call another time."

"You had better come in and wait," said the woman, "they have as much time to-day as they will ever have. They slave, Sir, from morning to night. As soon as they get their breakfast they go out and visit the sick; fever seldom leaves our congregation, for they are about the poorest and worst clad in Overbury. When they come back from visiting these plague-dens, for they are nothing better, they get their dinner and then go to the confessional! It's hard work that, Sir, and very wearing out I'm told, particularly when priests set about it over-fatigued, to begin with, from running through all the alleys and lanes in Overbury, places where not a breath of fresh air gets in!"

"But this is the forenoon, my good woman," rejoined the farmer, "and how do they happen to be hearing confessions now? I thought you said that they were always out at this time?"

"This is the eve of a feast-day, Sir," replied the woman; "perhaps you are not a Catholic, and so do not know that those who are going to receive holy communion to-morrow, must prepare themselves by confession to-day. But I must go now; for I think I hear one of the priests walking about. If it be, I'll send him to you. Go into that parlour, if you please, where you see the door open."

Blount did so, and found himself in a very plainly furnished apartment; the table was covered with books and papers, the walls were decorated with a few good prints, devotional groups, and heads of saints, chiefly taken from the old masters. A large crucifix stood upon the chimney-piece; the chairs were plain and not very comfortable; one of them was larger than the rest, and beside it was a prie-dieu. Blount had time to observe all these particulars ere the priest entered. He was rather a stout elderly man, tall and dignified, but at the same time plain in his manners; benevolence, good sense, and firmness, were legible on his countenance.

"That's the man for me!" thought the farmer to himself, as he rose and stammered, while the priest looked inquiringly at him; "I am told that you wished to speak to me," said he.

"Yes, your Reverence," said the farmer. "I, that is, Mr. Feversham! I mean, your Reverence, that we both are thinking of it!"

"I don't understand you," said the priest; "thinking of what?"

"I mean myself!" rejoined Blount, alarmed; for he began to remember he had no right to betray his patron, and that he ought only to speak for himself. "Why, dang it, Sir, it's no use mincing matters; I want to become Papist, and to belong to the one holy Catholic and Apostolic Church mentioned in the creed."

The priest smiled at this odd address, and then set about questioning Blount as to his motives, &c. On one point the farmer was obstinately silent, and that was as to how he had acquired his information and what had led him to think of the Catholic Church. "Honour bright," he always replied, when the priest touched upon the forbidden topic.

Mr. Howard was on the whole very much pleased, though a good deal amused with his new convert. He found him tolerably well instructed on most points, which, as he had no Catholic book but the Douai Catechism, surprised him a good deal.

"Have you no difficulties, Mr. Blount?" at length he said. "No objections to any part of our religion?"

"I am pretty well satisfied with most things," said Blount, "but I have written down a few small matters on a bit of paper here, that I am not just up to yet. I meant to have asked Mr. Fever—— your honour about them, if you please. Do Catholics ever worship images? I don't mean for to say that your Reverence does; but do the poor people? I have heard say that in countries where they were not so enlightened as in England, it was sometimes done by the Papists!"

"*Never*," replied the priest. "Catholics pay divine honours to God alone; they do not even worship saints and angels, in the Protestant acceptation of the word, far less their images and pictures. Human beings are naturally inclined to preserve and venerate pictures and statues of their ancestors, or of great men whom they admire and love; and are Catholics not to be allowed to do the same with regard to the Holy mother of God, and his favoured servants, the glorious saints and angels?"

"To show them respect such as a man shows to the portrait of his friend or relation, is a different thing from worshipping them, as I am sure I have heard they do," said Blount.

"If you mean by the word *worship*, paying divine honour to them, I, as a priest, assure you that Catholics do not. If, on the contrary, you give to the word the signification adopted in the Church of England prayer-book, I allow that Catholics do."

"What meaning does the prayer-book put on the word *worship*?" asked Blount, with curiosity.

"Nay," said the priest, "it is I that ought to ask you, what the man means when he says to the woman in the marriage service, 'with my body I thee worship.'"

"Why really I do not know," replied the farmer, "unless it be to show her respect; it can't be to make a goddess of her I should think."

"You have now explained the word *worship*," said the priest, "in the Catholic sense as applied to creatures; it simply means to show them respect, and this worship is altogether different from paying divine honour. This old-fashioned signification of the word *worship*, such as is understood in your prayer-book, or as the term is applied to justices of the peace, having fallen into general disuse among Protestants, has given rise to considerable misunderstanding between Catholics and those separated from them."

"Would it not be better, Sir, since Catholics do not pay divine honours to images and pictures, that they should not keep them in their churches to mislead people?" said Blount.

"The Church is of a different opinion," replied the priest; "for they are of great use in exciting devotion; the picture of the crucifixion, for example, sometimes speaks more forcibly to the heart than the most eloquent sermon."

"And perhaps, Sir, that is the reason why I have seen Catholics abroad, kneeling before an image or a picture—not that they were praying to them, I suppose, from what you say, but to keep them in mind of what these things were intended to represent."

"Exactly so," replied the priest; "and surely it is much wiser to place some pious image or picture in a church, the contemplation of which may excite devotion; than to have there an unmeaning monument to some dead magistrate or lord, whose life perhaps was anything but edifying!"

"That is most true, Sir," rejoined the farmer. "Now, in the very parish church at Overbury, there is a great staring representation of the lion and the unicorn just opposite the communion table! It has often struck me, that if a savage from the South Seas were to come to this part of the world and enter that church, he would directly think that these monstrous beasts were the gods that Englishmen worship."

"And in thinking so," interrupted the priest, smiling, "he would be no more uncharitable than Protestants are in affirming that Catholics worship the images in their churches."

"But, speaking of images," said the farmer, "since you do not worship them, what need have you for leaving out the second commandment, as you so often do?"

"I thought," replied Mr. Howard, "that you told me you had been studying the little Douai Catechism; your difficulty is tolerably explained there."

"Is it indeed, Sir?" said the farmer, "if it be, I took no note of it; besides, I am very sure that it calls the commandment that forbids cursing and swearing, the second. However, here is the little book, I have got it in my pocket."

The priest took it, and opening, read as follows: "The first commandment.—I am the Lord thy God, who brought thee out of the land of Egypt and out of the house of bondage. Thou shalt not have strange gods before me. Thou shalt not make to thyself any graven thing, nor the likeness of any thing that is in heaven above or in the earth beneath, nor of those things which are in the waters under the earth, thou shalt not adore them nor serve them. I am the Lord thy God, mighty jealous, visiting the iniquity of the fathers upon the children to the third and fourth generation of them that hate me, and showing mercy unto thousands of them that love me, and keep my commandments."

"You've done very cunningly, Sir," said the farmer, "for you have rolled the two first commandments into one."

"I've just read what is called the first commandment in the Douai Catechism; the verses word for word are as found in the twentieth chapter of Exodus," replied the priest.

"But would not it be much wiser, Sir," said the farmer, "to divide them into two, as the Protestants do? Besides, all the world knows that there are ten commandments, and if you join two of them into one you diminish their number!"

"I beg your pardon," said Mr. Howard, "we divide the Protestant tenth commandment into two; surely coveting your neighbour's wife is a very different sin from coveting his house, and common sense sanctions the division."

"I would rather divide the commandments as God divided them when he gave them to Moses," said Blount.

"Very good," rejoined Mr. Howard; "but how are we to know how God did? The commandments are given by Moses in verses like the rest of the Bible, leaving optional to commentators the method of dividing them. St. Augustine divided them as we do; and the Protestant method is sanctioned by St. Jerome."

"Well, as long as the whole substance is given, I will not quarrel with the division," said the farmer; "but you know, Sir, Protestants are apt to say that Catholics leave out the second commandment to cloak their own misdemeanours in worshipping images."

"If ever you hear it again," said Mr. Howard, "tell them it is a lie; for there is scarcely a Catholic catechism printed now-a-days, however small, which does not contain the commandments entire. If at any time they have been abridged, it has been in some very simple elementary book for children, as I have myself seen done in Presbyterian catechisms, and no fault found."

"Well, that is all perfectly satisfactory," said the farmer; "and now, Sir, if you will not be offended at my free way of speaking, I would mention a thing that I think both foolish and useless in your Church. What can be the object of preaching to honest English folks in Latin, to bamboozle them for no good end?"

Mr. Howard laughed as he replied: "We never preach in Latin to those who do not understand us. Our sermons in this country are all in English; and we try to make the great truths of our religion intelligible to every capacity. You are perhaps thinking of the Mass, which is always performed in Latin."

"Perhaps so," said Blount; "but would it not be quite as acceptable to God, though said in English?"

"Very likely," replied the priest; "but the Catholic Church, nevertheless, has good reason for retaining her service in Latin. It was the language in most general use during the times of the Apostles. Afterwards, when vulgar tongues were in a state of perpetual change, had the Church in different parts of the world made use of them, alterations and discrepancies would insensibly have crept into her services. As it is, by the use of Latin, these have been avoided. Many other advantages result from it. When priests or bishops travel abroad, they are as capable of performing their functions as at home. When a poor Catholic layman chances to be expatriated, wherever he goes he finds the Catholic service the same, and can everywhere take part in it."

"That *is* a fine thing," interrupted the farmer; "when I was a soldier in Spain, (for I served the king in my time, Sir,) it was beautiful to see the Catholic soldiers quite at home on the Sunday, and going into the papist churches, and hearing Mass with more comfort than they could have done in England, while we Protestants could not have found a church of ours in any place we passed through, though we had given a thousand pounds for it."

"I dare say not," said Mr. Howard, with a smile.

"But after all, Sir," continued the farmer, "it would be more satisfactory to Catholics, I should think, if they understood Latin."

"Most of them," said Mr. Howard, "understand it sufficiently to follow the priest through the service. All their prayer-books have got Latin on one side, and their mother-tongue on the other; so that a very small degree of attention will enable them to make out the meaning of the Latin words. Even supposing they do not, it is of little consequence. You must remember that the Mass is a sacrifice offered to God; the thing of importance is to be present at this sacrifice, and to join your intention with that of the priest. Even though you do not understand every word he says, yet, if you know the drift of it, and the object his actions have in view, it is sufficient. Under the Jewish dispensation, when crowds assembled to see the priest sacrifice an animal in the temple, do you suppose that those who were at too great a distance to hear the particular words he said, but who, nevertheless, joined him in his intention with all the fervour of their hearts, got less benefit from the sacrifice than those that could follow him word by word?"

"I should think it would come to the same thing," said the farmer. "The chief point, according to my judgment, would be joining with the priest in your own mind, and trying to be very fervent."

"Exactly what I should wish you to do when you come to hear Mass in the Catholic chapel," said Mr. Howard.

"There's a thing I am curious to know," said the farmer; "did all the Apostles say mass in Latin, or do you not think they sometimes used other languages?"

"Undoubtedly they used other languages, according to the country they were in," replied the priest; "though Latin was the one in most general use. Accordingly, the Greeks retain their Apostolic liturgy in old Greek, the Armenians in old Armenian, the Copts in old Coptic, &c., &c. The Catholic Church permits these languages to be retained, because the words of the liturgy have been transmitted in them from Apostolic times; but they are quite as unintelligible to the vulgar as Latin, having in each case become a dead language."

"I thought the Greeks had separated from Rome," interrupted the farmer, still ready to catch an objection.

"The schismatic Greek Church has done so," replied Mr. Howard; "but there is also a large body, termed the United Greek Church, in communion with Rome."

"Thank you now, Sir, very kindly, for all the good instruction you have given me," said the farmer, rising to depart. "When do you think, Sir, that I'll be fit to become a Papist? I am longing for the day when I'll belong to the great Church that worships God in the same way all over the world! Oh! it is a beautiful thing, Sir, for a Catholic to know that he has brothers in all parts of the earth, and that his religion is not merely in some little corner, like one of the Protestant sects! A man is twice a man, Sir, when he has a bond of union with his kind; and the larger his heart, and the wider the circle of his charity, the more I think of him! The Church that is spread all over the world for me! God bless Her!"

The priest smiled at the farmer's enthusiasm, and shook hands with him warmly, as he assured him that he would be happy to admit him into the Church as soon as all his scruples were satisfied. He recommended him, meanwhile, not to let the matter rest, but to search for as many objections as possible; it being much better to discover them now before being received, than that they should arise to torment him afterwards.

CHAPTER XXXIV.

"O, but they say, the tongues of dying men,
Enforce attention like deep harmony." SHAKSPEARE.

"The souls of the just are in the hand of God, and the torment of death shall not touch them."

During the last few weeks, considerable changes had taken place at the rectory. Harvey had got the offer of a tolerable living, and immediately decided upon giving up his fellowship and marrying. He had no difficulty in obtaining the rector's consent, who, however, frankly avowed that, did he believe him to be a true priest legally ordained according to the canons of the universal Church, he never would have agreed. Harvey did not at all like this mode of sanctioning his marriage, and tried to prove that he was a true priest, and as such had as good a right to marry as any other man.

"I am sure," said he, "that the most bigoted Roman Catholic could not maintain that it is forbidden by divine law for priests to marry."

"Allowing you to be right," replied the rector, "you know as well as I do, that the discipline of the Roman Catholic Church forbids priests to marry. Now, as I never can cease to hope, that with your enlightened views of Catholic truth, (I mean enlightened as compared with many of your brethren,) you will ultimately join the Roman Catholic communion. On doing so, were you a true priest, you would have to give up your wife; but being only a mere layman, it matters little whether you are married or single, and I have, therefore, no hesitation in trusting Mary's happiness to your keeping."

"And were I even to become a Romanist," rejoined Harvey, indignantly, "of which, however, there is little fear, I should think it my duty, as a priest whose orders could not become invalid, to give up my wife immediately and conform to the discipline of the Church I embraced."

"That could not be done," said the rector, with a smile, "unless you obtained the consent of certain other parties concerned. However, you would all have time to make up your minds long ere the Catholic Church would consent to ordain you."

Harvey found it a much more difficult matter to obtain Mary's consent than that of the rector. She was very unwilling to leave her father at such a critical period, when his health was so bad and his mind so ill at ease; but he joined his persuasions to those of Harvey, and at last she agreed. He was very anxious to see her settled before he gave up his living, and he fancied that the decisive step would appear less awful after she should be removed from experiencing any of the painful results which must accompany it. He himself did not fear poverty, and he hoped to find an asylum in one of the English Catholic Colleges, where, perhaps, he might be able to render himself useful as an instructor of youth. As for poor Lady Harriet, there was not a doubt that her brother would give her an annuity, and she might perhaps live one part of the year with the Earl, and the other part with Mary. To do Harvey justice, he acted very nobly on this occasion; and though Lady Harriet had never been a favourite of his, he expressed his perfect willingness to afford her an asylum should it be necessary. Mary was much touched by this generosity, but it was a bitter humiliation to her to marry him in such circumstances, and had it not been for the urgent solicitations of her father, she would not have consented.

We shall now join Mrs. Egremond and Miss Beauclerk, who are going out to take a walk, leaving Mary and Mr. Harvey to a tête-a-tête in the drawing-room, and Mr. Feversham in the library, lying on a sofa suffering from a severe head-ache.

"I am so glad there is going to be a marriage in the house!" said Miss Beauclerk, "it was getting so wretchedly dull! No amusement, no anything going on! I should hang or drown myself were I to live here always! But don't you wonder, Mrs. Egremond, that Mr. Harvey is going to marry at all, after what he said the evening that Mary was not with us, upon the excellency of celibacy?"

"Yes," replied the elder lady, "I remember him saying that, 'under a really effective church system, the priests would be, if possible, selected from those who had taken such vows.'"

"I am quite of his opinion," said Miss Beauclerk, "for did not our great Queen Elizabeth, the head of the English Church, take a vow of celibacy?"

"I must say," rejoined Mrs. Egremond, laughing, "that I think good Queen Bess would have done much better had she married and had a family, instead of flirting with so many suitors, even after she was an old woman!"

"But, don't you see," said Miss Beauclerk, "that, as Mr. Harvey so well explained, she was perhaps one of those who, unlike himself, have a vocation for a life of celibacy; though indeed he said that, in some cases, it was a 'fearful snare.' One would think that the dowagers who frequent May Fair agreed with him in these High Church views, they seem so anxious to get their daughters off. By the way, you know, of course, that I am to be one of the bridesmaids, and that everything about the ceremony is to be conducted according to the strictest and most recent Oxford views."

"You don't mean to say that any change is to be made in the marriage service?" said Mrs. Egremond.

"I don't know exactly," replied Miss Beauclerk. "I only heard Mr. Harvey say, that the marriage should be in Oxford style; which, I suppose, means being married in a surplice, as a friend of mine in Cornwall was: though another Puseyite clergyman in the neighbourhood was offended, and said it ought to have been in plain clothes, for it was as a man, and not as a clergyman, that his marriage took place."

Mrs. Egremond laughed. "Thank heaven," said she, "our evangelicals have no such nonsense about them."

"And do you know, Mrs. Egremond," continued the young lady, "when I am married I intend to have it done in the Puseyite fashion, it appears to me so much more firm and binding, not to speak of the extra solemnity. In another marriage that I saw myself, three clergymen helped to marry the couple—each one saying a little bit of the service; and the bride and bridegroom were part of the time in the centre of the church, and part of the time at the communion rails. It was so impressive, and so out of the common! I like it best, however, when it is a clergyman that is being married in his surplice; for it is just as if he were performing part of the service for himself! It is so independent marrying and being married at the same moment."

One evening, a few days afterwards, the farmer again called for the rector, but was told that he was suffering from indisposition, and able to see no one. Had Mr. Feversham been anxious for it, he might have seen Blount, notwithstanding his ailments; but the truth was, he had heard of his visit to the priest, and felt satisfied that he was now in excellent hands. He thought also that there might be an awkwardness in talking with him, now that he appeared progressing so rapidly, while he himself was hanging back. At this new disappointment, Blount's heart swelled; he had been uncomfortable ever since talking with the priest, until he should make the rector informed of the circumstance; and now he felt both sad and dispirited, as he turned away from the house. As he walked down the avenue, before he reached the gate, he began to think that it was a pity to lose the evening, when he so seldom had one to spare; so, instead of turning homewards, he set off towards Overbury, and called for Mr. Howard. Luckily, he found him at home; so he entered upon the subject uppermost in his thoughts without farther ceremony.

"Is it true, Sir," he inquired, "that papists think more of their own works or merits than of those of Jesus Christ? I read in a book the other day that, trusting to their own, they make Christ's merits of none effect. And that is the reason why they fast, and wear hair shirts, and scourge themselves, and do all the rest of their mortifications."

"The doctrines you describe," replied Mr. Howard, "are declared to be damnable heresies by the Catholic Church. We Catholics know that we are insufficient of ourselves even to think a good thought; and that the grace by which we are justified is given us purely on account of the merits of Christ. Nevertheless, through these merits of Christ the good works of a just man, proceeding from grace, are so acceptable to God, that, according to His promise, He regards them as meritorious, and is pleased to reward them. At the day of judgment each man will receive according to his works, so he must endeavour now by 'good works to make his vocation and election sure.' (2 Pet. i. 10.)"*

"Well," said Blount, "if the Apostle was right in recommending good works, Catholics must be right in doing them, so long as they remember that it is

* See Bossuet's exposition.

only through Christ's merits that these are acceptable to God; but I don't like to hear a man's own good works called merits, when I know that of themselves they deserve nothing. It is the name I quarrel with."

"You must not mind the name," replied the priest, "but regard the doctrine of the Catholic Church. She teaches, that of themselves our works are useless, that without grace we can do nothing, and that grace is the pure gift of God. When, by the help of grace we perform a good work, that work through the merits of Christ, and through them alone, will obtain a reward."

"But," urged the farmer, "do you not hold that some of your great saints had merits sufficient to obtain heaven, both for themselves and others, without Christ to help them at all?"

"Never," replied Mr. Howard; "their good works, like those of the meanest human being, were altogether worthless in themselves; but, being performed by the grace of God assisting them, they became meritorious through the death and passion of Jesus Christ, and through that only."

"But," rejoined Blount, "what do papists mean by talking of works of supererogation? Do not these merit for themselves without being beholden to Christ at all?"

"No," said the priest, "I repeat that nothing we can do is meritorious but through Christ. There are some good works, however, which though counselled are not commanded. These are called works of supererogation."

"I should like examples of them from Scripture, if you please, Sir," said Blount.

"Certainly," replied Mr. Howard. "The Bible teaches, 'he that gives his virgin in marriage does well; and he that gives her not in marriage does better.' Now, this better part, recommended but not enjoined by St. Paul, is a good work which may either be performed or not as we please, therefore it may be termed a work of supererogation."

"Now I begin to understand it," said the farmer; "a good work that we chuse to perform, which is not positively bid, is one of supererogation. I suppose, Sir, if done by the grace of God, and offered to Him through the merits of Christ, it will be counted meritorious, and obtain a reward."

"Certainly, Mr. Blount," replied the priest; "and to make the thing still more clear, I shall give another instance. The first Christians, as many of them as were possessors of lands or houses, sold them and brought the prices of the things that were sold, and laid them down at the feet of the Apostles, to be distributed to every one as he had need. Now, this was a most meritorious good work, but certainly not commanded."

"Therefore a work of supererogation," interrupted the farmer; "I see the whole thing very clearly now."

"I am glad of it," said the priest. "Is there any thing else you wish to ask me?"

"Oh, yes, Sir," said Blount, "there is a very heavy charge which I have heard brought against the papists, which I'd like if you would disprove. Is it true that the Pope claims authority to dispense with the laws of God, and absolve one from keeping the ten commandments? I never altogether believed it; but it is so often said, I sometimes feared there might be some truth in it."

"It is utterly false," replied Mr. Howard; "the Pope has no authority to interfere with the ten commandments, or any of the laws of God. The only dispensations he can give are with regard to the regulations of the Church on matters of discipline—such as the manner and times of fasting, whether holy communion should be received by the faithful under one or both species, what holidays are of obligation in different places, &c."

"Then the Pope," said the farmer, "could not give

leave to lie or forswear one's self, as I have heard say he could?"

"Certainly not," replied the priest; "Catholics are taught that every lie is a sin, and that it is damnable to call God to witness an untruth: such a thing must not be done to save a whole world by the Pope himself; still less could he authorize any one to do so."

"I've heard also," continued the farmer, "that the Pope could give leave to break faith with, or to murder heretics; and that a Catholic may cheat a Protestant whenever he likes, particularly if he does not tell a direct lie, but confines himself to equivocating and prevaricating; also, when he asserts a thing, he may make a mental reservation to the contrary."

"It is false," replied Mr. Howard; "sincerity and truth are strictly inculcated by the Catholic Church. Pope Innocent XI. prohibited teaching the lawfulness of any species of dissimulation, under pain of excommunication; and in 1826, the Catholic prelates of Ireland published a declaration containing the following words: 'The Catholics of Ireland, (and Catholics everywhere can make a similar declaration,) not only do not believe, but they declare upon oath, that they detest as unchristian and impious, the belief that it is lawful to murder or destroy any person or persons whatsoever, for or under pretence of being heretics, and also the principle that no faith is to be kept with heretics.' The British Catholic bishops have also declared that 'no power in any pope or council, or any individual or body of men, invested with authority in the Catholic Church, can make it lawful for a Catholic to confirm any falsehood by an oath, or dispense with any oath by which a Catholic has confirmed his duty of allegiance to his sovereign; or any obligation of duty or justice to a third person. He who takes an oath is bound to observe it, in the obvious meaning of the words, or in the known meaning of the person to whom it is sworn.'"

"That is all most satisfactory," said the farmer; "I see, too, from the last declaration you read, Sir, that Protestants have no right to say that Catholics must necessarily be bad subjects to the government. It strikes me, however, that in my little boy's History of England, it is mentioned how a pope deposed a certain king John!"

"No doubt," replied Mr. Howard. "During the middle ages certain popes acted on their right as feudal superiors, and thus maintained an order and justice in the intercourse between the various European kingdoms, in latter times no more to be met with. This is very far, however, from being an article of the Catholic faith, and is as much opposed by French Catholics, as by English Protestants."

"Well! to think of the lies that are told against Papists! They have much to answer for that spread them! Now, Sir, I'll ask one more question—are not Papists very much in the habit of leading bad lives, knowing that on their death-beds they can get absolution for all the sins they have ever committed?"

"Alas!" said Mr. Howard, "Christians of all denominations are in the habit of leading bad lives, and trusting to a death-bed repentance! But so far from Catholics having encouragement to do so, they are taught in their devotional books and by their clergy, that they must work out their salvation in fear and trembling, and by no means rely upon a death-bed repentance. Generally speaking, as men live, so they die; and it is to be feared that those who neglect God during their lives, will not find Him at their death. A priest is bound to give a dying sinner all the assistance in his power, by administering to him the last sacraments, and inciting him to sincere repentance, teaching him not to despair because God is merciful; but it has often been remarked by the Catholic clergy, that those who trust to a death-bed repentance are generally cut off by sudden death, or summoned to their last account in places where no priest is to be found to reconcile them with God. It frequently happens also that through the neglect of friends, ignorant, perhaps, of a sick man's danger, the clergyman is not summoned till the patient is too weak to make his confession, or perhaps in delirium unable to recognize his visitor, and therefore not in a state to receive the sacraments."

"Well, Sir, God willing, I'll not put off preparing for death till sickness comes," said the farmer; "what you have just told me will be a warning to me to take heed in time. But I fear, Sir, I am detaining you; I think I saw the servant look in just now and make a sign to you."

"You are right, Mr. Blount," said the priest. "I believe I am wanted. I purpose going to see a sick man, to whom my colleague administered the last sacraments yesterday, in my absence. I believe the poor fellow is well prepared for death, and in the happiest frame of mind. All the assistance we can give has been already rendered to him; but he is naturally anxious to see me once more before he dies, for he regards me as the means of his conversion to the Catholic religion, and I had the satisfaction of receiving him into the Church."

Blount rose to go away, but hesitated and looked wistfully at Mr. Howard. "Would you let me walk along with you till you get to the house," at last he said, "and explain to me the meaning of the last sacraments? But perhaps you think I make too free, and are displeased."

"Not at all," replied the priest, smiling, "I shall be very glad of your company; but I thought you wished to keep secret your visits to me; and what will your acquaintances think, should any of them see you walking with a Catholic priest?"

"They may think what they like, Sir," said the farmer, his countenance brightening; "I am ashamed, your Reverence, of having been ashamed, and now that I have made up my mind, I mean to tell all the world boldly that I am about to become a Papist, and that I shall feel proud to be called one!"

"You ought to term us Catholics and not Papists," said Mr. Howard, as they quitted the house. "*Papist* is a name of reproach which the Protestants give us."

"Is it indeed, Sir?" replied Blount. "I thought you had been called Papist after the Pope, which never could be a disgrace."

"True," said Mr. Howard, "the word comes from Papa, which is the Italian name for the Pope; and if you have a fancy for using it I won't quarrel with it. But did not you say that you wished to ask about the last sacraments?"

"Yes, Sir," said Blount. "I understood that extreme unction was the last sacrament; but you speak of more than one."

"Before receiving extreme unction," replied the priest, "the sick person must make his confession and receive absolution. This, as you know, is called the sacrament of penance. The viaticum, or holy communion, is also given to fortify his soul and strengthen him for the final conflict. For you must know that the devil besets a dying bed, and frequently torments the sufferer with grievous temptations, and particularly to despair of God's mercy; now, the last sacraments strengthen him to overcome them."

"But why do you call holy communion the viaticum?" asked the farmer. "Mr. Feversham never gave it that name."

"Mr. who?" asked the priest with some curiosity.

"I mean," said Blount, colouring, "I never heard the name viaticum before; what does it signify, if you please, Sir?"

"It means provision for a journey," replied Mr. Howard; "the strengthening food given to the soul before her last most important voyage, when she is about to be summoned to the presence of her Creator. When the sins of her past life are rising before her in dread array, and when the spirits of evil, knowing that their time is short, lose no means untried to make her peril her salvation even at the last hour. I am sorry that the sacraments have been already administered in this case, otherwise I should have taken you with me."

"Oh! Sir," said Blount, "I should like nothing better than to go with you yet, if you think that I should not be in the way. I should like to see a Catholic death-bed, and judge with my own eyes of the fruits of your holy religion."

"Then come in with me," said the priest, "we are just at the door."

So saying, Mr. Howard entered a dilapidated tenement, and after ascending a long staircase, knocked at the door of a miserable room. It was opened by a young woman very poorly clad, whom Blount immediately recognised as the wife of the blind man whom he had relieved a few days before in the Catholic church. He turned away his face and tried to keep behind the priest, for he did not wish to be recognised; but his precautions were needless, the room being so dark the woman scarcely took notice of him.

"How is he?" whispered Mr. Howard.

"Oh! very bad!" said the woman, in a low voice. "He brightened up a little after receiving the sacraments last night; but I see very well that there is not the least hope. He is dozing just now in the inner room, and I am trying to keep the children quiet here."

"We shall wait a little in hopes he may awake," said the priest, "and if he continue long sleeping I shall return to see him to-morrow."

"Thank your Reverence, kindly," said Mrs. Powell, as she dusted two chairs with her apron, for her visitors to sit down.

"I am not half pleased with you," continued Mr. Howard; "I understand that you have been in great distress since I saw you last, in want even of necessaries, and yet you never came near me to apply for relief, when you knew that I wished you to do so."

"Oh! Sir, I beg pardon," replied the woman; "but you see, Sir, William was very unwilling that I should go. He took it into his head that you might think he had turned Catholic in order to get charity; besides, he said that you had more people to take care of than you could manage already, for you were not over-rich yourself."

"Well," continued the priest in a dry tone of voice, trying to conceal the kindness with which his heart overflowed, under a somewhat gruff manner, "what did you do in your difficulties? Who relieved you? For I understand that you got help somewhere!"

"Why, you see, Sir," said the woman, "it's a long story; William took a great notion of the Blessed Virgin after all you had been telling him about her. And he said that if we would all trust her and love her entirely, she might do something for us. I spoke of going to a rich Protestant lady, that had been kind to him some time since, a Mrs. Egremond; but he would not hear of it. And one day that we had no meat in the house, and not even coals to make a bit of fire, he took it into his head that he could manage things better than me, and that he would get us money himself. I thought at first that he was going to play the harp in the street, and it put me into a great fright, for I knew that he was not able for it; and besides, he had not been over the door for weeks past. However, that was not the thing that he intended at all. So I said to him, 'William, where on earth are you going?' And he said, 'To the church, to the altar where the blessed sacrament is kept.' And I said, 'It would be a great deal better for you if you would go to Mr. Howard's house, or else to Mrs. Egremond to ask charity; for you won't find a loaf in the church for the starving children.' So he told me not to lose patience, but to dress the children and to come with him and see. And then he took the boys by the hand and told them, that when they got to the church they were to ask Jesus and his mother Mary to procure them some relief, and that if they would be good children and love Jesus very much, Mary would be sure to send it to them. Well, Sir, we set out, and to tell the truth, I was annoyed and worried with William's obstinacy in going to the church, when none of us had had any breakfast. But he always was obstinate and fanciful; however, in this case he had the best of it, and I was wrong, God forgive me! When we got to the door of the chapel, we saw an honest-looking farmer sort of gentleman, with a very pleasant face, loitering about."

Here poor Blount began to feel very uncomfortable, but Mrs. Powell quite unconsciously continued.

"And he got into talk with William, and William held forth to him, as you know, Sir, it is his infirmity to do, for he is fond of talking. But that day he talked in a beautiful sort of way, just as if an angel had been speaking out of him; and the strange gentleman seemed pleased, and followed us into the chapel; but William never asked charity, Sir, nor never thought of it. And then we left the gentleman at the door, and went forward near the altar; and William said the Litany of the Blessed Virgin, and I and the eldest boy repeated the answers, while the little one went wandering about the chapel. When the litany was finished, instead of coming away as I had expected, William began to beg and entreat the Blessed Virgin to show herself a true mother to him and his family, and to send us some relief; for he said, and I remember his words exactly, as I took notice of them at the time, 'My most dear mother, look down with pity upon us; you are our only hope and our only refuge! We have no one to look to but you! There is no one else knows our distress, and we mean to tell no one else; for we wish to apply only to you! Dearest mother, hear our prayer and send us relief! And, Oh! let it come speedily; for we trust in you and no one ever trusted you in vain!' Well, the words were hardly out of his mouth, when the little one came running up with a bright gold sovereign in his hand! I was so surprised I was like to drop, and William actually cried, he was so grateful to his good mother as he always calls her. I asked the child where he got it, and he said, that the pleasant gentleman at the foot of the chapel had put it into his hand, saying that his mother Mary had sent it. We looked for the stranger, but he was gone, and William took it into his head that it was an angel; but I told him that angels were not so common, and that the stranger was a good, stout, flesh and blood looking man, rather plain in his ways for a born gentleman."

"It was, indeed, very remarkable," said Mr. Howard. "I should like to know who the stranger was!"

Meanwhile the little boy to whom Blount had given the money in the chapel, was gazing wistfully at him as he sat in the farthest corner of the room with his back to the light. The sly little fellow walked round and round, in hopes of getting a clear view of his face; but the farmer always turned his head away from the side the child was at. At last the little rogue fairly jumped on his knees and got his face between his hands, and after taking a good look, exclaimed, "I have you now, I have you now! Mother, I have found him!"

"Hush!" said Mrs. Powell, in an anxious tone. "Remember your poor papa!"

"But he is here! he is here!" continued the boy in a loud whisper, "the good angel that Mary sent to help us!"

The woman started, and rushing to Blount, seized his hand with every demonstration of gratitude; but just then a feeble voice from the next room was heard, exclaiming, "Alice! Alice! What is this? Is Mr. Howard arrived?"

"Come, come! no more nonsense! Go to your husband, my good woman!" exclaimed Mr. Howard, anxious to spare Blount, who he saw was very much ashamed at being discovered; a smile was on his countenance and tears glistened in his eyes, as he regarded the farmer with lively satisfaction and approval.

"It is a happy prognostication for you, my good friend," whispered Mr. Howard to him, as they entered the dying man's apartment, "that the Blessed Virgin has selected you so early to be her messenger!"

"Here is Mr. Howard, and he has brought with him the kind gentleman that helped us in the chapel," said Mrs. Powell to her husband.

A gleam of pleasure illumined the sightless countenance of the harper, as he held out a hand to each. "God bless you both!" he faintly exclaimed, as he grasped them; "May He reward you who can do it better far than I."

"Are you happy?" asked Mr. Howard.

"Happy!" he replied, "who would not be happy, about to go among the glorious saints and angels, and be in the sweet company of the Mother of God, for ever and ever! O Jesus, I love you! O Mary! take me soon into the presence of thy dear Son, for my soul longs to depart and be with Christ!"

"Happy, happy man!" whispered Mr. Howard to Blount, who stood by the bed-side with his great eyes glistening.

"Would to God I were in his place, Sir," replied the farmer in a low voice.

"What shall I do unto my Lord, for all his goodness unto me!" ejaculated the harper, as though unconscious of the presence of his visitors. "I will praise Him, and love Him, and bless Him, through all eternity!"

"Once you get to heaven," said Mr. Howard, again taking his hand, "you must not forget to pray for the priest that instructed you and admitted you into the Church!"

"Indeed, I will not forget," replied Powell; "I never can repay what I owe to him! And when I get to heaven, I shall never cease to ask the Blessed Virgin to bless his mission, and to intercede for his flock. O Mary, my most sweet Mother! grant that he may be the instrument of saving thousands of poor despairing sinners like myself!"

"Will you pray for me too when you get to heaven?" humbly asked poor Blount.

"Yes, I will pray," said the harper, "that the Blessed Virgin may often employ you to be her messenger in relieving the afflicted—that you may be her son, and she your mother!"

The poor man was now seized with one of those violent fits of coughing which seemed as though they would rend his whole frame asunder; and Mr. Howard, who had been accustomed to attend the sick during the greater part of his life, gently raised him up in the bed, and supported him with his arm, like the most tender of nurses. The paroxysm was unusually long and violent; and when it ceased, the priest laid him back on the pillows, quite exhausted. It was evident that he could converse no more, so Mr. Howard contented himself with uttering a pious ejaculation now and then, in which it was evident from his gestures that the sick man joined.

"Of all the saints," said the good priest, "St. Joseph made the happiest death, for he died in the arms of Jesus and of Mary. Commit yourself, then, to his protection, and invoke his assistance."

The dying man raised his hand in token of assent.

"Jesus, Mary, and Joseph, I give you my heart and my soul," continued Mr. Howard, whilst the harper moved his lips, though no sound was audible.

"Jesus, Mary, and Joseph, help me in my last

agony! Jesus, Mary, and Joseph, grant that I may die in peace with you!" said Mr. Howard, who then paused, and listened to hear if Powell would respond.

"Jesus, Mary, and Joseph, I love you!" he at last uttered faintly in an indistinct whisper." He then shut his eyes, and seemed beginning to doze; but, after a few minutes, awoke, and stretching out his arms, exclaimed, "Oh, Mary, I am ready! Come quickly!" His breathing then became heavy, and it was evident that he was falling asleep.

"We had better go," whispered Mr. Howard to Blount, "we should only disturb him by remaining longer."

With soft steps they left the room, and bidding adieu to Mrs. Powell, descended the staircase to the street; where the farmer, after warmly thanking the priest for the happiness that had been afforded him of seeing the consolation of religion on a death-bed, took his departure, and hastened homewards.

The harper died that night, and so suddenly did his agony come on, that good Mr. Howard, though he rose from his bed to attend him the moment that he was summoned, arrived too late. Mrs. Powell, however, faithfully fulfilled the instructions which she had received in case of such an event. The blessed candle which the priest had left was lighted, holy water was sprinkled on the bed; and every now and then a little crucifix, the faithful representation of the dying Jesus, was pressed to the harper's lips. A pious Catholic neighbour hastened to assist the distressed family, and falling on her knees, and making the children follow her example, recited short acts of contrition, in which it was evident the dying man joined with his whole soul, though unable to speak. From time to time she then uttered ejaculations of love to God, and words of pious affection, such as—"Jesus, I love you." "My Lord and my God, have pity upon me." The harper after that struggled to speak, but in vain; while he pressed the hands of his wife and children, and then pointed to the crucifix which was hanging round his neck, as though recommending them to the protection of that beloved Lord who had died for him. There was evidently something which he wished to say, but was unable to utter. At last he got out the words, "Jesus and Mary!" after which he closed his eyes and expired.

CHAPTER XXXV.

"I know not in what manner the majority of them would rather err, and defend with pugnacity the opinions which they love, than receive without obstinacy what may be consistently advanced."

LUCULLUS.

THE rector and Harvey meanwhile continued their conversations together, each trying to convert his opponent, but each uniformly ended where he began, in the conviction that the other was wrong. At last, the younger clergyman bethought himself of a new course of proceeding. He determined henceforth to cease the attempt to reconvert his future father-in-law, and to confine his endeavours to persuading him to defer a little longer the momentous step he contemplated. Could he manage to delay the crisis, he hoped that something might occur to shake altogether the rector's unhappy resolution. Harvey also took the fact into consideration that many parties were beginning to look with suspicion on the opinions of the Oxford men, and to regard them as tending rapidly towards Rome. This was annoying both to him and his friends; and he feared that it would tell against him, should the announcement of his marriage be quickly followed by the news of his father-in-law's secession from the Anglican Church.

One evening, shortly before the marriage, the two gentlemen were walking together under a majestic grove of elms at a short distance from the house. Harvey was abstracted, for he was considering how best to introduce the proposal that was uppermost in his thoughts. After pacing up and down for some moments in silence, the rector cut short the thread of his meditations.

"What a curious anomaly is the present state of the Church of England," he observed, "claiming Catholicity, and yet not in communion with Catholic christendom!"

"Catholics abroad have at least our warmest sympathy," said Harvey.

"The sympathy of a few, but the hostility of the greater portion of your clergy," said the rector. "Do you really think that such a position as yours has ever been tolerated in former ages? Has it not uniformly been denounced?"

"These questions have nothing to do with the point at issue," replied Harvey. "Every age of the Church has its own especial and characteristic phenomena: suppose the Catholic Church really decided this matter with regard to the first fifteen or eighteen centuries, until she decides for the present time, you have no right to say what her fiat would be."

"The opinion of the majority of the Catholic clergy is against you," rejoined the rector.

"It matters not," said Harvey; "in no way are we bound to accept that judgment, however general: when it comes before us with a distinct and authoritative ratification, it will be time enough to consider of it. The Church of Rome has not hitherto done us justice; she has never investigated closely the existing state of the Anglican Church, nor sifted the evidence producible in favour of the saintly graces which thrive within her bosom. Let her make this enquiry, and found her decision upon it; our Oxford men will then regard that decision as worthy of very grave consideration."

The rector smiled while he replied: "So you mean to say that the Anglican Church possesses one at least of the marks of the true Church—that of sanctity."

"Decidedly so," said Harvey.

"Have you any men among your clergy of the present day," rejoined the rector, "whose lives will bear comparison with those English saints of Catholic times, whose memoirs are now publishing by your own party?"

"I allow," replied Harvey, who had a good deal of candour in his composition, "that the sanctity of the holy men in the Anglican Church of our own day is a different kind of religious excellence from that which appears in the heroic saints of old; not perhaps less admirable, however, when we consider the disadvantages of their condition."

"Nay," interrupted the rector, "I scarcely expected that you would confess having any disadvantages."

"Certainly it is a great disadvantage," replied Harvey, "not to be in perfect communion with the rest of the Catholic Church. Our position, nevertheless, is a very safe one, seeing that we earnestly desire a union with Rome, always premising that certain necessary concessions be made to us; and besides, what to me is the most consolatory thought of all, is that God appears to bless our present position by vouchsafing to us that sanctity to which I alluded: a proof that the grace of the sacraments, in our instance at least, overflows the *apparent* boundaries of the united Catholic Church. Believe me, my dear Mr.

Feversham, there are many clergymen who, like you, believe the whole cycle of Romish doctrine, and yet are content to remain in the Anglican Church, convinced by the graces bestowed by God upon her members that He *wills* them, for a time at least, to do so."

"Clergymen of this description," said the rector, dryly, "sometimes leave the Anglican Church."

"Very true," said Harvey, anxious to accommodate himself to the rector; "but that does not make it the less remarkable that their saintliness was produced and sustained so long within it."

The rector did not reply; and the two gentlemen paced up and down for some minutes in silence. At last Harvey recommenced:

"I entreat you, my dear Mr. Feversham, to consider the possible consequences of the step you are about to take; particularly the loosening of many domestic and social ties, the natural consequence of difference of communion. Do you contemplate the possible struggle of duty with feeling—perhaps of duty with duty, the obligation to steadfastness with that of natural affection, or of obedience to authority with that of deference to the voice of conscience?"

"I have considered all, and I am prepared for all," said the rector, in a hollow and constrained voice.

"Will not your peculiar habits and views," continued Harvey, "clash occasionally with the feelings and maxims of your new associates? Are you sure that you will find yourself among brethren who will feel for you, and directors who will understand you?"

"All such thoughts in a case of manifest duty, as I consider this to be," replied the rector, "must be treated as mere sinful temptations."

"Perhaps they are providential notices to pause," suggested Harvey. "I grieve—I grieve indeed," continued he, "to see you about to join a body of men, who are degraded in this country to the rank of a mere sect."

"It matters little whether you call the English Catholics a sect or not," calmly replied the rector, "as long as they enjoy *one* unspeakable advantage over you, that of being in communion with the whole Catholic Church."

"And far be it from me," said Harvey, "to depreciate the unspeakable blessedness of union with the whole Catholic Church. It is, as you well know, the nearest and dearest wish of my heart that we may all come, in God's good time, and in His own appointed way, to be one. But I dare not forestall that time, nor prescribe that way, as I think you seem inclined to do. Indeed, were I, like you, to seek the blessing of unity otherwise than by the road which my conscience points out, it would in the end prove no blessing to me."

"I, on the other hand," said the rector, "in joining the Catholic Church, follow the dictates of my conscience."

"But, my God!" rejoined Harvey, "why *should* you leave our communion—why *should* you join the Church of Rome? Have you not a place to fill, and work to do, in the Church of England?"

"It is highly dangerous," replied the rector, "to remain a moment longer than is absolutely necessary in a Church which, even you must allow, possesses few or no safeguards against the inroads of heresy, and uses even less than she possesses."

"But don't you see," continued Harvey, "that, notwithstanding all our disadvantages, there are many promising signs to be found in our position. Our Church seems continually on the verge of a crisis, which her good angels interpose to arrest. It never 'is,' but always 'to be' crushed! Depend upon it there is a strong and vigorous vitality about her, which will enable her to stand not only the assaults of her foes, but the violent remedial efforts of our good friends at Oxford, which, however they may shake her in the meantime, must in the end raise her to a state of vigorous health, unprecedented in her annals."*

"Then, perhaps," said the rector, "you consider the present tumult and disorder which pervade the church to be a sign of good?"

"Decidedly so," replied Harvey; "principles and habits which have grown through three hundred years cannot be uprooted by one gentle and peaceful effort; and Protestantism is a demon which will cruelly 'rend the body from which it is preparing to depart.' (Ward.)"

"You are a strange being, Harvey," said the rector; and the principles which you express appear to me not altogether consistent. However, I am tired of argument, and shall give up the field, only asking you one question—how does it happen that to-day you have expressed yourself so anxious for union with Rome, provided she make certain concessions, whereas I distinctly remember that, some weeks ago, you solemnly asserted, that 'union was impossible?'"

"Union is impossible," said Harvey, "as long as Rome so obstinately refuses to make the slightest concession; however, I hope with my whole heart for better times, and to despair of them would, I think, be giving way to a temptation of the devil. At any rate, my dear friend, I beg and implore you to delay leaving our Church for some months longer. The good which you may have it in your power to do by thus temporising is incalculable. By your example and teaching you may spread true Catholic doctrines around you, and thus pave the way for a reunion between the churches. Between ourselves," and here Harvey lowered his voice to a whisper, "there are certain clergymen of my acquaintance, men whom I esteem and venerate, but who go much farther than I do, that believe everything commanded to be be-

* Great part of the preceding conversation is taken, with some alterations, though in certain places word for word, from Mr. Oakley's "Reasons for not joining the Romish Communion," in a letter to a Roman Catholic friend, published in the English Churchman.

lieved by the Council of Trent, and yet retain their livings and outwardly hold allegiance to the Church of England; because, as they wisely observe, the time is not yet ripe for change, and they can do more good by spreading Catholic opinions among their flocks, than by openly professing Romanism."

"Far be it from me," said the rector, "to judge such men, who perhaps in the sight of God, are better far than I; but nevertheless, they appear to me to deceive their own consciences by sophistry and false reasoning; I know not how they can reconcile it with their sense of honour, to remain in one Church while they teach the doctrines of another. As for me, since my mind has been in doubt, I have carefully refrained from teaching in public, and the only person of my congregation to whom in private I opened my mind, was one whom when a mere youth I perverted from Catholicity. No, no! it is against my English notions of honour, for a clergyman who is in heart a Roman Catholic, purposely to convert his flock to that Church under the guise of teaching them Anglicanism."

"Well," said Harvey, somewhat put out, "I was wrong perhaps in proposing such a line of conduct for your imitation, and I by no means defend them, for their opinions are ultra, and they go far beyond what I am inclined to do. All I would say is, that any thing is better than leaving the Anglican Church at a crisis like the present, when minds like yours, my dear Mr. Feversham, may go far in effecting a reconciliation between her and the Papacy. How much more glorious to assist in bringing about such a happy consummation, than as a single individual to sever yourself from the Church which has so long nourished you, to become but a mere drop in the ocean of Catholicity. My dear friend, think *twice*, nay *ten* times, before you fling away the advantages of your position. Enter immediately into a correspondence with our Oxford men; act not as an individual absorbed in the selfish pursuit of his own peace of mind, but act for England and for her Church."

"I will do nothing hastily," said the rector.

CHAPTER XXXVI.

"No fight—no victory. No victory—no crown."

Maxim of Father G——.

A WHOLE year had elapsed, and the rector had kept his promise to do nothing hastily. After Mary's marriage, he went about from one watering place to another, accompanied by Lady Harriet. Medicinal springs have cured many ailments in their time, but, alas! in the catalogue of the wondrous cures effected by them, no where do we find mention of relief afforded to a mind diseased; how then could Mr. Feversham hope for convalescence through their means? According to Harvey's desire, he entered into correspondence with several of the Oxford men, particular friends of his son-in-law. This engaged much of his thoughts and attention, and afforded him considerable pleasure, for he flattered himself that he was gaining some influence over these gentlemen, who certainly watched his steps with deep interest. Harvey also encouraged him in the belief that by delaying a little longer to enter the Catholic Church, he might probably have the satisfaction, after a year or two, when certain difficulties should be smoothed away, of inducing some of these clergymen to act along with him, and make their peace with Rome; whereas, by pressing forward too hastily, he might lose the influence he had already acquired, and render their conversion and that of Harvey more hopeless.

"Act not for yourself alone," said Harvey over and over again, "but taking the beautiful motto of St. Ignatius for your own, do all for the greater glory of God."

Alas! we are not allowed to do evil that good may come, however brilliant the prospect; and no hope of future advantage can excuse the man who delays leaving an heretical communion. Salvation is only to be found in the true Church, though that Church has mercifully included in her pale those who being baptized in a heretical communion, are separated from her not by wilful schism but through ignorance. What hope can there be, however, for those who after being convinced of the truth of Catholicity, delay from prudential or any other human motives to enter the fold of safety, should death attack them unawares, and find them still among the ranks of heresy; ours is a merciful God, but His patience can be worn out.

We shall now drop this painful subject, and reminding our readers that a twelvemonth has passed since the events recorded in the preceding chapter, turn at once to a more agreeable picture, that of Mr. Howard the Catholic priest, who is just leaving the chapel-house on a mission of charity. He is going to visit a poor debtor, who has been wrongfully thrown into prison by an unprincipled relation, who claimed a debt which had been already paid, but of which payment the proofs could not be found. The man was a convert to the Catholic religion, and had been received into the true church by Mr. Howard himself about ten months previously. Since that time one disaster had followed another, for whom the Lord loveth He chasteneth. Let us hope, however, that brighter days are in store for him; for though it generally happens that converts are severely tried at first, yet in the end they receive a hundred fold greater happiness than before, even in this world.

"I am glad beyond measure to see your Reverence," said the poor man, starting eagerly forward as the priest entered, and grasping his hand which he shook warmly; "it is very, very kind of you, Sir, to come so often to see me. I was getting rather down-hearted yesterday, when I saw the fine day, and the sun shining, and the clear sky, and felt the fresh breeze on my cheek, and heard the birds singing away as merrily, poor things, as though there was no sorrow near them. It is a great trial, Sir, being cooped up this way instead of striding along at the tail of my own plough, and whistling as cheerily as any of the larks in the sky above me; however, God's will be done."

"Yes, my good friend," said Mr. Howard, "I know well that the want of air and exercise must be a great trial to one like you, accustomed to the country and to labour in the fields. You must remember, however, that it is God who sends you this affliction; try to forget that it has come upon you through means of your relation, and embrace it joyfully as proceeding from the hands of a kind and merciful God, who has especially sent it to you as a means of acquiring great merit and of expiating the temporal punishment due for the sins of your past life."

"Well, well, Sir, I will try to forget from whom the injury came," replied the debtor, "and I will try also to look upon it as sent from God purely for my good. But there is a favour I would ask, Sir, and that is, that you would never call him my relation again, unless you want to set up my corruption. Our family has always had its faults; there have been hasty fellows, drunken fellows, quarrelsome and wild fellows among us, but there never was one mean, dirty, shabby fellow like him. No, no, your Reverence, he is not my relation, though he calls himself my son-in-law. He was only married to my step-daughter, thank goodness; and not a drop of my blood runs in his veins, praise be to God."

"Well, I shall be more careful in future what I call the gentleman," said Mr. Howard laughing; "and now tell me what you have been about since I saw you."

"I have read a great piece of the life of St. Francis Xavier that you lent me," replied the debtor. "Oh! it is a beautiful book, Sir; that man was a hero, if ever there was. I'd have liked to have served under him. At first I thought what a fine cavalry officer he'd have made, leading a charge, and dashing into the ranks of his enemies; and before I knew where I was, I cried out 'hurrah,' and made all the debtors start. My face got very hot, when they asked what was the matter; that sobered me, and then I began to think that St. Francis had chosen in reality the very part that I proposed, and which nature had intended for him, since he became the great warrior of the cross, and the soldier of Jesus Christ."

"You are right, John," said Mr. Howard; "St. Francis was a true soldier in spirit, and what is more, he joined an order founded on military principles."

"Indeed, Sir," replied the man, "I like that, and I wish you would tell me something about it; they were called Jesuits, were they not? For what were they instituted?"

"To labour," replied Mr. Howard, "in the conversion and sanctification of souls, to train up youth in piety and learning, to defend the faith against heretics, and propagate it amongst infidels.* They were the great champions of our Church who stemmed the tide of the Reformation, the 'forlorn band who

* See chap. 18th, of Challoner's Catholic Christian Instructed.

gained a great day.' They were the first opponents of the slave trade who *died* to prevent it; the founders of a commonwealth in Paraguay, which realised all that has ever been dreamt of Utopia; sages in the art of government, the protectors of the poor and oppressed Indians, the boldest and most successful missionaries of modern times. In every walk of life they excel, as preachers, men of letters and scientific philosophers, and in nothing more than as instructors of youth."

"They must be universal geniuses," replied the debtor; "but the thing I admire most is their military cast."

"That," replied Mr. Howard, "was the reflex of the soldierly character of their founder, St. Ignatius. In his youth he had been a brave knight, and when he bid adieu to his well loved sword, to use the words of an able writer,* 'his military mind conceived the design of levying a spiritual army, the general of which should be Jesus Christ himself.' To this end he wrote a book of meditations called, 'Spiritual Exercises.' You must suppose yourself armed and on the battle field. Christ calls you on one side—Lucifer on the other. The two hostile banners flaunt the sky. The trumpets are calling: 'Say, soldier, under whose banner will you enlist?' An important question, and involving grave considerations! Lucifer tenders present pleasures which will pass away, and which are yet mixed with bitterness even while they last. Jesus Christ leads the way in suffering as in fighting. He asks not his meanest follower to bear half as much as he has himself endured. Present sufferings he proffers, but which will also pass away; and which even while they last, are blended with ineffable consolations. *Soldier, which side will you choose?* And those sufferings blended ever with a certain sweetness, when at length they will have

* Miles Gerald Keon.

passed entirely away, must give place to scenes and to emotions less transitory—to everlasting joys, to crowns that fade not, and to triumphs unfollowed by reaction! *Once more, soldier, which side will you choose?'* "*

"Have not I chosen already?" cried Blount, for it was he, starting up with enthusiasm under the influence of Mr. Howard's kindling glance. "Yes, Sir, now that I am so happy as to be a member of the one, holy, Catholic and Apostolic Church, I will be a faithful soldier of Jesus Christ, and stand by him until death, so help me God!"

"But, my dear Blount," rejoined Mr. Howard, with a smile of pleasure on his countenance, as he marked the impetuosity of the new convert, "you must remember that a soldier of Jesus Christ must suffer more frequently than fight. It is very plain that fighting would suit your temperament better than suffering."

"No question of that, Sir!" interrupted Blount.

"Nevertheless, most merit is to be gained by suffering," continued the priest; "besides, it is what God appoints for you at present, and you must submit because it is His will."

"I will try, Sir," said the farmer, sadly. "Many a scrape I got into in my youth, owing to my roving disposition, so it is a fitting punishment for me now to be confined within four walls, and I shall just offer it to God, through the merits of Christ, in expiation of these same offences. God knows how much better I like to hear the lark sing than the mouse squeak, as an old Scotch soldier said, so may be He'll reckon it more merit for me to sit patiently here, than if I were a poor sickly atomy of a weaver, or man-milliner, that never knew the taste of fresh air except on a Sunday! But the biggest trial was what I had yesterday, when my wife and Neddy came

* See No. 3 of Oxford and Cambridge Review, article on the Jesuits, by Miles Gerald Keon.

to see me. They had just passed a gray mare drawing a cart. Poor thing, her knees were broken, and she was as thin and starved as possible. The man that drove her was lashing her, and Neddy was as mad at him as he could be, only his mother kept him quiet. Just then they crossed the street, and the dumb beast saw Neddy and winnied to him, for many was the time the boy had rubbed her down and fed her! It was my own old gray mare, Sir, that I used to be so proud of, the best trotter in the country, that fetched a good price when my farm stock was sold! God knows how they had treated her afterwards—but there she was with her knees broke, and only fit for the kennel! When Neddy and his mother came in, he was blubbering as if his heart would break; and I would fain have joined him, only I thought shame to give such a bad example to womankind! So I held my tongue, though there was a lump in my throat."

Mr. Howard soon after this took his leave, and we shall take the benefit of his absence to relate the events which had latterly befallen the farmer. Soon after Mr. Feversham's departure from the village, Blount was received into the Catholic Church by Mr. Howard. A great deal of bad feeling was excited in the parish by this step. Had he joined any other denomination of christians, it would have been otherwise; nay, had he even professed himself an infidel and denied God altogether, it would not have caused so much surprise, and certainly would not have drawn down upon him the same amount of angry reproaches as he now had to undergo on every side. The curate of the parish, Mr. Hounslowe, a keen Puseyite, was the only person who let him alone; but there was not a single dissenting minister within ten miles round, who did not either pay him a visit, or write him a letter adjuring him to have nothing to do with the abominations of the Church of Rome! The farmer took it all very quietly, had an answer ready for every one that personally attacked him, and coolly whistled as he threw the letters which he daily received into the fire. Fortunately for him, the dame was by no means so exasperated as he had expected. Very sorry she was that he should have left "the glorious Church and State by law established," but then, as she told her neighbours, she had the consolation of knowing that he had entered another which possessed a very fine "hierarchade," consisting of all sorts of clergy from curates up to cardinals, and that had an excellent old man at the head of it, more dignified than Queen Victoria, who after all was but a woman! Now the Pope had been head of the Church, even before the Bible was all finished; at least so Blount had told her; and for her part she had a great respect for antiques, and thought that since her husband must leave the Church of England, he had made a better choice than she could have expected. So much for the dame; but unfortunately all those connected with Blount had not the same liberality. The steward upon the estate where Blount had his farm, was a brother of Mr. Longab, and a very zealous man. He was not a Methodist, having invented a church perfectly new in its principles, in which he himself occasionally officiated as high priest. Certain little peccadilloes in which he privately indulged, were beginning about this time to be whispered among his flock. Anxiously he looked about for some means of reinstating himself in the public good opinion, and it occurred to him, that the easiest method of passing for a saint was to have an extreme horror of popery, and to show his detestation not only of that iniquitous church, but of the individuals belonging to it. Accordingly he preached against Blount, he spoke against him and annoyed him in every way he could. Unfortunately for the farmer, the gentleman who owned the estate resided abroad, so that it was impossible to obtain redress for many oppressive and vexatious exactions. There is an old proverb that it is easier for the injured than for the injurer to forgive. Accordingly the farmer found it impossible to mollify his persecutor, whose ill-feeling at last took the form of implacable hatred. It had happened that a short time previously, Blount, relying upon the long lease by which he held his farm, had expended a good deal of money on making certain improvements, which were not expected to bring in any return for a year or two, though after that, they would greatly increase the products of the land. Unfortunately, the crops failed the first harvest after the farmer had declared himself Catholic, and he was consequently obliged to crave a little delay in paying his rent. To his surprise this was refused, and a flaw being pointed out in his lease, he was suddenly obliged to leave his farm. His stock was hurriedly sold by the unjust steward to great disadvantage; so with only a few pounds in his pocket, poor Blount was obliged to leave the house which had sheltered him in affluence and comfort during so many years, and with the dame and Neddy occupy a small cottage in the neighbourhood, going out to the farmers who lived near, as a day-labourer. It was a beautiful sight to witness his contentment and resignation under these heavy afflictions. God, however, in His mercy, vouchsafed him certain consolations. Neddy learned with eagerness and delight his father's religion, and often when for a moment he felt down-hearted, comforted him by his childish remarks, which breathed a faith and simplicity that both surprised and delighted his father. The dame also was changed for the better. Seeing her husband's trials, she now endeavoured to controul her temper, naturally quick; for she said that he had enough to suffer without her helping to torment him. She also talked less and worked more than she had done before—her conduct appearing far less eccentric and more rational than formerly. The farmer now began to think that after all he was not so much to be pitied, and that he would yet get on very well, particularly after Mr. Feversham should return, who would probably do something for him. Unfortunately, however, it happened that he had a wealthy unmarried brother, with whom he had quarrelled some years previously, for which reason Blount felt a delicacy in asking him for assistance in the hour of his distress. Jacob Hogg knew this, and was always urging his father-in-law to apply to him. Now Mr. Hogg had long been intending to take a pleasure trip either to the continent or to North America. He had now got a good deal of money in his hands, some of it Mrs. Benson's, which he had not yet transmitted to her, and some belonging to other friends and neighbours, who had been beguiled by his seeming sanctity to trust it into his keeping. He also proposed to fail shortly, and declare himself bankrupt; these and various other little reasons would render it exceedingly convenient for him to make his pleasure tour at as great a distance from his old friends as possible. It struck him that a few hundred pounds more in his pocket would be no bad thing, and as he was very sure that his father-in-law had lost the receipt for the payment of Mrs. Hogg's dowry, he fancied that by getting him thrown into prison for this alleged debt, his brother might be induced to pay the money. It is needless to enter into the details of this iniquitous proceeding; it is sufficient to say that Blount at last became an inhabitant of the debtor's prison, and that his brother, though appealed to by Mr. Hogg unknown to the farmer, maintained a dignified silence throughout the whole transaction.

CHAPTER XXXVII.

"A cousin o' mine, a puir dwiny atomy o' a cratur, gaed out to the Indies as Scudgy to wash the dishes, in ane o' thae gran' India men. An' whan he was there, he took to convertin' the heathen, and made a hunder thousan' pun'." *My old Nurse.*

It happened one day that Dame Blount and Neddy were longer than usual in paying their accustomed visit to the farmer, and the good man began pacing up and down in great impatience; for having nothing in particular to occupy his time, he very naturally conjured up a few fears lest anything should have happened to either of them. He had expected them at least an hour, when Neddy came rushing in followed by his mother, who walked with great dignity and pomposity, as she always did when she had any thing to communicate.

"Oh, father!" cried Neddy, "mother has got a letter; and you'll not guess who wrote it! its from a grand lady that keeps company with kings and queens and princesses as thick as blackberries!"

"Don't let on, Neddy, who it's from," interrupted the dame, "I'll read it first and let your father guess. I made out the writer before I opened the letter, though it's not her handwriting on the back. That is what kept me so long this morning; it took me nearly an hour looking at it through the light and turning it round and round and cyphering the seal; for I was determined I'd not open it till I gathered who it was from—which at last I did, when I discovered a wild savage man on the seal, that at first I had taken either for cupid or a monkey!"

"Well, dame, let's hear," said the farmer laughing, "I can almost guess it myself now; though it's sooner than I expected to hear from Deborah."

"The letter is dated," said the dame seating herself, blowing her nose and clearing her voice, "from the Pickmanbone Islands, August, 184— 'My dear sister, you are by no means the person whom I would choose to write to, had not my mind undergone a great change, and been emptied since my departure, of many narrow and sectarian notions. I have now discovered that there are many pious missionaries who are not Methodists; indeed, it appears to me that all connected with the London Missionary Society, are regenerated characters, cleaving fast to the truth as it is in Jesus. This being my firm conviction, I have been induced by a pious blacksmith, a Mr. Tompkins, who is settled here as teacher and minister of God's word, to give up all exclusive connection with Methodists only, and henceforth loving every one whose election and predestination are made sure, stand or fall by the London Missionary Society, of which Mr. Tompkins is an honoured member. I mean by this no offence to the Methodist connection, some of whose ministers are rich and flourishing men out here—loving all as I do because they are vessels of election. As soon as you have read this letter, which I purposely write above your comprehension, I beg you will lend it about among my old friends and admirers, and in particular get it read in the meeting-house, if not from the pulpit, at least in the vestry. After which will you carefully enclose it to the secretary of the London Missionary Society, to be published in their annual reports. I shall not waste time in detailing the events that occurred during the voyage, since I have already told them to Mr. Tompkins, who means to make use of them in his own missionary report. My pen shall take a higher flight, and forgetting my individual self, give a statistical, diplomatic, fiscal and colonial detail of the grand position of the missionaries in these isles, as sovereigns, lawgivers, ministers of justice, and preachers of the word. To begin at the beginning, in reading over the missionary archives, I was struck with admiration at the wisdom displayed in the selection of the site of their labours. The captain of the expedition receiving instructions to be guided in his choice by 'the safety of the women, probability of introducing improvements, supply of provisions, and the products in sugar, cotton, and sandal wood.' This was truly being wise as serpents, as well as innocent as doves! Then their admirable prudence in taking care of their own safety! In some of the islands they took on shore two swivels, eight muskets, one blunderness, nine pistols, and nine swords; fifty-six gun-flints besides those in use; powder, ball, drum and fife! though, praise be to God, 'gunpowder and the gospel were not carried in the same packet!'* Some popish priests have occasionally set foot here, and had the impertinence to say that such precautions were not apostolic. Now I say, let them go, miserable creatures as they are, with nothing but the clothes on their back and the breviary in their hand, to wherever the soil is uninviting and the people ferocious. Good enough for them any day! But let us London Society missioners stick to the fat places of the earth, where there are no 'inhospitable climates, absolute governments, established prejudices,' or 'difficult languages,' lands flowing with milk and honey, and sending splendid returns of oil and cotton to the societies at home; not to speak of the riches which the missionaries gather for themselves! Just to think of a Mr. Oakes, one of the first missionaries to Australia, having by his honest industry amassed a large fortune—upwards of '*one hundred thousand pounds being to be divided amongst the*

* See Campbell's Maritime Discovery and Christian Missions.

family! That is what I call preaching the gospel to advantage! Then there is a Mrs. H. wife of a Wesleyan missionary, 'will possess considerably above ten thousand pounds!' When will the pope of Rome's missionaries be as respectable, or make as much money! In this respect our missionaries beat the apostles themselves; but indeed in every respect they are a stage beyond them, and have introduced improvements unknown in the barbarous first ages of Christianity; at least so Mr. Tompkins informs me. For example, 'in no island of importance has Christianity been introduced without war.'* An excellent method, I opine, for grounding it deeply in the minds and hearts of the inhabitants. Then every 'serious inquirer after truth' is bound to possess a copy of the scriptures, and pay for it too!† A thing which as far as I can gather from the Bible, the apostles were never sharp enough to enforce. Then it is beautiful to see the perfect system of taxation which the missionaries have introduced. The natives are ordained to pay a poll-tax amounting to eight shillings per family. The men are ordered to labour *three* days in each month for the *government*, and if there be important public work to be done, then there shall be *six* more working days, really *nine* days in each month, without pay or food. The missionaries are not such fools but they can turn a pretty penny out of these privileges! Then every imaginable sin is punished by a fine according to its enormity.‡ The Bible says, 'where sin abounded grace did much more abound;' but I say, that in this case it should be, where sin abounds money comes in; and what is more, goes into the pockets of the Lord's people that have to do with the government. Another proof of

* See the testimony of Williams the missionary, as quoted in the 18th Portfolio.

† See vol. 2. p. 231. Ellis's Polynesian Researches.

‡ For these laws and system of taxation, see the authority of Mr. Simpson, quoted in 18th number of the Portfolio.

missionary wisdom which strikes me with admiration, is the abolishing of old customs and sports even to 'running, wrestling, throwing the spear, &c., under the pretext of idolatry, gambling, or time ill spent, (so that even swimming is no longer an amusement,) and the consequent change in the habits of the people, have been powerful agents in depopulation.'* Glorious thought! Truly the ways of providence are wonderful! Fulfilling the scriptural injunction to increase and multiply, it is astonishing how the children and grandchildren of the missionaries fill the land, and how by the mysterious regulations of Infinite Wisdom the savage population are dying away, and making room for them to take their place! But enough for the present of public affairs; I shall put off till my next letter giving a sketch of that sweetly-domestic and highly virtuous vessel of election, Queen Pomata, to whom I have the honour of being privy counsellor, though as yet I can understand but little of what she says. Suffice it to say, that she owes her sovereignty to the missionaries, who take the chief management of her affairs, and that her enemies are base enough to give her a shocking character, and to say that an addiction to ardent spirits is her least fault. But saints have been reviled and slandered from time immemorial, so I am determined not to believe a word of it, particularly as there is some talk of Mr. Tompkins arranging a marriage between her son, the prince royal, and my own little Betsy. God's will be done! I am resigned to become the grandmother of kings and princesses in Israel. Mr. Tompkins is highly indignant also at the behaviour of Jacob Hogg, in not sending out the remainder of my money as he promised. Tell Jacob that if he do not bestir himself, and that quickly, Mr. Tompkins, who I trust will soon have a legal right to interfere as my protector, intends to blazon his character as a

* Simpson's Sandwich Islands, pp. 9—16.

defaulter, and a wronger of widows and orphans, in all the pages of all the missionary magazines that will be published in London for the ensuing year. And now, dear sister, rejoice with me at our approaching alliance with royalty, and at my close contact and delicious intercourse with kings, queens, missionaries, and other grand dignitaries out here. Praise be to God for all His mercies! Hallelujah! Amen.

"Your loving sister,

"Humble though uplifted,

"DEBORAH BENSON."

CHAPTER XXXVIII.

"The sign of the cross will be in heaven when the Lord shall come to judge. In the cross is salvation; in the cross is life; in the cross is protection from thy enemies; in the cross is infusion of heavenly sweetness; in the cross is strength of mind; in the cross is joy of spirit; in the cross is the height of virtue; in the cross is the perfection of sanctity. There is no health of the soul, nor hope of eternal life, but in the cross.

"For priests alone rightly ordained in the Church, have power to celebrate." THOMAS à KEMPIS.

A WHOLE fortnight elapsed ere Mr. Howard again had leisure to visit farmer Blount in his prison. When at last he did go, he found him in high glee; for he had just been holding an argument with one of the debtors, and when a man fancies that he has the best of it in a discussion, it always raises his spirits.

"They were laughing at me, Sir," said Blount, "because I always make the sign of the cross when I say grace before meals; and one impudent fellow declared that he had never seen such a brazen-faced papist in his life. Most of the kind that he had seen before, used to do it like gentlemen with their thumb across a button hole, so that nobody could tell what they were after. But he said I did it with such a flourish from my forehead to my chest, and from shoulder to shoulder, just as if I was proud of it; and he wondered I was not ashamed. So I told him that I did it that way on purpose to show that I gloried in it, for the cross was the standard of Jesus Christ, and those that were ashamed of Christ, Christ would be ashamed of at the last day."

"You answered very well, Mr. Blount," rejoined the priest: "It is miserable to see how Protestants dislike and contemn the sign of the cross. How unlike the first Christians, who were accustomed to do it on all occasions, as Tertullian says, 'at every step, at every coming in and going out, when we wash, when we sit down at table, when we light a candle, when we go to bed, whatsoever conversation employs us, we imprint on our foreheads the sign of the cross!'"

"When Protestants make little of the sign of the cross," said the farmer, "it looks as if they were ashamed of believing in a crucified God. Now I think we cannot make it too often, to put us in mind of the death and passion of our Saviour. Indeed, I told them all so, and some of them said I was very right; but just then the same forward chap that had first attacked me, cried out, 'You may defend making the sign of the cross if you like, but there is one thing that you cannot defend, and that is holy water.' And then he made all the fellows round him laugh, describing how his grandmother, that was a Papist, used to sprinkle herself and her bed, and indeed many another thing that belonged to her with holy water. Then some of the debtors asked what holy water meant, and I said blessed water, so they all began to laugh; and I said that there was just as much sense in blessing water as in blessing meat, which all pious Protestants did before they ate. And then I explained how the Catholic Church blesses everything she makes use of, altars, candles, vestments, &c. &c. by way of begging God that such as religiously use them, may obtain His blessing."

"You might have given them Scripture for it too, Blount," said Mr. Howard; "for in their own Protestant Bible, St. Paul writing to Timothy in the fourth chapter says, that 'every creature of God is good, for it is sanctified by the word of God and prayer.'"

"Does not the Church believe," continued Blount, "that evil spirits fly from the sign of the cross and from blessed things?"

"Certainly," replied Mr. Howard, "and that is one reason why Catholics so often dip their fingers in holy water, and make the sign of the cross upon their persons. That is also the reason why candles blessed in the church are lighted beside dying people, and holy water is sprinkled on their beds."

"The Catholic Church seems to care for every thing," replied the farmer; "her children are surrounded by her blessings till the last, and even beyond the grave, since she continues then to help the poor souls by her prayers. Till I became a Catholic, your Reverence, I was always mortal afraid of dying, but I don't think I should be so frightened now."

"You have no reason now," replied the priest, "but you would have had reason for terror, had you delayed your conversion. There is a melancholy instance of the kind just now occurring in what formerly was your neighbourhood. A very amiable man, a clergyman of the Church of England, who has long been suspected of a leaning to the Catholic Church, but who through timidity and a certain indecision of character, put off from year to year openly confessing his principles, has now returned to his rectory dangerously ill, and from what I hear, his deathbed is so beset by his clerical friends, that there is little or no chance that he will be allowed to summon the aid of a Catholic priest. Had he ever given me the slightest encouragement, I would go to visit him now; but as it is, I hardly dare intrude."

"Mr. Feversham!" exclaimed the farmer, turning very pale. "O, Sir! Sir! For heaven's sake go to him! I know he is in heart a Catholic! O, do not let him die like a dog, without making his confession and saving his soul!"

"How do you know whom I mean?" asked Mr. Howard, gazing at the farmer with surprise.

"I felt sure it could be no other," replied Blount. "I saved his life when I was a boy; he was the kindest of masters to me when I was his servant; and he is the person that I told you converted me to the holy Catholic Church with his own hands before ever I came to know you, Sir!"

"Then this was the Catholic friend of whom you so often spoke," said Mr. Howard, "whose name you kept such a secret?"

"Yes, Sir," replied Blount; "but there is no more need for secresy now. Oh! Sir, for God's sake go to him, and force your way in whether they will admit you or not! Tell him that his faithful servant sent you to him! And, Oh! Sir, fight your way in, if they won't let you in peaceably! God pity me, being in prison here, or no power on earth could keep me from him!"

"But perhaps he does not want me," said the priest, gravely. "Besides, he has had an attack of paralysis, and I am by no means sure that he is now in possession of all his faculties!"

"God have mercy on him!" exclaimed the farmer, bursting into tears. "My dear, dear, kind master! Oh! that I could lay down my life for his! If they would but let me out of prison, though it were only to get the length of his chamber door, that he might have one Catholic near him in his distress! Oh! Sir, to save a soul, could you not get in by the window, if they will not let you in by the door! Don't stand on ceremony with them, Sir, but get in some way, though it should be in a trunk or a portmanteau, and I'll bless you till my dying day! I'd cut off my right hand to get you in. O go, Sir! Go! for God's sake!"

"Do not be so impetuous, my good Blount," said Mr. Howard to the farmer, who was pacing up and down the room in his agitation, as if he could knock himself against the walls that detained him so much against his will. "I shall certainly go to Mr. Feversham, and that directly. Meanwhile you must pray hard that God may procure me admittance."

"That I will, Sir," replied Blount. "I'll not rise from my knees till I think you have got there and spoken to him. God speed your Reverence, and grant you success!"

Mr. Howard set off immediately on leaving the farmer; luckily his horse was saddled and ready for him when he reached the chapel house, so that no time was lost. As he rode up the avenue and approached the rectory door, he felt a little awkward, for he feared that he might be regarded as an intruder. Repressing this feeling, as unworthy of one on such an important mission, he knocked at the door and asked for Mr. Feversham. The servant replied that his master was dangerously ill, and unable to see any one; besides, at that moment there were two clergymen with him, his son-in-law Mr. Harvey, and a friend from Oxford, the famous Mr. Camden, and that he rather thought they were about to give him the sacrament! They had got candles lighted in the room, though it was day-light, and Mr. Camden's own man had told him that his master intended hearing the rector's confession!

With a heavy heart, Mr. Howard turned away after receiving this information, and slowly and sadly returned to Overbury.

The footing on which the rector stood with Mr. Camden, now demands some explanation. As we already mentioned, a long and interesting correspondence had been carried on for some time between Mr. Feversham and the heads of the Puseyite movement in Oxford. Thanks to the skilful management of Mr. Harvey, neither party exactly understood the sentiments of the other. Both acting by his advice, temporised a little, in hopes of bringing round their correspondent to their own opinions. The rector kept in the back ground his contempt for Anglican ordination, and did all in his power to persuade the Puseyite clergymen to join him in a body, and make arrangements for reunion with Rome; or at least to try if the Papal See might not be persuaded to move a step forward to meet them, and thus smooth away some of their difficulties. The ultra Puseyites, on the other hand, enlarged much on the possibility of clergymen in the Church of England conscientiously retaining their livings while holding every Roman doctrine. Probably if Mr. Feversham and these gentlemen had met in person, their correspondence would have changed its tone. As it happened, the rector's bad health and frequent illness, on several occasions prevented the meeting which both parties desired. And yet it would be unfair to say that either side was uncandid. Mr. Feversham believed them to be much nearer Catholicity than they actually were, and they, on the other hand, flattered themselves that they would be able to retain him permanently in the Anglican Church.

While at Cheltenham a week or two previously, the rector, in addition to his other complaints, had a threatening of paralysis, and as soon as he was able to be removed, was hurried to the rectory by Lady Harriet, who declared it was intolerable to take charge of a sick man at a watering place. She wrote both to Mrs. Egremond and Miss Beauclerk, requesting them to await her in the country and assist her to nurse Mr. Feversham. These two ladies kindly agreed, and had every thing arranged for the invalid's comfort before his return. Mrs. Harvey, who, had it been possible, would have flown to her father at the first intimation of his danger, was unfortunately unable to undertake the journey. A week before Mr. Feversham's seizure, she had been thrown out of a carriage and severely bruised. Such was her husband's anxiety on her account, that he not only kept secret from her the melancholy tidings of her father, but also remained watching her sick bed, until her physician assured him that there was no further cause for alarm. Then, and not till then, he quitted her on the plea of urgent business, and passing on his way near the town where Mr. Camden resided, had little difficulty in persuading that gentleman to accompany him. They only arrived at the rectory the evening before Mr. Howard called, and were unable then to see Mr. Feversham, as he was too weak to speak. The next morning he appeared a good deal revived, and was allowed to see them; but we shall delay telling what passed on the occasion, until we describe Mr. Camden. He was thin, pale, and his countenance was of a strikingly intellectual cast. His fine features were emaciated with fasting, and his body was broken down with the mortifications to which he subjected it. At least so his admirers accounted for his premature infirmities. He looked between fifty and sixty, but in reality was scarcely past forty. He sometimes smiled but rarely laughed, and the predominant expression of his face was a saintly melancholy, which at times, when in a fit of abstraction, was almost painful to behold. In his youth he had intended to marry, but had been jilted, and for the last fifteen years he had declared his conviction that celibacy was better than matrimony for an *Anglican priest.* His sermons were very popular, and much frequented by the young men of his party, who looked up to him as to an oracle. They were singular from their near approaches to Catholicity, and from the ingenuity with which Mr. Camden hovered on its brink, and yet never advanced farther; sometimes appearing about to fall down into its terrible abyss, and then, by a skilful sophism, recovering himself and clinging faster than ever to the rock (not of ages, but) of three centuries, the Church of England! The present position of the Anglican Church gave him very great uneasiness, and if possible increased his melancholy. But, far from looking upon it as a reason for quitting her communion, he was accustomed to say, that "the lowering aspect of things around, was a call from God, to aim at still higher and stricter obedience, and to open new paths of labour and self-denial." He used also to tell his pupils "that the response of all who have made this trial had been most wonderfully harmonious; the more they have laboured to chasten and deny themselves, the more they have experienced, not a restless and uneasy desire for fuller privileges, but the very reverse; their treasure has been increased of heavenly peace and joy in believing."* Poor Mr. Camden! He might speak in this way, but no one who examined his countenance, which expressed an unutterable melancholy, could be deluded into the belief that he himself felt peace and joy in believing.

During the painful and weary journey between Cheltenham and the rectory, Mr. Feversham had been in a sort of stupefaction, scarcely appearing to notice anything that happened around him. Once he

* See Ward's Ideal of a Christian Church, page 570.

had roused himself a little, and beckoning to his attendant, whispered, "I want a priest to be sent for —a Catholic priest." But as he almost immediately afterwards fell into a dose, little attention was paid to what he said. Lady Harriet overheard him, but merely remarked, "Poor man! Harvey will do all that is necessary for him when he gets to the rectory!"

Now it so happened that Mr. Camden had pleased Mr. Feversham more than any of the other Puseyite clergymen with whom he had corresponded, and he was the one of whose conversion he had the most sanguine hopes. On being informed that he and his son-in-law had arrived, his countenance expressed the most lively joy. The next morning, as we have already mentioned, he was a great deal better, and eagerly asked to see them. The physician in attendance sanctioned this request, but warned the two gentlemen at the same time, on no account to fatigue the invalid, and if they had anything particular to say, to be as brief as possible. Harvey entered first, and was deeply affected on beholding the change which illness had wrought upon his father-in-law. As soon as he could command himself, he whispered, "Our mutual friend, Mr. Camden, is here, and has something of great importance to say to you. Shall I admit him?"

The rector faintly smiled his assent, and Harvey went out for Mr. Camden.

"My dear father-in-law is dreadfully changed," he whispered, "and scarcely able for any exertion. Do not, my dear friend, exhaust him by conversation, but try to prepare him immediately to receive the holy sacrament."

Mr. Camden pressed the hand of his friend and softly entered the sick man's apartment. Going up to the bed he took Mr. Feversham's hand in his, and kneeling down, ejaculated in the words of the prayer-book—

"'O Lord, look down from heaven, behold, visit, and relieve this thy servant. Look upon him with the eyes of thy mercy, and give him comfort and sure confidence in thee!" Then remembering Harvey's caution not to waste time, he stopped short, and rising up, continued, "My dear brother in Jesus Christ, the grievous sickness with which it has pleased a most merciful God to afflict you, has been sent by his fatherly hand, to remind you that you must prepare for giving in your last account, ere the great portal of eternity opens to admit you. Answer me then truly and candidly—are you now ready and willing to receive the last sacrament from the hands of a priest of the holy Catholic Church?"

"God knows how joyfully," faintly murmured the dying man, who, alas! misunderstood him. "But where is the priest that I may confess to him?"

"Here, here! in this house, in this room!" said Harvey, who was present during the foregoing scene, a silent listener.

"God in heaven bless you both," whispered the rector. "Leave me now for half an hour while I prepare myself."

The two gentlemen did so; and the elder clergyman going up to his own apartment, rang for his man servant, and desired him to open his portmanteau and take out the various things necessary for administering the sacrament, without which Mr. Camden never travelled. He then changed his dress, putting on the vestments, in which he was accustomed to perform his priestly functions.

"All is ready now, Sir," said the man.

"You may go for the present," replied Mr. Camden, "I shall wait here while Mr. Feversham prepares to make his confession."

The servant went down stairs, much pleased and edified by what he had heard, for like his master he was a strict Anglican Catholic, and no sooner had he entered the servants' hall, than he told the news in strict confidence to the other domestics. Meanwhile Harvey was giving orders to prepare the apartment as soon as the rector should be ready; nor were candles forgotten which were to be lighted during the administration of the sacrament. Just then a visitor was descried from the window of the servants' hall coming up the avenue towards the house.

"That's an Anglican clergyman!" exclaimed Mr. Camden's own man with great dignity. "You may know him by the cut of his coat and his turned down shirt collar. I should know an apostolic Anglican priest among a thousand!"

"Mr. Harvey has just given orders," rejoined the footman, who usually opened the door, "that no one is to be admitted. But if he belongs to the same sect as the Puseyites, I'd better go and ask before sending him away."

"Stop a bit if you please, Sir," interrupted Mr. Camden's own man, with a patronizing air, elevating his eye-glass, and scanning Mr. Howard, who just then passed the window. "After all, I suspect I have been mistaken. That fellow is low, quite low, decidedly vulgar! Never saw an Anglican clergyman in my life in such a coarse black suit! Dolly my dear, look here!" continued Mr. Camden's man turning to the chambermaid, who evidently regarded him with mingled awe and admiration. "Look here, while I teach you how to know an Anglican clergyman! Their countenances are all thin, pale, and penetrating. That fellow there, now standing at the hall-door, is dressed like a coarse imitation of one of them; though he wants the ethereal neatness and spiritualized elegance with which I strive to inoculate my master. But it is in the face chiefly that you can discern the difference!"

"Lawk, Sir, how can that be?" inquired Dolly in amazement.

"That is just what I want to point out to you," replied Mr. Camden's own man. "The Anglican clergymen are generally interesting and melancholy beings, consumed by a sorrow which the world neither knows nor can understand, which indeed I account their great charm. Now, that fellow at the hall-door there, (just turning away upon my life,) is as robustuous and hearty as if he were sure of his salvation, and never had a doubt. Vulgar fellow, not a spark of gentility or carewornness on his countenance; depend upon it he is a schismatic."

"It seems to me," said Dolly, looking after Mr. Howard, "that he goes down the avenue far less cheerily than he came up."

All was now ready, Mr. Howard had been dismissed, a dead silence reigned through the house, the attendants raised the rector up in bed, and propped by pillows he sat, while a gleam of happiness illuminated his countenance; for now he believed that he was about to be reconciled to that holy Church which had so long possessed his love and his faith, though, alas! not his outward allegiance. How it had come to pass that a priest should be there he knew not, he cared not; now was no time to ask questions. He was weak, very weak, and must husband all his strength for the trying ordeal he was about to pass through—that of confessing the sins of a long, and (must we say it,) mis-spent life. The follies, not to say the crimes, of the wild young cavalry officer rose in dread array before him, and the fearful responsibilities of his latter career, his moral cowardice, his procrastination, all assumed a deeper dye at the moment before confession, than he had ever anticipated.

"God will accept of my shame in satisfaction for the sins of my past life," thought the sick man, and feeling that his strength was fast ebbing, he nerved himself for the effort, and ejaculating a short prayer to Jesus and to Mary, desired the priest to be summoned.

The attendants quitted the apartment—the door

opened, and a man in priestly vestments entered. "Brother in our Lord Jesus Christ," he exclaimed, "I come now to bring peace to your soul—that peace which passes all understanding!"

The rector tried to raise himself, and held out his hands towards his visitor. It was not till the Anglican clergyman had quite reached his bedside, that he recognized Mr. Camden; but when he did, the change that came over his countenance was appalling! It literally became black! He sank upon the pillows, and waving Mr. Camden away with his hand, who, shocked and terrified, tried to support him, had only time to cry out,—

"A true priest! A true priest! I will none of this man!" when a convulsive change passed over his features, and he fell to one side, helpless, passive, and insensible, in the arms of Mr. Camden! Dreadfully shocked, the latter rang the bell violently and called for assistance; fortunately the physician was not far distant, having merely gone to the house of a gentleman in the neighbourhood. He was summoned immediately, and on his arrival pronounced that a dangerous paralytic seizure had taken place. The rector continued insensible during the whole day, the only sign of life being his heavy breathing. Lady Harriet fell into hysterics on hearing what had occurred, and it required all Miss Beauclerk's patience and care to manage her, for she insisted upon rushing down stairs and throwing herself into the arms of the poor dying rector! Mrs. Egremond installed herself as nurse in the sick chamber, for which post she was admirably qualified by her composure, gentleness, and care in literally fulfilling the doctor's orders.

Poor Mr. Camden! It would be difficult indeed to describe his feelings; wounded in the tenderest point, grieved beyond measure and depressed, he paced moodily up and down the grove near the house, where the cawing of the rooks, and the falling leaves of autumn, harmonized with his melancholy. In about an hour Harvey joined him, and related the opinion of the physician, after which Mr. Camden described his own scene with the rector. In conclusion he said, "There has been a sad mistake somewhere, Harvey. God knows who has been to blame! Had I been aware of the true state of circumstances, no earthly inducement should have brought me here —and still less would I have exposed myself and the venerable church of which I am a member, to the shame and confusion which have this day fallen upon us!"

To this speech, Harvey made a deprecatory reply, in the course of which he cast some blame upon the rector.

"To blame Mr. Feversham would be unjust," said Mr. Camden. "I feel no ways inclined to find fault with others for leaving the church, as long as they do not criticise me for remaining in her. If Mr. Feversham has not been able to find 'peace of mind,' and 'freedom from mortal sin,' in the Anglican fold—if 'the service of our Church' has been 'a burden' to him and not 'a privilege'—if 'the Sacrament' has been 'a dead ordinance' and 'the preaching an unbearable torture'—then, in God's name, let him leave us; we do not wish to keep him! Though, after all, I think he might have given our system a more fair trial!"

"Indeed he might," said Harvey, who, had he chosen, might have pleaded in the rector's favour the long and weary years during which he had studied and pondered over the subject, not to speak of the tedious and miserable twelvemonth which he had lately passed, throughout which he had deferred accomplishing his fixed purpose, solely at the instigation of his son-in-law! "To say the truth," continued he, "I always thought that Mr. Feversham showed a great deal of pride, in attributing his 'own defects to deficiency in our church's ordinances, rather than to his own past and present habits of sinful neglect!' "*

"Very likely," replied Mr. Camden. "Pride is in every case the forerunner of a fall! O, if the discontented members of our church would but realise as they ought to do, her glorious pre-eminence over the common protestant sects! and observe the attachment to our own communion, peculiar to ourselves among the religious professions of this age and country! Others can change from sect to sect, without misgiving; we cannot! If Mr. Feversham did not feel this, he ought at least to have remembered that his brethren feel it, 'and he should have guided himself at least for a while, by the direction thus given to his brethren.' "

"Don't you think, too," continued Harvey, "that there is a sort of nameless shudder which members of the Anglican Church feel, when about to leave her communion? Something of the kind is alluded to by Mr. Newman in his sermons."†

"Undoubtedly, I think so," replied Mr. Camden. "And I also agree with Mr. Newman in saying, 'that where individuals *have* left us, the step has commonly been taken in a moment of excitement, or of weakness, or in a time of sickness, or under misapprehension, or with manifest eccentricity of conduct, or in deliberate disobedience to the feeling in question, as if that feeling were a human charm, or spell of earth, which it was a duty to break at all risks, and which if one man broke, others would break also.' "

The two friends now paced up and down a few minutes in melancholy silence, which was at last broken by Harvey.

"Should my father-in-law recover his conscious-

* See Ward's Ideal of a Christian Church, page 572.

† At the time the above was written, Mr. Newman, Mr. Ward, and the other Anglican clergymen from whose works we have quoted, were still members of the Established Church.

ness before your departure," said he, "you will speak to him again—will you not? Perhaps you may succeed in bringing him to reason."

"God forbid that I should make the attempt," replied Mr. Camden, "particularly after the distressing scene which I witnessed to-day. In any case I would let Mr. Feversham alone, as there is no doubt that as a Roman Catholic he is secure of salvation. I mean to set out this evening and return to my parish as quickly as possible. I pity you, Harvey, from the bottom of my heart—for, should the rector again become sensible, you will have a distressing part to perform. You cannot in conscience refuse to send for a Roman Catholic priest to satisfy the dying man!"

"O, that I could accompany you, Camden!" exclaimed Harvey. "What will our Oxford friends say if they hear that my father-in-law received the last sacraments from a Roman Catholic priest, and I in the house!"

Poor Harvey was in great distress, not that he feared for Mr. Feversham's soul, but because he dreaded the opinion of the world!

The long and weary day at last drew towards its close; and the time for Mr. Camden's departure approached; Harvey's spirits got lower and lower, while the rector hovered between death and life. Had it not been the fear of what people would say, Harvey would have prepared to go with his friend, for he felt that his presence at the rectory was of little use; and he was also anxious to rejoin Mary. His wishes were realized in a way he little anticipated, and most painfully. About half an hour before the chaise ordered for Mr. Camden arrived at the door, the post bag was brought in. It contained a letter for Harvey, which was addressed in a strange hand. Eagerly breaking it open, he read the sad news that his wife was dangerously ill, having given birth to a dead child. Of course he instantly prepared to accompany his friend, and nothing could exceed his alarm and anxiety; for he was tenderly attached to Mary. Before setting off, the two clergymen left the most pressing injunctions with Lady Harriet, that in case of Mr. Feversham recovering consciousness, a Catholic priest should be immediately sent for to see him. All the reply she made however was an hysterical giggle.

Before leaving the rectory, Mr. Camden's own man took a most pathetic farewell of Dolly, the chambermaid, who by the way though simple, was a remarkably pretty girl. Though she had only known him four-and-twenty hours, she wept abundantly at parting, for she said that "Mr. Camden's gentleman was the most interestingest, melancholiest, green complexioned, man she had ever come across, and the most like to an immortalized sperrit of any human she had ever see'd!"

As for the too fascinating valet, he assured Dolly, that had he not unfortunately been of opinion that celibacy was a higher state than matrimony, he would have taken her attractions into consideration! But remembering his position as the own gentleman of Mr. Camden, the great oracle of the Anglican Catholic branch of the Church in the realm of Great Britain, he felt he had a duty to perform, both to himself and his neighbours.

"I shall never forget you, Dolly," he said, pressing her hand; "but like the phœnix, I must die unwedded, an Anglo-Catholic martyr!"

As the gentlemen drove from the door, Mrs. Egremond left the chamber of the invalid to pay a visit to Lady Harriet. She found her giggling violently, and the paroxysm ended in a flood of tears as she entered.

"Is it not odd, Mrs. Egremond," said Miss Beauclerk, who with one arm was supporting Lady Harriet, as she lay on the sofa—"Is it not extremely odd, that both the clergymen have left us, leaving orders to send for a Catholic priest as soon as the rector becomes sensible!"

Mrs. Egremond started back in horror, while Lady Harriet with difficulty controlling herself, exclaimed, "God pity me! I am a miserably used woman, when even clergymen of the Church of England—one of them my son-in-law—conspire against me! They wish to make out the poor, dear, innocent rector to be a Roman Catholic; for what reason I know not! Just as if I, unfortunate creature that I am! had been the wife of a popish priest for so many years without knowing it! But that shall never be—it is all nonsense! I will die across the threshold of his door, rather than let a priest get admittance to him!"

Poor Lady Harriet here got worse and worse, and at last screamed and struggled so violently, that it was all the two ladies could do to hold her. At last she became quite exhausted, and shutting her eyes, reclined back on the sofa apparently asleep. Then for the first time Mrs. Egremond was able to question Miss Beauclerk, who gave but a very imperfect and garbled account of the events of the day.

"For my part," said Mrs. Egremond, in a whisper, "I think there is but little chance of the rector becoming sensible again. He seems to me too far gone! Poor Lady Harriet may spare herself all uneasiness about the priest, for Mr. Feversham will never see him!"

"I do not know that," said Miss Beauclerk. "The doctor seemed to think otherwise. You know while there is life, there is hope."

"Very true, my dear," replied the elder lady, "we must not despair. Should he revive, I would counsel poor Lady Harriet to send immediately for dear Mr. Sharples, who has more consoling views of gospel truth than any man I know. He is peculiarly suited for the occasion; he knows so well how to improve the opportunity both to the sick and to their friends!

He never says anything about works or righteousness, but holds entirely by faith."

"Then he is just the person for poor dear Mr. Feversham," said Miss Beauclerk; "for we all know how few good works he did, at least openly."

"He is suited for all sinners," said Mrs. Egremond gravely, "smoothing as he does the path to heaven, with the words 'only believe and thou shalt be saved.'"

"There shall not a clergymen of any kind enter this door," cried Lady Harriet, starting up in another paroxysm; "they have killed my poor dear husband already; and not a soul but the doctor shall get leave to see him till all is over."

CHAPTER XXXIX.

"—— Whatsoe'er may be,
Of excellence in creature, pity mild,
Relenting mercy, large munificence,
Are all combined in her." DANTE.

"But have I now seen death? Is this the way
I must return to native dust? O sight
Of terror, foul and ugly to behold,
Horrid to think, how horrible to feel." MILTON.

MR. HOWARD heard the news of the rector's paralytic seizure early the next morning, ere he had time to visit the prison. Thanks to the garrulity of the servants, the intelligence spread like wild-fire of the rebuff experienced by Mr. Camden, and his subsequent departure with Harvey. The dissenters with Jacob Hogg at their head, gave out that Mr. Camden in trying to play the part of a Popish priest, in all the grandeur of candles and vestments, had so incensed the rector, that he had first knocked him down and then fallen into a fit. Of course this story was disbelieved by all who had known Mr. Feversham. Among the many erroneous statements, one thing seemed clear, that the rector had not received the sacrament from the Anglican clergyman. This gave very great consolation to Mr. Howard as well as to poor farmer Blount, who had been almost frantic when the news first reached him, that his kind and honoured master was in such imminent danger. When the first storm of his grief subsided, he sank into a moody silence, from which Mr. Howard at last roused him, by proposing him to join in saying the litany of the Blessed Virgin for the unfortunate Mr. Feversham. They accordingly knelt down and commenced. Never did poor sinner pray with more fervour for the remission of his own sins, than did the farmer on this occasion for his friend and benefactor. At first his words were choaked with sobs, but gradually as the prayer continued, his voice became clearer and firmer, until at last when they reached the conclusion, his words rung out so heartily in the last responses, that Mr. Howard was surprised. They had scarcely risen from their knees, when Blount began to speak.

"Oh, Sir!" said he, "a good thought has struck me. I was reading in one of the little books you lent me, that when Catholics are anxious for anything, they often try a nine days' prayer—a novena I think they call it; and that they generally get what they want by that means—if they ask with faith something for the glory of God. So, Sir, I have it all as clear as daylight. We'll get the rector in his senses again, and a priest will admit him into the church."

"How will you manage it?" asked Mr. Howard, half amused by the farmer's simplicity, and at the same time greatly touched and edified by his child-like confidence and faith.

"Why, Sir," replied Blount, "you will offer mass every morning during nine days, for Mr. Feversham; I and my little boy will say a whole rosary for him daily, and I don't doubt either, but what I'll get my dame to say the memorare to the Blessed Virgin, for she is much softer and more teachable in her nature lately; and though she is of the established Church still, it is not the first time I have wheedled her into saying Catholic prayers! Oh, Sir! we'll succeed when we are all at it! for who ever asked the Blessed Virgin in vain, as the memorare says. Should I be wrong, Sir, to pray also that I might get out of prison by the ninth day, and see the rector before he dies?"

"You can pray for what you like, Blount," replied Mr. Howard, "as long as you add, if it be for the honour and glory of God, and in conformity with His holy will: otherwise I am sure you would not desire it."

"Indeed I should not, Sir," replied the farmer; "I wish to do the will of God in all things—even to remain in prison if He desire it. But I think there would be no harm in speaking of getting out, when I am praying to the Blessed Virgin at any rate. She will not release me from prison if it be not for the glory of God that I should see the rector. But I may as well put her in mind of the thing, that she may consider of it."

"Do as you please," replied Mr. Howard smiling; "I have great confidence myself that our prayers for the rector will be heard; as to your getting out of prison I shall leave that alone."

"Well, any way," said the farmer, with something

between a smile and a sigh. "Our heavenly mother is a good mother, and a kind one, and she never could find it in her heart to disappoint us about the rector, when she can so easily get all we want by asking her dear Son for it. Why, Sir, I know by myself how it will be—if I had a dog that trusted me as entirely as I do her, I would rather suffer a deal of pain than cheat him of the bit of bread he asked for in his kindly and trusting way."

* * * * * *

Time passed on, the fourth day had arrived, and there were still very bad accounts of the rector. The physician said that he had no hope, and that he would probably breathe his last quietly without any warning. Mr. Howard, who was acquainted with the medical gentleman, happened to meet him in the street, and heard this opinion, as he was on his way to meet Blount. He was, therefore, somewhat shocked when the farmer at his entrance rushed up to him with the greatest glee, and shaking his hand warmly, shouted—

"Hurrah, Sir! wish me joy! I'm getting on! *She's* hearing me! You know whom I mean!" and then lowering his voice so as not to be overheard, he continued, "things are going on capitally. Jacob Hogg has fled the country with another man's wife and lots of other people's money! My step-daughter, Sarah, is liker a wild cat than anything else, she is so mad!"

"You talk, Blount, in a most unbecoming manner," said Mr. Howard; "for my part I can see nothing to rejoice at in a fellow-creature committing mortal sin."

"Ah, your reverence!" exclaimed the farmer, quite abashed, "I was not thinking of that; all that struck me was, how cleverly the Blessed Virgin was arranging for letting me out of prison on the ninth day—that is next Saturday! For you see, Sir,

Sarah is stark mad with indignation against Jacob, and has been hinting to her mother, my dame that is, that the receipt for the money I am now in prison for, is in existence still—and that the innocent must not suffer for the guilty—and that if I'll make no inquiries into it and not blame her, perhaps she may find it among the papers Jacob cast on the back of the fire, the day before he ran off, but which she, smelling a rat, picked out of the blaze when his back was turned. Oh, Sir! it is wonderful the ways of Providence!"

Into this affair, however, we shall enter no further, except to mention that the receipt did actually make its appearance, and that a friend of Mr. Howard's, a county magistrate, got a statement of the circumstances prepared, to lay before the court then sitting, in hopes of obtaining an immediate order for the farmer's release. But, alas! notwithstanding these efforts, poor Blount was still in prison on Saturday morning, pacing up and down in great excitement, sometimes a prey to despondency, and sometimes shaking it off, telling his wife and Neddy, who were almost as anxious as himself, that it was wrong to despair; the Blessed Virgin could do what she liked still, and Saturday was not over yet.

The ninth mass had been said for the unfortunate Mr. Feversham, and Mr. Howard was debating within himself how he should next proceed, when just as he was about to sit down to breakfast, a knock was heard at the door, and presently a gentleman was announced. It was the physician who attended the rector. He looked very grave; for he was a conscientious, though liberal Protestant, and did not at all like the unpleasant errand on which he came. After shaking hands with Mr. Howard, whom he had often met in the houses of the sick poor, where he attended gratuitously, he proceeded to inform him that his patient, Mr. Feversham, had wonderfully revived the preceding evening, and appeared now in perfect possession of his faculties. He had left him about eleven o'clock, and just before that, Mr. Feversham, dismissing the attendants, had spoken to him in private. He had declared himself a Roman Catholic, and earnestly implored him to bring a Catholic priest out with him the next day to hear his confession and give him the last sacraments. "I am sorry," continued the physician, "that with one part of Mr. Feversham's request I cannot comply, that of bringing you with me. For I had no sooner left the rectory last night, than I was summoned to see a gentleman in the same neighbourhood suddenly taken ill. I was obliged to remain with him the whole night, and quitted him only two hours ago. Ere I returned to town, I called again on Mr. Feversham, whom I found enjoying a refreshing slumber, which I thought it best not to disturb. I am now going ten miles out of town, and shall not return till late; I am glad, however, that I have seen you and been able to deliver my message in person."

Mr. Howard thanked the good doctor for the trouble he had taken, and assured him that he would instantly set out to see Mr. Feversham.

No sooner said than done. Within an hour and a half from the time when his visitor entered, the priest was at the door of the rectory. He gave his card to the servant, and desired him to mention that he was a Catholic priest, and had been sent for to visit his master. The man showed him into a parlour, and then went up stairs to deliver the message. On his way he met Miss Beauclerk, who eagerly seized the card, which she regarded with great curiosity.

"So it is a Catholic priest who is down stairs—the man above all others I most wish to see!" she exclaimed as she turned the pasteboard round and round. "Well, you need not disturb your master now," she continued, "I know he is asleep. Lady Harriet is reading a novel, and Mrs. Egremond is writing a letter, so I'll go down stairs and entertain the priest till Mr. Feversham awakes."

So saying she rushed past the servant, in her usual impetuous style, and only stopping a moment at the door of the parlour to arrange a rebellious curl, entered with great dignity, while she regarded Mr. Howard with mingled curiosity and awe, something like what little boys feel on first being ushered into the presence of a rhinoceros.

"Mr. Feversham is now asleep," were her first words after saluting Mr. Howard; "if you will have the goodness to remain till he awakes, your name shall then be mentioned to him."

"Certainly, Madam, I will do so with pleasure," he replied.

Some conversation then ensued upon the rector's illness and its cause, in the course of which Mr. Howard made the discovery that his companion was a very odd young lady. Miss Beauclerk did her utmost to make herself agreeable to the priest, and after discussing Mr. Feversham till the subject was exhausted, touched upon an infinite variety of topics, in order to amuse her companion, such as Puseyism, poetry, railways, music, national cookery, fasting, monastic austerities, and ship-building. It was all in vain, Mr. Howard would not be fascinated!

"Do you know," at last she exclaimed, "you remind me for all the world of a proud prelate of the middle ages!"

"How so?" asked Mr. Howard, with some curiosity.

"Because you look half stern, half savage, just like the stone bishops with mitre and crosier, such as one sees on old monuments—or like St. Senanus when he sent away the lady!"

Mr. Howard's colour was slightly heightened by this compliment; nevertheless he laughed heartily. Miss Beauclerk noticed both circumstances, and it encouraged her to proceed, for she thought that she had made a hit.

"Come now!" she continued, "do give me a lesson, and inform me how you Catholic priests have such marvellous power in reading the human heart! Or if that would take too long, do tell me at least if you are not a Jesuit? Are there female Jesuits? And is there any reason why I should not become one? I like nothing so much as mystery and a dash of romance—and you Catholic priests are such romantic creatures! Ladies have no weapons compared to yours—the stiletto and the breviary!"

Mr. Howard had great difficulty in keeping his gravity at this speech, nevertheless he managed to answer, "I am no Jesuit, Madam, and am not aware that any female Jesuits exist. On any other occasion I should be happy to reply to your catechism, but at present my time is precious. Would you have the goodness to inquire if Mr. Feversham is yet awake, I fear it is getting very late."

"Certainly, Mr. Howard," replied the lady rising to ring the bell. "But in your delightful company time passes so quickly! The very sight of a Catholic priest overpowers me with a flood of romantic and chivalrous associations! Bare-footed friars, triple crowned popes, incense, bells and inquisitors, pass in warlike array before my mind's eye, and transport me into the bewildering and spirit-stirring past, until I forget the present and imagine myself surrounded by the shades of all that is heroic and great in the papacy and in the tomb!"

Mr. Howard looked impatient, and just then the door opened, and the servant, after receiving Miss Beauclerk's orders, informed her that Lady Harriet desired to speak with her.

We shall now ascend to the chamber of the invalid; his sleep was uneasy and broken; at times he fancied himself wandering through a wilderness thickly strewn with pitfalls; a violent storm raged, and in the lull between the blasts of the hurricane the howling of numberless wild beasts could be heard, as if greedily searching for prey. They got upon his track, they pursued him—he fled. With difficulty avoiding in his terror the snares so thickly scattered on his path, he at last succeeded in reaching a noble and stately palace. The ravenous animals howled with rage and disappointment, as they beheld him approach so near the place of refuge. Fear lent wings to his feet; for he felt that these were not ordinary beasts of prey; he had a dreadful and oppressive idea that it was not his body that these monsters sought—theirs was nobler game! They thirsted for his soul, and longed to seize the immortal part that never dies, and damn it for all eternity.

"Mary, mother! help! help!" he cried in his mortal agony. Just then a fair and gracious lady opened one of the lattices in the highest part of the palace, and waved with her hand to the suppliant. Alas! the lattice was all too high for him to reach! He tried to climb, but at every step slipped back! The ravenous monsters came nearer and nearer, their howl rang in his ears, and he almost felt their hot and pestilential breath on his cheeks. The lady from above looked down with pity, and shook her head as though to say, "You err in the mode which you attempt!" Then with a bright smile she pointed to the portal of that noble palace, where stood a man in black array, beckoning to the poor hunted wanderer to approach. 'Tis true a gulf black and repulsive lay between—but what of that? The man in priestly garb held out his hand to guide him over it, and admit him into the fold of safety and of peace. When suddenly just as the sick man stretched forth his hand to grasp that of his friend, Lady Harriet appeared and with a loud scream pulled him back, so that they fell together into the abyss. The hellish monsters darted after—there was darkness and woe unutterable—when with a convulsive gasp the rector awoke.

It was some moments before he could realize the blissful certainty that it was only a dream. As soon as he recalled his scattered senses, he signed to the attendant to approach and said,—

"The Catholic priest must be here by this time, it seems to me I heard his voice just now. Go down instantly and send him up."

The servant departed; but was long in returning. The rector grew very impatient, and violently rang the bell which was placed within reach of his hand. Voices as though in altercation were heard upon the stair-case. Then the hall door closed, and a horse was heard galloping away. The rector's heart sank within him. A painful misgiving oppressed him. He had no longer strength to call out or to ring again. His brain reeled—once more he felt Lady Harriet seize him, and down, down they both fell together into the dark profound! With all this he was conscious of what took place in his apartment, and at length became aware of the door opening, and heard Mrs. Egremond advance to the bed and say,—

"I am very sorry, Mr. Feversham, that there has been any misunderstanding; but it seems before your message came down stairs, Lady Harriet had sent away the priest, as she considered you too weak to be disturbed just now."

The rector heard no more—his mind wandered! Jesus and Mary have mercy upon his poor soul!

CHAPTER XL.

"———— The world has seen
A type of peace. And as some most serene
And lovely spot to a poor maniac's eye,
After long years, some sweet and moving scene
Of youthful hope, returning suddenly,
Quells his long madness—thus man shall remember thee."
Mores Catholici.

"Thou that hast looked on death,
Aid us when death is near,
Whisper of heaven to faith,
Sweet mother hear."
MRS. HEMANS.

"Man of strange words, and some half-maddening sin,
Which makes thee people vacancy, whate'er
Thy dread and sufferance be, there's comfort yet—
The aid of holy men————."
BYRON.

"OH, pray, Sir!" exclaimed the farmer, as Mr. Howard detailed to him the ill success of his mission. "Pray! pray! pray! Let us storm heaven by our prayers! Saturday is not done yet—it is only two o'clock; the Blessed Virgin cannot help hearing us!"

"I shall not give up hope, that I promise you;" replied Mr. Howard. "To-morrow I will call upon Dr. Roscoe who attends Mr. Feversham, and in his company will doubtless gain admission to him."

"To-morrow may be too late!" said the farmer, mournfully shaking his head.

Just at this moment Mrs. Blount entered, looking

very sad and agitated. "Oh! Blount, I have bad news to tell!" she exclaimed, without noticing the priest. "John Richards, the groom from the rectory, riding Mr. Feversham's best horse, passed me at full gallop as I was coming up the High-street, and pulled up a few steps farther on, at Dr. Roscoe's door. I ran to hear the news, and he said that the rector had turned awfully worse, and that the doctor must come without a moment's delay. But the doctor was not in, and his servant said that he would not return till late. "He will not find my master alive then!" said the man. So he mounted again and galloped off like mad to the other side of the town, to try and find Dr. Gibson, who visits Dr. Roscoe's patients when he is in the country."

"Oh, God help us!" cried the farmer, dropping on his knees. "Mary, mother, I rely upon your assurance, that no one ever asked you in vain! And I claim your promise and will not give it up!"

Mr. Howard stood a few moments lost in thought, and his lip trembled as he watched the farmer who knelt before a little black crucifix which he had given him, while silent tears dropped heavily down his cheeks.

"Such confidence must prevail!" said he to himself, at last. "Faith like this man's is all powerful! Continue to pray," he added turning to the farmer. "I go now to take other means." So saying, the good priest left the prison, and walked as fast as he could to a distant part of the town. He felt that it would be wholly useless to attempt seeing the rector again in present circumstances. His only hope was, that the dying man might continue in life till Dr. Roscoe's return, when he proposed instantly to accompany him to the rectory. Mr. Howard expected that day an old and intimate friend to arrive from London, an Italian ecclesiastic who had studied with him many years previously in the Roman College. This gentleman had written to him a few days before, stating that he was then in London, and that important business calling him to the neighbourhood of Overbury, he would, if convenient, make his head quarters at the chapel-house. Mr. Howard in his anxiety for the rector, forgot all about this, and instead of returning home to meet his friend, who was expected to dinner, took his way, as we have said, to a distant part of the town. Now it so happened that a convent had lately been established there, chiefly owing to the exertions of the good priest, who was confessor to the nuns. These ladies had lately arrived, and had not been in Overbury more than three months at the time of which we speak. They were, in consequence, neither much known nor heard of in the town; but their prayers and good deeds ascended up daily to God, a well pleasing sacrifice. It was to obtain the prayers of these holy women, that the priest now approached their dwelling. On reaching the door, he asked to speak with the Superioress, Mary Teresa, whose family name was one of the most ancient of England's untitled aristocracy. She soon made her appearance in the parlour, a stately lady, considerably advanced in years, with a pale sweet countenance, at times illumined with such a bright and sunny smile, as made one think how lovely she must have been in youth. She listened with deep interest to the recital of Mr. Howard, who without mentioning names, merely spoke of the dying man as a clergyman in the neighbourhood. When he had finished, she replied—

"We go into the chapel at five o'clock to recite the divine office, and I promise you that all our prayers shall be offered for the unfortunate clergyman, that God may grant him admittance into the Church before his death. But you have not told me his name—is it a secret?"

"There is no need to keep it secret," replied Mr. Howard; "the clergyman is called Feversham. He belongs to the old Catholic family of that name, and was brought up in the ancient faith during his boyhood."

"The ways of Providence are wonderful," exclaimed the superioress, turning ashy pale, and catching hold of a chair to support herself. "I knew that the object of so many prayers could not be lost. There is hope—there is great hope—God himself has sent you here to give me consolation, and a special answer to prayer............

"For thirty long years," she continued, "I have never heard mass nor received holy communion without making earnest mention of Mr. Feversham, and imploring God for his reconversion. He is the son of my mother's brother, my playfellow in childhood, and the favourite pupil of the director of my early youth—Father Lefevre. About the time he entered the army I retired from the world to the convent in France, whence our sisters and myself have been transplanted here. Though so many years have passed since I heard of his fall, not a day has elapsed without my earnest prayers that God would yet have mercy on his soul. Thanks be to God, and to our Holy Mother, that have sent you to ask the prayers of our community. I look upon it as a pledge that they will be heard."

Much consoled, Mr. Howard now left the convent and hastened homewards. To his surprise he found that his Italian friend had not arrived, nor had any letter of apology been received from him.

We shall now return to the chamber of the dying man. We have said that his senses wandered, and his brain reeled. Had God deserted him? Was this the punishment for his moral cowardice—for his delay? Only for a short time does God vouchsafe His grace to the members of a false church. When they refuse to make use of it, when they procrastinate, alas! how frequently is it withdrawn! The faint-hearted rise from their easy couches too late; and, like the children of Israel, find that the manna has melted and disappeared. But it is not for us to decide what final award a dying man deserves. Let us remember that God is merciful, and loves to answer the prayers of His servants. Had there been ten righteous men abiding in the doomed city, it would have been saved.

Such a painful change was visible on the rector after the priest's departure, that Mrs. Egremond thought it but right to warn Lady Harriet of her apprehensions, and immediately to send for medical assistance. Mr. Feversham spoke a great deal, but incoherently; he talked of the days when he was a boy, and played on the green banks of his native river—of the old chapel where he served at mass, of the grey-haired priest that used to take him on his knee, kind Father Lefevre—of his mother's rosary, and the cross attached to it, which she taught him to kiss—of his father's blessing while on his dying-bed; and his last injunction, to be faithful to God, and to his Church, and to remember those pious ancestors who had suffered fines, imprisonment, scorn, nay, in one instance, *death itself*, in defence of a holy cause!

All these things did the rector speak of in his delirium; but his words were indistinct, and little comprehended by those around him.

Five o'clock at last struck, and at once he grew calm; his words were no longer heard, and perfect silence reigned. Mrs. Egremond on tip-toe stole towards the bed, for she almost feared, from the sudden change, that the worst had taken place. On looking at the rector, however, his countenance appeared tranquil; he breathed, while his lips moved, though what he said was inaudible. Reassured, she sat down beside him.

Meanwhile an important change had interiorly taken place. No sooner had the good nuns begun to pray than the confusion and chaos in his brain subsided. His ideas arranged themselves of their own accord; he knew where he was, and what passed around him, and he was able to take a clear and lucid view of his whole position; he comprehended what had occurred, how the priest had been dismissed, and he realized the difficulty of sending for him again, opposed as he would be by those around him. He felt that he had not many hours to live, and what was to be done must be done quickly. Mrs. Egremond left his bed-side, and walked to the other end of the apartment, where she sat down, and conversed in whispers with Lady Harriet and Miss Beauclerk. The rector determined to try one fervent appeal to their compassion, which he trusted would not be unavailing. He opened his lips, and tried to say, 'Send for a priest;' but his weakness was so great, he could not make himself heard. Again, and again he tried; but in vain. His senses, sharpened perhaps by the near approach of death, became painfully acute. He could overhear Mrs. Egremond say, "Poor man, we must take care that he be not again disturbed; he will probably slip away quietly without any further struggle."

The rector felt that human aid there was none. Now were of avail the beautiful lessons which a mother's love had inculcated on his boyhood—long forgotten and long disregarded; but which now in startling vividness recurred to his mind, as though they had been uttered but yesterday. As death approaches, the distinctions of time recede from our view; to the dying man the long-forgotten past is blended with the present—all seems one short day, the prelude of the true life, that of eternity. Was it his guardian angel that struck the chords of old association, and like sweet music caused to steal upon his ear the soft words of his mother as he knelt an innocent child by her lap?

"Mary will answer you whenever you ask her aid."

The dying man prayed with his whole heart; he

felt that his heavenly mother was his only hope, his last chance. No, not *chance,* that word is misapplied; for he felt *sure* that Mary would hear him. Oh, how deeply he realized that without her he would now be in despair—in dark dreary despair, a foretaste of hell! With her to help him he felt assured; for was she not the sinner's friend? and how many souls has she not saved, when on the brink of eternity they have called upon her!

With his eyes shut, and his soul absorbed in mental prayer, the poor rector lay motionless in bed—happy, yes, very happy. He no longer cares to speak, no longer wishes to implore Lady Harriet to send for spiritual aid. It is all the same to him whether she summon a Catholic priest or not; he knows so well that one will come in God's own good time. The Blessed Virgin herself will provide for him the minister of God, to receive him into the true Church. All he has to do now is to wait patiently, and *trust,* yes *trust,* in one that never disappoints those who confide in her.

Six o'clock struck; seven, eight, nine, were in succession announced by the time-piece. Still the rector lay in silence. Those around him thought he was insensible, but they were mistaken: for his mind was never more clear than now. He was not even impatient; for what is the use of impatience, when one is certain that an all-powerful and beneficent being is arranging everything for our greatest good?

Nine o'clock struck, as we before said; the nuns were just finishing their evening prayer, and offering it all to God for him—when, hark! the rector's quick ear detected the sound of carriage-wheels, and the clatter of horses' feet. It came nearer and nearer. It must be on the avenue approaching the house. The rector smiled, for he knew who was coming. He heard the carriage-door open, and the steps let down, and a man with hurried tread entered the house.

Now for the first time Mr. Feversham found his

voice, and in a loud clear tone that startled his listeners exclaimed:

"Let all of you leave the room, and send the minister of God to me."

In amazement they obeyed, while a dark complexioned man in a Catholic priest's soutain, whose jet black hair and piercing eyes betrayed his southern origin, with eager steps passed them on the landing-place, and without waiting to be announced, hurriedly entered the sick chamber. Lady Harriet stared in astonishment, while the servant whom he had preceded whispered to her,

"It is Monsignore Geroni."

We must now return to poor farmer Blount, whose feelings can be better imagined than described. After Mr. Howard left him, he paced up and down saying the rosary, in which he was joined by little Neddy, and if truth must be told, by the good dame also, who though she did not altogether approve of the Popish practice, yet in a case of such great emergency, esteemed it lawful to adopt any means of doing good to the rector. Sometimes the farmer stopped, and sitting down wrung his hands, giving way though only for a moment to despondency; but in a few minutes he always roused himself with the remark, "I'll not be the one to give up first any way. The saints always got what they wanted, because they prayed so long, so I'll keep at it till something better turn up;" so saying and taking little Neddy by the hand, he would pace up and down resuming his prayers.

The prison clock struck the hour of five. "Oh! that time, that time!" exclaimed the farmer. "It is a melancholy thing when each new hour brings decreasing comfort; Oh! Mary, Mary! hear us quickly."

Just then the door opened, and an official belonging to the prison informed him that an order for his release had arrived.

"God be praised," cried the farmer, "there are no

friends like heavenly ones." "Neddy, you rascal," he continued turning to the child, "if this don't teach you faith, I'll disown you for my son and let you die a heretic."

The boy laughed and so did the dame, but soon the farmer's glee evaporated, as leaving the door of the prison they entered the street, for he thought upon the rector. Bidding adieu to the boy and his mother, and desiring them to return home, he hastened to the chapel-house, in hopes of inducing Mr. Howard to accompany him immediately to the rector. To his great disappointment he found him in the vestry hearing confessions; and such was the crowd of poor creatures that besieged the door, that Blount, in spite of himself, was obliged to wait a very long time indeed, before he could get to speak to him. The priest was well aware that it was useless to go to Mr. Feversham, until accompanied by the physician; so to keep the farmer quiet, he despatched him to Dr. Roscoe's house, to watch for that gentleman's return. Poor Blount! That weary evening was the longest he ever spent in his life. At last a few minutes after nine, the physician returned, and was immediately hurried off by the impatient farmer, who had already provided a carriage by Mr. Howard's orders, who was waiting in considerable suspense at the chapel-house. They drove as fast as they could, but an hour elapsed before they reached the rectory, and looking at his watch, Dr. Roscoe saw it was a quarter past ten. They found the hall door ajar, for in the confusion of Monsignore Geroni's arrival, no one had noticed to shut it. A death-like silence reigned.

"Is he dead?" whispered Mr. Howard awe struck.

"The Blessed Virgin would not disappoint us," replied Blount half reproachfully.

Softly they ascended the stair-case following the doctor, who led the way to the sick room. But what was their surprise on entering, to behold the rector's bedside surrounded by the whole household, both ladies and servants, some of them on their knees, and others standing, but all deeply affected. A stranger in priestly garb was reading in English though with a foreign accent, the recommendation of a departing soul; Mr. Howard looked hard at him, and after a moment recognized the Italian ecclesiastic whom he had not seen for so many years, but whom he had that day expected. Overpowered with astonishment and gratitude to Almighty God for his wonderful dispensations, he knelt down, and joined from the bottom of his heart in the prayers which the good priest was reciting.

He had just come to the words, "Let his soul rejoice in thy presence, and remember not his former iniquities and excesses, the unhappy effects of passion or evil concupiscence; for although he hath sinned, yet he hath not renounced the Father, Son, and Holy Ghost, but hath believed and had a zeal for God, and faithfully worshipped him who made all things."

"Alas, alas!" exclaimed the dying man, "at these words the fiend mocks me............O, Mary! come to my aid, thou knowest I die a Catholic. I have been received and admitted into the One, Holy, Catholic, and Apostolic Church; plead my cause before God, and let not the enemy reproach me for having denied the faith."

"Mary, Mother, hear him, hear my poor master," sobbed the rough voice of the faithful Blount, who had managed to get close behind the Italian ecclesiastic. The dying man recognised the voice, and turning upon him one kindly smile, he gave a deep sigh, and uttering the word "*Mary*," expired. That last look remained engraved on poor Blount's heart, and many were the prayers he said, and when his circumstances improved, the alms he gave for the repose of the rector's soul.

Monsignore Geroni was the first to discover that all

was over, and began immediately the prayers for the dead. " Come to his assistance all ye saints of God; meet him all ye angels of God; receive his soul and present it now before its Lord. May Jesus Christ receive thee, and the angels conduct thee to thy place of rest. May the angels of God receive his soul, and present it now before its Lord.

" V. Eternal rest give to him, O Lord; and let perpetual light shine upon him.

" R. May the angels of God present him now before his Lord.

" V. Lord, have mercy on him.

" R. Christ, have mercy on him.

" V. Lord, have mercy on him.

" Our Father, &c.

" V. And lead us not into temptation.

" R. But deliver us from evil. Amen.

" V. Eternal rest give to him, O Lord.

" R. And let perpetual light shine upon him.

" V. From the gates of hell

" R. Deliver his soul, O Lord.

" V. May he rest in peace.

" R. Amen.

" V. O Lord, hear my prayer.

" R. And let my cry come to thee.

" Let us pray.

" To thee, O Lord, we recommend the soul of thy servant, that being dead to this world, he may live to thee; and whatever sins he hath committed in this life through human frailty, do thou in thy most merciful goodness, pardon through our Lord Jesus Christ. Amen."

CHAPTER XLI.

"The mass was sung, and prayers were said,
And solemn requiem for the dead;
And bells toll'd out their mighty peal,
For the departed spirit's weal."

MONSIGNORE GERONI while in London, after despatching his letter to his friend Mr. Howard, announcing his intention of dining with him on the Saturday, received some interesting intelligence, with regard to the ultra-high church party, which induced him late on Thursday to start for Oxford. He dined on Friday with some of those earnest and thoughtful men, whose longing hearts throb so anxiously for reunion with the mother Church; but who, alas! a mystery to themselves and to the world, are content to *wish* but not to act. There he met Mr. Camden, who eagerly embraced the opportunity of conversing with him. They talked of things of high import to England and to Christendom. Mr. Camden hung upon his words, and regarded him with an interest, nay, a veneration, scarcely warranted by what worldlings would have considered their relative position. It was with a sigh when the party broke up, that Mr. Camden rose to bid the Italian adieu. There was a charm, a fascination in his company; could Mr. Camden account for it? Yes, his heart against his will confessed the truth in a still small voice, which he struggled not to hear. He was a priest of the one holy Catholic Church, he came from Rome, from the mistress of Christendom, whose faith embraces the world. He knew the whole truth, and he *professed* the whole truth.

"O object of envy!" were the words which rose unbidden in the mind of Mr. Camden, as he compared the priest's position with his own.

When the two friends bid each other adieu—for, though they had met for the first time but a few hours before, yet a link had sprung up between them of warm interest—Monsignore Geroni alluded to his intention of spending a few days at Overbury. On hearing this, Mr. Camden started, and drawing him aside, rapidly and in few words, though with ill repressed agitation, informed him that a clergyman in whom he felt much interested, was now dying in that neighbourhood. Mr. Camden's servant, a few minutes before his master joined the party, had communicated to him the contents of a letter which he had just received from one of the Reverend Mr. Feversham's domestics.

"Feversham!" repeated Monsignore Geroni to himself; but with characteristic Italian caution, his face neither changed, nor did he show any other indication of surprise. Mr. Camden then proceeded to state that the rector was desirous of professing himself Roman Catholic, and being admitted into the Church before he died; but that his death-bed was jealously guarded by his relatives, and it was most unlikely they would comply with his wishes. The servant who had written this account to Mr. Camden's man, had gathered his information while waiting at table on the ladies of the family; and at the time he wrote his master was insensible.

"Do, for God's sake," continued Mr. Camden, "get admittance to this gentleman, should he recover his faculties before his death! Use my name—my influence—anything in short to effect this purpose. I would not for all the wealth and power England could give, have this man's dying agony on my conscience!"

Monsignore Geroni needed no further persuasion, but assuring Mr. Camden that he would do all in his power for the unfortunate clergyman, bade him a kind farewell. Mr. Camden followed him to the door, and as soon as he was concealed from the view of the rest of the company, dropped on his knees before him and asked his blessing. Much touched by this beautiful and unexpected humility, Monsignore Geroni bestowed it with a heartfelt prayer to the Blessed Virgin that she would look down with pity on the Anglican clergy, and above all, take under her special protection the sad and weary searcher for truth who now knelt before him.

The Italian was delayed longer than he had anticipated on his journey, for he had to go much out of his road to find the Catholic bishop of the diocese and get permission to hear Mr. Feversham's confession, &c. At Overbury he received such intelligence of the alarming state of the dying man, as induced him to travel post-haste to the rectory, without waiting to call on Mr. Howard, and announce his arrival.

The late Mr. Feversham's elder brother, a good and pious Catholic, with whom he had held little or no communication since he had deserted the faith of his fathers, was in the South of France during the rector's last illness. On hearing of his danger, he hastened homewards, but arrived too late to close his brother's eyes, though in time to witness his funeral obsequies. These were conducted in the most Catholic manner. A solemn mass of requiem was sung, at which many ecclesiastics and several bishops assisted, invited by the pious care of the elder Mr. Feversham, who gloried in making public the return of the erring wanderer to the true fold. The poor of Overbury long had cause to bless the rector's name, such liberal alms were bestowed by his relative for the repose of his soul. Nay, he did more—when he heard from Mr. Howard of the touching attachment which poor Blount had manifested to his brother, and when he called to mind how in his boyhood he had saved that brother's life, he immediately offered him a farm upon his estate, in a distant part of England; the very spot where his childhood had been spent; not only establishing him upon an excellent homestead at a low rent, but advancing him capital to stock it. A few months after Blount's removal, the good dame called upon the successor of Father Lefevre, and of her own accord asked to be instructed in the Catholic religion. She was shortly afterwards admitted, to her husband's great joy. Little Neddy is now studying at a Catholic college, and says that he wishes to be a priest. His father is delighted with the idea, but tells him that it will be time enough to talk of it when he becomes a little older. Jacob Hogg, if report speaks true, has become a popular preacher in the United States; crowds flock to hear him, and his principal admirers are among the fair sex. His particular forte seems to be conducting revivals. Mrs. Benson is now married to Brother Tompkins, the pious gentleman, by trade a blacksmith, and minister of the gospel, as mentioned in her letter. She is also the happy mother-in-law of a black prince of the blood.

As to Mrs. Harvey, it was some months ere she recovered her health, after hearing of her father's death. About that time she was visited by her Catholic uncle, Mr. Feversham, who brought her a long and very touching letter from the superioress of the nuns at Overbury. This deeply affected her, for it gave a circumstantial account of various things connected with her father's last illness. Many prayers were said for her conversion; and her name was inscribed at the Archiconfraternité in Paris. Before the summer was over, she declared to her husband her conviction that the Roman Catholic was the only true Church. Harvey was aghast! His position as a clergyman of the Church of England; his Anglican friends—what would they say? It was dreadful! He was a kind husband, however, and much attached to Mary. What opposition he might have made, we know not, had circumstances remained as they were; but it fortunately happened, at this juncture, that a rich relation died, and left him a great deal of money, so that he was no longer dependent upon his living for support. He immediately gave it up, and went abroad; where he had the satisfaction of knowing, as he often said to his friends, that his wife was a member of the true Church. Had she remained in England a Roman Catholic, she would have been a schismatic! He seems intending to reside permanently on the continent; but he has as yet taken no steps towards following Mary's good example.

When we last heard of Miss Beauclerk, she was paying Mrs. Harvey a long visit in Rome, where she and her husband were spending the winter. She came to Italy, as she confessed to her friend, chiefly in the hopes of making the acquaintance of some Italian bandit, in order to finish her life as a young lady with a little romance, ere settling down into a sober English matron; for she was now engaged to Mr. Pulteney, the young gentleman with the fine property, with whom she used to flirt so much before he went to confession to Mr. Camden.

As the rector's life had been insured, and the interest of the amount, which was considerable, settled upon Lady Harriet, she remained in very comfortable circumstances. She preferred residing in Bath to living with Mary and her husband, as she said that the sight of an Anglo-Catholic clergyman, since the poor rector's death, always gave her a fit of blue devils.

Mrs. Egremond still resides in Overbury, but performs so many good works, and is so charitable and beneficent, that it almost looks as if she were beginning to question if by faith *alone* we are saved. Strange to say, she has had many private conversations lately with Mr. Howard, who, since the night on which Mr. Feversham died, has been a frequent visitor in her house.

O my most sweet Mother, whose dear child I would wish ever to be, if thou art pleased with my feeble attempts in this book to procure thee honour, deign to obtain for me from thy Divine Son, that Protestants reading it may be induced to seek for the One True Church—that Catholics may learn in all their difficulties and dangers to have recourse to thee!

RICHARDSON AND SON, PRINTERS, DERBY.